CONDEMNED TO LIVE

A PLEASURE CRUISE CHARTS A
COURSE FOR MURDER IN THE
GALAPAGOS ISLANDS

A NOVEL BY

NORMAN MALAMUD

Barringer Publishing, Naples, Florida April 2010
www.barringerpublishing.com
Cover, graphics, layout design by Lisa Camp
Editing by Elizabeth Heath

ISBN: 978-0-9825109-7-1

Library of Congress Cataloging-in-Publication Data
Condemned to Live/by Norman Malamud

Printed in U.S.A.

DEDICATION

Condemned to Live is dedicated to
my wonderful daughters Shari Pacer
and Hillary Wiegand for their support;
to Craig Terkowitz for his valuable knowledge;
to Gail Dimaggio and my colleagues at
Hodges University workshop writer's group
and of course to Judith May Malamud.

CHAPTER 1

Trevor Jase Carr stared down at the handcuffs the guard snapped tightly about his wrists. The majestic surroundings he had taken for granted in the tranquil environment of the Galapagos Islands abruptly vanished from his memory, taking with them his precious freedom.

Gazing blankly at the canvas body bag the medics carried out of the rafting lodge, Quito's Prefect of Police, Fernando Hernandez, spoke to Carr, the man he had accused of strangling his wife. He tweaked his unruly mustache. "I don't understand," he said. "You admit you almost strangled your wife in a fit of sexual passion, or blind rage as you so aptly put it – because of her infidelities, and you expect me to believe you did not kill her? Enlighten me. What does 'almost strangle,' mean?"

A shadow crossed Trevor's face as he glanced at his friends, ashamed but unyielding, trying to defend himself against the charge of murder. "I know it sounds crazy, but it's the truth. She was the cause of all our problems, starting with the wild party on the yacht, when she drugged us by lacing the drinks with Ecstasy, to her sleeping with every man she could entice. She was always on the prowl, trying to satisfy her sexual appetite. I'd had enough. I snapped the moment I caught her having sex with..." He pointed to Tom Floater, the rapids guide, "him."

"Yes, yes," the commissar said, unconvinced. "Senor Floater has confessed to the indiscretion, but the finger marks on your wife's throat and the bruises on the lower part of her body are more than enough evidence to arrest you for her murder."

Trevor, justifying his innocence, raised his voice in frustration. "She was a sex-driven animal. I did try to choke her, but at the last minute I realized what I was doing. I let her go. She was scared... and yes, she was bruised, but I swear she was alive when I left. I had polished off a fifth of scotch. I was confused. My head was jammed up, so I took a walk on the beach to clear my thoughts..."

"This is not going anywhere," the commissar said.

"Then give me a lie detector test. I'll take any test you want. I'm innocent, I tell you."

"Even if you took the test, the results would not stand up in court." He stroked his chin thoughtfully. "I suppose when you walked on the beach, as you said, to cool off, no one saw you."

Silence.

The commissar's brows displayed his suspicions. "I thought not," he said. "I'm afraid I must take you into custody, Mr. Carr."

The group who participated in the events aboard the yacht watched with compassion. "Just one moment," Judy intervened. "I was with T J... I mean Mr. Carr, on the beach last night. I overheard the commotion from his room, and when he left to walk on the beach, I followed him. I was worried."

"No!" Trevor shouted. "Judy, don't get involved." He turned to the agent. "She's only trying to protect me. She wasn't there."

Judy stood her ground; though she heard her husband, Beau, warn her to stay out of it. "I was with him," she said. "I'll swear to it if I have to!"

"Of course you would," the commissar said. "But that doesn't erase the fact that he choked his wife. You are under arrest, Mr. Carr."

Hernandez focused on the suspects involved in the murder, mentally calling to mind the dossier he had printed out on the database management system, summarizing the backgrounds of the individuals.

All Caucasians, US citizens, long term married

Beau Blessing: Age: 48, Author

Judy Blessing: Age 24, Artist/Designer

Trevor Jase Carr: Age 44, CEO–Startech Industries

Pamela Ann Carr: Age 27, housewife, now deceased

Lawrence Anthony Bartoni: Age 29, Pharmacist

Kaitlin Sara Bartoni: Age 25, housewife

Thomas Alva Floater: Age 28, Australian citizen, Rafting Guide, single

"I must request that the rest of you not leave this district until further notice. There will be questions that must be answered. You will be questioned and detained!" He eyed the group, mindful of their dejected expressions.

Commissar Hernandez was well aware of crime in Quito. Murder, robberies and rape had become every day headlines. Having recently taken over the position of Prefect of Police, he promised to rid the city of crime, but the murder aboard the yacht only complicated the already problematical situation. The principality relied heavily on United States tourist trade for its source of revenue, placing him in a precarious position. He decided to treat the prisoner with finesse – for now.

Trevor pleaded. "Please Commissar; I'd like to speak with my friends for a moment. Just one minute to say goodbye." He raised his hands. "I'm handcuffed. I promise, I won't do anything foolish." With reluctance, the commissar nodded to the guard.

Trevor's usual composed stature and good looks diminished as he walked to the far end of the room. He whispered hoarsely. "I don't want this to get out. Not yet. It could cause a drop in my company's stock. Listen, I have friends who own the Shangri-la Hotel and Casino in Atlantic City. They're intelligent, well-informed private eyes... well, actually that is not their main business, the hotel is. But they've worked with the C.I.A., and Interpol in Europe and in the States. Contact them. They will be the perfect pair to come to my aid. They're the only ones I can trust to get me out of this mess."

"What are their names? How can we get in touch with them, and will they come here?" Judy asked.

"They'll come. They're that kind of people. Call the Shangri-la Hotel and Casino, in Atlantic City, New Jersey, and ask to speak to Ceil Spiegel."

CHAPTER 2

The tourists shivered as the wind whipped about their heads on Atlantic City's boardwalk, but the moment they entered the Shangri-la Hotel and Casino, the glittering lights, the clanging of the coins falling into metal pockets, and the chatter of the patrons made them forget the dismal weather outside.

Ceil Spiegel, grande dame and owner of the hotel, was known to everyone as Ceil, from the bellhops to the mayor of Atlantic City. She flitted from one regular patron to another, greeting and schmoozing in her inimitable, gracious manner. Dressed in a pale blue La Croix cocktail gown, her blond hair wound in a French knot, the attractive, five foot one proprietress eyed the bartenders, waitresses, housemen, croupiers and cashiers at a single glance. Her outgoing, charming demeanor didn't fool anyone who knew the lady. Underneath this charismatic façade lurked a cunning, hard-nosed businesswoman who looked twenty years younger than her birth certificate confirmed.

Ceil smiled at one of the casino's steady customers. Her smile was cordial, but her voice sent a signal of caution to the woman who tossed a hundred-dollar bill at the croupier in exchange for chips. "How are you doing, Elinor?"

Elinor, now in her early forties, wore a pin striped man-tailored suit, high boots, and a buttoned down shirt. Her fedora cocked over one eye told anyone near by to think twice before fooling with her. "I've seen better days, Ceil. But I've seen worse ones too. Stick around, you bring me luck."

The dealer drew a card, "Twenty-one, house wins."

"Shit," Elinor grumbled, meaning it.

"I guess I didn't bring you luck this time," Ceil said, shaking her head. "How about I buy you a cup of coffee, or better yet, lunch? How long have you been at the table?"

Elinor pulled another C-note from her purse and tossed it at the croupier, avoiding Ceil's stare. "Been here? Let's see. Oh, about a thousand dollars worth of minutes, you might say. You're not going to give me one of your sermons, are you? My luck is going to change. I dreamt I was going to make a killing today."

Ceil signaled Harold, the dealer, and he tossed Elinor's bill back to her. Elinor sat up in her chair. "What's the matter, Harold? I didn't print the money on my computer. It's a genuine one hundred percent U. S. Treasury, guaranteed century note." She eyed Ceil. "Oh, I get it. Harold gets a nod from the boss, and Elinor's not welcome at the Shangri-la, right? Well, there are other casinos in Atlantic City that will be only too happy to take my dough."

Ceil replied. "No doubt they will. "Let's not get into a hassle. How long do I know you?" She didn't wait for an answer. "At least three years, right? I remember because you gave birth to the twins about then, and you cried bitter tears because you lost all the rent money, gambling. And to make matters worse, Louis walked out on you because of your habit."

Elinor removed her sunglasses, resting them on the brim of her hat. A nervous tick started her eye-blinking non-stop. Grabbing a cocktail from the tray of a passing waitress, she turned to Ceil. "Go ahead, rub salt in the open wound. You're going to tell me how you helped me out of a hole, and I said I'd pay you back, and never did. So you're entitled to give me a piece of your mind." She slid her sunglasses back over her eyes, stood, and made a turn toward the door. "I can take a hint. I'm going. You'll get the first installment as soon as I make a killing."

Ceil took hold of Elinor's arm. "Not so fast, lady! Listen, I want to ask you something."

Elinor hesitated. "If you want me to tail someone, or climb a tree taking pictures of an unfaithful husband, I don't do that any more."

"It's nothing like that, Elinor. Let's go into the dining room. By the way, when did you eat last, and who's with the kids?"

"I may have had a burger here, last night, or was it the night before? Whatever. The kids? The kids are in nursery school." She eyed Ceil with suspicion. "What's on your mind? I hope you're not going to offer me a job."

Ceil held Elinor around her waist and steered her into the dining room. "Sit down Elinor," she said. "I have a proposition to make to you. An offer you can't refuse."

At their suite in the hotel, Meyer stood facing Ceil. "What kind of shtick are you pulling now?" he asked. "I saw you gabbing with Elinor. If you loan her money again, please, don't tell me, I don't need the aggravation." He shook his head as he hung his jacket in the spacious walk- in closet of their penthouse apartment in the Shangri-la. Ceil allotted this particular walk-in closet to him. The other three were hers.

"She's not a junkie, Meyer. She's had a hard life, and gambling has become an obsession with her. It's a disease. An addiction. It took a lot of guts for her to get out of the rackets. You ought to know. Look how much you had to pay to walk away clean. Anyhow, I think she can be helped."

He shook his head. His six-foot stocky frame hovered over her. "I don't have an addiction, or a disease. This may come as a surprise to you, my philanthropic wife, but it's the gamblers that keep us in business." He rolled his eyes. "Does that mean that you have to support half the deadbeats with a gambling problem in Atlantic City? Why don't you open up a gambling shelter like they do for the needy? You could rehabilitate them, and loan them money at the same time." He couldn't resist teasing her. "You know, there is an organization known as Gamblers Anonymous. Why don't you send her there? You can go with her and applaud when she stands on the podium and says, "My name is Elinor, and I'm a compulsive gambler. This is my sponsor, Ceil, and if anyone needs cash, she's there for you." Raising his arms to form a stop sign, he continued. "Don't shove, everyone will get their share." He sighed deeply, showing his frustration. "If you want, I'll write a letter of recommendation."

She protested, politely. "You think your kibitzing is cute, don't you? So, I try to help out a few people. What's so bad?"

"What's so bad is you're getting a reputation for being a soft touch, Mother Teresa."

Slipping out of her dress, Ceil walked to her closet and hung it next to her two-dozen evening gowns then changed into a black lace negligee. He admired how she had kept her figure so trim for a lady in her early seventies. Returning to him, she sat down, patted the bed, and motioned for him to sit beside her. Her eyes held his. Smiling warmly at the man who would give his life for her, she said. "For years you've been telling me the same old story. And for years I've answered you in the same way. When are you going to give up? I can't see someone suffer and not help them. I just can't. Yes, I've been taken advantage of. But think of the ones who straightened their lives out. That's worth a hundred losers. We don't know what we have until we lose it, and then we wonder why we didn't do more with our lives when we had the chance."

He took her hands in his and stared lovingly at her, his eyes filling with tears, his heart full of affection. "There's only one like you, Ceil. So tell me. What did you promise Elinor? A year's free chips at the Black Jack table?"

"Never stop, do you? Always with the jokes, huh, Meyer?"

"You said you fell in love with me because of my sense of humor. You forgot already?"

"You're right about that. It's just that..."

"Uh, oh. Here it comes. Okay, let's get it out in the open. I know that look, Ceil. Lately, I noticed that you're antsy. Want to tell me why you're walking around with your head up your ass?"

"Nice talk, Meyer. Very eloquent. So if you're so smart, Einstein, you tell me."

"You're restless. You love running the casino, but you miss the excitement of our past work, and you thrived on our side hobby of locating lost relatives."

"Hobby? I'd hardly call it a hobby. Maybe it did begin as an adventure, but it did take off." She lay down on the bed and stared up at the ceiling.

"Do you remember how it started, Meyer?"

"Do I remember how it started?"

"That's what I asked you. Why do you always answer a question with a question?"

"I wasn't answering a question, I was making a statement."

"Whatever. Well?"

"Well, what?"

"Are you trying to be cute again or are you playing with my head? Just answer the question. Do – you – remember – how – we got into the private eye business? Just give me a yes or a no."

"Yes."

"Good," she said, a hint of tolerance in her tone. "So tell me."

He stood up and waved a mock fist at her. "For two cents I'd give you a good one right in the noggin."

"You just try it," she countered, laughing. "And you'll be emasculated so fast you'll be singing soprano."

He jumped on her, pinning her hands to her sides, kissing her passionately. "You wouldn't do that and spoil our sex life, now would you?" He rolled off, and she spooned tightly against him. "Sure I remember how we got into the private eye business," he said. "Like it was yesterday. It was at the dinner you threw for Spencer Chadwick, when he ran for district attorney of Atlantic City. He heard about our so-called moonlighting work. It was after we helped the police chief, locate that ... what's his name? The guy who had three wives in three different states."

"Jacob Mulholland," she recalled."

"That's the one," he said. "And when Spence's daughter was kidnapped and raped by the bastard, he asked us as a personal favor to work with the police. What a wild goose-chase that bum led us on. But we finally caught up with him."

"Well, am I right? Is that what's bothering you? You know, we could take a sabbatical from the hotel and go back to sleuthing. Which reminds me. I have to tell the accountant to mail our private investigator renewal license checks, or they'll lapse." He laughed.

"Let me in on the joke, Meyer, I could use a good laugh."

"I was remembering how hard we studied in order to pass the test at City Hall and how worried you were."

She rolled her eyes. "Wrong, Sherlock. Correct me if I'm missing something here, which by the way, I'm sure I'm not, but it was I who was worried about you passing the test."

"Big deal. So your brain retains more than mine. You want me to go sit in the corner?"

"You're very smart, Meyer. You have a suspicious mind and that's an asset for a private eye. I wish I didn't trust everyone the way I do. I should have furthered my education."

"Furthered your education? Are you nuts? You passed the bar on the first exam, and built an empire by making the Shangri-la the most profitable establishment in A.C. Even The Donald wanted to buy you out, and have you take over his non-profit enterprises. What you have, you can't get from school. People like you who have special instincts don't acquire it in school. It's God-given."

"Well thank you, sir. That's the nicest thing you've said to me in a long time."

"Don't snow me," he said. "I know how shrewd you are. You can spot a phony at ten paces. Stop fishing for compliments."

"I guess that's what makes us a good team," she said, knowing he was right.

"You know, Ceil," he said. "There are probably a lot of cases the chief would be glad to assign us. And if you feel you don't want to work for them, I could contact some of the boys. They always need someone to cover their asses. Especially now that the government has come up with sophisticated bugging devices."

She shot up in bed, a wave of fear pulsing though her body. "No! Not the mob. Thank God you're through with that scene. I shiver every time I think of your involvement with them."

"Hey, don't turn your nose up at them. That's where I made all my money, and some of it went to get you started in this hotel. You forget so easily."

She reached into a drawer, pretending to look for something. After rearranging the articles the same way they originally were, she closed the drawer and stood to face him. Watching her, he said, "Don't get so upset, it was only a suggestion. Ceil, what are you futzing in the drawer for?"

"I have every right to get upset. I don't forget so easily, as you said. I could never understand how you just fluff off what the mob does. Okay, I know you personally didn't rub anyone out. Or so you tell me. But I can't get it through my thick head how you and everyone else watch movies like *The Godfather*, or the *Sopranos*, with such zeal, like you're condoning their behavior."

Holding out his hand in protest, he said, "Whoa there. Aren't we getting a little carried away? What makes you think we condone the murders? Why are you making so much out of it? Okay, I won't go there, I promise. Settle down, will you? For God's sakes, it's only a story."

"Only a story," she said with irritation. "Get real. I suppose what we lived through during the Holocaust, was only a story too." Tears of pain streamed down her face as memories of the past flashed thorough her mind.

He was at her side at once, embracing her, knowing that she, unlike he, was not able to put the past behind her, and he couldn't blame her; he could only take her in his arms and comfort her until she pulled herself together. "How about we go down to the kitchen, and let the chef fix you a hot corned beef sandwich, and me a hot pastrami? I hear he just received a barrel of kosher pickles from New York. Mmm, doesn't that make your mouth water?" He felt her tension dissolving as it always did with time. "We can top it off with a double-thick chocolate malted."

"You always know how to bring me back," she said, planting a kiss on his cheek. "I'm sorry, I didn't mean to take my frustrations out on you."

"So, who should you take them out on, Mario Puzo? I'm always here for you, Ceil, like you are for me. Now shall we partake of the food I discussed?"

She dabbed at her eyes with a tissue, hugging him. "I wish I could forget the past as you have," she said. "I forgot there was a time I would die before mixing dairy and meat."

"It's not easy to forget, and we never will. The trick is to live with the memories without letting them get the best of you. We have a good life. No, we have a great life. And I promise I'll never say anything again, no matter how many deadbeats you help out. Now that we're back to ourselves, you want me to start the ball rolling? I could put the word out that we're in the private eye line of work, again."

"Honestly, I don't know what gets into me. The casino is more than a full time job. I do miss working on cases, but I worry about the casino, always afraid it won't run without me."

He shrugged. "C'mon, you've got competent people running it for you. And what about the times we schlepped around the states and in Europe for weeks at a time? When we came back, it was still here." Meyer placed his hands on his hips. "In fact, there were times the take in the casino improved. So don't give me that bull that without you the casino would fall apart. Let's eat. All this talk has given me a big appetite. Mmmm, I can smell the pastrami from here."

They ate in the hotel cafeteria exclusive to the employees. Ceil liked mingling with the help, and they with her. She kibitzed with them, asking about their children and how their lives were progressing, and if there was something she could do, or, if they were in need. The odors and chitchat reminded her of home. She was well aware there isn't a better place to be than the kitchen, to know what's going on in your business.

"Chin Lee, " she said to the head chef. "How do you get the corned beef to taste so good? Soy sauce?"

He waved a hand of dismissal at her. "That's very funny," he answered laughing. "You tell me how to win at the tables and maybe I tell you my secret ingredient. Deal?"

"Quit while you're ahead," Meyer said, taking a big bite of his pastrami sandwich, the mustard dripping from the side of his mouth. "Where's the malted?"

Ceil wiped his mouth with a napkin. Shaking her head, she said, "Such a slob. Don't talk with a full mouth." Looking at the counterman, she added, "Eighty-six the malted."

Meyer waited until he finished chewing. "No malted? You full already? Have an egg- cream."

"I'll have a diet Dr. Brown's celery tonic. It will ease my conscience and I can save on the calories at the same time."

As they ate, the loudspeaker announced, "Mrs. Spiegel, long distance telephone call, Mrs. Spiegel."

Picking up the wall phone, she said, "This is Mrs. Spiegel."

"Uno momento por favor," the operator chirped, as a click could be heard. "Your party is on the line, Senora."

"Hello, is this Mrs. Ceil Spiegel?"

"Yes, this is she. Who is this?"

"My name is Judy Blessing, and I'm calling about a friend of yours, Trevor Carr."

"T.J.?" Ceil, asked anxiously. "Has something happened to him? Where are you calling from?"

"From the city of Quito, in Ecuador."

"South America? What's wrong, and why are you calling for him? He's not dead, is he?" Ceil asked, concerned from the obvious tremor in the woman's voice.

"No, he's not dead," Judy, said. "But he has big problems. He's been arrested for the murder of his wife."

CHAPTER 3

The three of them – Judy, her husband, Beau, and Lawrence, sat on the deck of the luxurious yacht, *Isabella*. The faint scent of hibiscus swept by the southern winds crossed their nostrils, but today it meant nothing.

The chef stood nearby, patiently awaiting their luncheon order. Ordinarily, the women would be gaily chatting or dishing one another; the men would be discussing the day's scheduled agenda, most likely contrary to the women's. But today was not one of those happy days. The three hopeful couples, who started out to mend their marriages, were now reduced to being mere visitors in a strange country.

Resembling a suave character plucked from a chapter in an Agatha Christie novel; a silk scarf wrapped flamboyantly about his neck; a cap that rested over one eye, Beau Blessing, the aspiring author, broke the silence. "Amid the turmoil we've encountered on this so called vacation at least we've got one good thing going for us," he said. He took a sip of the martini the steward served and smiled with approval as the liquor slid pleasantly down his throat. Placing the glass on the table under the umbrella that shaded the group, he attempted to swat a fly hovering over the hors d'oeuvres, but the steward scooped up the fly before Beau could snag the insect. "Getcha next time," Beau sang.

Judy rolled her eyes. "You know something Beau," she said annoyed by his attitude, "You constantly surprise me. The only good thing that could happen today is if you'd just shut up. T.J.'s been arrested for murder and you're carrying on like you don't give a damn. Don't you care what could happen to T.J.?"

Lawrence Bartoni interrupted. "Go easy Judy . We're all upset. He's putting on an act. Of course he cares. We all do. Even Kaitlin, in her condition, is concerned." He tuned toward Beau, but projected his voice toward Judy. "If Beau didn't care he wouldn't be drinking so much.

"I'm sorry Judy ," Beau said. "And, I apologize to you too Lar, but I keep remembering how T.J. made some serious moves on Judy. She *is* my wife. On the other hand, Pamela was a cold-hearted bitch. T.J. had every right to get rid of her."

"*If* he did get rid of her," Lawrence interjected. "Look, we can all take the blame. We all contributed to the fiasco. And, did it ever occur to either of you that the authorities might accuse one of us for the murder of Pamela? Let's pray the Spiegels can get T.J. out of this mess.

Beau shook his head. "It's not going to be easy. This is not like the law, as we know it in the States. They throw you in jail for just eyeing a policeman."

The captain interrupted. "Mr. Bartoni, the hospital is on the phone. I'm afraid it concerns your wife, Kaitlin."

CHAPTER 4

On that bleak night when Kaitlin O'Connor was four years old, she sat curled in a fetal position sobbing in a locked bedroom closet in the trailer home she shared with her mother. She held tight to her teddy bear, Pinky, as she heard her mother yelling through the closed door. "You'll stay there until I get back, and you know what you're in for if you wet yourself!"

Kaitlin wiped the tears that fell from her cheeks onto Pinky's furry head. She looked through a crack in the door, and listened as a door opened, and closed with a thump.

Charlene O'Connor shouted into the narrow living room that doubled as a kitchen. "Is that you, Mac? Fix yourself a drink and make me one, too. This one's hit the dust. And don't water mine down. If I want soda pop, I'll drink Pepsi. And another thing wise guy, don't start lecturing me on how much I drink." She dabbed her exposed breasts with a powder puff and stepped into her mini dress.

Mac McGinnis, her current lover, a burly truck driver with a face that resembled a tame grizzly bear, grunted. "I don't dilute your drinks, Charlene. The way you're hitting the bottle your taste buds must be numb. What are you doing in there, anyhow? Get a move on, will ya? I promised the guys I'd shoot a game of pool before we eat." He carried the drinks into the bedroom and placed the glass into her eager hand. He threw her an icy look and shook his head. "You look like shit Charlene, been guzzling the booze nonstop again?"

She spun around. "Piss off, Mac. You don't pay the rent on the old homestead; so don't start acting like you got a right to insult me. Try slipping a wedding ring on my left hand, and kick in with some do-ray-me, so I won't have to waitress at the diner, – then you can have the privilege of mouthing off."

"Don't start that crap again, Charlene. I told you a hundred times. I ain't ready to settle down." He knew his affair with Charlene had seen better days and that it was time to move on, and soon. "Things change once you get hitched. And I don't get off on anyone telling me what I can and can't do. Once a guy takes those wedding vows, he's stuck for life. Forget it. And besides, you're unpredictable. You drink too much. It makes you sloppy. Snap it up, will ya?"

She gulped her drink and set the glass down. "You're so full of shit, Mac. You talk big like all the losers. You got two things on your mind. Playing pool, and getting your rocks off."

He scowled. "If you're going to get crazy, Charlene, I'm telling you right out—I had a rough day and I'm not in the mood for your shit. Stop bitching or I'm gonna walk."

She stood, smoothed her dress and gave herself a quick check in the mirror. Grabbing the drink from his hand, she downed it. "Yeah, yeah," she said, staring at him, and waving a hand of dismissal. "I've heard that story before, Buster. But you never forget my address, do you?" She took his arm. "Let's go. I'm getting thirsty. The brat's been getting on my nerves all day."

Kaitlin, watching from the crack in the closet door, held her breath.

Mac looked around the room. "Where's the kid, at a friend's house?"

"No, she's being punished."

His eyes searched the room. "Kaitlin," he called out. He eyed Charlene. "What do you mean she's being punished? Where is she, in the bathroom?"

She tugged at his arm. "None of your business where she is, Mac. C'mon, let's go."

Kaitlin's whimpering sounded from the closet. "Don't tell me you locked the kid in the closet again. What the fuck is wrong with you? Were you gonna keep her in there 'til we got back?" He extended his hand and glared. "Give me the fucking keys, Charlene. How would you like it if I locked you in there?"

"I told you, Mac. Butt out. She's not your responsibility. If you're in such a hurry to play pool, let's get a move on. The kid has to learn to listen to me. She can wait until we get back."

"Who do you think you are, Joan Crawford?"

Her eyes became slits. "I told you, Mac. Butt out. No harm in setting her straight while she's young. That's how my mother brought me up, and . . . "

He guffawed. "Yeah, and look how you turned out, Ms.-Mother-of-the-Year-rummy."

She poured a glass of vodka, downed it in one gulp, and sneered at him. She shot back, "Get lost, pervert. If you're not coming, I'm taking my car and going to The Hangout by myself. There's lotsa dudes that would die to get into my panties." She sneered at him. "No low down, dirty truck driver's going to tell me how to raise my kid."

His eyes shot arrows at her, his fists clenched, ready to strike. "Unlock the damn closet, and let the kid out, Charlene, or I swear, I'll break it down."

Grabbing her purse, she brushed past him, and scurried out the front door before he could stop her. Starting the engine, she yelled back. "Go to hell, pussy, and don't come back, or I'll call the cops and tell them you deal drugs."

Mac peered out the window, watching her drive over the curb, missing the fire hydrant by inches. She floored the gas pedal, leaving rubber on the pavement, and sped away. He walked to the closet and spoke to Kaitlin. "Listen to me, Kat. I don't know where your mother hid the key so I'm going to have to make a big bang and kick the door in. You hear me, kid? You understand what I'm saying?"

Silence.

"Hey, Kat. You know me. Remember, we went to the zoo and I bought you peanuts to feed the animals? It's Mac, your Uncle Mac, the man who takes you for a ride in the big truck. You don't want to stay in the dark, musty closet, do you? Be a good girl and tell me you hear me. I don't want the door to hurt you when I bust it open."

Her breath came in short gasps. She answered almost inaudibly, "I hear you. Is Mommy here?"

"No, she's gone. Now listen to me, Kat. Move to the end of the closet, because when the door opens, it's going to come at you, and I don't want you to get hurt. Understand?"

"Ye . . . yes, Uncle Mac. Are you sure Mommy isn't here?"

"I swear, Kat. Now go back in the closet as far as you can, and cover your ears. There's going to be a big noise. I'll count to three, and then I'm going to kick the door in. Okay?"

Her voice thin and fearful, she clutched her teddy bear to her chest. "Okay, Uncle Mac."

"Here we go. One . . . two . . . three." The door split into pieces, and there in the corner of the closet sat Kaitlin clutching her teddy bear, Pinky. Her tear stained cheeks chaffed from crying, and her large saucer shaped eyes looked up at the man she knew only as Uncle Mac.

Picking the frail child up, he held her gently in his arms, patting her head, trying to comfort her.

She sobbed. "Can I be with you Uncle Mac?"

"Well, let's get you settled first," he said, taken aback by her question. "We'll see. Do you have to go to the bathroom, or maybe you're hungry? Did you have dinner?" She shook her head. "Bitch," he mouthed, thinking of Charlene. He checked the refrigerator which contained a moldy loaf of bread, three six packs of beer, and a bottle of milk that had soured. "Tell you what, Kat. Go to the bathroom and wash that pretty face of yours, and then Uncle Mac will take you to McDonalds. Would you like that?"

She didn't have to reply; her smile, and the gleam in her eyes gave him his answer.

He grimaced, troubled at the thought of what he would do about the situation he found himself in. Thoughts of his troubled childhood flashed in his mind, reminding him of his father's cruelness towards him.

Kaitlin walked out of the bathroom and stood staring up at Mac, her face filled with curiosity. "See," she said, holding her hands up to him, "Nice and clean."

He smiled approvingly and reached for the doorknob. But before his hand could grasp it, the door flew open, and Charlene, crazed from drinking, burst into the room. The door's impact caught him off balance, sending him crashing against the wall. She screamed hysterically, "Kidnapper! Call the police! He's taking my baby!"

Kaitlin ran to the closet and crouched in terror. Mac picked himself up and closed the front door. He grabbed hold of Charlene and shook her violently. "Get a hold of yourself you drunken whore! Nobody's taking your kid. We were only going to McDonald's to get her something to eat. Whadaya do with the money I give you?" He shook his head. "Now, that was a stupid question, wasn't it? It all goes for booze, right?" He picked her up and flung her on the couch. "You no-good slut. Starving the kid so you can drink yourself to death. I'm taking the kid and reporting you to social services. She'll never see her next birthday staying with you. Did you look at her? She looks like a concentration camp victim." He walked to the closet where Kaitlin sat shivering, holding tightly to her teddy bear. "Don't be afraid kid," he said with tenderness. "Uncle Mac is going to take you where you'll be safe. Here, take my hand. Don't be afraid."

Kaitlin poked her head out of the closet. Mac extended his hands, but she suddenly drew back, her face drained of all color.

"It's okay, Kat. Don't be afraid." Her eyes grew wider, and she gasped. But, it was too late. The steam iron came crashing down on his head, splitting his skull. Blood splashed on the wall, her face and dress, and over her most precious possession, Pinky, her teddy bear.

CHAPTER 5
15 Years Later

Moving shadows from passing vehicles flickered on the ceiling above Kaitlin's infirmary bed, sending anxious thoughts through her mind. Having been told she had Hodgkin's disease distressed her, but the problem of how her husband would hold up to the news bothered her more.

Kaitlin imagined a million things, among them that hospitals were nerve-wracking places. In the dark you can hear the moans of sick patients and in the light when you find the bed next to yours vacant, you wonder if your roommate was released, or had died during the night.

Tears rested in Lawrence Bartoni's eyelids as he paced up and down the hospital waiting room. "Sit," his grandmother, said, her thick Italian accent evident. "You're wearing a hole in the floor."

Lawrence's mother intervened. "Leave the boy alone. Can't you see how upset he is?"

Mrs. Bartoni's mother-in-law snapped. "What am I, blind? Only married a year, and she's sick already. I bet she won't be able to have children either." She shook her head. "I suppose this means that I won't get to be a great-grandmother." Her mouth curled to one side. "It must be from her side of the family. They carry the infirmity." She scowled at her grandson. "An orphan you had to marry with a name like Kaitlin, and Irish yet. Not enough nice Italian girls in Brooklyn? All the Irish do is drink, and you never know who they're sleeping with. I told you before you got married she looked sickly. I could see it in her eyes, always so frail, like a bird with a broken wing. "

His mother's eyes flared hatred at her mother-in-law. Speaking between clenched teeth she raised her voice to her husband. "Tony, get her out of here before I strangle the old..."

"C'mon mama," Tony said, taking hold of his mother's arm. "You're getting out of hand. I'll take you home."

Grandma shook his hand loose from her arm. "What's everyone so sensitive about? What did I say so wrong that your wife is so touchy? If you had listened to me in the first place, we wouldn't be sitting here worrying about this Hodgkin's thing." In a self-aggrandizing way, she stood and started for the door, shouting at her son, "Anthony, stop pulling my arm. I'm going. I can take the bus. I have tokens. I got along all these years without..." Her voice faded as she walked down the hospital corridor, grumbling. Without warning, she stopped short, turned around, and called out in a loud voice. "Wait. You'll be sorry when you need money. I don't forget so easy."

When he returned, Tony put his arm around his son. "I'm sorry. I tried to keep her home, but you know her. She promised she'd behave."

Lawrence's mother shook her head. "Behave. She doesn't know the meaning of the word. I told you years ago, Tony. Your mother should be in a home with disturbed bitter old ladies like her."

"Okay, you two," Lawrence said. "Let's not get into a family feud. We're all concerned with Kat's test results." The swinging doors parted and the doctor walked toward them.

They stood by and the doctor raised his hand. "Please," he said, a half smile on his face, "be seated."

"How is she?" Lawrence asked.

The visitors in the waiting room hushed and Dr. Ludwig suggested they go to a more private area.

Once settled in a circle of chairs in a private room, the doctor spoke. "How much do you know about Hodgkin's lymphoma, Lawrence?"

"Just what we touched on in school. I've tried researching it since Kaitlin was diagnosed . . . but every time I started, I chickened out."

"As painful as it is, we do have to face up to it. Hodgkin's lymphoma is a cancer of the lymphatic system. The lymphatic system is an intricate disease-fighting network that is spread throughout the body. Tumors develop from white blood cells which are called lymphocytes, and begin growing without restraint, often at different locations in the body."

"Yes, yes," Mrs. Bartoni said, impatiently. "Please, Dr. Ludwig, skip the mumbo jumbo and tell us how serious it is – and what can be done?"

"We've only begun testing."

Mrs. Bartoni bit her lip. She started to speak, but her husband interrupted. "Marie, let the doctor finish, will you?"

Dr. Ludwig, smiled. "Let me be brief. We've done a complete physical examination, plus blood work and urine tests. We have yet to schedule an M R I, which will scan the abdomen..." He waited for their reaction. "If this is too upsetting, perhaps we could discuss it later in the day."

"I'm okay," Lawrence said, flicking his eyes from his mother to his father, and back to his mother; but he wasn't okay. He was far from it. Kaitlin had a life threatening disease. It left him irresolute, powerless to come to her aid. It weighed heavily on his mind.

Mrs. Bartoni gasped. "Oh my god! Does this mean she may need chemotherapy?"

Lawrence faced the doctor. "Level with me. From the urine and blood tests, just how serious is her condition?"

"I'm hopeful that it can be contained. The sooner we start, the better Kaitlin's chances will be. Now, if Kaitlin agrees."

"I think it should be done now," Lawrence said. He followed Dr. Ludwig out of the waiting room and into the corridor, leaving his mother in tears, his father trying to comfort her. "How much does she know, doctor?"

"Only that she has the disease, but I have the feeling she knows more than she's letting on. She's never discussed, or hinted about feeling ill?"

"Lately her demeanor has been different. Mood swings, like from happy to moody, and that's not like Kaitlin."

The doctor frowned. "Did she ever complain about sudden high fever? Severe constipation, mental confusion, numbness, drowsiness?"

"Maybe constipation and drowsiness from time to time, but I didn't think it was out of the ordinary."

"Don't blame yourself. Those are common symptoms for many minor illnesses. Hodgkin's can go undetected for quite a while before any extraordinary symptoms occur." They approached Kaitlin's room. "Here we are. Want me to go in with you?"

"No, thanks doctor."

"Very well. I have patients to see. Be gentle with her."

"Yes. She's going to put on a gutsy performance for me."

The doctor smiled. "I surmised as much from the discussions she and I have had. She may look frail, but she's strong willed, isn't she?" He stroked his chin thoughtfully. "And yet, at times she seems so vulnerable."

"She *can* be unpredictable. She does get depressed from time to time. But she always comes around." Suddenly, Lawrence stopped short.

Sitting on a visitor's bench across from them sat his grandmother. She caught his eye. "I didn't mean to yell at you, Larry," she said tearfully. "I mean, about Kaitlin. It's just that your mother, she makes me lose my temper." She rose, walked to her grandson and tilted her face up for him to accept her kiss. "I'm going home now. Forget what I said before. Diciamo le cose che non significhiamo. You understand, Larry. We say things we don't mean." She sighed, turned to leave, but couldn't resist adding, "Your mother, she still makes me crazy. And – about my will, we'll see."

Amused, Dr. Ludwig turned and walked away. Over his shoulder, he called, "Your wife's waiting. We'll talk later."

Kaitlin's face lit up the second her husband entered the room. Her eyes shone at the sight of him; her outstretched arms waited to embrace him. She took in his distress. Running her fingers through his hair, she kissed his cheek and spoke softly. "Lar, it's okay. I'm going to beat this, you'll see. Even the doctor said I have a good chance of recovering."

He sat down beside her, holding on to her hands. "I'm such a big baby. I'm falling apart, and you, the sick one, are comforting me. There's something wrong with this picture."

"Stop carrying on. It's only natural for you to worry about me. I'm going to try my best to keep an optimistic outlook, and you have to promise me that you will too."

He melted into her eyes, thinking of the same haunting eyes that had attracted him to her two years ago, when they collided in the Brooklyn Public Library on Eastern Parkway, Brooklyn, New York.

CHAPTER 6

I t wasn't her hair that attracted Lawrence Bartoni to the girl he bumped into at the library. Her hair was nothing special. Mousy brown in color, cut too short, with bangs that lay unevenly on her forehead, or needed to be styled, or blow dried, or better yet, started over with a fresh cut. Neither was it her face, which housed an adorable turned up nose and baby doll lips that curled up at the end of her mouth. It was her eyes that held Lawrence transfixed – large and round as saucers, which reflected a pure, honest, innocent soul. As he bent down to retrieve her books his breath quickened and he knew this was the girl with whom he wanted to spend the rest of his life. They dropped to the floor at the same time. "I'm so sorry," he said.

She answered coyly. "I'm so clumsy – always bumping into things."

"No, it was my fault," he insisted. "I'm a klutz. Here, let me help you." He offered his hand and helped her up.

She quickly slipped her hand from his. "Well, if you insist, you can take the blame," she said, enthralled. She lingered a few seconds before turning and colliding with another passerby. "Oh my God!" she exclaimed. "Not again."

Lawrence sprang to her assistance. "Excuse us," he said to the startled victim who scowled and went on her way. Picking up her books again, Lawrence tucked them under his arm and smiled. "Are you going or staying?" he asked.

"If you're staying, I'll escort you to a table. If you're going, I suggest you let me walk you out. I wouldn't want you crashing into anyone else."

"I was leaving. Were you?" she asked.

"That depends on you."

"On me? Why?" she asked.

"I'm very sensitive to girls who need someone to take care of them." He looked at her hoping she wasn't offended.

Mustering her strength, she said. "Well, I can't offend you, can I? You may carry my books."

He took her books, his head feeling light, his heart doing flip-flops. "Wanna get married?" he blurted, out of the blue. "I could run home and get your parent's permission."

Ordinarily, by now, she would have been out the door, blushing and too flustered to think of having a conversation with a perfect stranger, much less a good looking young man; but his reassuring, gentle manner gave her the courage she needed. She stifled a giggle. "I live with my aunt. I'm an orphan. How about your parents? Wouldn't it be proper to get their permission, too?"

The mention of the word orphan saddened him. He wondered if she was really an orphan. It wasn't easy reading her. "Pop digs graves, and mom is a bag lady. Now, my grandmother – we keep her locked up in the attic, and let her out every other Saturday, so she can go to her witch's coven. On Sundays we untie her so she can make an Italian feast for the entire family." His head bobbed up and down. "When you meet my grandmother, you'll understand." By her smile he could tell she enjoyed his humor.

They stopped at a bench outside the library and he motioned for her to sit. Looking deep into her eyes, he felt a wonderful euphoric explosion bursting throughout his very being. He moved closer to her and touched her cheek. When she didn't show signs of resistance, he inclined his body toward her and tilted her face up to his, and on impulse, kissed her.

Her face paled. "Why did you – do that?"

His cheek on hers, he said, "I don't know, and I don't care."

She remained motionless. Finally, she mustered enough courage to speak. "I'm not used to doing anything so bold... and in a public place."

"I'm sorry. I don't know what came over me. I shouldn't have moved so fast."

"You don't understand. It's me, not you. I don't go out . . . well, that is, with men, and I don't have girlfriends. I guess I'm a loner. Most people frighten me. Always have." Feeling flustered, she added, "I don't know why I'm telling you this. I'm all mixed up. I should go."

He held onto her hands. "Not a chance."

Her breathing slowed. "Why?" she asked.

"Because, I don't even know your name."

From her hospital bed, Kaitlin shook Lawrence. "Lar, are you all right? You seem a million miles away. Stop worrying. I'll get through this Hodgkin's thing."

"I was thinking about the first time we met. Remember? At the library."

"Of course I remember. You were quite aggressive. You threw me down on the bench outside the library and practically tore my clothes off."

"Get-outta-here! As I recall, you were the one who pursued me, pretending to bump into me. Portraying yourself as the shy, virginal, innocent waif, when what you really wanted, was to get your hands on my bank account."

"That's right, all twenty-two dollars and fifty-one cents, if I remember correctly. What a shy little twit I was. Scared of everything and everybody."

He kissed her fingertips one at a time. Tears welled in his eyes. "Oh Kat," he whispered, his voice breaking. "I don't know if I can do this."

She straightened up and placed her hands on his shoulders. "Now you listen to me, Lawrence P. Bartoni. No more sulking and childish carrying on. Get yourself together. What if it were you?"

"I wish it were."

"Stop!" she warned. "It isn't you, and you can't change it no matter how hard you wish you could. You're not listening. Stop brooding. I need you to work with me." She leaned close and rested her cheek on his. "I don't mean to hurt you Lar, but we have to be realistic." Her eyes pleaded for his understanding.

He straightened up. "I'll do anything you want. I love you with all my heart. In fact, you are my heart. Okay, I promise. I'll give it my best shot." He turned away afraid she would see his troubled expression. "By the way, did Doctor Ludwig tell you he wants to start your treatment as soon as possible?"

"Yes, and I'm glad you brought it up. We have to talk."

His eyes widened. "Talk? What's there to talk about? If you're worried about me, don't. I told you I'd be strong."

"I'll have to undergo tests and probably chemotherapy, and whatever, but I thought delaying it a month wouldn't make such a big difference."

He was taken aback. "What? Why in the world would you want to delay the treatment, even for a day? Didn't you hear what the doctor said? It's important to start as soon as possible." He shook his head. "I don't understand."

"Listen, I spoke to the doctor and he didn't exactly challenge my suggestion of postponing the tests for a while. Which leads me to believe that a couple of weeks is not going to make a difference, or he would have insisted otherwise. It's my decision."

"Now I really don't understand. Kat, why would you want to wait when it might make even the slightest difference?"

"Listen, Lar. When we were married we didn't go on a honeymoon because you had to finish your thesis, and then I came down with the flu. We never had a honeymoon. I want to take this time to go away because... well, we don't know when we'll be able to do it again... not in the immediate future, anyway." She sighed, watching his face pale. "It will only be for a week, and a week can't possibly have an effect on my condition."

He sprang up. "Kat, I'm trying, but what you are asking is ludicrous. If we go away for a week and you get sick... I'd never forgive myself for giving in to you. Please, Kat. You can't ask me to do this."

"Yes, I can Lar. Stop overreacting. I want this. Maybe it's hard for you to understand, but this disease I have may be curable, and it may not. I want us to have this special time together, to keep with me in my heart forever. It may sound foolish to you and it may be only something a woman can identify with, but it's very important to me. Please, don't fight me, Lar. Try and see my point of view. I never asked you for anything, don't refuse me this one time, please. One week is not going to make a difference, believe me."

He looked into her eyes, those soulful eyes that now swallowed him up. "Okay darling, " he said with reluctance. "If that's what you want. Where would you like to go?" he said grimly. "Hawaii, Bermuda, Jamaica?"

"The place we've always wanted to go. The Galapagos Islands."

CHAPTER 7

Trevor Jase Carr feigned sleep. The soft rustling of his wife's negligee as she slid silently off the bed and closed the door beyond her confirmed his suspicions. Upon hearing her muffled laugh in the adjoining room, he was certain of it. He struggled with his conscience. *Does she want me to catch her talking to her lover? Face it man. You know damn well she's been screwing around. You've grown apart, and your marriage has fallen apart.*

Stealthily pulling the covers aside, he walked to the bar, picked up a glass, placed it to his ear and leaned against the wall, but the only sound that reverberated through the wall was a subdued giggle. Eyeing the phone again, he picked it up with care, placed his hand over the mouthpiece and listened.

"What was that?" his wife asked, concerned.

The voice on the other end of the line answered. "I'm mixing a martini, Polly Paranoia. You're jumpy tonight. Concentrate on me, sweetheart. I'm so hot for you. I wish you were here with me."

"I feel the same, but we'll just have to wait until the weekend, T.J.'s going out of town."

He sighed. "Mmm. I can feel your voluptuous breasts rubbing against big John. Please, Pamela, I love it when you talk dirty to me. Don't stop. C'mon baby, make me come."

Trevor grimaced. He placed the phone gently in its cradle, sat down on the bed and placed his head in his hands. Heartsick, his eyes roamed to a picture of her when she was eighteen and crowned Miss Virginia. It brought him back to a time when he thought their love was as sacred as their wedding vows – until death do we...

CHAPTER 8

The sun darted in and out of the gray billowing clouds, echoing Pamela Ann's lackluster mood. She frowned.

"Jesus, Pammy," her mother said. "I don't know what in the world is wrong with you. It's your wedding day and you're carrying on like a spoiled brat. I just don't understand you." She shrugged. "Not that I ever did." She sat alongside her daughter, who was brushing her hair obsessively. "For God's sakes, put the brush down and look at me when I talk to you. You're pouting like a two year old, just as you always do when you can't get your way. I..."

Pamela spoke over her mother. "Mother, please! Spare me the sermon. Save it for the old biddies at your tea socials. What a laugh. Your not understanding me is an understatement. Can't I have wedding jitters without you lecturing me? And how many times have I asked you to call me Pamela? Pammy is so juvenile. Go attend to the guests, or see if the hors d'oeuvres are hot, or cold. Better yet, get lost."

Mrs. Heller gave her daughter a long serious look. "Don't you take that tone with me, young lady. I've endured nineteen years of your childish fits, tantrums, and shenanigans. And another thing... why didn't you give Harry a little respect and have a Unitarian wedding? Or at least a priest and a rabbi."

Pamela threw her hairbrush across the room. "Fuck off, mother! Out! Now! You know as well as I that he's not my biological father. My father was probably some guy you picked up in a bar. Didn't they have condoms in the old days? This Jewish Mafioso character you married and tried to pass off as my real father just doesn't cut it."

"I'm going," her mother said, shaking her head, the hurt and exasperation crossing her face. She walked to the door, opened it then turned on her heels. Her patience at an end, she scowled at her daughter. "You little bitch. You're just an ungrateful little monster who doesn't appreciate a thing she has. Harry has given you everything you ever asked for, and honest to goodness love, too. I don't envy T.J. one bit. Jesus, what a catch. Top of his class. Built like superman, and better looking than any actor in Hollywood. But then again I suppose you'll screw up your marriage just as you do everything else you put your hands on." She closed the door, sighing a breath of frustration.

Pamela walked to where the hairbrush lay and picked it up. Sitting at the vanity, she continued brushing her hair, smiling at her image in the mirror. "Foolish, overbearing pain in the ass. They should put mothers over forty to sleep forever." A knock at the door startled her.

"Pamela," T.J. said. "What's wrong? Your mother is very upset. Did you have another argument with her? Are you all right? Can I come in?"

"Don't you dare, T.J. It's bad luck for the groom to see the bride before the ceremony. Mother and I had one of our usual falling-outs. Wouldn't be a normal day if we didn't. Now why don't you go back downstairs? I'm expecting the bridesmaids any second, and I don't want you around."

"Pamela, are you sure you're okay? You don't have one of your migraines, do you?"

She rolled her eyes. "T.J., I'm just fine. Now be a good boy and get out of my face. Go entertain the guests." Her voice softened. "Please, darling."

"If you insist," he said. As his heels clicked on the stairs, he wondered if he was being paranoid, or if lately her personality had changed. He chalked it up to prenuptial jitters.

Pamela sat admiring herself in the mirror. *"Mother was right about one thing. T.J. is the best catch in Virginia. Then again, there's Edward. He's pretty hot too. Might as well get this over with.* She stood admiring her form in the mirror and spoke to her image. *And besides, who said I have to eat vanilla ice cream forever, when there are so many other flavors to sample.*

❖

T.J. lay on his back staring up at the ceiling, mulling over the many indiscretions in which he had caught, but never confronted Pamela. Thoughts ran through his head as he focused on the ceiling. The night-light cast eerie shadows on the walls, playing tricks with his imagination. *Was I so weak-willed, knowing she cheated and to just let it go, pretending it never happened? I'm C. E. O. of one of the most prestigious corporations in America – make critical decisions all day – and I can't call my wife out for cheating on me.*

His eyes burned and he blinked a tear that fell onto his pillow. He wished he could go to the CD player and put on a Nina Simone recording to accompany the morose mood he was in.

Knowing Pamela might return from her imprudent telephone call at any moment, he settled for a deep hopeless sigh. *If I had taken her mother's advice when she warned me to keep her in line, I wouldn't be in this predicament. Face it. This marriage is kaput.* The longer he thought about her constant cheating, the angrier he became.

Upon hearing the door open, he pretended to be asleep. The satin sheets made a whooshing sound as Pamela slid cautiously onto the bed.

Seething with anger, he inclined his body towards her, propped his face on his elbow, and uttered a disgruntled sigh.

"Hi sweetheart," she said demurely. "I thought you were asleep."

"Now, did you really?" he snipped. Anger flashed in his eyes. "Into telephone sex, are we? Did you talk dirty to him, Pamela? Did he cry out, 'take me' – like I do – when he came? Why didn't you go to his apartment and give him a blow job?"

She sat up, pretending to be genuinely surprised by his sudden accusations. "You're crazy. That was Rebecca I was talking to. You know how she gets when she drinks and has a few hits – she's off somewhere in la-la land, rattling on about her perverted experiences. I was only humoring her. Why are you carrying on like a suspicious husband?"

"Give me a break. The masquerade is over. How long did you think I would let you get away with the shit you've been pulling? You want to rub pussies with Rebecca, okay, I can overlook that, but . . . " He jumped off of the bed and threw his hands up. "I've given you enough time, hoping you'd come to your senses." His fury escaped him; it vibrated around her. "I've had it! It's over!" His fists clenched, his eyes full of hate for her, he paced back and forth muttering obscenities. Suddenly he stopped short at the foot of the bed and stared down at her. "That's it!" he barked. "Tomorrow morning I'm calling Bill Rallings. We'll be divorced in a month."

She reached for her negligee, and threw it over her shoulders, walked to the night table, opened the music box and removed a cigarette. She was distressed, thinking he might be serious. She tried to disguise her nervousness as she lit the cigarette, but her hand trembled. *Have I overstepped my bounds, not covered my tracks? Well, I'll just call his bluff.*

"You can't prove a thing, T.J.," she said, her tone acid cool. "Oh, I'm not saying that I haven't had a few . . . flirtations. You know how impulsive I get. But you've always been so open-minded about our sex life, and if you suspected that I was, uh, promiscuous, you should have spoken up. It's your fault too. If you had told me, maybe I would have...anyhow what's the big deal? Okay, so I had a fling here and there."

He rolled his eyes.

"And besides," she continued, "You have no proof."

He grinned from ear to ear. "Wrong! There's been a private eye on your trail, or should I say tail, for a while, Pammy. It will all be on the table when we go to court. By the way," he teased, "you take a fantastic picture."

The blood drained from her face. "You didn't," she said with a tone of uncertainty lingering in her voice.

His smile was smug, as his head bobbed from side to side, "I did, Pammy baby. I did."

She cringed when he called her *Pammy,* but knew it was not the time to anger him further – it was time to convince him to drop the idea – regain the upper hand. "Okay, so you have me nailed to the cross. But, did you ever think that I might . . . just might have done the things out of desperation?"

"Really? Could have fooled me."

"I'll level with you. Please, sit. I can't stand you hovering over me with that smug look on your face."

"My smug look has good reason to be there. And to tell you the truth, I'm not interested in furthering this conversation." He turned to leave.

"T.J., please hear me out. I'll only take a moment, and then you can go."

Her voice was throaty. "You must have some feeling for me after all these years."

"Yeah? What about your feelings for me?"

She started to speak but the grandfather clock struck twelve midnight with a resonance of finality, and she stopped short. He stood waiting to hear the lame excuses she was about to spew.

"You're right," she said soberly. I have been cheating on you, but not for the reasons you think. I've always had this deep-rooted insecurity. I've always hungered for a father image. Or, it could be my medication. Whatever the cause, it's left me wanting to fill a void, a void that's never satisfied. It could be the pills I take to help me cope with depression." She looked at him for sympathy. "Yes, it's the pills. They make me edgy, short tempered. They change my personality."

He eyed her warily.

She continued. "Maybe your standing up to me is a good thing – a wake up call for me. You've been more than patient with me; more than I deserve." She gazed at him, her eyes pleading. "If you give me another chance I'll try real hard to get my act together. We did have something special, didn't we? Let's get it back? Please. Give me this one last chance."

He struggled with his conscience. There had been good times. No, there had been great times. Was there a chance he could forgive her, or was it a lost cause? His resolve started to slip away and with it his anger.

"There are certain conditions you'll have to live by."

"Name them," she said, conscious of his unexpected change of heart. "Whatever you say."

He shrugged. "Okay, I'll give it a try, but I am telling you right off, no second chances. I don't want to be watching you all the time." He squinted at her. "I mean it, Pamela. I get to check all prescriptions. You just can't keep taking drugs indiscriminately."

"I promise. You'll see. Maybe we can recapture some of the good times we use to have."

His gaze grew distant. "Well, if you don't fuck around, maybe you'll have more for me."

She paused, and then moved closer to him. "Shall we seal it with a kiss?"

Silence.

Taking advantage of his hesitancy, she quickly pecked him on the cheek.

His voice was gentle, but he let her know his hurt. "One more thing. I want you to see a shrink. If you want, I'll go too."

"Anything you say, T.J."

She thought of running to him, caressing and intoxicating him with her womanly allure, but quickly changed her mind. It would be too obvious, too sudden. No, she'd play it cool. Win him over first. He had too much on her. "You know, T.J., it might not be a bad idea if we started this truce by taking a vacation. Somewhere quiet – peaceful – just the two of us. We could rekindle the old flame?" she said, posing it as a question. "What do you think?"

"I'll make the effort if you'll hold on to your end of the bargain. You know getting off the pills is not going to be easy." He stared her down. "Pamela, I'm dead serious. No more screwing around!"

"I'll try, I really will. Have any favorite places you'd like to go? Hawaii, Europe, skiing in Switzerland? We used to have fun skiing San Moritz, and Zermatt. Mmm, I can see you're not turned on."

"Not really."

"I've got it. Remember, you told me you'd love to visit the Galapagos Islands, and I poo-pooed it because I said it would bore me; there was nothing to do but look at strange animals. Let's go there. If I can give up Elizabeth Arden, and..." She held his gaze. "And, my deceitful indiscretions, you must know I'm serious."

He felt some of his tension leaving. "We could do that," he said, eyeing her guardedly. "I'll make the arrangements."

"No. Let me research it. You're much too busy at the office. We can charter one of those exclusive yachts, with a Captain, a chef, and crew. I think I could really get into it, and it would be a good test for me."

"If you insist."

She took hold of his hand and led him to the bed. "And now, will you allow me to make up for all the loving you've missed?" She smiled seductively at him and let her negligee slip to the floor, revealing her exquisite body.

Her hands caressed his face, slowly wandering down his back, pressing him firmly against her. Trevor moved through the motions, moaning and sighing at the proper times, but his mind was not into it, and neither was his heart. He wondered if all her previous deceitfulness had finally caught up with him.

After Pamela had fallen asleep, Trevor felt depression take over. He lay awake staring at the shadows on the ceiling. Flashes of the past clouded his consciousness, and memories of his dead son entered his mind.

CHAPTER 9

"But, mother," Pamela, argued, "T. J's been out every night this week. Don't they do business during the day anymore, or are they too busy playing with themselves?"

"Really, Pamela. How crude. They have a huge business to run."

"Stop living in the past, mother. You know as well as I what goes on at those so- called meetings." Her face darkened as her outrage boiled over. "Stop living in the past. This is the twenty-first century. What you need is some intrigue. A young stud that will flush out the cobwebs in your sex organs."

Mrs. Heller's face reddened with embarrassment. Kissing her grandchild as if to wash away anything he might have heard, she placed him in the playpen and turned to face her daughter. "You've become so gross ... so insensitive. I hardly know you anymore. Look at what your stepfather has done for you. This grand house, the automobiles, and T. J's position as junior vice president with the firm. Can't you show a little appreciation?" She walked through the bedroom to the nursery, lifted the baby out of the crib, hugged and kissed him, then called out. "He's not crying now. I think he's getting over the colic."

"He never cries when you're around. As soon as you leave he'll be screaming bloody murder."

Mrs. Heller laid the baby back into the crib and walked to her daughter. "Perhaps if you showed a little more tenderness towards him he'd feel more at ease.

"Are you quite finished with how I should raise my child and how ungrateful I am?" Pamela asked, her hands placed firmly on her hips. "And if you say, 'Where did I go wrong,' I swear I'll..."

"...You'll what? Strike me? I'm going to make an appointment with your psychiatrist. And, why may I ask, did you stop seeing him?"

"He's a quack. Never talks to me."

"He's not supposed to talk. You are." Scrutinizing her daughter, she added, "What happened to you, Pamela? You've lost that warmth. Even with the baby... you're so distant."

"Aren't we being tactful. Why don't you just come out and say what you mean? I've become a cold-hearted bitch. Well, it suits me, and if you don't like it, you can just fuck off."

Her mother stiffened. "I didn't want to do this, but you're forcing my hand. I'm going to talk to T.J. Maybe he can straighten you out. God knows, I can't."

"That's a laugh. T.J. worships me."

Pamela laid the brush down on the vanity and stared into the mirror. Arguing with her mother was stupid. It could cause a rift with her stepfather and possibly alienate T.J. This altercation was counter productive. Control. She had to take control and make up with her mother – her parents could still be useful to her. Faking tears, she flung herself on the bed and pretended to sob. "Oh Mother, why do I say such horrible things? What comes over me to make me behave this way? I'm so high strung. Nothing satisfies me. I get upset at the least little thing and hate myself afterwards, and I'm such a disappointment to you."

Mrs. Heller shrugged. Her daughter's role-playing was something she had endured for years. She was tired of overlooking, forgiving and trying to understand. Her last hope was Pamela's marriage to T.J., but in her heart she knew her daughter was a bad seed. "Let's call it post partum syndrome," she said. "Many women experience it after giving birth. Maybe the doctor can give you something to relax you. It's the colic. Max has been practically crying non-stop. If you like, I'll take him for a few days."

She hugged her mother. "No, thanks anyhow. I can manage." She dabbed at her eyes with a tissue. "Thanks for being so understanding. You'd better go. You'll be late for the ladies garden meeting." She ushered her mother to the door, kissed her on the cheek, and forced a smile. "I'm going to the kitchen and make myself a cup of tea. I'm beginning to feel better. I'll call you later, and Mother, you won't mention my little tizzy fit to T.J., or Dad, will you? They have enough on their minds."

Her mother sighed as she closed the door. Predestined doom clouded her mind. As she always did when she felt frustrated and helpless, she called for God's help. "Please, Lord," she whispered. "May your light surround me, your love enfold me, and your power protect me. And God, please help my daughter find the right path."

Pamela sat at the kitchen table sipping her tea, listening to her son's shrill crying. Walking to the nursery, she stood at the entrance and screamed at the top of her lungs. "Shut up, you little bastard. You're driving me crazy." Her yelling frightened the baby, and he cried louder. Putting her hands to her ears, she walked back to the kitchen and sat down at the breakfast table. "Every time that God damn nurse is off, the brat pulls one of his tantrums," she yelled. His shrill cries penetrated her head like a dozen corkscrews. She yelled toward the nursery. "I'm getting a migraine, Stop that howling!" She slammed her fist down hard on the table, causing the teacup and saucer to fall to the floor.

Rising from the table, she entered the nursery where the stench of feces overwhelmed her. Turning chalk white, her eyes bulging, her senses out of control, she screamed. "I just changed your fucking diaper two hours ago. Phew, you stink. I think I'm going to throw up."

His non-stop wailing pierced her eardrums. Pointing a finger at him, she cried, "Listen you little bastard, I've had it with you." Her reasoning fading fast, her mind a blur of flashing lights, she picked the infant up and shook him violently, not stopping until his eyes rolled upward in his head and he became silent. Then she laid him back in the crib. To make sure the infant was dead she placed a pillow over his face and held it firmly. Turning him over, she laid him face down to make it appear that he had suffocated on his own.

She returned to the kitchen, heated water, brewed the teabag, poured herself another cup of tea, sipped it, placed the cup lightly on the saucer, took the dustpan and broom out of the utility closet, swept all the remnants of broken china into the dustpan, vacuumed, making sure the floor was clean of any slivers; all the while humming, "It's going to be a great day."

She speed dialed her mother. "Hi, Mother. Listen, I need you to do me a big, big favor. I have an appointment at the dressmaker, and it's Bridget's day off. T.J. and I have a charity affair tomorrow, and I want to wear my new dress. T.J. thinks it's too risqué – says I look like a hooker. Anyhow, what do men know about fashion?"

"Take a breath, Pamela. You're rambling."

What? No, I'm not rambling. Anyhow, I need a favor. Could you come over and watch little Max after the garden meeting? I think he's over the colic. He's quiet now. And Mother, I want to apologize for the way I carried on this morning. Tell me you forgive me."

Mrs. Heller swallowed hard. "I forgive you."

"You're so tolerant. Gotta run. I have to shower and change. See you soon."

Lost in thought, Claire Heller placed her cell phone on the seat of the limousine. Her daughter's flippant attitude, profanity, and mood swings worried her.

An inner voice told her something was wrong. She tapped on the enclosed partition that separated her from her chauffeur. "Roger," she said, "Turn the car around. I want to go back to my daughter."

The fifteen-minute ride seemed like hours as tension set her mind spinning. Finally, the limo pulled up to the circular driveway, as a cold sweat broke out on Mrs. Heller's forehead.

Peering down from the upstairs window, Pamela spotted the limo pulling up to the house. She raced down the stairs, out the front door, stepped into her car, waved a hurried goodbye, and yelled to her mother, "See you." The tires screeched as she drove out of the driveway, causing gravel to sputter onto the flowering bougainvilleas.

Mrs. Heller didn't wait for the chauffeur to open the limo door. She sprang out of the car, rushed up the steps, leaving the front door ajar. There was a deathlike silence as she ran through the foyer into the living room, headed for the nursery.

A noxious odor of feces permeated the room. Lowering her face, she smiled lovingly at her grandchild, and turned him over on his back expecting to change his diaper. Upon feeling his cold, lifeless body and his glassy eyes staring up at her she drew back in terror.

Panic struck. She stood frozen unable to move. Finally, she pulled herself together and walked to the window where the chauffeur stood waiting for her. Her frantic tapping on the windowpane drew his attention. He dashed into the house, where he found Mrs. Heller, her body trembling, unable to speak, holding the dead baby.

The dark mahogany conference table overflowed with platters of assorted sandwiches, hors de oeuvres, pitchers of iced tea, hot coffee, and trays of assorted pastries. The board members sat, their eyes focused on Trevor Jase Carr, C.E.O. of Perfect-tech Industries.

"So Gentlemen," T.J. continued, "I hope I have made myself clear. Just because our profit margins have doubled and the stock has rocketed to new heights, do not for one-minute think we can sit back and just collect royalties. The industry has become litigious – the competition is fierce." His eyes locked with each of the twelve board members in turn, sending them a clear message that their jobs were on the line. He continued with, "Let's not get complacent."

The members stiffened in their chairs.

"Am I clear?" T.J. asked.

He looked for affirmation as his private secretary tried to get his attention. Interrupting a board meeting was strictly forbidden. T.J. sensed her urgency. He took her arm and led her to the outer office.

T.J. met the chauffeur at the front door as soon as he pulled up to his home. "How did it happen, James?"

"I can only tell you Mr. Carr, that your mother-in-law came to baby-sit and found the baby . . . dead," he whispered.

"Where's my wife?"

"From what Mrs. Heller said, she went to have a dress altered. I think your mother-in- law's in shock. I took the liberty to phone for Dr. Livingston. Should be here any minute. I didn't call the police; I wanted to wait for you. Did I do the right thing?"

"You did, James. Thanks."

T.J. rushed to the nursery to find his mother-in-law crying hysterically. "The baby! Oh God, the baby! I should've come earlier. It was my fault." She swayed from side to side with grief. "She had to go to the dressmaker – the charity affair – why did she have to go to the damn dressmaker?" She sobbed. "The dressmaker is more important than the baby."

Tears streamed down T.J.'s cheeks. He picked the lifeless child up and held him in his arms. He breathed air into the baby's mouth, but it was too late. He wept convulsively, pacing the length of the nursery, clutching the child tightly. "Max, my son," he sobbed, "You didn't have a chance to live. Not a chance – not a lousy chance. I love you Max, wherever you are." He stopped, turned on his heels, and faced his mother-in-law. "What dressmaker, Mother?"

She spoke between sobs. "You know . . . the charity ball . . . She had to have the gown altered for tomorrow night. What does it matter, now?"

"The charity ball isn't until next week," he stammered. He laid the baby in the crib, sat down, close to his mother-in-law, and put his arm around her, trying to comfort her. Looking back at the infant, he wondered why Pamela had left so suddenly.

CHAPTER 10

Judy Blessing studied her husband as he pushed the mashed potatoes from one side of his plate to the other. "Why the sour puss, Beau? Writers block?" Silence.

Placing her napkin on the table, she rose, stood over him, pecked him on his cheek, and massaged his shoulders. "C'mon," she whispered in his ear, her breath warm, her voice tender, "This isn't the Beau I know. What happened to, 'Mr. Laugh everything off'? You're the one who preaches about life being too short, and depression being bad karma germinating evil cells throughout the body."

Beau lifted his head and smiled up at this beautiful redheaded woman with piercing green eyes, who he adored.

He never quite understood what she saw in him. Yes, he knew he was handsome, and from what people had said, distinguished looking, especially with his hair graying at the temples. He was well built for a man who was twice her age, with a winning boyish manner and a terrific sense of humor. But, Judy was more than just beautiful. People noticed her; even did a double take, wondering who this captivating woman could be. He was puzzled that her insecurities overshadowed her diverse talents and good looks.

"Where are you, Beau? I asked you what happened to Mr. Happy?"

He laughed. "That my dear is advice I give, not take. It doesn't apply to me."

She sat down beside him. "I know what your problem is, and you're wrong."

He rolled his eyes. "Is this going to be a long lecture? Should I put the computer to bed?"

Ignoring his banter, she continued. "You've been writing for five years and you've finished three manuscripts." He frowned. "Stop making faces. I'm being honest. I'd tell you to get a job in Target, or chauffeur people to the airports, or catch and mount butterflies, if I didn't think your writing was good. I read two to three books a week and I tell you Beau, yours are better than a lot of them. They've been published and once an author has one successful book on the best seller list they're a shoo-in for anything else they write."

"I know you're right Jude, but my problem is..."

"Stop right there, Beau! If you're going to bring up that you won't be around to see your work published, I swear, I'll leave you." She shrugged. "Save the clever remarks for your novels. Honestly, sometimes you make me so goddamned mad. Do you know a single writer that wrote a best seller right off the bat?"

He nodded. "Has to be. Just can't think of one off the top of my head."

"Even Dean Koontz struggled and wrote five manuscripts before he broke through. You know what you need?"

"Yeah, a miracle or an introduction to Spielberg."

"I'm serious Beau."

"So am I."

"It takes time for a first time author to get published." She sulked. "I have enough aggravation at work without coming home to a depressed husband."

"You call designing clothes, work? You're lucky. God gave you talent. To you, it comes naturally. Your sketches of the shmatas are works of art. I can sit straining this brain forever until I get a thought that makes sense."

"You're so full of it. You don't give yourself enough credit. Your imagination is spectacular and you're very bright. On the other hand, your sentence structure leaves a lot to be desired."

"Well, excuuuse me. I didn't have a daddy to send me to an Ivy League school." He placed a clump of potatoes on his fork and aimed it at her.

Shaking her head, her irritation evident, she said, "You just dare to let that potato go and it will be the last childish prank of your life. Honestly Beau, sometimes I think you never grew up, just enlarged."

Setting the fork down on his plate, he crossed his eyes and stuck his tongue out at her. "Now that hurts," he said pretending to cry. "You know how sensitive I am. You are perhaps suggesting that I am immature?"

"You're also full of shit. I adore your sense of humor. That's the first thing I admired about you, but once in a while it would be refreshing to hear a serious thought come out of that mouth. When you write, you're a different person... so together."

"Okay, from now on I'll be serious in our conversations and humorous in my writing."

She rolled her eyes. "I give up. Forget we ever had this conversation. I'm going downstairs to work."

He pointed a threatening finger at her. "*You* are not going anywhere until you kiss me. By the way, Jude, before our little repartee you mentioned something about what I need."

"I have a vacation coming and since you're stymied with your writing I thought it might be a good time to get away. You can get your gray matter together and I could just veg- out. How about it?"

"Great idea. Maybe I'll get inspired. Where to?"

"Laura, my assistant went to the Galapagos Islands last year and raved about it. I've checked with the travel agency and it sounds wonderful."

She teased. "You *have* heard of the Galapagos Islands, haven't you?"

"The Galapagos Islands? Of course, they're off the coast of Corfu, near Greece, right?"

She stared him down.

"Okay, okay, just kidding."

"So what's new?" she countered.

He stood, folded his arms, pulled back his shoulders and spoke with authority. "The Galapagos Islands are a cluster of thirteen volcanic islands about one hundred and fifty miles west of the coast of Ecuador in South America. One can see the Giant Tortoises, Green Sea Turtles, Marine Iguana, and Land Lizards, cruise the islands on a commercial boat, or hire a yacht at fifty thou with a crew of seven to cater to one's every desire."

"You sneaked my brochures, didn't you?"

He nodded. "You know you can't hide anything from me."

Her face lit up. "A yacht? Wow! Way to go. I'd love to do that. Please, can we at least think about it? I'll be your slave forever."

"We'll see."

"My parents used to say, we'll see, and it always ended up, 'no.'"

He stepped toward her and took her in his arms. "Did I ever make you a promise that I didn't keep?"

"No."

"Then, I promise."

"How did I get so lucky to have you as my husband?"

"Beats the shit out of me. I had younger and more beautiful women banging my door down. Poor judgment on my part, I guess."

He ran from the room, she at his heels. When he let her catch him, he twirled her in circles and kissed her. "I don't want you to get a swelled head, but I was the lucky one."

"I'm so excited," she said. "But Beau, promise you won't get angry if I ask you something."

"Uh, oh. What's it going to cost?"

"Well, I know how you are about money and you are inclined to be a little... uh...frugal. Well, let's say, careful with expenses."

"You're being very tactful Jude. I'm cheap and we both know it. What is it?"

"Can we go first class? Like hire our own yacht? All the other trips we made were so...like the Air Pakistani flight to Paris, where there were no assigned seats and we had to race for them and gasped for air until they turned the air conditioning on. Jesus, every time I think of how small the seats were – made for elves. And the time we..."

"Stop! You're defaming my character. Okay, I'll let you make the arrangements, but it will have to come out of your bonus. Agreed?" She pouted then smiled. "Absolutely."

"I'll kick in too," he said sighing.

She kissed him repeatedly. "Bless you, Blessing."

"Stop mauling me," he grumbled lightly. "And you know I hate that 'bless you, Blessing' line. I've heard that stupid line all my life. Now if you will excuse me, I have to attend to my husbandly chores – clearing the dishes."

"Let me help," she urged.

He raised his hands. "No! Thank you very much. You make more of a mess.

We made an agreement. The house is my responsibility, and bringing home the moolah is yours. By the way a first class tour of the Galapagos Islands, chartering our own yacht with a captain and crew – as I said before, you're talking at least around fifty thousand big green ones. Dat'sa lot of dinero, kiddo."

"Beau, I want this to be a very special vacation. It's your birthday and it's the big one. Let's splurge. I've been all over the world for the company, checking to make sure the garments are ready for production. But we haven't gone anywhere together."

"Thanks for not mentioning the birthday number." He stroked his chin in thought. "You know Jude, you could've, and still can make extra money," he said, referring to cash payoffs, dinners, or trips to exotic places manufacturers give buyers for giving them business above and beyond the legal ethical boundaries. "Bad judgment on your part. If you play it smart, you could retire early and I wouldn't have to be a half-assed writer."

She protested loudly. "I wouldn't take a dime from a manufacturer. That's dishonest. And you should be the last to talk about ethics. If you hadn't been so greedy trying to make a fast buck, I could have retired, too," she said with wounded anger.

He agreed. "I'm sorry. You're right, and we're paying for it. You wouldn't have to support me, if I wasn't such a fuck-up."

She hurried over to embrace him. "Honestly Beau, I didn't mean to hurt you. It's just that you make me so mad."

He kissed her tears. "I know you didn't, but it's true. We wouldn't have to worry about money if I'd been a mensch."

"I'm going to give you the same sermon you give me when I get depressed. We're healthy, have a beautiful home, and we love each other,... well, this week anyhow. I know that you'll get published one of these days. And besides, we do have money invested in the stock market. We could tap into that."

He raised his voice. "We are not touching that money! That's for you when I –
She threw her hands to her ears. "Stop!"

"Jude, honey-bun, you're going to have to face up to it sooner or later."

She raised her voice. "I don't want to talk about it! Okay, forget about the stock. I'm going downstairs to work." As she descended the stairs, she muttered. "God, he's so damn cheap."

"What was that?" he called to her.

"I said, 'As you sow, so shall you reap.' Just an old saying sweetheart."

Beau walked into the kitchen, loaded the dishes into the dishwasher, dialed start, and sat down. Angst-ridden, he put his elbows on his knees and let his forehead sink onto his palms, his thoughts drifting to a dark time in his life.

CHAPTER 11

Seymour Blatt viewed the garments that hung on the display wall in the New York City showroom, and turned towards his partner. "I tell you, Beau, this spring line's a winner. Those whores who call themselves buyers better leave paper or they're as dumb as I think they are."

Beau glowered. "You know Sy, you have the biggest mouth in the garment industry. Judy's a buyer. Do you consider her a whore too?"

"Aw, C'mon, Beau. Judy's my favorite person in the whole world. How you lucked out with her is something I'll never understand." He poked him playfully in the ribs. "I've seen your shlong in the steam room and it can't be that." He clapped Beau on the back. "I would think after five years, you'd be used to my shtick. You know how irresponsible I can be." Seymour walked to the window and looked down at the throngs of people on Seventh Avenue, scurrying home.

A dark shadow crossed Sy's face. His breathing quickened. "Listen," he said. Let's have a couple of hits before we close shop, okay? It's been a long day. There's something I have to discuss with you... about finances.

"Finances? You never bother me with the financial end of the business. Orders are coming in from all over the country, and some big ones from major department stores."

Seymour avoided Beau's eyes. One look at Seymour and all expression left Beau's face. "Uh, oh. I'm getting bad vibes. You have that funny look on your face, like when you've done something you shouldn't have."

Sy stuttered. "The... the sales are great, but...

"So?" Beau screwed up his face. "What are you talking about? I'm aware of every order we get. I think you need a vacation, or a weekend to rest up. Lately, you're mind is somewhere in the clouds."

Seymour walked to the bar and removed a cigar box. "Pot, coke, or both?" he asked.

Beau stared at Seymour, with concern. "Pass on the drugs, Sy. Maybe vodka. Something tells me I'm going to need it." Seymour poured the liquor, added a splash of cranberry juice, two ice cubes, and handed Beau the glass. He downed the drink. "Okay. Talk. What's it this time? Did Betty catch you in a motel with one of the buyers? Or did you lose a bundle at the track again?"

Seymour lit a joint and took a few deep tokes, then emptied two dots of coke on the table, scooped it up with his pinky and inhaled one into each nostril.

Beau cast a dubious eye at Seymour. "Jesus, its only Thursday, Sy. Aren't you starting early? At least wait for the weekend."

Seymour refilled Beau's glass. His smug expression faded into one of severity. "Drink up, then I'll talk."

"You're scaring the shit out of me, Sy. Have you been snorting all day?"

Seymour's voice was heavy. "All fucking day, all fucking week, and all fucking month." He moved closer to Beau. Biting his lip, he muttered, "I haven't had the balls to tell you what I did." He snorted again.

"Hey, take it easy. You're going to overdose and I'm not taking you to the hospital. I promised Judy I'd take her out to dinner. You didn't murder anyone, did you?"

Seymour walked to his desk, hesitated, and then turned back and faced his partner. "I wish I had. I wish to God I could go back and undo what I did." His eyes watered. "But I can't. And the worst part of it is – I deceived you."

Inwardly cursing, Beau took a chair next to Sy. "I'm on the verge of strangling you Sy. What the hell are you talking about? What did you do?"

"I know you're going to hate me for the rest of your life, and I can't blame you."

Beau's face flushed with exasperation.

"All right, all right, I'll tell you. You're going to find out anyhow." He puffed profusely at a joint. "I wrote fake orders. Big ones. I've been doing it for a while."

"What? Fake orders? What are you talking about? Orders have to be written on the store's stationery, or on our order pads with confirmations with delivery dates to follow. What are you saying?" Beau let out an arduous sigh. "Oh, Sy. You didn't ... Never mind, I can see from your face that you did. How did you get hold of their order copies?" He shook his head.

"Another stupid question. Knowing you, I'm sure you managed it. But Sy, why? And how did this finagling get by the factors' bookkeepers?"

"They advance us the money to keep the company going as long as they see the orders coming in, and we *are* a solid company. They've been our factors for over five years. Why should they suspect anything?" His face grew pale and his hands shook. "I bet heavy. I mean heavy – at the track, basketball, hockey, and any action or event I felt I could make a killing. But my luck ran out. I got deeper and deeper in debt, and as a last resort, like a schmuck I went to the mob figuring I'd pay them back when I won. But I kept losing and losing, and the amount I owed just kept growing and growing – plus the compounded interest they demanded... well, it got to a point where I just couldn't cover it." He covered his face with his hands. "I started to drown. I didn't know where to turn...so I kept taking money from the business to pay them off until..."

"...Until the factors called you on it and you had no way to explain yourself. Is everything gone, Sy?"

"Everything and more."

Beau's fist pounded the table. He shouted. "Fuck! Fuck! Fuck!" He grabbed Sy by his shoulders and shook him. "The mob! I can't believe it."

"They're paid off."

"Do you have any idea what you've done? We are going to jail! Why didn't you come to me – talk to me? We *are* partners. You've done some crazy things, but this..."

"I was too ashamed. You've always been so straight with me, and such a gem. I didn't have the heart. I kept hoping that I could somehow pull us out of it. Turn things around." His head bobbed up and down. "I didn't think. I didn't think."

"No, you didn't. You became lost, Sy. You spent all day at the track with the bookies and too much screwing around – and the drugs... It's the drugs that did you in. All the hard work we put into this business to make a nest egg for our future, and now it's down the fucking toilet. Jesus, Sy, we had millions."

Seymour Blatt sobbed uncontrollably. His hands reached out and encircled his partner, holding him tight. "You don't have to worry," he wailed, "I'll tell them you had nothing to do with it. I swear. I'll take full responsibility. I'll put it in writing."

Beau gulped down the rest of his vodka, and half filled another. "I don't know what to say, Sy. I'm numb. I have to call Judy. I need her strength right now."

Seymour clenched Beau's arms. "One more thing, Beau. I know you're going to see to it that I have the best lawyers, but just in case... watch after Betty and the kids. Please. You know the safety deposit box where we stash the green we skimmed from the cash sales we made?"

"You mean you didn't touch that? You must have been high."

"I did take some – about a hundred thou. There should be five hundred and fifty thou left in cash. I've been so out of it I forgot the money was there."

"Well, how fucking lucky can we get. We'll need it for the lawyers."

"You'll be in the clear, I promise you. Just make sure you invest some of it for Betty and the kids. I hope that someday you'll have it in your heart to forgive me."

Beau listened to the hum of the dishwasher as the cycle turned to off. He removed the hot, dry dishes from the dishwasher, and returned them to their proper place in the kitchen cabinet, all the time thinking about Sy's face after the police had driven him to the morgue to identify Sy's body, after they fished him out of the Hudson River.

CHAPTER 12

On the flight from New York to Miami, Trevor was cool toward Pamela, but when the plane touched down at Miami International Airport, his mood changed from discontent, to doubt, and finally to forgiveness. He hadn't harped on her, hoping the promises she made were sincere, and not made under the influence of the pills she swore she threw out the morning after they reconciled. But her sudden trips to the lavatory during the flight left him skeptical. Having gone this far, he decided to give it one last chance. Acting suspicious of her every action would only threaten their already shaky situation.

They walked hand in hand to the first class lounge where they relaxed and refreshed themselves before boarding the flight to Ecuador.

The moment the customs inspector in Quito, Ecuador, stamped their passports, Trevor took Pamela's arm and led her to the waiting limousine. Pamela was overly attentive for a while, and then suddenly became lost in thought for a short period of time. He wondered if stopping the pills abruptly was too much of a shock to her system. He knew addicts had to ease off gradually. He thought. *Why, didn't I consult her doctor before we left?* The tightness in his stomach reappeared.

The recurring dreams of their baby Max, who died so abruptly, also weighed heavily on his mind. How many times had he asked himself if Pamela had something to do with the infant's death? The fact that the baby did not resemble either of them haunted him to the point of frustration.

Fortunately, at the moment, Pamela was cheerful, attentive and loving to him, and once again he was happy knowing there might be a glimmer of hope that they might get their lives back on track. There was no sense watching her every action, it would only make her uneasy, and he more suspicious, and would eventually destroy what they were trying to achieve. He smiled, convincing himself he was not the Pill Patrol, or Big Brother spying on her every move.

"Why the broad grin?" she asked.

"Was I grinning?"

"Yes, but as long as you're happy, I don't care." She searched the surrounding area. "Now, where's our guide?"

"Right beside the limousine," he said."

"That's the driver, silly. Every group has to have a guide. It's the law. He will be with us throughout the trip. Didn't you read the brochures I gave you?"

"Did I have time? I had to juggle my office schedules, and even so, I left a million things undone."

"You don't say. I remember the time we went to Paris and I asked you if you were worried about leaving work at the office, and you said, 'fuck'em. It will be there when we get back.'"

"I didn't have all the responsibilities I have today." Noticing the man heading toward them, he asked, "Who's the dapper dude coming our way?"

"Has to be our guide. Stop frowning. If you're worrying about me, forget it. You're the only man in my life. Don't make me uncomfortable. I promised, didn't I?"

"What makes you think I was thinking about that?"

"I'm not sure. Maybe, I'm a little paranoid – or guilt is rearing its ugly head."

The guide strolled up to them and extended his hand. His black eyes seemed to be laughing. His mouth turned up at the corners – his smile warm and cordial. "Hello, hello, Mr. and Mrs. Carr. I am your guide. Call me, Santiago.

It is island that I am named for. I apologize for my lateness, but the pangos had leak and had to have reparation. The landing was wet," he added, looking down at his dripping, rolled up pants.

"Where to now, Santiago? The hotel?" Trevor asked.

"Overnight at Swiss Hotel Quito. Tomorrow morning we fly to island. We lucky – you charter special plane. No stop at Guayaquito. Go directly to Isabella. El Capitan waits for us there. Magnifico, grande yacht for only two passengers." He raised his eyebrows. "And, for Santiago too. Yacht has ocho cabins." He held up eight fingers. "Seven crewmen, and you have private cook. We eat good." He patted his stomach. "Big shot Americans. I am honored to be your guide."

"And we are honored to have you as our guide," Trevor countered amused.

"I love him," Pamela said. "It's a perfect start to our vacation."

"Don't love him, just let him be our guide," Trevor said, winking. Then followed up with, "Just kidding. Just kidding."

CHAPTER 13

T he water sparkled from the sun's reflection as the yacht's stern cut a path, parting the blue green waters. Aboard the yacht *Yolanda*, Brooklyn born Lawrence Bartoli sat in a lounge chair, leaning forward, anxiously awaiting his wife, Kaitlin to emerge from their third class cabin. Disappointed at not seeing her, he sat back, nervously tapping his fingers on the arm of the lounge chair .As she ascended the stairs, his face brightened, and he waved. "Over here, Kat," he called. "How are you feeling? Better?" He regretted allowing her to talk him into booking the cruise, but when she looked at him with those engaging eyes, there was no way he could refuse. He wanted to ask her to cut the vacation short, but it was a moot point now, knowing what her answer would be. He eyed her mindfully. "That's the second time today you threw up."

"Lar, move over. We have to talk." He slid over as she spooned herself close to him.

He whined. "What's wrong? You want to go home? You're not feeling well. I knew it. You're white as a sheet. Let's get off at the next island and go to Quito, and then..."

Kaitlin put her finger to his lips. "Cool it, Lar. You're carrying on as if I were on my death-bed."

He shivered at her remark.

Trying to calm him, she rambled on. "I'm pale because I threw up. I feel much better now. In fact, I feel great. I love the smell of the sea air. I read somewhere that everything started from the sea."

"Sure, sure Kat. That's very interesting, but I'm worried about you." He snuggled closer to her. "I know when you go off on a tangent that you're avoiding something. Come clean." He squeezed her hand. "Are you getting worse?"

"No, I'm..." She turned towards him, their faces only a breath away. "Lar, I'm pregnant... I think."

Lawrence's jaw dropped. He stuttered. "I ... I... don't know what to say. My first thought is that I should be happy... but..."

"Your second thought is... how will I be cured of the disease and still have the baby, isn't it? I don't believe in abortions." His complexion paled. "It's going to be all right, Lar. Maybe I can still have the baby."

He gritted his teeth. Not believing his ears, he turned towards her, and shouted angrily, "Are you out of your mind? Have the baby? You can't be serious! You're playing with fire. You don't know what your saying." He sulked. "It's my fault. I should have known better." Passengers turned to see what the quarrel was about.

"People are watching, Lar. Keep your voice down. What do you mean, you should have known better?" she asked with reservation. "You used a condom. Accidents happen. It's nobody's fault."

He ran his hands over his face. "It is my fault, Kat. Remember last month when we made love and I ran out of condoms?"

"Uh huh, I remember. You ran to the drugstore and bought some. So?"

"Well, there's something I didn't tell you. I mistakenly picked up the wrong ones."

"The wrong ones?"

"You know I'm... uh... well endowed. Well, the condom was too small, but I used it anyhow."

"But you would have known if it tore, wouldn't you?"

"I looked at it afterwards to make sure... but there's always a possibility... I'm such an asshole. How could I do that?"

"The question is, why would you do that?"

His voice filled with guilt, he inhaled and let it out with a long sorrowful sigh. "I didn't think. I was selfish. The tightness of the smaller condom felt so good, and I thought... well, what's the difference? I put your life in jeopardy."

"Now Lar!" she declared with a hint of anger. "Don't fall apart. I'll be okay. They perform miracles today." Aware of his sensitive nature, she took his face in her hands and kissed the tears. "Just think. I'll have twins."

"Twins?"

"I'll have you, and the baby. That adds up to two babies, doesn't it?"

He held her tightly as the knot in his stomach told him that she wouldn't have the baby – now or ever.

CHAPTER 14

A light summer breeze blew in from the east, bringing with it the scent of jasmine, roses, lilacs, oranges, and cinnamon. The potpourri aroma drifted into the grass and wood- covered makeshift shelter where Trevor, Pamela, Judy and Beau sat across from each other, waiting for their accommodations to be completed.

Judy returned a polite smile to the attractive blond lady, and sized her up and down, wondering from the diamond Rolex watch, Cartier love bracelet, and large diamond ring – if she might be one of the members of her country club.

Pamela poked Trevor, whispering, "Do you know them? They look so familiar."

He glanced at Judy and Beau, shaking his head. "No, I don't think so. Good looking, aren't they? Like out of Cosmopolitan. Maybe they're models." He smirked. "Mmm. Beautiful, isn't she?"

Pamela's eyes narrowed at Judy, showing a hint of jealousy. She ran her tongue over her lips. "Stunning man," she said, looking at Beau. "So distinguished looking. Must be a dignitary. The lady made a good catch. Has to be her lover. I bet he's keeping her in some high-rise ivory tower, like

Rapunzel."

T.J. drew back. "Careful Pamela, your fangs are showing. Aren't you being a bit catty? Remember, you promised to behave." He quickly glanced at the couple. "I think they look great together."

"Yeah, like father and daughter," she said in a hushed tone. Pamela let her wrist drop, exhibiting her diamond bracelet, and eight carat canary yellow diamond ring, the facets twinkling as they reflected off the sunlight.

Not pleased with his wife's criticism, Trevor focused on Judy. His eyes followed her every curve, starting with her kelly green silk blouse with the top two buttons open at the neck, exposing a trifle more than just a hint of cleavage; her flawless, alabaster skin which revealed her breasts as they rose and fell to the rhythm of her every breath; down to her crossed, shapely legs, reminding him of the old Vargas drawings from his mother's collection that he used to get off on. A large brimmed hat the same color as her blouse shaded most of her face. She raised her head, her green eyes catching Trevor's stare. She smiled at him, her eyes lingering more than necessary for casual acknowledgment, and then returned the smile. She quickly looked down, embarrassed and avoided his eyes while squeezing Beau's hand.

Observing their guide and another guide having words with the captain, she asked, "What's wrong, Beau?"

I'm not sure Jude. From the little Spanish I know, all I can decipher is, 'you're wrong, it's mine.'"

"Beau, shouldn't you go and talk to them? And why are you so nervous?"

"I'm not nervous. Stop fretting. Give them another minute. I'm sure they'll straighten it out."

Across from Judy and Beau, Pamela showed her agitation by tapping her foot. "T.J., what the hell is going on? Get over there and find out why we're spending fifty thousand dollars to wait like third class tourists to board the yacht." She glanced at Judy and Beau. "And why is that couple sitting over there like they're also waiting to board?" She shut her eyes tightly. "You know what? I bet we're all booked on the same yacht."

Trevor and Beau stood and started walking to where the three men argued. Greeting one another, they exchanged glances. Beau extended his hand to Trevor. "Hi, I'm Beau Blessing. Don't tell me we're both booked on the same yacht? That's impossible."

Trevor smiled and shook hands with Beau. "Jesus, I hope not. Not after all the planning my wife went through making the arrangements," he said, watching Pamela and Judy approach. "Let's get to the bottom of this."

The guides talked over one another as the captain raised his hands and shouted, "Silencia, por favor!" He faced the men, trying to keep the situation from getting out of hand. "Please excuse the confusion, but evidently there has been a blunder. This has never happened to me before, but for some reason you are both booked on the yacht. He held up a printed itinerary. "I have the manifesto right here. See, it states one couple, but I have two reservations for this date, and..."

Pamela grabbed the itinerary from his hand and read it. "I don't believe this," she complained. "How could the agents be so stupid? What do we do now? Flip a coin to see who stays and who goes, while the losers try to book another yacht? God only knows what kind of scow we would end up on."

The captain shook his head. "You will not find another yacht available at this time of the year. It is high season. The only yachts, if there are any available, would be on a third class line." He eyed the four travelers and began gesturing. "I know you would not be interested in traveling that way. I would be very grateful if anyone has any suggestions. Perhaps we could go aboard and have champagne and hors d'oeuvres on deck, to at least get out of the sun and talk it over?"

Pamela sighed. "Well, I certainly can go for a good stiff drink."

Judy, nodded, "I'm with you."

The captain, relieved for the moment, extended his hand to Pamela and to Judy.

Trevor and Beau exchanged shrugs and ascended the gangplank. "What line of work are you in?" Trevor inquired.

Beau clapped him on the back. "I'm a travel agent," he joked. "I work real cheap. Want me to fuck up your next vacation?"

They sat eyeing each other. Beau broke the silence. "Well," he said, his eyes flicking from Pamela to Trevor, his hand resting on his wife's arm, "Are we going to be civilized about this situation, or are we to become antagonistic and insult each other, hoping that one of us will get disgusted and leave?"

Trevor waved a hand. He focused on Judy, but directed his voice to Beau. "First things first. I dislike speaking to strangers without knowing their names. I'm Trevor J. Carr. This scintillating lady by my side is Pamela Ann, who likes to be called Pamela. Never Pam, and never, never, Pammy, if you want to live to see tomorrow." Pamela rolled her eyes. "To my friends I am known as T.J."

"Eloquently put," Beau said. "I'm Beau Blessing to my friends, and I always speak to strangers. And if you make one remark about 'bless you Blessing, you're dead meat. This devastating creature at my side is Judy Blessing, my child bride. With that out of the way, what are we going to do about our predicament?"

"Now is the time for clear-cut logical sense," Trevor said, raising his brows at Beau. "Don't you agree? I vote for the ladies to make the decision."

"Absolutely, T.J.," Beau countered quickly. "This does call for, as you so aptly put it, clear-cut logical sense."

"They're playing with our heads, Pamela."

"Fucking with our heads is more like it," quipped Pamela.

"Whatever," Judy, said, slightly taken aback by Pamela's language. "Let's say for conversation's sake that we agree to share the yacht, which has eight double cabins, seven crew members, and the captain, who by now must be tearing his hair out. We could go our separate ways. We do have our own guides. I don't see any other solution."

Pamela nodded in agreement. "We could sleep in a different cabin each night and not bump into each other the entire trip." She smiled flirtatiously, admiring Beau's stature and good looks as sexual fantasies played in her head.

"I doubt that," Judy said. "The yacht isn't a battleship." Glancing from her husband to Trevor, she raised her eyebrows, waiting for a sign of confirmation. Trevor started to speak, but Pamela cut him off. "Forget about them, Judy," she said. "They asked us to make the decision, and we did. Who cares about what they have to say?"

"I'm not sure. I usually let Beau make the decisions."

"Get over it. Where were you raised, in China?" She leaned toward Judy. "You're going to put the American woman's fight for freedom back a hundred years, but we can confer on that later." She extended her hand to the center of the table. "Done deal, guys?" she suggested, not expecting resistance. "Now where is the waiter with the champagne?"

"You asked for vodka straight up, and he's the steward, not the waiter."

Trevor said. They all shook hands. "We have to concede, Beau. The opposition is getting out of hand. My wife can be quite outspoken. Comes from being spoiled by wealthy parents." He leaned over and pecked her on the cheek.

Pamela, shot back. "What's wrong with saying or doing what you feel? I may be a bit impulsive, but I'm honest. And, Mr. Big Shot, computer executive, if my wealthy parents hadn't given you a shot in the ass, you wouldn't be CEO of Startech Systems today."

"Are you really the bigwig at Startech?" Beau asked, surprised and impressed.

Trevor grimaced at his wife. "I don't go around bragging about it..." he pointed a thumb at his wife... "like she does, for a few reasons. I don't want people liking me for my money. More important, they might take it into their heads to kidnap Pamela, and that would just break my heart." He ducked as she threw a napkin at him. "You see, we have a fantastic relationship." He turned to Beau. "Since we're getting along so famously, how about you? Do you really have control over her? I get the feeling she leads you around by the nose. Not that you don't prefer it that way. Or is it an act for our benefit?"

"I make the moves, but with her approval, though we do have our disagreements. Sometimes the age difference rears its ugly head, but not for long. We've had hard times financially, and there are always unsuspected surprises that come up, usually when you think all is going smoothly. You know as well as I, that you have to work at a marriage or it will slowly deteriorate. Right? We practically bankrupted our life's savings for this trip."

Trevor, remembering Pamela's indiscretions took her hand in his. "That's why we're here, to work on our marriage."

Feeling the conversation was becoming too personal in too short a time, Judy spoke up. "Gee, what I would do not to have to get up every morning, go to work, and take the crap I have to from people inferior to me. I used to pretend I was rich. I would go out and buy whatever I wanted, until the bills became outrageous, and my father constantly gave me heat about having to pay them. Then I met Beau, and he paid all my bills. We laugh about what my dad told Beau. "She's *your* responsibility now. You deal with it.'"

Beau threw his hands up. "And I did. I was financially successful then." Taking hold of Judy's hand, he smiled and said, "But it was worth it."

The captain approached, apprehensively. "Are we? Uh. Have we made a decision, perhaps?"

"We have," Trevor said. "We have decided to share the boat."

"Fantastico," he exclaimed. "I have taken the liberty to have the two, what we call 'luna de miel' suites, made up. They have the finest appointments and are next to each other."

"Really?" Beau said.

"Uh... next to each other?" Judy, said reluctantly.

Knowing Pamela, Trevor's demeanor showed signs of concern. "Very well," he said with trepidation.

Pamela's smile concealed a smirk. "How thoughtful of you, captain," she said. "Mmmm, sounds cozy."

CHAPTER 15

The early morning had been hazy, but the sun broke through, promising the tourists another beautiful day to explore the islands. Kaitlin shifted her weight from one foot to the other, impatiently waiting at the bathroom door, which they shared with the couple in the adjoining cabin. The slow rocking of the boat made her nauseous, and although she hid how she felt from Lawrence, she wondered if taking the trip might have been a mistake. The adjoining bathroom door closed with a soft click and Kaitlin sighed with relief. She turned the knob and came face to face with her neighbor. The surprised woman smiled warmly at her. "I'm so sorry, dear. I thought you and your husband were up and about. Sharing a bathroom is so inconvenient. Traveling on a third class boat does have its drawbacks. I can wait. You go ahead and take your time." Noticing Kaitlin's pallor, she asked, "Are you feeling poorly? Can I help?"

Kaitlin managed a half smile. "I'll be all right. Thanks for letting me in first."

"You go ahead dear. I know how it is when you're... that way, having had four daughters of my own. You know what I mean, don't you, dear?" She closed the door and called back, "Don't be bashful, dear. If you need any motherly advice, just knock on my door."

The cool water felt good on Kaitlin's face as she splashed. *How did she know I was pregnant?* She looked down at her flat stomach. *I better get up to Lar before he comes looking for me.* She walked to the upper deck feeling a wave of nausea, but as she stepped out, the sea air filled her lungs, and she felt better.

Lawrence eyed her with concern. "You all right, Kat?"

She moved towards him, smiling brightly. "Never better, Lar. Want to share the chair?"

He extended his arms to her. "Come here, I've got something for you."

She nestled in his arms and turned, her bottom pressing against his privates. "I think there's something very wrong with you," she said, giggling. "After two years you should be tired of me."

"Are you crazy, Kat? No pun intended. I could eat you up all day long. All I have to do is look into those unbelievable eyes of yours, and I'm a goner."

"We just did it this morning, you sex fiend. Are you sure it's me, not just that you're sex driven?"

"Listen, sweetheart. I know you're not feeling well, and I can abstain if you don't feel like having sex. I love you too much to pressure you. You come first, and always will. I'd never force myself on you." He kissed the nape of her neck. "There are other ways a man can satisfy himself."

"I know, Lar." She rubbed her bottom against his hardness.

"You know what? What's so funny?" he said, becoming more aroused. "And stop teasing me."

"I know you play with yourself all the time. I don't mind. Honestly. We've never discussed it, but its okay, really." He backed away from her. "You don't have to be embarrassed Lar. I want more than anything in the world for you to love me the way you do. After all, we're married. We shouldn't have any secrets from each other. That's the one thing I couldn't stand."

"You never have to worry about that. I'd cut it off before having sex with another woman. I swear on... you just tell me who, and I'll swear on their life."

"I believe you, Lar. You don't have to swear on anyone's life."

"But that would make it official," he joked. "I know. How about my grandmother's life? Everyone wants her dead anyhow." He moved closer to her again, and she in turn, pressed closer to him. "I love you so much, Kat. You have no idea how much," he added, as he rubbed hard against her.

She waited until she felt him soften. "Make any friends while I was gone? I know you like to socialize."

"Actually, I was talking to that guy over there. He told me about this terrific tour that takes you down the rapids. I've always wanted to do that. But it can wait," he added, remembering her condition. He felt bad for mentioning it.

"Why does it have to wait, silly?"

"Forget it, Kat. I'm such an ass for even suggesting it. We can do it another time. There are places in the States where we can go, when you're feeling better." Shaking his head in disgust, he struck his hand to his forehead, admonishing himself. "What a schmuck I am. I wish I would think before I speak."

"But Lar, I want to go. It could be fun, and I'm feeling better all the time, really."

"No, I won't hear of it. It's too dangerous."

"But it's not too dangerous for you? I tell you I'm okay." She looked at him with those big innocent eyes. "Pleeease. I'll be especially good to you." She raised her brows suggestively. "As much as you want, Lar." She nudged him lightly with her elbow. "C'mon, don't be a spoiled sport."

He melted as he always did when he looked deeply into her eyes. "You never refuse me. I'm just so worried about your Hodgkin's, and now you being pregnant..."

The little old lady who shared their bathroom interrupted. "Feeling better, my dear?" she asked. "Young man, you should take better care of your wife. Poor dear was as pale as a ghost. Why I thought she..."

Her husband cut her off. "C'mon Doris, we don't want to miss the sea turtles," he said pulling at her arm. "When are you going to learn to mind your own business? Always putting your two cents in where it isn't wanted."

"Are they the people who share our bathroom?" Lawrence asked, annoyed. "And when did she see you pale as a ghost? Are you hiding something from me, Kat?" He sat up, his face darkening as his anger boiled over. "I've had it! This is it! You don't fucking complain about anything. If someone bumps into you, you apologize. How can you be so passive? Don't you have an opinion about anything? If the steak is tough, you'll sit and struggle with it. You're paying good money, why should you put up with it? You let everyone get ahead of you at the checkout counter. I hate sharing a bathroom, and this, what they call a yacht, is not what I thought it was going to be." He wanted to stop reprimanding her, but he couldn't control himself. "You cater to my every whim like I was some kind of king. I'm not taking the chance of you getting sicker here, where there are no doctors, no hospitals, no fucking anything! I should've never let you talk me into coming here. I haven't had a peaceful moment since we left the States. I don't know when you might just... enough is enough." He ran his hands over his face. "Please, Kat, be reasonable. If something should happen to you, I'd never forgive myself."

She held him close to her breast. "Shush, baby," she said looking around to see who might be watching. Finding that they were alone, she lifted his chin and held his face in her hands. "Let's talk about this before we go any farther. You want to go home? Okay. We'll go home. Personally, I think you're taking this whole thing too seriously, but I understand how you feel. You're sensitive and over emotional, but I love you anyhow." She blinked back tears. "You're caring, loving, and sensitive to my needs. You're not afraid to cry or show affection, and you have heart. Ask any woman if she would choose an inhibited, self-indulgent macho- man, or someone like you, and you'd be the winner for sure."

"What has this got to do with your illness?"

"You're overreacting. If I'm pregnant and I admit I do show signs of it, one week is not going to make any difference. Let's face it. There's no doubt they'll have to abort the baby. Chemotherapy and having a baby is a definite no-no. You have to stop watching and worrying about every little move I make. There's no reason to fall apart and run home. If you want to go, then we will. Personally, I want to stay. It's not the Hodgkin's that's acting up; it's the pregnancy and the morning sickness. I can deal with that if you'll just not... go to pieces all the time. We made a deal, Lar. We weren't going to mention the Hodgkin's until our vacation was over. Let's have the best time of our lives, right now."

"You're right as usual," he said, pulling her closer. "C'mon, give this marshmallow a big kiss, and don't look at me. You know I get lost in your eyes. And how come you're so much stronger than I?"

"You have your good points and I have mine. Combined, I think we make a great team."

CHAPTER 16

Beau closed the cabin door and viewed his wife. She stood in the center of the room, her eyes fastened on him. "What?" he said loudly, his face grim. "You're not happy with the accommodations?"

Wrinkling her mouth to one side she cast a dubious look his way. "Lower your voice, Beau. I'm not sure how thick these walls are. The accommodations are great. It's sharing the yacht with the Carr's that worries me."

He paled. "Really? They seem like an outgoing fun couple. And we don't have to associate with them if you don't want to."

"If *I* don't want to. Does that mean you do?" She didn't wait for his reply. "Oh, he's nice enough. In fact, he's very sweet. It's that man-eating wife he's married to that makes me cringe. How he tolerates her must be the eighth wonder of the world. Maybe we acted too hastily by agreeing to share the yacht."

He stepped closer, eyeing her. "Well, well. My sweet unassuming wife is showing a side of her I've never seen."

"Bullshit, Beau. You've seen all my sides. Don't tell me you think this woman is Miss Goody Two Shoes in disguise? You men can be so blind."

"Get over it, Jude. They evidently have had a bad time of it and are trying to make things right. Why are you condemning her? It's not like you to..."

She overrode his words "... to see a self centered, egotistical, spoiled brat, for what she is? And why may I ask are you taking her part in this discussion?"

"This discussion is getting out of hand, Judith. You tell me how we can resolve this predicament and I'll be only too happy to comply."

"So it's Judith, is it? Which means you're either angry, upset, or can't see my point of view, which kills you."

He slammed his hand against the wall. "I don't think I want to pursue this goddamned conversation. It's not setting a suitable mood for a holiday."

She turned away from him, removed her jewelry and began to undress, hoping he would overlook the disagreement, and calm down and take an interest in her. "I'm going to take a shower. Maybe by the time I finish, you will have come to your senses."

Oh God, he thought, *I've upset her and I didn't mean to.* As she walked away, he called to her, "I haven't seen the bathroom. Is it very large?"

The bathroom door closed and after a second, she opened it a crack. Peeking out, she held one hand on the door and extended her leg and showed a tinge of pubic hair. "It's quite cozy. Why do you ask? Is there something you'd like to check out?"

"I'm not one to force myself on a lady, unless I'm invited. I have morals, you know."

"Your morals don't go any higher than your stomach, you phony. Get your ass in here before I come out and give you the spanking of your life."

"Mmmm, promise?" He was out of his clothes in a minute flat and joined her in the shower. He bit on her ear, embraced her, and pressed his body close to hers. "Why do you aggravate me, Jude? I told you a million times there's no one as beautiful or sexy as you. Wherever we are, everyone looks at you – men and women. That insecurity of yours gets me so goddamned mad."

"That's because you're so secure, you can't understand why anyone else can be... unsure of themselves."

"You've got so much going for you. Beauty, brains and that unbelievable talent of yours... If I had one tenth of what you have, I'd..."

"Don't stop what you're doing, it feels so good."

"I won't stop if you promise to think better of yourself. Okay?"

"Whatever you say, Beau. I'll try."

He stopped short. "Hey Jude, go easy on the jewels. I want this to last. "
Caressing his buttocks, she thought, I'd better keep him satisfied before that witch makes a move on him.

CHAPTER 17

Pamela fluffed her long blond tresses with a towel. "I think it's going to work out real well, T.J., don't you? He seems to be a very nice man, and so good looking. A perfect gentleman."

"And I suppose I'm not? Take it easy, Pamela. They're a happily married couple. And despite the age difference they seem right for each other." He tried to read *her* thoughts. "You haven't mentioned her. Too much competition for you?"

"Don't be obnoxious. I can see she's attractive."

"Attractive? Give me a giant break, Pamela. The lady is to die for. Not that I'm falling down slobbering over her, but face it, she's more than just attractive. But then, so are you. Why make it a contest? They seem to be sincere, nice people, and since we're going to share the yacht, let's not make it an 'I'm richer or more handsome or smarter scenario,' okay?"

"Don't give me a Sunday sermon. I only said she's attractive. Okay, she's very attractive. Does that suit you?"

"Forget it, it's not important. What is important is that we all get along. This isn't a cruise ship. Like it or not, we made an agreement to share the yacht and we are going to see them quite a bit. Let's make it a happy vacation. You do remember why we came, don't you? You do like her – and him?" He grinned awaiting her answer.

"Stop carrying on. I'm not going to throw him into the sack. I'm only saying that there's something to be said for maturity. And I would like to see Miss Judy without makeup. Bet there's a big difference." She sat at the dressing table admiring her reflection in the mirror, turning her face from side to side. "T.J., do you think I need an eye job? I'm starting to notice my age."

He stood behind her and kissed the top of her head. "You're crazy. You don't need a thing. Stop carrying on. You are very beautiful and very sexy, I might add." He cupped her breasts with his hands. "Want to fool around?"

"Oh, T.J., I'd love to but I just got my period."

"I don't mind."

"Well, I do," she snapped. Knowing she made a mistake, she smiled and said, "But if you like, I could go down on you. You always loved that."

His silence was loud. "It's okay, I can wait. I'm going to take a shower."

In the shower, he wondered if this vacation was going to solve any of their problems, or if this vacation a mistake. He worked the soap over his body, masturbating until he came to a climax, whispering excitedly, "Yes! Oh yes, Judy."

CHAPTER 18

Judy, Pamela, Trevor and Beau sat under a large multi-colored umbrella, having breakfast and chatting cordially. A cool ocean breeze blew from the east, offsetting the rising temperature. Billowing white clouds floated in the azure sky creating a scene Turner would have gladly painted.

"Well, I must admit the menu is more extensive than I had expected, and the food is exceptional," Pamela said, her eyes flicking from Trevor to Judy, then to Beau, where they lingered for a few seconds longer than necessary. "I must compliment the chef."

"More coffee?" the steward asked, his eyes glued to the short shorts that clung to Pamela's thighs and the bra top that barely covered her nipples.

Without answering, she moved the cup and saucer toward him intimating that she did. After pouring coffee for the others, he smiled politely, nodded, and walked away. Pamela, cognizant of his butt, smiled.

Judy, her large brimmed hat shading her flawless complexion, giggled aloud. *I'd love to photograph her.*

Trevor, who sat opposite her, found it difficult to take his eyes off of Judy. "Want to let us in on what you're giggling about?"

Judy sipped her coffee slowly. "Just a passing thought."

"Care to share it with us?" Trevor asked.

"My wife has a habit of having conversations with herself." Beau said.

"I bet you talk in your sleep," Trevor said, visualizing her lying naked on a bed with him next to her.

"C'mon Judy," Pamela chimed in. "Now you have me curious too."

"Well, since you people are not going to let me rest until I tell you... I was going to wear the exact same outfit that you're wearing, Pamela. I put it on, but got cold feet. Now I'm glad I didn't wear it."

"You're kidding," Pamela said. "You're nuts. Why in the world wouldn't you wear it? You have a fantastic figure."

"Thanks, but I'm a bit shy."

"That's not fair," Trevor said, to Beau. "If my wife can go scanty, so can yours. After all, we're sharing the yacht."

Beau smiled. "But we're not sharing wives, T.J."

Pamela frowned. "Listen, Judy, you're on an island away from the rest of the world. If ever there was a time to let your hair down, this is it. Jesus, haven't you ever gone to a nude beach?"

Judy's cheeks colored. "No!"

Pamela shook her head. "I bet you never slept with a woman, either."

"Pamela!" Trevor shouted, glowering at his wife. "Jesus, that's outrageous. I think you -"

Judy cut in. "Please don't make a big deal over it." She leaned towards Pamela. "I don't criticize what people do sexually. It's just not my preference." A far away look came into her eyes. She turned to her husband. "Although years ago when Beau and I took a little sea plane from Manhattan to Fire Island, we did get real stoned, and there's another time that... but I don't remember what happened." She eyed Beau.

"Don't look to me to bail you out of this one. I'm not telling. I'm saving the story for the future. In case you get out of line."

Pamela stood. "You have to tell us. I'm not going to rest until I find out the details of Miss Judy's sordid past."

"I'm afraid you'd be disappointed, Pamela," Judy said.

Her hands placed firmly on her hips, Pamela stood her ground. "Okay, change into the outfit and I'll drop the subject. C'mon, we're on holiday. Loosen up."

Judy looked to Beau for support, but he only shrugged. "I think you should wear it. You paid good money for the La Croix, but if you feel uncomfortable, don't. I want what Judy wants. I mean it's her call. She's the one who's going to be on exhibition," he said, wishing she would.

"Well, only on the yacht. I couldn't wear it in public."

"That's a step in the right direction, Judy," Pamela added. "I can assure you that by the end of the vacation, I'll have all your inhibitions up in smoke."

Santiago, the guide inched up to the table. "If you would like to see the animals, I suggest we get started."

"I haven't seen the other guide," Beau said.

Trevor smiled. "Since we're getting along so well, I took the liberty of paying him off. No need for two guides. Okay with you, Beau?"

"Sure. It's your money, why should I fight it?"

Trevor nudged Pamela playfully. "You better change, we wouldn't want the sea turtles to get aroused looking at you in that outfit."

CHAPTER 19

It was almost high noon when the tour guide pulled a checkered handkerchief from his shirt pocket and wiped the perspiration from his forehead. The temperature had risen to ninety-nine degrees as Kaitlin and Lawrence stood among the crowd of eager tourists listening to the guide's discourse on wildlife in the Galapagos Islands.

"As you know, the island we are on is called Isabella, and we are in the area of Tangus Cove, which is a protected natural harbor used as a haven for ships over the last three centuries. If you look closely at the rocks, you'll see the inscriptions of dates and ship's names bearing witness to the whalers who landed here." Noticing the tourist in the rear edging towards him, the guide gestured with his hands. "Please, those in the front, move in, so those in the back can hear me." He continued, his voice sounding like a well-rehearsed recording. "I will not go into the species of birds until we get to see them, or, if one happens to come to us, as they often do, make sure to cover your head." He waited for the laughter to stop, and continued. "The dry area behind the beach is visited by giant tortoises and by large iguanas, which can grow as large as four feet. We will get to them shortly, as we will to the penguins."

"I don't believe it," Kaitlin said. "Penguins in the tropics? How do they exist?"

Upon hearing her, the guide smiled. "That is the most common question asked. They are a smaller species of penguins, which live in the cooler waters of the Archipelago, and are unique to the Galapagos, and are the only penguins found on the equator. They escape the tropical heat by nesting in deep lava caves."

Kaitlin fanned herself with her brochure. Taking quick notice, Lawrence took her hand and whispered. "Are you too hot?" He held up a bottle of water. "Take a sip, honey. You have to drink a lot when it's this hot." He steered her towards a stone bench. "You know what you need, Kat? A big hat to keep the sun from getting to you, like those ladies over there are wearing."

Kaitlin turned towards where Santiago was explaining the rock formations to Pamela, Trevor, Judy, and Beau. "Look at them, Lar. They must be movie stars. Do you recognize any of them?"

"They look impressive all right, but I don't think they're anyone special. Probably well-to do people on vacation with their own guide."

"We have our own guide. What's the big deal?"

"The big deal is, they don't have a crowd of tourists bumping into each other like we do. And I bet they have their own yacht with their own bathroom."

"Why Lar, you're jealous."

"Fucking right," he said with conviction. Her mouth dropped, knowing he used profanity only when he was angry. "I'm jealous and pissed that we have to share a bathroom, and you can't get to it when you're sick. And you have to stand in the hot sun. Damn right, I'm jealous."

Taking his hand, Kaitlin spoke softly but firmly. "Lar, you promised you wouldn't get emotional. I'm coping with the inconveniences. Can't you try harder? Nothing is going to happen to me. As soon as we get back, I'll have ... well, the doctor will tell us what to do about the baby. Now, we better get back to the group, they're way down the road." Holding her hand out to him, she blew out a deep breath."

Pamela and Judy smiled casually at Kaitlin, as she and Lawrence strolled towards them. But as Trevor and Beau stepped aside to let them pass, Kaitlin suddenly felt faint and swayed unsteadily. Trevor, acting on impulse caught her as she went limp. The ladies immediately came running.

"Oh my God," Lawrence gasped.

"Get her out of the sun," Judy called out as Trevor carried Kaitlin to the shade of a mangrove tree.

"I have seen this many times," Santiago said. "People do not understand our climate. She may be dehydrated."

"She's not dehydrated," Lawrence said, his voice cracking as he gently stroked Kaitlin's cheek. Kaitlin responded, her eyes wide with wonder and embarrassment looking up at the group leaning over her. "Kat, honey, are you all right?" he cried.

"She'll be all right as soon as you get some liquid into her," Pamela said.

"She's had lots of water," Lawrence said dejectedly. "She's pregnant."

Kaitlin smiled, her face showing embarrassment. "What a stupid thing to do. I'm fine. Lar, help me up."

Judy stood over Kaitlin. "Sit for a minute. Getting up too fast is not the best thing to do."

"I feel so foolish. Please, don't worry about me. I don't want to spoil your day." She focused on Lawrence. "Lar, are you okay? You're shaking."

"What do you expect me to do, a jig? Of course I'm shaking. You just won't listen to reason. Will you go home now? What are you waiting for, to get sicker?"

Kaitlin addressed the group. "I'm sorry to put you folks through our problem. My husband gets very nervous when I'm not feeling well. Please, you don't have to stay with me."

Lawrence lost control. He raised his voice. "I suppose I haven't got a reason to be nervous?" His eyes shifted from Kaitlin, to the others. "No, don't go. I want you to stay. I need someone to tell her she's crazy. – that I'm not overreacting every time she gets morning sickness and throws up, or, passes out, and can't get into the bathroom in time because we're booked on a cheap cruise ship, with rotten food, and have to share a bathroom."

"Why did you come in the first place, knowing she... by the way, what are your names?" Trevor inquired.

"I'm Lawrence Bartoni, and this is my wife, Kaitlin. Why don't you tell them why Kat?" Frustrated, he let his emotions overflow. "Never mind. I will. She made me promise to go on this vacation because she's sick."

"Most women experience the same symptoms when they're pregnant," Judy said with compassion. "It will pass."

Lawrence held Kaitlin's gaze, then stared down at the earth. "The pregnancy is the least of it. She has Hodgkin's disease."

Surprised, Pamela and Judy spoke in unison.

"And she's pregnant?"

"Why don't we go somewhere, cool off, and sit for a while?" Beau suggested.

"There's a small bistro, over there," Santiago said, pointing down the road. "But what about their tour? The guide will get into mucho trouble if they are missing."

Trevor took Santiago aside, dug into his pocket, and removed a roll of bills tied together with a rubber band. He peeled off a hundred dollar bill, and handed it to Santiago. "Let's give the kids a real honeymoon. Fix it with their guide, and get the info on what cruise they're on. Have all their luggage brought to our yacht. I'll settle with their travel agent later. And meet us at the bistro."

Pamela took her husband's arm. "I'm proud of you T.J. That was sweet of you." Judy locked arms with Trevor, and Beau took Pamela's arm. *Maybe, I judged Pamela too harshly, she thought. There might be a good side to her.*

Kaitlin and Lawrence followed behind, their arms around each other unaware of the arrangements Trevor had made for them.

Trevor turned back and smiled at Beau. "I did the right thing, didn't I?"

"Having their things moved from their poor accommodations, to our yacht? Absolutely," Beau answered, winking at his newfound friend. "Didn't cost me a dime."

Trevor smiled at Judy, tightening his grip on her arm. "You agree?"

"You have a good heart, T.J.," she said, returning his squeeze, wondering why in the world she did that, and why she felt a sudden attraction to this stranger.

CHAPTER 20

Plaques of varnished fish with glazed eyes mounted on the walls of the quaint bistro stared down at the patrons. Santiago, back from settling with the guide to have the Bartoni's belongings moved to the yacht, gave Trevor a thumb up sign. He sat down at the bar, and conversed with the owner, a thin, bearded man who resembled Rip Van Winkle. His wife, a pretty but more than pleasantly plump woman, wearing a low cut peasant blouse and bright red skirt, stood smiling at the three sober couples. "Le gusta la vino?" she asked.

"Do you have hard liquor, like vodka or scotch?" Beau inquired.

"Vino, Okay? No comprende," she said, grinning. She turned to her husband for help.

He placed a glass of sangria in front of Santiago and spoke in Spanish. "Deben ser Nueva York. Diganosa sus turistas sangria, cerveza y agua del servicio del onit ninguna cargo franco el agua." He guffawed loudly.

Trevor shouted at Santiago. "What was that all about?"

Laughing, Santiago translated. "He said your clients must be from New York. And to tell the tourists we only serve sangrias, beer and water. No charge for the water." Santiago tilted his sombrero. "You must taste the sangria; it is the best in the world. They make it themselves. Believe me, nothing like it anywhere. If you like, he will make iced tea for the young lady."

"We don't have much choice," Trevor said to the group. "Shall we?"

Judy looked around. "I think we should. You know, when in Rome... how about iced tea for you, Kaitlin?"

"Yes, thank you. What about you, Lar?" she asked, hoping he had calmed down. "You should try the beer, you're always interested in tasting different kinds of beer."

Lawrence mellowed. "Beer it is then," he said, still feeling somewhat ill at ease for sounding off.

"I'll try the sangria," Pamela said, her eyes flashing to the mounted fish. "God, those fish are depressing. This place is out of a novel I read about survivors whose plane crashed on a barren, deserted island and they had to eat each other because there was no food."

"Now there's a happy thought," Judy said. "Beau, you should use that in your next book. You could title it, 'Eat or be Eaten.'"

The owner's wife set the iced tea, a huge glass of beer, and two large pitchers of sangria filled with fruit on the table and stood waiting. Trevor shouted to Santiago. "Do we ask her to join us or is she waiting to be paid?"

"She's waiting for you to taste the wine. They take a great deal of pride in their wine and she won't leave until you sample it and give your opinion."

"Does she pour, or do we?" Trevor asked.

"One of the women has to serve. There's a superstition that if a man pours he will lose face."

Pamela rolled her eyes. "I'm containing myself, but I may throw up."

"Why don't you do the honors?" Judy said to Kaitlin.

Kaitlin stood. "I'm flattered," she said, raising the pitcher. "It's heavy, but I can manage. I'm stronger than I look. Should we toast to something?"

"You make it up," Beau said. Staring at her, he added, "Look at those eyes. Don't they remind you of that artist that draws women with large eyes?" He sighed. "Just beautiful. You know, Jude, you should sketch her."

"Please, you're embarrassing me," Kaitlin said, her face flushed. She raised her glass and toasted. "To very kind and thoughtful friends," she toasted. "If I may call you my friends."

"And back to you, our new young friends," Trevor toasted.

It's a done deal, Trevor thought. *Your belongings are being carried aboard the yacht as we speak.*

Beau closed his eyes as he sipped the sangria. He turned to the woman. "Delicioso," he exclaimed, holding his glass out for more. "Best sangria, I ever tasted. Filler-up."

"Wonderful," Pamela said as Judy and Trevor drank theirs.

"The beer is very good too," Lawrence said. "How's the iced tea, Kat?"

"Fruity, but very tasty."

Judy held the glass of wine up to the light. "Look at the color. It's magnificent. I don't think two pitchers are going to be enough, the way you guys are chugalugging."

"Oh yeah? You're on your second. Slow down, Jude," Beau said, finishing his. "It's only early afternoon." He squinted at her. "And we don't want you getting high. We can't take a chance of those horny iguanas getting hold of you. They would love to eat you up."

Pamela started to speak, but Trevor cut her off. "Don't even think of it," he said. "We have youngsters here."

Lawrence finished his beer and held his hand up for another. "You have to be kidding," he interrupted, leaning over and pecking Kaitlin on her cheek. "We're not that much younger than you all."

Beau smiled. "Maybe them," he said thumbing toward the others. "But I could be your grandfather."

"You're crazy," Pamela said, her eyes smiling longingly at Beau. She spoke to Judy, but her eyes focused on Beau. "I bet your man is one hot stud in bed."

Trevor rolled his eyes wanting to reprimand his wife, but Judy spoke up. She finished her drink and turned to Pamela, "In bed? Like an eighteen-year-old battering ram. And, thanks for the compliment. I admire your taste in men."

Pamela shrugged. "I'm getting to like you more and more, Judy. You're getting loose. I told you I'd have that effect on you." She eyed Lawrence, admiring his youthful muscular body while touching her knee to his underneath the table. "Now folks," she said, "What are we going to do about our fledglings? We can't permit them to go back to that scow they call a yacht." She faced Judy. "Judy, help me out here."

Judy looked at Kaitlin. She thought of her having to deal with the Hodgkin's disease and being pregnant at the same time. Looking from Beau to Trevor, she pleaded silently for confirmation of her thoughts. "Well guys, help the ladies out."

Trevor screwed his mouth to one side. "I'm in agreement with what you're suggesting, but don't you think before we decide, we should check it out with the recipients. Did it ever cross your minds that they might prefer to be alone? What do you think, Beau?"

"Absolutely," he said, his head bobbing up and down.

Lawrence stood. He burped. "Oops, Sorry. Now listen up. I know you all have our interests at heart, but you are discussing Kat and I as if we're invisible. Worse – as if we were orphans in need of a home. Okay, so I made arrangements, the cheapest I could find because we couldn't afford to go first class. As it is, we had to borrow money from my parents." His voice cracked. "Anyhow, I don't understand how you can get us better accommodations when the island is booked solid. I know Kat wants to stay and I do too, as much as I worry about her - but it's not possible."

Kaitlin broke in. "Now Lar, don't get emotional. They are trying to help us." She sipped her iced tea, not knowing what else to do. "I don't know what to say, except, thank you for offering."

Pamela stood. "Then it's settled. There's nothing more to discuss. You and Lar will join us. We have our own yacht. And, you'll have your own bathroom. In fact you can have five bathrooms. Agreed, everybody?" She didn't wait for an answer. "Trevor, get the cash out and tell Santiago to square the details with their guide and cruise director."

Trevor laughed. "I'm way ahead of you. Their luggage is on the way to our yacht as we speak. Right Beau?"

Beau, his eyes trying to focus, nodded.

"Boy, you sure take charge," Judy said. "No wonder you're so successful."

Pamela stood. "He's a fucking wonder boy."

Kaitlin and Lawrence sat, staring at each other.

"I have to go to the little girls room so badly," Pamela said. "The sangria is starting to flow. Judy, come with me, I hate going to strange bathrooms by myself."

On the way to the bathroom, Judy took hold of Pamela's arm. "Aren't you playing the dorm mother a bit thick, dear? What's going on in that devious mind of yours? If you're thinking of Lar, be careful. And if you're thinking of Beau, I'll kill you so fast you won't know what hit you. Jesus, Pamela, T.J. is a great catch, what's wrong with you?"

"That's exactly what my mother said on the day of my wedding. What's wrong with you?" She tossed her hair to one side. "Don't worry about Beau. As much as I would love to have him, I'll abstain. But Lar is kind of cute, don't you think?"

"What makes you so outrageous?"

"We don't have that much time, Judy."

"If you must cheat on T.J., at least stay away from the family, so to speak. I saw you eyeing the steward. Now there's a hunk."

"Thanks for trying to keep me straight. And as far as the steward is concerned, I've already had him."

Judy rolled her eyes. "Figures. What took you so long? We've only been on the yacht for two seconds."

"I need to get my sea legs. By the way, now that we've bonded, I've been meaning to ask you something."

"What?"

"Well, if you want to curb my appetite with men, maybe we could get it on."

Judy sing-sang. "I don't think sooo."

She winked at Judy. "Yeah, that's what they all say. The vacation is just beginning."

CHAPTER 21

Judy plopped down on the bed. "Thank God, the water is calm," she said, sighing. "I think I'll skip dinner. What ingredients do they put into the sangria? My head is spinning."

"Who would have thought it?" Beau said, sarcastically. "You had enough to float a battleship. Seems lately, you and the grapes are bonding."

"Let's not get into bonding, Beau Blessing. I may have had a few more than I should have, and so did we all, but that didn't keep you from sneaking peeks at Pamela."

A shadow passed over his face. "So we're back to the Beau Blessing shit, are we? Now I know you're drunk. You're obnoxious side rears its head when you drink too much."

"I may be a bit inebriated, but I'm not blind. Beau, love of my life, tell me something?"

"Don't sweet-talk me. And if it means we are going to get into one of our spats, the answer is no. But you'll ask anyhow?"

"What is it about women like Pamela that make men wild with desire? I know she was Miss Virginia in the stone-age, but what makes you guys rise to the occasion?"

He folded his arms. "Afraid of the competition? Don't be. She may have been Miss Virginia, but you could be Miss World. How about taking a shower to sober up? Honestly Jude, I hate conversing with you when we are not on the same wave length."

"I like conversing when I've had a few drinks. Gives me the nerve to say things I ordinarily wouldn't say."

"Sometimes we can say too much... and then you may be sorry." He walked to the bed and bent over taking her face in his hands. "Can we please change the subject? How about you sleep it off and when you get up you'll be the old Judy. Okay?" He kissed her gently on the lips.

She returned his kiss. "Want to fool around?" she asked, her eyes closing.

"Sure," he said. "Soon as you wake up. You'll be refreshed, then."

She sat up. "You don't want me. You don't think I'm pretty anymore. What was it you said at the bistro? Oh yes. 'You should sketch Kaitlin. Look at those eyes, they're as big as saucers.' Another thing, watch out for that man-eater, Pamela. She's hot for you. I think there's something radically wrong with her. Her eyes widen abnormally, as if she has... what is that affliction called? I think it's a lack of vitamin A... I think it's called... starts with an X. I'm too out of it to remember. I caught a glimpse of all the pills she carries in her bag, when we were in the ladies room. Jesus, she's a walking pharmacy. How she got through customs with the stash is beyond me."

He shook his head, annoyed with her nonsense. "You're talking pure dribble," he said. "I'd be a fool to make a move on anyone else when I have someone as lovely as you."

"I'm lovely? You used to say I was beautiful."

He shrugged. "I love you, and you are beautiful, and that is the end of this conversation. I'm going on deck to get some air."

Her eyes closed as he opened the cabin door. He was up the stairs unable to hear her muffled voice, saying, "This vacation has all the earmarks of turning into a sexual orgy, Beau."

The sun drifted in and out of the clouds casting ominous dark shadows on the water. As Beau reached the lower deck, an uneasy feeling crept through him. He stopped short, observing the Captain exiting cabin twelve. Unable to avoid the captain, who was now upon him, he waved a tentative hello. The captain smiled graciously. "Did you enjoy your morning in Isabella, Mr. Blessing?"

"Unbelievable," Beau said, wondering what the captain was doing in cabin twelve. "Uh... the giant tortoises, and iguanas, they were something else."

The captain buttoned his jacket and straightened his tie as he spoke, a hint of nervousness in his manner. "You cannot communicate with animals anywhere in the world like you can in the Galapagos. It is a very special place. And the sangria is also very special."

"Yes," Beau agreed. "It is a special place," he answered, wondering how the captain knew that they had sangria.

"And now if you will excuse me I must attend to a slight mishap in the galley." He threw up his hands. "It appears the chef is having one of his hysterics because some seafood was not included in the shipment of fish. He is a perfectionist and quite temperamental." He shrugged. "It is not an easy task commandeering a yacht."

"I should think not," Beau said, walking away.

Making sure the captain was out of sight, Beau guardedly walked to cabin twelve and with his ear to the door, listened, then tapped softly. The door opened a crack, and upon seeing him, Pamela grabbed his hand and pulled him inside. She poked her head out and looked up and down the passageway. Closing the door noiselessly, she smothered him with kisses. He resisted her advances, holding her at arms length. Staring down at her, his voice intimidating, his eyes showing anger, he said, "Where's T.J., and what the hell was the captain doing here, Pamela?"

She knitted her brows. "Beau, silly baby," she cooed. "T.J., Lar, Kaitlin, went fishing. The captain was walking by and noticed I inadvertently left the door ajar. He peeked in to see if anything was wrong. I understand he inspects all the cabins every day to make sure they are attended to properly. This is a luxury yacht, baby, and he expects a big tip when we depart. You're awfully suspicious. C'mon, loosen up. Why so gloomy? Judy not putting out? Well, I'm here, and no one can satisfy you the way I can." She let her negligee fall to the floor and stretched out her arms to him. Noticing he was reticent, she lifted her right breast and tongued it, smiling at him coyly.

"I know you, Pamela. You're the type who behaves for a while, but I'm beginning to think you're slipping back into an old pattern. And what's this I hear about drugs in your bag? Didn't you tell me that you were weaning off of them?"

"So she blabbed about my pills, did she? So what? They're all legitimate. If you want, I'll show you the vials, all certified prescriptions by verifiable doctors. You're beginning to sound like T.J. It's boring. You were so cool in the city. Don't worry; T.J. and Judy will never catch on to our affair in New York."

Beau felt uneasy. "I thought going on the yacht... having you and Judy, playing games with T.J., would be challenging... fun. But, now it's becoming too much."

She put her fingers to his lips. "I love when you get angry, Beau. Don't waste it. Show me your anger. Take it out on me. I want to feel you hard inside of me. Make me lust for you. Drive me wild." She pulled him close to her groping for his penis. "Oh there you are, you devil," she said. "Come on out, and let me make you big and strong."

She took his member into her mouth as he sat on the bed and removed his clothes, not missing a stroke until he was naked. Her eyes searched his. She pulled hard, her mouth tightening around his member. His eyes rolled in his head; she squeezed his testicles until she felt his body stiffen and his pleasure erupt. She didn't let go until his breathing became normal. Embracing him with her arms, she snuggled close to him. "You're the best I ever tasted. I never get enough of you."

"How about you? Even Steven."

"I just want to lay here beside you. The wine took a lot out of me. I'm content. But I do have to use the little girl's room. Don't move until I get back."

"Not to worry. You drained me dry."

He pretended to sleep as she crawled into bed. His mind raced thinking about how stupid he was to let himself get involved with her in New York, and what an asshole he was to let it go this far. Where are your brains, he wondered? *You have Judith, a gem of a lady, and you let yourself get sucked into a no-win situation that has to blow up in your face. She's going to mess up your marriage, for sure. The lady is dangerous. I've got to think of a way to detach myself from her. Of course she didn't want sex with me. She's probably still sore from fucking the captain. He recalled how when he first entered the cabin the bed was unruffled. No doubt about it, Beau Blessing, one way or the other, you have to break it off. But how?*

CHAPTER 22

Having put her clothes in the spacious closet, Kaitlin, with a dejected expression on her face, walked to the window and looked out. Lawrence studied her, hoping she wasn't going to get sick again. *Her damn moods are getting to me.* Walking up to her, he encircled her with his arms. "What's the matter Kat?"

"I'm okay, Lar. The yacht is something else, isn't it? And this room, I could live here forever."

"Then what's wrong? Thinking of what you have to go through when we get home? You're the one who keeps telling me not to worry. This is sort of a switch, isn't it?"

"It has nothing to do with my health." She pulled away from him and stared out the porthole.

Her depressed tone annoyed him. "Give me a break, will you?" He picked up a magazine and flung it across the room. "If it's not your health, then what the hell is it?"

A look of surprise flashed across her face. "Why are you mad at me? I'm only trying to tell you about -"

"About what? Honestly, Kat, since you became pregnant, you're acting strangely. Well, at least since we got here."

"About the people. I mean the women."

"You've lost me. I think they've gone out of their way to accommodate us. Especially you. It's you they felt needed more conveniences because you're not well. This is not like you. You're usually so compassionate. So caring. Judy and Pamela adore you."

"I know that. You don't understand."

He collapsed into an armchair. "Okay," he said, provoked. "I give up. Why don't you enlighten me?"

"Let me put it this way. Look at them and look at me."

"Okay, I'm looking. What am I supposed to see?"

She walked to the closet mirror and turned towards him, striking a models pose. "Imagine Judy and Pamela standing alongside me." She waited for his response. "See what I'm getting at?"

"So they're glamorous. So what? You're still very pretty. You just don't use all the makeup they do. And you don't dress up like they do. You know, so revealing."

"Even if I did, I couldn't look like them. And, we can't spend money on clothes like they can afford to."

"I'm not sure I like where this is going, Kat. I'm getting irritated. What's this all of a sudden with the glamour bit? I love you just the way you are. I wouldn't want you any different."

"That's pure bullshit," she blurted. "You don't want me any different because you're afraid."

Surprised by her accusation, and more so because she used profanity, he said, "That's right. How did you guess? I'm afraid that you'll be discovered by a talent scout who will whisk you off to Hollywood, where we would get divorced because every stud there would be running after you. Get real, will you? I told you, I love you just the way you are."

"You still don't understand. Not only do I feel like the poor relation, I feel so inferior to them. They are so cultured, so worldly. You know they've asked us to join them tonight. Judy said they were going to dress, and to them that means formal. What am I going to wear, my torn jeans and come as a bag lady? And you don't even have a suit."

"So we won't go. We can stay on deck and watch the moon and have sex.

We have each other. And we can eat in our room." He bit his lip seeing the forlorn look on her face. His heart went out to her. "How about it, Kat? I'm sorry I yelled at you. You're just as good or even better than they are, and it kills me to see you so upset. You have more than enough on your mind."

"You're right, but I do like them. Especially Judy, and Beau and T.J. Judy's a super lady. And T.J., he's special."

"Oh, is that so? Don't tell me you've got the hots for him? I think these men are having an effect on you."

"And maybe, these ladies are having an effect on you. I see the way you look at Pamela. I bet if she let you, you'd..."

"...Jump on her bones? Get out of here," he said thinking how erect his member became when Pamela pressed her knee against his, beneath the table at the bistro.

A knock at the door ended their conversation. Lar opened the door, his breath taken away as Judy stood smiling, wearing the revealing bra top and short shorts she said she didn't have the nerve to wear in public. "May I come in?" she asked. "Lar, the men are having cigars and drinks on deck and asked me to make sure you joined them."

Pamela stuck her head into the room. "Hi Kat," she said her voice cheerful. "I'm here too. We girls have to talk some trash."

Noticing Kaitlin's teary eyes, Judy paused. "Goodbye, Lar. See you tonight at the get- together," she said, ushering him out the door.

As he moved to go, he felt Pamela's rear end rub against his crotch. "Oops," she said. "Tight squeeze, isn't it?"

"Hey, grab a chaise," Trevor said blowing smoke rings in the air, as Lawrence approached. "Kicked your ass out, did they?"

"Just as well," Beau said casually. "You wouldn't want to be in on their conversation. Probably tearing us apart."

"Beau," Trevor said, leaning towards Beau. "Are you sure we've never met before? Your voice seems so familiar. It's been driving me up a wall."

Beau felt a pang of guilt, but showed no outward signs of emotion. "I hear that all the time. Guess my voice is ordinary." He lifted the humidor and offered Lawrence a cigar. "Do you smoke? Finest Havana money can buy. Not that they're mine." He flicked his thumb at Trevor. "Money bags over here is doing the honors."

"Fuck you, Blessing," Trevor joked; aware of Beau's pointing a warning finger at him.

Beau smirked. "Maybe he doesn't smoke, T.J.," he said turning to Lawrence. "It's an older more mature man's pleasure."

"Well, I used to in college, but yeah, I'll try one," Lawrence said, feeling intimidated by them.

"How about a drink?" Trevor asked. "I know you do that. You'll have to help yourself, we told the steward to take off. Hate having him hanging over us all the time. Right, Beau? And I don't like the way he looks at the women. Like he was fucking them with his eyes." He sipped his brandy. "Bar's open, Lar, don't be bashful. Brandy, beer, wine, scotch, and any fucking thing you want."

"I'm not bashful, T.J., and I'd appreciate it if you and Beau didn't treat me like I was a kid, or your son. I *am* twenty-eight. And just because you've got money and position, doesn't make you better men than I."

Beau lifted his glass. "Hear, hear," he toasted. "I'll drink to that. Good for you, Lar. See, T.J., the kid has balls, after all."

"Cool it," T.J. chided, leaning towards Lawrence. "Don't be so sensitive, Lar. I was only kidding. Actually, I think highly of you, and you *are* a better man than me – more sincere. I have to admit. I was telling Pamela that if I had a son, I'd want him to be a lot like you."

"What does a lot mean, T.J.?" Lawrence asked. "Are their character traits about me you would change if I were your son? Like standing up to you?"

"That is exactly what I mean. Just the fact that I'd like a son similar to you isn't enough for you, is it?" He sipped his brandy. "Light the cigar and finish your drink. You have a lot of catching up to do. Beau, and I have been drinking for over an hour."

"Lay off of him, T.J.," Beau said. He watched Lawrence polish off his glass of Brandy. "Hey, Lar, go easy. Don't get ahead of us; I'm not playing nursemaid to you two." Thinking he might have offended Lawrence, he immediately changed the subject. "You mentioned that you're a pharmacist. Where did you go to college?"

Lawrence tried not to choke on the cigar. "Arnold and Marie Schwartz College of Pharmacy. It used to be called Brooklyn College. Top ten in my graduating class." He reached for the vodka, but decided on a coke instead. He eyed T.J. "The lower part of the ten, I might add, *dad.*"

"Whiz kid, huh," T.J. said. "Know anything about physical education? You look like you work out."

"Funny you should say that. I wanted to major in Phys. Ed. My parents talked me out of it. More money and security in being a druggist, they said. But I took a few courses." He set the coke on the table and poured himself a scotch, aware of Beau's watchful eye. "I'll only have one, *dad,*" he said, smiling falsely. "I promise to behave myself."

"Glad to hear it, "Beau countered. "For a minute, I thought I would have to send you to your room without dinner."

T.J. laughed. "That's more like it. Now you're getting mellow, Lar."

"Why did you ask about Phys. Ed., T.J.?" Lawrence asked.

"Well, the stockholders have been bugging me to enlarge our health club facilities at the Startech complex, and I've been looking for someone to set it up and run it." His eyes narrowed at Lawrence. "Would you be interested?"

Lawrence's heart skipped a beat. His eyes widened with excitement, then he edged closer to Trevor, and set his drink on the table. "Interested? Are you kidding? I'd kill for an opportunity like that. I'd move Kat out of Brooklyn so fast... and give her the things she deserves... wow!" He turned to Beau. "He's not fucking with me, is he Beau?"

"You've known him almost as long as I have, but I think he's sincere. Just make sure you get it in writing."

Trevor gave Beau the finger. "You understand you'll have to take a few courses, get certified as a trainer, and whatever else is needed to make you qualify for the job. And don't think I'll make it easy for you. The board of directors will be watching your every move. And every one of them has a son-in-law, nephew, or dumb spoiled, rich good-for-nothing relation that will be vying for the position. You'll have to prove yourself on your own merits."

Lawrence's voice quavered with excitement. "I can do it. I know I can. It's something I've dreamt about. I'll be good at it. You won't be disappointed in me, I promise."

Beau stubbed out his cigar in the ashtray. "You'll do real well," he said. "You have the makings of a first class administrator. Wouldn't you agree, T.J.?"

"That's up to Lar," he said, thoughtfully. "If he plays his cards right."

"Well, I'm ready for the Jacuzzi. Anyone else?" Beau said.

Trevor waved a hand of dismissal. "And sweat away all the good booze? Uh, uh. Catch you later. By the way, the ladies seem to be cooking up some kind of formal dinner party for tonight. I overheard Pamela talking to the chef this morning. I'll be damned if I'm getting dressed in formal attire on my vacation."

Beau nodded in agreement. "I'm with you, T.J."

"Guess I lucked out," Lawrence said. "The best I have is a pair of navy Dockers. Don't think it would go over with the ladies."

"How about if we go along with them, but find another dress code, just to have some fun," Trevor suggested.

"I don't know," Lawrence said. "Won't they get pissed?"

"Now is the time to assert yourself, Lar. I learned the hard way, and you can save yourself a lot of heartache if you listen to me. Once you let them run your life, you've lost your manhood."

Beau knitted his brows. "Jesus, T.J.," he said. "Don't take your marital problems out on Lar. There are a few of us whose wives don't..."

Trevor's face flushed with anger. "Where do you get off..." he began, but stopped short, realizing that it was common knowledge that Pamela fucked around. He stood and faced both men. "Sorry guys. That was the liquor talking, not me. Beau, if it's okay with Lar, we'll meet you in the Jacuzzi in a minute. You're right. I have to sweat the booze out. We'll be drinking at the party. Try to think of something we can wear tonight while you're playing with yourself in the tub."

"How serious are you about the offer I made you, Lar?" T.J. asked.

"Totally awesome. Couldn't be more serious. It's the one bright spot I've had in ... a long time. Why? Don't you think I can do it?"

"Oh, I think you can do it. I wonder how badly you want to do it."

"I don't understand. I just told you how serious I am."

"A while back you said you'd kill to get this job."

"Oh, you mean I have to do away with all the competition? No problem, I'm from Brooklyn. I'll put a hit out on them." He smiled, but it quickly dissipated when he looked into Trevor's cold black eyes.

Trevor clapped him on the back and placed his arm around Lawrence. "Listen," he said. "You don't have to worry about the nincompoop board of directors. I can make you rich. More, I'll make sure that Kaitlin has the best medical care money can buy." Glancing around, still embracing Lar, he drew him closer, checking to see if anyone was within hearing distance. Tilting Lawrence's chin close to his, their faces almost touching, he said, "My offer doesn't come without a pay back. Do what I want and I'll make all your dreams come true."

CHAPTER 23

"You're what? Did I hear you say you're taking an upper?" Trevor asked.

Pamela stepped into a silk chemise, teasing him with her voluptuous body, knowing how much he would have liked to take her right then and there. "You heard me, T.J., just one to keep things going. The girls are dressing for tonight's dinner in one of the empty cabins. Why do you have that sour expression on your handsome face? If you keep it up, you'll get deep creases and before long you'll resemble a dried prune. You're not by some chance thinking that I might be having a clandestine affair with one of the crew, are you? Or are you wondering about the captain? I know you're suspicious of him."

His face darkened with anger, certain from her posture she had hit the pillbox. "Damn it, you're pushing me too far, Pamela. I'm warning you, I'm not going to tolerate your outrageous behavior and your bitchy sarcasm. And, another thing..." He scurried into the bathroom and flung the cabinet door open. "Where do you stash the drugs? You promised you'd ease off the stuff, but I can tell from your personality shift, you've been popping pills and intend to fuck anyone that is walking, crawling, or standing still. When you're high, there's just no reasoning with you. You're on a crash course straight to hell."

"Get out of my bathroom, you son of a bitch," she screamed. "And keep your filthy hands off my things. What gives you the right to accuse me of anything? You fucking loser. If you're not happy, get a divorce." Her eyes widened abnormally as she tried shoving him out of the bathroom, but he shook her off and she lost her balance, and found herself on the tiled floor. Looking up at him she shouted, "Go on get a divorce! I'll take you for everything cent you have. You'll be the laughing stock of Startech. I'll tell them you're gay. That should keep you in good standing with the stockholders."

His voice fired back at her. "You'll stop at nothing, will you? Even make up lies." His face flushed with anger. "And don't think I'm not suspicious about the baby – yes, the baby – that you probably smothered to death." She paled. "You remember, Pammy, the basketball player you screwed when I was away on business. I wondered why you wanted the baby cremated so fast."

She tossed her head back as if erasing his words. Picking herself up, she walked calmly to the mirror and checked her makeup. She turned and stared blankly at him. "Prove it, big shot. Don't fuck with me, Trevor. I'll make your life a living hell. You know I can. And another thing, I'm not forgetting you just struck me and threw me to the floor."

He ran to the closet and pulled her makeup case from the shelf and turned it upside down. The pills scattered over the floor. She rushed in, and fell to her knees trying to retrieve them. "Idiot! You know I need them. I can't function without them. I'll go crazy. Do you want to be responsible for what I might do? I could harm myself."

He pounded his fists against the wall, all the time wishing it were her he was beating. "Harm yourself?" he said, feeling sick to his stomach. "I wish you would." She shrank back with fear. He walked slowly to where she stood, placed his hands around her neck and pressed lightly. She gasped in horror. He whispered hoarsely, "I wish you were dead, Pamela. I never wanted anything so badly in my life." Her eyes grew wide with terror as his fingers tightened around her neck. "I want you dead so desperately, I can taste it."

A knock at the door brought Trevor back to his senses. He instantly released his grip on her and went to the door. Opening just a crack, he asked, "Yes?"

"It's Judy," she said, pushing past him. "Sorry I had to break up the lovers spat, but I had to intervene before the neighbors call 911." She looked at Trevor with disappointment but compassion. "We're in the next cabin. Beau said if I didn't interfere, he would. Is this something that can be patched up, or do we have to call out the militia?"

"I need a minute to pull myself together," Pamela said. "Please stay."

"Take your clothes, T.J.," Judy commanded. "And anything else you need, and join Lar and Beau in our cabin. Kaitlin and I will change here."

"I don't need anything," he said, avoiding her eyes, ashamed the blowup was overheard and especially, because of what she might think of him.

"Good," Judy said, grasping his arm and leading him to the door. "I'm sure Beau has anything you might need. He's such a stickler when it comes to grooming." Her eyes shifted to Pamela. "I'll be right back. I'm going to get my clothes and make up. You okay, Pamela?" she asked, as they headed out the door.

"Lose the bastard," Pamela called out as she gathered up the dispersed pills and tossed them into her make up box.

Judy returned with her evening gown and makeup bag. "I'm sorry, Pamela, but we couldn't let it go on any longer. It was getting out of hand. I thought you two were here to make things right."

"I'm just fooling myself. They'll never be right."

"Listen, I'm not asking to hear your story, and I sure as hell don't want to get involved. But we are thrown together on this vacation and we have to figure a way to either make peace or part ways"

"Like it or not, you are involved. And so are Kaitlin and Lar. I know you mean well – you're a terrific gal. Look, I'll level with you. The truth is... I'm sick. Not physically – mentally. Something just snaps, and I get these wild impulses to misbehave. And it's always sexually." She held Judy's gaze. "I don't have to tell you. You've seen me in action. This uncontrollable urge to seduce every man I meet takes hold of me, and I can't seem to do anything about it. I need my pills, and the strange thing is that after I take them, I feel this terrible gnawing deep down in my very being... a feeling of endless loss... a craving that begs to be filled until the next time. And then it starts all over again." Resisting the urge to cry, she stared down at the floor and back up to Judy, and said, "I've never opened up to anyone, except you. Not even my mother."

"It's high time you did. Maybe it's a warning to seek help. How you went on with this illness is something I don't understand. I can't believe T.J. wasn't aware of it. Didn't he try to get you help?"

"T.J. is actually a sweet man. Sometimes a little deceitful, but I suppose that's why he's so successful. I fooled him into thinking I was going to a shrink, just as I fooled my mother and everyone else. If he tried to strangle me just now, he had good reason. I drove him to it. Look at me now. Normal right? Like a different person, that's how quickly I can change and become the heartless Jekyll and Hyde. I'm sure the pills have a lot to do with the change in my personality, but I just can't get off of them."

"I'm not a shrink Pamela, but this much I do know. You have to ease up on the drugs and rid yourself of that other person, the one that's overpowering the sane Pamela, and the sooner, the better. You have to go somewhere to detox. You can afford it. There are places that cater to addicted people."

Pamela stood. "I can hear the shrink now. 'Will the sane Pamela come out now?'" she said, half smiling. "Okay, I promise as soon as we get back, I'll see one."

Judy looked toward the door. "Kat will be here any second. Can you get through the evening, or should we call it off? We could all just hang out."

"No, let's not spoil everyone's evening. We promised Kat a complete make over." She took hold of Judy's hand. "Thank you is not enough. But there is one more thing. T.J. thinks the world of you. I can't face him. I'm too ashamed. Would you talk to him for me? Sort of mellow him, so we can get through the night."

Judy hesitated. "I don't know, Pamela. This is really none of my business. I -"

"Please," Pamela said, her eyes pleading.

Sighing deeply, Judy nodded reluctantly. "I shouldn't, but I'll try."

Pamela smiled with relief. "Come in, Kat," she said. "The door's open."

CHAPTER 24

What a schmuck you are, Trevor thought, studying his image in the mirror as he shaved. Losing your temper and letting Pamela get the best of you was a stupid, stupid move. And trying to strangle her was more stupid. For a man who heads a multi-billion dollar- conglomerate, you're acting like a moron. Have to get the heat off of me and make up with her. It shouldn't be too difficult, once she starts popping pills again. She's sure to make a move on some guy tonight. I have to come up with something brilliant in order to dispose of the bitch. She'll never get better, and I'll never be free of her until she disappears from the face of the earth.

He thought about his talk with Lawrence, thinking Lawrence would never refuse his offer. *It's a chance of a lifetime for the pharmacist from Brooklyn. He'll agonize over it for a while, but he's sure to come around.*

T.J. yelled into the sitting room, "What's happening gentlemen? You guys better come up with something, it's getting about that time."

"You'll see when you get out here," Beau replied.

Trevor combed his hair, tightened the towel around his waist and stepped into the sitting room surprised to see Beau and Lawrence draped in bed sheets. He smiled. "Now, how did you know that's just what I was thinking of? And where did you get the hairpieces?"

"Yeah, you thought of it. Bullshit!" Beau said. "Your imagination doesn't go further than a micro chip. And they're called wreaths, not hairpieces. Actually it was Lar's idea, with a little help from Santiago."

Relaxed comfortably in a lounge chair, Lar, trying to look impressive, puffed on a cigar. "It's nothing new. In Jamaica, the men parade around drinking rum swizzles and yelling, toga, toga, toga. Afterwards, they have a contest to see who draped the best toga."

"I know I shouldn't ask, but what is the prize?" Trevor asked. "A convertible Corvette?"

"Yeah, fat chance. The winner got a free weekend. The runner-up got free drinks for the rest of his stay. Except the contest was held on the night before we left."

"Unfortunately," Beau said, "Judith and I went to one of those places. Big mistake. I had to practically fight the horny fuckers off when everyone got high."

Trevor knitted his brows. "Who told you they don't get high now?"

"I meant, when we did. It wasn't our kind of vacation. We had to line up for breakfast, lunch, and dinner. Judith was mad as hell, which was surprising, because she's an extremely easy-going lady, but she was right. Vacation is when you want your meals served, not a smorgasbord where you have to line up like in the army. But there was a highlight to the vacation. We didn't have any connection to get some grass, so Judith, believe it or not, goes to the desk clerk, and asks right out, if he knew where she could get some pot. Boy, did he blow her off. We knew the island had lots of resources, but I was squeamish. I pictured me in jail on bread and water, with the rats biting at my ass, and worse, Judy tied by her wrists, with some sweaty pimpled-faced guard putting it to her. But the next day, as we were swimming in the ocean, this big dude, sporting an oversized cap, swam up to us and said, 'Hey, mahn. Got some nice red buds for you. Make you and the lady feel real special." Judy and I connected immediately and we all walked onto the beach. He took off his cap and removed the grass wrapped in a brown paper bag. I gave him ten dollars, and he gave me enough pot for a year. As he walked away Judy called after him. "How about the rolling paper?" He didn't even look back. He walked into the water and started swimming. When he was almost out of sight, he laughed and yelled back at us, 'use the brown paper bag, mahn', and we did. "Some toga vacation that was."

Lawrence walked to the bar and poured himself a scotch. "Anyone else?" he asked. "You should put that in one of your novels, Beau. You know something else, if we want to follow the rules we're not supposed to wear underwear. Like the Scots, they don't wear anything under their kilts."

Trevor and Beau exchanged glances. "I'm game," Beau said.

Trevor gave a thumbs-up gesture, but his mind was on Lawrence. He tried reading Lawrence's body language, wondering if his aloof cigar-puffing demeanor and his drinking so freely was an indication that he decided to accept his proposition. He smiled confidently. Reaching for a cigar, he held it up and lit it, all the while eyeing Lawrence intently. "Like the cigars, huh?" He turned to Beau. "I'm beginning to think that our young man has a taste for the good life, Beau."

"You'd better not pull his chain, T.J. Lar thinks the job you offered him is a sure thing. Disappointment can be a bitter pill to swallow. It won't be easy going back to filling prescriptions after you think you're going to be the big cheese trainer of Startech Industries."

"What are you talking about? I have all the confidence in the world in Lar. If I say the job is his, it damn well is. You can be a witness to it. Want me to put it in writing? What are you, anyhow, his lawyer?"

"No, just his friend, and yours too. Only trying to keep the record straight."

"So now you're his father, too. Jesus, how lucky can a guy get? Three fathers, no less."

Lar blew smoke rings into the air. "Gentlemen," he said. "Is it necessary to speak about me as if I were somewhere else? Don't get me wrong. I'm flattered. No one except my parents ever held me in such high esteem. I'm overwhelmed. Don't stop. I love it."

"Listen to the snotty kid, putting on the airs, will ya Beau? Remember, Lar, I told you it wouldn't be easy. Of course, if you go along with the advice I give you..." His mouth tightened and he spoke intently. "If you're smart, you'll listen to me. I promise you. It will be a shoo-in." He waited for Lawrence to reply.

Lawrence rested the cigar in the ashtray, locked eyes with Trevor, and said, "Whatever you say, T.J. I appreciate this chance, and I give you my word, I'll do whatever you ask of me." He knew from Trevor's pleased expression they had consummated the deal.

The telephone rang and Beau picked it up. Not waiting for the caller to speak, he said, "We know, we know. The natives are restless." He looked to Trevor, who still wore the towel around his waist. "The gentlemen need at least ten more minutes to make their entrance."

"Listen, Beau," Judy said. "I know you. Don't get carried away. No outrageous stunts, okay? Call us when you're in the dining room, and make sure you go easy on the booze. We need you guys to be sober when we show up."

"Mmmm, and what are you vixens scheming? You're not planning to spring out of a cake, or come wrapped in cellophane, are you?"

"You wish," she said, and hung up.

"What's that all about?" Lawrence asked, as he tucked, tied and draped a sheet around Trevor, who stood with his hands in the air.

"You're pretty good at this," Beau said, admiring Lawrence's handy work. "That was Judy. She wanted to know if we were ready. You heard the rest."

"I've had enough courses on dressing dummies in med school. I'm an expert on how to dress." He turned toward Beau. "You don't think they'll really come in cellophane, do you?"

"Whoa!" Trevor yelled out, squirming as Lawrence pinched his skin while tying a knot. He teased, "You'd like to see them wrapped naked, in cellophane, wouldn't you?"

His eyes shining, a tinge of excitement crossing his face, Lawrence lied. "Uh, of course not."

"Bullshit!" Trevor said coolly. "Every man wants to run his hands over another woman. It's just one of those unspoken subjects. Like masturbating. Everyone whacks the bishop, but no one admits it." He studied his appearance in the mirror, his eyes surveying the toga, then, he focused on Lawrence. His eyes lingered. "Let's be frank, Lar. You can't honestly look me straight in the eye and tell me you haven't thought of having sex with Pamela?"

Lawrence swallowed hard. Beau intervened. "Stop fucking with him, T.J. I'll answer for both of us. You're getting a little carried away. I don't know where this conversation is going, but if it is a swapping party you're thinking of, forget it. I, myself, have thought of fucking Pamela," he said, his eyes avoiding Trevor's. "But as you so eloquently said, 'we all think about it, but won't admit it.' You can't tell me that you haven't wanted to get Judy in the sack. Maybe that's where we should leave it. In our imaginations. I think your argument with Pamela has unnerved you. Let's forget we ever had this conversation," he said amicably, watching the tension in Lawrence's face ease up. "Let's just get through the evening."

Trevor's demeanor stiffened. "Sure, easy for you to say. Get through the evening and then what? You both have solid marriages, while mine is in the shit-house. Let's face it. We all know what's going on. You don't have a wife that fucks everything in sight. Is that plain enough?"

Beau became tense, his conscience reminding him he was not above reproach. Having been Pamela's lover in New York, he found himself in the same position as Trevor, wanting to dispose of her, also. Suddenly it came to him. "Lar," he said. "Nothing personal, and nothing to do with you, but I'd like a minute alone with T.J. You can't go to the party without us; it would give our toga surprise away. So, would you mind using the adjacent cabin for a few minutes?" Lawrence glanced at Trevor, reading his approval. Beau waited until he heard the cabin door close, poured Grand Marnier into two brandy snifters and handed one to Trevor.

"Look, Beau," Trevor said. "I know you mean well, and I appreciate your concern, but if you're going to lecture me on why I should go on with this marriage, you're wasting your time. You don't really believe that we can patch things up, do you?"

"Drink up, T.J. I have something to tell you, and you have to try to control your anger until I finish, if that's possible.'

"I don't think I could be angry with you, Beau. I'm fond of you." He smirked. "If you're going to tell me you fucked Pamela, I'm not in the least miffed. You're just one of many. In fact, I wouldn't blame you, knowing how she can seduce men. She can be quite irresistible when she wants to lure you into her web. She sends out sexual pheromones that draw you to her like a magnet."

"There's more. Do you remember when you said my voice was familiar? I fluffed it off, saying that I have a common voice and so many people sound like me?" Trevor started to speak, but Beau held his hand up. "You're right. I did do Pamela, but not here. And not on the Galapagos Islands."

Trevor looked puzzled, then his eyes widened. His brain connected the telephone voice the night Pamela slid out of bed, with Beau's voice. He sprang from his chair, anger flashed from his eyes, his face grave, his fists clenched, he lunged at Beau, ready to strike, then suddenly stopped dead in his tracks. "Well fuck me," he said, laughing so hard his eyes flooded with tears. He walked to the bar, picked up a bottle of Grand Marnier and refilled the glasses. He placed his hand on Beau's shoulder. "Maybe your guilty conscience had a little to do with your confession, but stop me if I'm wrong. The reason you came clean is because in the beginning it was passion, then intrigue, so you went along caught in her trap, just like the others. When she arranged this vacation for four, instead of two, bribing the travel agent to book us on the same yacht, it didn't take long to discover what a sick puppy you were involved with, did it? And now you're scared shitless Judy might find out, and ruin your happy little nest." Not until he finished speaking did he remove his hand from Beau's shoulder.

Beau took a deep breath and let it out slowly. "I was such a fool," he said, looking sadly at Trevor. "Do I have your word as a gentleman to keep this between us? Judith would be devastated, and my marriage – well, it would be history."

"No problem. Just remember, we can lick this thing. I've already worked out a few strategies. We have to combine forces. Think about it. You'll see I'm right. In fact, you don't have a choice. We know too much about each other than to be stupid and pull apart at this stage of the game. Do you want to know what I've planned?"

"Unless you insist, I'd rather not. Not yet."

"As you wish," Trevor said, extending his hand. "And Beau, you won't make this your next novel, will you?"

"It could be a best seller," Beau said thoughtfully. "I wouldn't do a thing like that." But his mind was already formulating the first chapter. "Listen, we better get Lar in here. He must be wondering what this is all about."

"Don't concern yourself with Lar. He knows a lot more than you think," Trevor said as he tapped on the wall of the adjacent cabin.

"Jesus," Lawrence said, looking at his watch as he entered the cabin. "The ladies are going to skin us alive. I was reading a tourist guide while I waited and they have one-day water- rafting trips down the Rio Toachi. I'd love to do that. We could fly to Quito and then to Rio Toachi, and raft down the river for two hours, but I don't know about the ladies."

"Sounds good to me," Beau said.

"Me too," Trevor agreed, an idea flashing through his mind. "Let's talk about it tomorrow. Sorry to keep you waiting, Lar. We had a lot to work out. You don't want to hear about it."

"You guys think you're so fucking smart," he said smugly. "I don't know why you sent me out of the cabin. I had my ear to the wall, and heard every last word you said."

Trevor and Beau exchanged glances and broke into laughter. "You might be sorry you had your ear to the wall, Lar." He poked Trevor. "You better keep an eye on this one, T.J. You just might be working for him someday."

CHAPTER 25

The luminous reflection of the moon cast shadows on the rippling current as the three men jubilantly drank, puffed cigars, and joked with one another. Lawrence bolted from his chaise. "What the hell was that?"

Springing up, Trevor, and Beau peered over the side of the yacht as a splash of water sprayed them. "It's the Loch Ness monster," Beau said jokingly. Trevor lifted his toga and wiped his face with it.

"You're flashing, better drop the toga," Beau, quipped.

Lawrence dabbed at his face with a tissue. "I think it was one of those giant iguanas. Scared the shit out of me. Did you know that they are the only sea-going lizards in the world?"

"Fascinating," Pamela said sarcastically, as she and Judy appeared, dressed to the nines, breathtaking in their evening gowns. "The iguanas are the highlight of my day," she added, turning to Judy. "Remind me to write it in my diary."

"Great costumes, guys," she said, rolling her eyes at Pamela. "And for this we had to hole up in our cabin for an hour. Well, Greek warriors, how do we look?"

The men stood, admired the two exquisite women, and felt a little foolish in their bed sheets as the ladies paraded in front of them, looking like movie stars at a premiere. Pamela, her bruises covered with make-up, her blond hair teased wildly about her face, wore a silver sequined gown. Slit thigh-high, her plunging neckline cut a V to her belly button, leaving her breasts exposed almost to her nipples. She wore backless, spiked 'come get me' shoes.

And Judy, not to be outdone, wore a semi-transparent black chiffon confection with a tight bustier and fluffy skirt that stopped mid-thigh.

"Absolutely smashing," Trevor said to his wife, but his eyes were on Judy. He poked Beau, as he walked to Pamela. Pecking her on the cheek, he searched her eyes for forgiveness. "Wanna call a truce?" he asked softly, nibbling at her ear, hoping to win her over.

"Sure," she said, but as the words left her mouth a wave of depression and a craving for drugs came over her.

"Unbelievable," Lawrence said sitting down quickly, afraid his erection would be seen. "Where's Kat?"

"Ah, ha, we thought you'd never ask," Judy said. She gestured toward their cabin. "And now ladies and gentlemen, it gives me great pleasure to introduce that femme fatale, the envy of every woman, in all her finery, the one and only... Gypsy Kaitlin."

Kaitlin, completely made over, every inch the glamour girl, wore a black silk one shouldered skin-tight gown borrowed from Pamela's wardrobe. Very much resembling Natalie Wood, she walked shyly out of the shadows into the light. Eyes widened, jaws dropped, and gasps were heard as the men stared, amazed at her transformation. Kaitlin, her eyes sparking, wondered if she looked as beautiful as the women professed she did.

Trevor and Beau walked to Kaitlin. "Well, where have you been all my life?" Trevor said, "You're the stuff dreams are made of."

Beau pushed him aside and extended his arm to her. "Don't bother with the riff raff, my dear. A classy woman of your stature and beauty needs a mature man of culture, who knows how to treat a lady."

Trevor stepped to her other side and slid his arm under hers. "Pay no attention to the man behind the sheet. I can give you diamonds, rubies, emeralds, and untold wealth; I will be your love slave." They escorted her to a chaise, feigned dusting it and stood at either side of her. "Would her Highness like a drink?" Trevor asked.

"Or perhaps an aperitif," Beau added.

"Or how about a fist full of knuckles," Lawrence said standing alongside of them. "Have we forgotten her Highness is betrothed to the handsome prince?"

"Fuck off, prince," Trevor said.

"Yeah, fuck off," Beau mimicked. He took a napkin and slapped Lawrence with it. "I challenge you to a duel, the winner to lay claim to the royal beauty,"

Judy placed her hands on her hips. "Okay, you vultures, that's enough. Give Lar a chance to digest the new Kat," she said, noticing Pamela walking away. "Ladies room?" she asked sarcastically. "Need any help?"

"No thanks. I'll be right back."

Lawrence sat staring at Kaitlin. "What's wrong?" she asked.

"Wrong? I didn't realize how beautiful you are." She knitted her brows. "I mean I always told you how pretty I thought you were, but now, well you look older." She bit her lip. "No, that's not what I meant. Not older, more sophisticated. It's just that I... well, it's sort of a shock."

She looked at him; her eyes making his heart melt as they always did. "You're not saying it to make me feel good, are you?"

He moved closer to her. "Gee, Kat. The way you look, no, I'm even more in love with you. You're so sexy, you just turn me on so, I could just..."

"That's enough of that," Beau said, intervening. "Time to eat, drink, and be merry. You can screw your heads off later. Now is the time to partake, and concentrate on the fabulous dinner the chef has prepared. But first..."

"But first," Pamela said, returning from her cabin, "we have to break open the Dom Perignon. Let's make this a night to remember."

All eyes turned toward Pamela, exchanging glances, aware she was high. Trevor winked knowingly at Beau, then took Pamela's arm and led her into the dining room. He felt pleased she was making things so easy for him.

Dinner went exceptionally well. The conversation was light, mostly about Kaitlin's transformation. Lawrence kept reassuring Kaitlin he loved her new look, but inwardly he wasn't sure he liked the change. The thought of other men being attracted to his wife brought his insecurities to light. But for the moment, her bout with Hodgkin's disease and her pregnancy were forgotten, and that made him happy.

Pamela's behavior was beyond reproach. Her performance as the attentive wife and charming hostess led them to believe that perhaps when she left so suddenly, she hadn't taken drugs, but Trevor knew better. To him, her charming behavior was the calm before the storm.

"Judy mentioned river rafting. What about it?" Pamela asked.

Beau took a second helping of tiramisu and sighed. Smiling smugly, he pointed his fork at Pamela, then Kaitlin, and lastly at Judy. "Now ladies," he said, "The time has come for you to prove that you are one of the guys."

Judy lifted her fork and pointed it at him. "And what makes you think we want to be one of the guys?" She looked from Kaitlin, to Pamela, and back to Beau. "Bouncing down some stupid river is not my idea of proving anything, but a way to commit suicide. It's the last thing in the world I would like to do." She made a sour face.

Beau scowled. "That's a piss poor attitude. You women talk such a good game about women's rights and how far you've come, but when it comes down to it, you really belong in the kitchen, bussing the kids to and from school, and having dinner ready when your man comes home after a hard day at the office."

She gave him the finger. "You're so full of it, Beau. Ladies, don't listen to him. He's baiting us. You men want to go bouncing down the river, be my guest."

Trevor raised his hand. "Hold on, Judy. It could be fun," he said, hoping he could get her to change her mind. "At least come with us. You don't have to go rafting, you can stay in the lodge. If Pamela goes, will you?"

Judy looked at Pamela. "You mean to tell me you would consider doing it?"

Pamela shrugged. "Well, I have thought about it. It might be fun. I've heard it's a thrilling adventure."

Lawrence spoke up. "Please. I'm dying to go. Judy, please don't nix this. At least say you'll think about it." He looked at her, his eyes pleading, and then turned to his wife. "Kat, I don't think it would be wise for you to go down the river. You and Judy can wait for us. It's only an hour ride. Okay?"

"If the ladies go, so will I, but please, no flack about my being sick, okay? I haven't been nauseous or thrown up all day. I think I'm over the worst of it."

Lawrence threw up his hands. "One day and she's cured. Gentlemen, maybe Judy is right. It is a guy, thing. They don't want to go, and they'll be bitching and moaning and carrying on and spoil it for us."

Trevor sent Lawrence a threatening look. "I'm not sure I agree with you. Pamela wants to go. Why don't we take a vote? Personally, I don't think anyone should be left alone for two hours. Pamela, you spoke about rafting before, so I take it you're serious about it."

"Okay, okay, I'll go!" Judy announced. "But forget about the rafting bit. I'm sure they have a lodge where Kat and I can hang out until you get back. Lar, you did say it was an hour ride down the rapids, didn't you?" His head bobbed up and down with excitement. "For one hour we'll manage."

"You may change your mind, Judy," Trevor said. "I've done it, and it's not as dangerous as you think." His anxiety level rose as their eyes held for a moment, certain he was becoming obsessed with her. "I'm surprised. You appear to be the sports minded type of woman."

"To me, sports minded is working out in the gym and being aware of my health," she said, running her fingers through her hair. "I have to think long and hard about the rafting."

"I'll research the particulars," Lawrence said. "Wow! I can't wait."

"Good, then that's settled," Pamela said. "Now, let's party. Everyone into the lounge, I'm going to make my specialty. Pamela's B. B. special."

"Oh God," Trevor moaned, "I've had her B. B. before. It's potent."

"What does the B. B. stand for, and what's in it?" Kaitlin asked.

"She won't tell," Trevor replied. "But knowing Pamela, it probably stands for ball-buster."

Pamela waved a hand of dismissal at her husband. "You'll love it, and I promise I won't make it as strong as I usually do. I have all the ingredients. I made sure the steward stocked the bar to the hilt. Now, everyone into the lounge, while I do my thing." As they left for the lounge she called out to them. "And ladies, I don't know about you, but afterwards I'm changing into something more comfortable. I feel overdressed. How about it?"

Judy answered. "Good idea, Pamela."

Pamela hummed as she started preparing her concoction. Speaking aloud but softly, she took a large glass shaker and proceeded to add the ingredients. "A little bit of this, and a little bit of that, a little shake, and lo and behold, the B. B. special is almost ready." Sneaking to the doorway, she looked around making sure no one was around. Satisfied, she walked back to the bar. *And now, to complete the magic brew. All that's needed is a dash of rapturous delight.*

Her eyes filled with anticipation. She removed a zip-lock bag, emptied four Ecstasy tablets onto the bar, and pummeled them with the flat end of a knife until a powdery residue remained.

Her heart stopped for a second as Trevor yelled from the lounge. "Want any help?"

"Be there in a jiff," she shouted back, scraping the powder into the concoction. She picked up the remaining particles with a wet finger, sucked on it, and closed her eyes with delight.

Lifting the tray that held six glasses and a glass shaker, Pamela started towards the lounge, excitement circulating though her body. *Wait until they get a taste of my B. B. laced with Ecstasy. They'll crave sex, their endorphins will explode, and their heads will... well, their heads will just follow their uncontrollable impulses.*

An ocean breeze ushered Pamela into the deck area. Her hips swayed sensuously to the background of Frank Sinatra singing, *"Fly me to the moon, and let me play among the stars..."* Holding the tray out to them, she smiled promiscuously.

"Well, this calls for a toast," Beau said.

"Here, here," the group said in unison.

"You're the writer, Beau, make a toast," T.J., called out.

Beau winked at Judy. "Well, here's goes," he said. "To all the ones who have come before me, and to all the ones who followed after..."

They all interjected with, "Boo! Boo! Boo!"

Lawrence spoke up. "Beau, that sucks. I mean really sucks. Give us something legitimate. No wonder you were never published."

Beau placed his hand to his heart. "And I thought you were my friend, Lar." He feigned tears."

"Uncertain if he had hurt Beau's feelings, Lawrence said, regretfully, "I was only kidding."

"He knows it, Lar," Judy cut in. "He's putting you on."

"Okay," T.J. said. "Enough of this B. S. Let's drink up. It's party time."

Kaitlin chimed in. "What about the toast?"

"Screw the toast," Beau said. "Let's drink."

Pamela smiled, thinking, *they've consumed a glass of my concoction, and they're already three sheets to the wind.*

Lawrence admonished Kaitlin, but she insisted on drinking.

Judy finished her first potion and held her glass out for another. "Oh, oh," she said.

"The shit really hit me." She set the empty glass on the table and put her hand to her forehead.

"Let me take you to the cabin." Beau said, annoyed.

T.J. sprang up quickly and rushed to Judy's side, offering his hand. "Relax and enjoy yourself, Beau," he said. "The situation is well in hand."

Pamela quickly grabbed Beau's hand. "T.J.' is quite capable, Beau. Judy will be okay. Let me freshen your drink."

Wavering, T.J. held Judy tightly about her waist, escorted her down the stairs and stopped at the first cabin, where he hesitated. "I'm not quite sure if this is the right one, Judy," he said, his hands stroking her derriere. "Jesus, all the cabins look alike."

"It doesn't matter, as long as I can lie down. I'm okay, a little dizzy, and yet..." He swung the cabin door open, bent down, and swept her up in his arms. Kicking the door shut with his heel, he carried her into the cabin, and laid her down gently on the bed. Her arms held tightly around his neck, she sighed sensually. "I'm just tingling all over. You're not going to leave me here all alone in this strange room?" Her eyes grew wide as she held onto his neck with both hands.

"Of course not my dear," he breathed in her ear, as his lips brushed softly against hers. "That would be very rude indeed. But first we have to remove your gown. Wouldn't do to get it all messed up, would it?"

"Gown? Oh, yes, my gown... my gown."

Running her fingers along the outline of his face, she began to nibble on his ear. "I'm not the shy little girl I pretend to be, T.J. I fooled them all into thinking I'm so proper, but I'm not. I can prove it, if you'll let me."

The effect of the drink put them into a state of euphoria. His skin tingled with a million wonderful sensations, and his voice echoed pleasantly in her ears. "From the moment I saw you, I knew I had to have you."

"Me too. Beau's okay, but he's a big baby. You, you're a real man, a mature man – a magnificent man. I'm sure you know how to satisfy a woman. Undress me slowly. And with each piece of clothing you remove, touch me there, then kiss it. I want to feel your lips all over me."

His breathing increased as she spoke. "You're making me so hot for you, keep talking. I love the way your voice sounds. It's such a turn on."

After her last piece of clothing was strewn about the floor, Trevor, moved in slow motion, untied his toga and let it drop to the floor. "Lay down beside me," she said, and propped herself up on her elbow running her fingers with a feathery touch from his toes to his thighs, teasing him as she skirted around his genitals. He closed his eyes feeling as if a thousand hands were touching him. When she felt he was becoming too excited, she mounted him, her knees on either side of his thighs, and rested her head on his stomach.

She caressed him, touching his ear, his nose, rubbing his lips and inserting her finger lightly into his mouth. He tried sucking her finger in, but she removed it and continued touching his nipples, pinching them, all the while searching his face. He moaned aloud as her fingers wound around his pubic hairs entwining them into ringlets, and when she grabbed his member he clenched his teeth and panted, "Easy, not yet baby, not yet!" He winced, trying to hold back, unsure if he were imagining it, or if he was having an orgasm.

"You're not ready yet," she assured him. "Cool down. You're very high."

"I never want to cool down. It's heaven, and I want to take you – now. If I don't, I'll just float off into the heavens and never come down. Please. I can't stand much more."

"No, you'll have to wait, I'm not ready."

His mind spinning, Trevor sat up. "I can't wait. I have to be in you, now. I'm losing my mind." He didn't wait for her to answer. Jumping up, he pinned her arms at her sides and pleaded, "Don't make me force you. Let me in there – in that sacred place I long for. I know you want me as much as I want you. I wanted to satisfy you more, but my body is so sensitive, I can't control it. I'll make it up to you, I promise."

"Then do it. I would have liked to make it last longer, but it's okay," she said, eyeing his penis. "My God, you're so big and hard."

"Yes, tell me how big and hard I am," he said as he released his grip on her and lifted her high into the air, holding her there. She came down, and he aimed his member at her vagina entering her with one plunging thrust. "Tell me you want me," he shouted. "Please, for the love of God, tell me! Tell me! I want to hear you say it."

"I want you! I want you!" she shouted. She began to withdraw afraid it would all end too soon, but his pleasure was too great. He grabbed her buttocks and pushed in and out of her so violently she felt herself reaching a climax. She screamed, "Now! Now! Ooooh, my God, Oh my God."

"Yes, yes, push it up, baby," he yelled, as he pounded her harder and harder, shouting, "Oh baby, I'm on fire." He bucked fiercely, his orgasm so strong he thought he would die at that very moment. He laid her down on the bed and dropped down alongside her, his heart pounding, his lungs gasping for air.

She moved closer to him, listening to his heart pounding. Sensing something was wrong, she asked, "What's the matter? Are you alright?"

"I'm not sure," he said fearfully. "I can't catch my breath... my heart is racing, and my mouth is dry."

"I'll get you some water. Just stay there and relax." Fear gripped her as she poured water into a glass and brought it to him. "Here, drink," she said.

Suddenly the door burst open. Beau, Pamela, Lawrence, and Kaitlin barged in, drinks in hand, feeling no pain. Beau ran to his wife, pushed Trevor aside, and nestled her body close to his. "Here, drink this baby," he said as he poured the B.B. liquid into her mouth. She made a gurgling sound as the fluid slid down her throat. "Did he satisfy you, Judy? Was he better than me? Well, let's compare, okay?"

Her eyes half closed, she asked. "Beau, is that you? Why are you swaying? I missed you Beau. He finished so fast and I wanted more. Much more. I need someone to satisfy me, now."

Lawrence intervened, downed the rest of his drink, and asserted himself. "No Beau!" he cut in. "No way! You had your chance. Now it's mine. I've been lusting for your wife for too long. Find yourself someone else." He shook Trevor. "You've got a hell of a nerve, leaving Judy unhappy."

Lawrence shrugged. "Sorry Kat, I just can't pass up this opportunity. I'll get back to you." Resting on his back, he raised his arms to Judy. "Show me what T.J.'s been lusting after, and what Beau's been raving about."

Pamela mouthed off. "Oh no you don't. I'm not playing odd man out. Move over, Judy, I'm going to show you what a real ménage e trios is. Okay Lar. Let's see what you can do with two ladies."

"Guess that leaves you and me, Kat," Trevor said, his hands working their way up and down the hollow of her back. I've got my breath back and Mr. Johnson is standing at attention. I've been having fantasies about you from the moment I saw you transformed into a luscious beauty. You're not the helpless little waif you pretend to be, are you?" His hand moved from the small of her back to the nape of her neck, and before she realized what was happening their lips blended in perfect harmony.

"Let me help you relax," she said. "I too have wanted you, as much as you wanted me. But all the beds are taken, unless..." She looked down at the floor and back at him.

He shrugged. "Why not? The carpet is thick, you can rest on me." The carpet felt soft and they moaned as their bodies enmeshed with passion. "I can't wait," Trevor said. "You're so beautiful, your body is so unbelievably irresistible."

CHAPTER 26

Judy looked up to see Beau, his face distorted in pain, his eyes showing hurt and disappointment, glaring down at her.

He cried in his sleep, "No! No! Jude! Don't! Please don't!" Beau's voice caught in his throat as he struggled to speak. "No! No! Jude! Don't! Jude! No!"

Awakened suddenly from a deep sleep by his sudden outburst, Judy sat straight up in bed. She reached over and shook him gently. "Beau, Beau, wake up," she pleaded, her hands trembling, her heart racing. "You're dreaming." She kissed him softly. "Beau, please wake up, you're having a nightmare." She wiped the perspiration from his forehead hoping it was a nightmare and not a heart attack.

"What? ... Where? ... Jude," he stammered, his eyes blurred, trying to focus. Relieved that he responded, she dabbed the beads of perspiration from his forehead and kissed him gently on his cheek. She sighed with relief. "Poor darling, you were having a bad dream."

He sat up and embraced her tightly. "Bad dream?" he asked, not sure he was awake. "It was so real. I had the weirdest..."

"Beau," she exclaimed. "You're squeezing the life out of me. Are you sure you're all right? You're shivering." She felt his forehead wondering if he had a fever.

"I'm not sick, I just feel as if I'm still dreaming. Hold me darling, please."

Sliding down alongside him, she placed her body close to his and cradled his head on her breast. "You have a hangover from last night's festivities. I'm sure it was Pamela's concoction that put everyone over the edge. That woman is some piece of work." Breaking away from her, he sat up, placed his hands on her shoulders and looked into her eyes questioningly. "Jude," he said with hesitation, afraid to ask, afraid of what her answer might be. "Do you remember anything about last night? I mean, everybody was stoned, not just me, right?"

Turning away from him, she gazed thoughtfully out the window and sighed, then faced him. "I guess we were all high, but that's what parties are for." Quickly changing the subject, she suggested, "You should have something in your stomach, Beau."

He started for the bathroom, but she caught hold of his hand, stopping him in his tracks. "It's not this cabin," she said. "We moved during the night. Or should I say this morning?"

Standing in the nude, he confronted her, feeling a twinge of guilt, suspicious as to why she was avoiding conversation about the night before. "I know that look, Jude. What's up?"

"Do we have to talk about it now?"

"Please, Jude. My head feels like it's in a vise. Am I hallucinating?"

"It doesn't matter, it's over."

"What doesn't matter? What's over?"

"We all got carried away. We were very... chummy. We hugged and kissed, and I guess became intimate."

"Intimate?"

"Intimate! Intimate! Are you deaf? Don't make a big deal over it." She walked to the bathroom hoping he would drop the interrogation. "I'm going to take a shower. Why don't you get some rest? We're supposed to tour the islands today and we haven't eaten yet."

He blocked the bathroom door. "Oh no, you don't. Hold it right there. You're not doing a thing until we clear up this mess."

She bit her lip. "Stop overreacting, Beau. There's no mess to clear up. I told you. We all got smashed and I guess, played around."

"You mean like played spin the bottle, or are you suggesting we had a ménage a six, swap your mate, sex orgy?"

"Stop giving me the third degree," she said angrily, plopping down hard on the bed, the tears resting on her lids, waiting to fall. "You were there."

"I know that, but it's all so fuzzy."

"I don't remember, and what I do remember, is hazy. And why are you making me feel as if I was the only one who participated."

He glared at her. "Now, that I think of it, T.J. was the one who took you to a cabin when you felt dizzy. Then Lar came back after checking on you and,... I don't exactly know, but he said something about you being well-taken care of... by Trevor... and then Lar and Pamela and you... I think, got it on. Or was it Pamela and Lar and Kaitlin... Jesus, I'm so confused. After that I'm not quite sure about anything, except... except maybe, you fucking Trevor? It's all so hazy. I seem to remember T.J. carrying you somewhere. But, I didn't take Kaitlin anywhere. I couldn't ...I wouldn't... Not Kaitlin. One thing I am sure of, that bastard T.J. has been trying to make you since we boarded this yacht and..." He stopped short and ran his hands over his face. "My God! It wasn't a dream! It was real." His mind clicked into focus as his eyes locked with hers. "Then it was real when I screwed Kat. Jesus, Jude, I respect Kat. I can't believe I did that. "

"Try Pamela, too," she confirmed. "She told me she was hot for you and Lar. I'm sure she arranged the whole scene, starting with drinks, which no doubt she spiked with some drug to get everyone stoned out of their minds."

"I'm sorry I accused you Jude. I'm just as guilty. We had no control over the situation. How are we going to face them?"

She put her hands to her hips. "We're going to face them the same way they're going to face us. I can assure you no one is going to breathe a word about last night. But I have to tell you, Beau, I have it in for that bitch for pulling that stunt. And when I get a chance, I'm going to bury her. Meanwhile I'm going to play the game as if nothing happened. And I advise you to do the same."

"Jude? Are you quite certain that you... did it too? I mean... with Trevor?"

"As sure as you are that you did it with Kaitlin and Pamela. Let's not pretend like it never happened. We have too much going between us to start having doubts. Now you lay down, I'm off to the shower."

He called after her, "Jude?"

Waving a defiant finger at him, her teeth clenched, she warned, "Don't ever think of asking me if he was better than you, or I swear, I'll deck you."

CHAPTER 27

Trevor and Pamela chatted with Kaitlin and Lawrence about the day's itinerary. Beau and Judy, who looked spectacular in a halter-top and short shorts, approached the breakfast table. Flashing her most endearing smile, Judy lowered her sunglasses and greeted everyone, her eyes lingering on Trevor a trifle longer. "Mohnin," she said, her voice taking on a southern accent. "I think it's going to be a glorious day." The steward held her chair as her eyes danced from one couple to the next, and rested on Pamela. "You must give me the recipe for that B.B. cocktail you served last night, Pamela. I've never had a better night's sleep. No hangover, either." She leaned closer to Pamela. "Come now, tell us the secret ingredients. I bet you put vitamins in it. It's amazing, I'm raring to go." She would have loved to expose the bitch and tell everyone what she thought was in the drink, but used restraint. She would wait for the proper time to avenge herself. Turning her attention to Kaitlin, she said, "The new you is sensational." She sipped her orange juice, enjoying the little charade she was acting out, as Beau looked on, his smile showing approval.

"What's on the agenda for today? The frigates, iguanas, penguins, or the seals?" Kaitlin asked.

Pamela, who remained subdued throughout the conversation, spoke up.

"Well, get her," she said, keeping a low profile, sensing Judy's demeanor, thinking that she was a tad too upbeat. Since everyone was in a pleasant mood, she played along, as did the others. She turned to Lawrence. "Isn't Kat a world of information? How lucky can you get, Lar? A wife who's shed her cocoon to became a beautiful butterfly is also a world of knowledge."

Kaitlin stifled a giggle, but held back, feeling Lawrence's leg as a warning, pressing against hers. They had a morning of, 'you did, I did, and so what, we did,' for two hours, finally deciding to call it a draw by kissing and making up, happy she was feeling well from the previous nights frivolity.

Trevor kept a calm deportment, fighting his impulse to drink Judy in with his eyes. But he, too, was aware of the importance of keeping the waters calm in order to attain his goal. He paid attention to his wife, making sure that he didn't over do it, but just enough to keep her oblivious of his intentions.

"Well, Kat," Judy said, "Looks like we'll have to fire Santiago and hire you as our naturalist guide."

Santiago walked up to the table. "Good morning all. I heard that, and I'm sorry to inform you but I am unfireable. Nevertheless, on this glorious day we are going to see, boobies, boobies, and more boobies. All the fledglings have left their mother's nest and are trying their wings." He snickered. "I would suggest a covering of the head in order to avoid the... uh...deluge, shall we call it?" He pointed to a chair. "May I?"

"You don't have to be so formal, Santiago," Trevor said, looking around at the group. "What's after the boobies, boobies, boobies, and more boobies?"

"In that case, I would like a cup of coffee," Santiago said. "I was so involved in the details of our day's activities this morning I haven't had a chance to eat breakfast."

Trevor motioned at the steward who immediately poured Santiago a cup of coffee. "Bring him breakfast too," Trevor said.

"Oh no, I couldn't," the guide said halfheartedly.

"Oh yes, you could," Trevor countered. "Now what's on the agenda today?"

After ordering a breakfast of orange juice, pancakes, eggs with sausages, and eyeing the rolls and croissants on the table, he sipped his coffee, wiped his mouth with a napkin and flicked an eye around the table. "Usually," he began, "our itinerary is held to a strict schedule, but since we are on a ... well, flexible schedule, I would like to discuss some points of interest which I have previously omitted...of course with your permission." He shared a cabin with the steward and was well aware of the gossip that circulated among the yacht's crew concerning the passenger's conduct, but knowing his place, he kept the gossip to himself. He hesitated as the steward refilled his cup of coffee.

Beau, realizing Santiago's dilemma of whether to eat or talk came to his aid. "We will understand if you eat and talk, Santiago. You're among friends. It will save time."

Born a fisherman's son, Santiago Pascador Riviera, was too ashamed to mention his middle name, since every one in school had teased him and called him 'fishy.' Nevertheless, he took pride in his work as one of the most respected nature guides on the islands. He had studied the guidebooks until he memorized every word verbatim, and although his discourse sounded flat and rehearsed, his personality more than made up for it.

Ignoring the chuckles and comments, he continued his monologue. "The Galapagos Archipelago are a cluster of thirteen volcanic islands located just under the equator, the oldest islands being four million years old and the youngest, which are still in the process of being formed, are considered to be one of the most active volcanic areas in the world."

He ignored Pamela's comment of, "That's nice," as she rolled her eyes. He continued speaking.

"Since man has not populated these islands, the animals have little fear of humans. This has been maintained by making the area a national park of Ecuador, limiting the number of human visitors, and providing paths which separate the animals from the viewers."

"We should write that into law in the States," Beau chimed in. "We could use separation between animals and humans in some of our neighborhoods."

"He's talking about animal animals, not human animals, darling," Judy announced.

"Well, when one of those human animals tried to grab the gold chain from your neck and almost choked you on Madison Avenue, did you consider that piece of shit a human, or an animal?"

"Drop it, Beau. You're interfering with Santiago's presentation."

"Be that as it may," Santiago said. "The islands are the safest place where one can live. I will not bother you with more details, except to say that Charles Darwin was the first to make a scientific study of the islands in 1835, and for four years explored the geology and wildlife of South America, maintaining that the islands were the inspiration for all of his ideas and the basis of his research. And in order to get us on our way I will add only one more brief comment. The rest I will tell you as we go."

"Now be a good girl," Trevor said humoring Pamela, feeling that she was bored before they even started the day's excursion. Putting his arm around her, he squeezed her closer, whispering in her ear, "If you behave, I'll buy you that yellow diamond you've had your eye on at Harry's."

"You have a jewelry store called Harry's?" Lawrence asked.

Judy giggled. "Yeah. Harry Winston on Fifth Avenue, in New York."

The creases in Santiago's brow deepened, showing his impatience. "Please," he said. "Allow me just one more moment and then we can depart. The Archipelago's fauna, which means animals of a given region, and their emphatic uninhabitability, are another feature of these Isles. Hence, little but reptile life is found here. Only the giant tortoise, the lizards, the immense spiders, the snakes, and the strangest anomaly of outlandish nature, the iguana, is heard. No voice, no howl. The only sound of life heard here is a hiss. Except for the chirping of the boobies and their relatives. He chuckled, waiting for them to laugh, which they did to humor him. "And I was going to tell you the effect that El Nino has had on the islands, but I think from your impatience, it is best left for another time. Bye the bye, I have completed the arrangements for your trip down the rapids for the day after tomorrow."

Lawrence's face lit up. "I can't wait. I hope it's one of those long rides down the rapids, not one of those Disney theme park children's slides."

"No need to concern yourself, Mr. Bartoni. I personally have ridden the rapids and it is," he said, stopping short as he noticed Judy's disturbed expression, "gentle in places and a rough in others, but not dangerous in the least. They allow children over the age of fifteen to ride the rapids."

"Now, don't cop out on us, Judy," Pamela said. "You said if I went, you would, too."

"What I said was, I might consider going if the women went, but I'm still not sure."

"Well, if Judy's not going, neither am I," Kaitlin said.

"Well, I'm going," Pamela said. "It could be fun."

Judy sulked. "So now I'm going to take the heat for being a poor sport, right?"

Everyone shrugged except Trevor. "I don't think it's fair to force anyone to do anything against their will," he said, looking directly at Beau, his brows raised, waiting for him to reply.

"Personally Judy, I think you can handle it, but I won't make up your mind for you." He spoke to Pamela and Kaitlin. "I think you should go. I'll stay behind with Judith and keep her company."

Trevor winced. "This is getting out of hand," he said, seething at the thought that Beau would get to be with Judy, and not him.

Santiago drained his coffee and sat back, sated. "Not to worry," he said. "No problem. I took it upon myself to reserve the entire boat. No decision has to be made immediately."

"Sure," Judy said falsely. "Now I'll be labeled the bad seed. Okay, I'll go. I won't be happy, but I'll go."

"Really, Judy," Kaitlin said. "You don't have to go if you're afraid."

"Uh, uh. I said I'm going and that's the end of the conversation," Judy said, stuffing a Danish into her mouth. "The hell with the calories."

"Yeah," Pamela said. "Like she has to worry about calories."

Santiago found his opening to the conversation and cleared his throat. "May I continue? The day grows short, and we already have a late start. I wanted to tell you about the island, but I can do that as we sight-see."

"I'd rather hear about the rapids," Lawrence said, impatiently.

"Lar," Kaitlin warned. "Are you forgetting that we are guests?"

He looked at her with concern. "Listen, I'm not so sure you should be going down the rapids in your condition. Just because you're feeling better is no reason to..."

She quickly put her hand to his mouth. "I'm going, and I don't want to hear another word," she said with conviction. Lawrence, taken aback by her sudden display of self– confidence, looked at her, dumbfounded.

"Way to go, Kat," Pamela said, "Judy, are we, or are we not unbelievable? Not only did we make her pretty on the outside, but our feminist influence has given her the strength to stand up for herself."

"I'm not so sure I like the change,' Lawrence said. He smiled, but was more than annoyed by his wife's sudden display of power and embarrassed by her reprimanding him in front of the men he wanted to impress.

"Shall we?" Santiago suggested, "The boobies await us."

CHAPTER 28

The morning dragged into the afternoon, and the afternoon into the early evening without Judy realizing the evening had arrived. The upbeat morning rush she felt during the day's adventure on Santa Cruz Island now all but dissolved. Even the main center of human activity in the islands where the six hundred pound giant tortoises that live in their natural surroundings, sometimes for over a century, or the grassy Pampa zone, representative of the moist higher elevations of the islands housing a unique genus of plants, all endemic to the Galapagos Islands, or the Charles Darwin Research Station, that documents the natural and human history of the islands, that she had looked forward to seeing, now held no interest for her.

Santiago, knowing their partying could last until dawn, suggested they turn in at a decent hour, so when they arrived in Ecuador early the next morning to raft down the Rio Toachi, they would be refreshed and ready to go. Judy feigned a headache, excused herself, and insisted on dining alone in her cabin. She talked Beau out of staying with her. She walked away from the group, seeing the look of anger and disappointment on Trevor's face.

The indiscreet happenings of the previous night weighed heavily on her mind. She rested in bed waiting for the steward to bring her dinner. Was it possible, she wondered, that all the promiscuity of the night before had occurred, or was it a dream, like Beau had originally thought when he awoke from his nightmare?

She questioned herself. *I'm no angel, that's for sure, but why did I let myself become entangled in a mad sexual orgy? You know damn well why, she answered. You were drugged, and so were the others. And, you might, just might, be attracted to T.J.*

A knock on the door brought her out of her thoughts. "It's Miguel, the steward, with your dinner, Mrs. Blessing."

"Come in, Miguel. The door is open," she said, not bothering to get up. He wheeled in a cart with a setting of silver, glassware, and a bottle of wine. Breasts of guinea hen were encased in a glass bell, and included a side of two new potatoes and asparagus au gratin.

He stood and held a chair for her. "Would you like me to pour the wine and serve?" he asked, a hint of suggestion in his voice, and a roguish expression on his face.

My God, she thought. *He's coming on to me.* "Thank you," she said coldly. "I can manage."

He shrugged with disappointment and turned to leave. "If there is anything madam wishes, she has only to ring the kitchen."

"Madam will do that if she so desires, but at the moment madam wishes to be left alone." She went to the door and held it open for him. The moment he was out the door, she snapped the lock and leaned against it, thinking *Jesus, what happened to the vacation we planned? This is like something you read in a novel, it just doesn't happen. Well, maybe it happened to Kathryn Hepburn in the movie Summertime, but not to me, and not in the Galapagos Islands.* She poured a glass of wine and sat down at the table. *It's that bitch Pamela. She's the cause of all this turmoil. Turning this excursion into a fuck-fest. The nerve of her to manipulate and involve us in this sexual free-for-all she cooked up, just so she can screw every man on board.*

The more she thought about Pamela, the more incensed she became. Visions of schemes to get even with her – going as far as doing away with the lady – ran through her mind, but the knock at the door shook her back to reality. *If it's that pervert Miguel, I'm personally going to see to it that he gets fired.* "Yes," she said flatly. "Who is it?"

A tiny voice answered. "Judy, it's me, Kat. Is it a bad time?" she asked, nervously glancing around to see if anyone was near.

Judy opened the door wide enough for Kaitlin to know she was welcomed. "I thought it was that sex crazed Miguel who Pamela has been toying with. Come in. Anything wrong?"

"Oh, I feel fine. Except I have a problem, and there isn't anyone here that I feel comfortable talking to... that is, except you."

"Need some motherly advice?" Kaitlin shook her head, and Judy continued. "I'm glad you're here, Kat. I need to talk also. Did you have dinner?"

"They're just starting to serve, but I told them that I had some snacks before and wasn't hungry. I felt so strange. No one said, 'what's wrong?' Or at least, 'don't you feel well?' Not that I'm looking for attention but..."

"How about sharing? There's more than enough for two, and you're thin enough.

Let's get some food into you. Suddenly, I'm hungry." She offered Kaitlin a glass of wine.

Kaitlin shook her head. "Since last night, I've sworn off drinking, and I shouldn't be anyhow, with the baby and my illness."

Judy stared hard at the pretty young girl who had this heavy burden to carry. "You are going to eat and I'm going to serve you, and don't give me a hard time. So tell me, what's the problem? Lar giving you a bad time?"

"He's only part of it."

"Don't tell me, let me guess. Pamela, the slut. She's the other part, isn't she?"

Kaitlin nibbled on the Guinea hen. "This is delicious," she said, looking sadly at Judy. "How did you know Pamela was my problem?"

"Get real, Kat. Pamela is everyone's problem. And your other problem is your dumb, naive husband who is getting his rocks off with her. Don't be shocked Kaitlin. Mine is also blinded by her sexual charms. We're lucky there isn't a chandelier on the yacht or she'd be swinging from it."

"But why? What do they see in her that we don't have? I do everything that Lar asks me to. He tells me that he never gets enough of me. And gee, Judy, how could anyone compete with you? You have to be the most gorgeous creature ever."

"Thanks, Kat, but beauty has nothing to do with it. The male animal is just that, an animal. He picks up the scent of a woman and if it is forbidden, dangerous, raunchy, or illegal, he will lust after it. You don't have to worry, Lar will never leave you; he needs you more than you need him. He just doesn't have the brains enough to know it. None of them do."

"Wish I could believe that, Judy. He's so impressed with T.J., and your husband. He's changing. He has this big shot attitude, smoking cigars, drinking and..."

"...And screwing Pamela. Listen, this too shall pass, and very quickly." She eyed Kaitlin. "Do you despise the bitch as much as I do?"

"More, if that's possible. I couldn't tell anyone but you, but I've been thinking of bad things. Like throwing her overboard."

Judy smiled slyly. "Glad to hear it. I thought I was alone, but now... want to join forces? Of course, only if you're really serious about what you just said."

"I'm dead serious."

"Dead is the key word here, Kat. I'm not fooling around. Listen, I have a plan. Tomorrow we leave for the rafting trip. Now, this is what I have in mind." Their eyes locked in an agreement of silent understanding.

Kaitlin breathed a sigh of relief, but it was short lived. Observing an ironing board in the far end of the room she hesitated and asked, "What in the world are you doing? Don't tell me you're ironing."

"Just a touch up," Judy giggled. "I was considered the best little presser in my family." She lifted the iron and held it above her head. "See, it even spits steam."

The blood drained from Kaitlin's face as Judy stood helplessly by. Eyes wide with fear, Kaitlin tottered backwards and crouched down on the floor in a fetal position, reliving a moment in her childhood when she was four years old, locked in a closet by her drunken, abusive mother. She visualized her mother hand raised, clutching an iron, crashing it down on Uncle Mac's head. Then she passed out.

CHAPTER 29

RAFTING DOWN THE RIO TOACHI RIVER

The grass hut was decorated with rural, handmade bamboo furniture that was bound together and patched up by a local fisherman, who was more than likely moonlighting as a carpenter. The room was large, with folding chairs lined up in rows to accommodate large groups of rafters. Multi-colored sisal rugs scattered on the dirt floor were ragged, but nevertheless lent a warm ambiance to the rustic atmosphere. The group sat on a three-piece sectional bamboo couch with flowered cushions, chatting and awaiting the rafting guide. Hearing voices, they all turned toward the grassy hemp curtain, which parted as he entered.

"Gud mornin, ladies and gentlemen," he said smiling, his Australian accent evident, the dimples in his furrowed, tanned face gave him a boyish, but roguish expression. "We expect perfect weather conditions for our rafting adventure tomorrow morning down the scenic Rio Toachi," he announced. I'm your guide, counselor, and nursemaid. My name is Tom Floater, no pun. It's real awright."

The seven onlookers smiled as they sat listening with anticipation. Tom's eyes moved from one to the other as he continued speaking. "But, please call me Tom. While you are here you are under my strict supervision. I am responsible for your welfare from this moment up to the time of your return to the yacht." He folded his arms across his chest, his well-developed muscles bulging under his athletic, knit shirt. "I want to take a few minutes to familiarize you all with some pertinent information. Since you are my responsibility, I must impress upon you how seriously I take my job, and the obvious reason for my concern, is, of course, your safety. Rafting is an exciting sport, but it can have unforeseen moments." Judy and Kaitlin exchanged glances, as did Trevor, Lawrence, and Beau. Tom Floater unfolded his arms, his warm smile assuring them that he would keep them safe. "Please understand, this is not said to alarm you, but to prepare you to handle any unexpected situation that may arise." He placed his hands on his hips.

Pamela studied the handsome tour guide, who stood six foot three, and had a build that was the result of regular workouts at the gym. Her sexual juices started flowing as she turned and smiled at Trevor. "I'm glad we came, T.J. This is just what the doctor ordered," she said, turning back to Tom and envisioning him naked.

He spoke directly to Pamela. "I suggest goggles for protection from the sun's rays, ma'am."

"Pamela," she said smiling, flashing her pretty whites.

Returning her smile, he said, "Then I suggest you wear them, Pamela. We wouldn't want the glare of the sun to hinder your ride."

"Ride?" she said under her breath, her breathing increasing as she envisioned him riding her. He returned her smile, his expression hinting that the trip was not going to be as boring as he thought it would be.

Judy rolled her eyes, thinking, here we go again; Kaitlin sighed with frustration at Pamela's brazen behavior; Lawrence sulked, feeling a hint of jealousy; Beau frowned, wishing it were all over; and Trevor, concealing his feelings, put his arm about Pamela, affectionately giving her free reign to her promiscuity.

Turning his attention to the others, Tom continued. "Those of you who have rafted before know what I am talking about. Newcomers are wise to be on the alert. For instance, life jackets must, and I repeat, must, be worn at all times, in or near the water. The pontoon is safe, but sometimes the river likes to kick up her heels a bit. You never know when she may decide to throw a few unexpected breakers at us. In order to ensure that everyone understands the precautions they must take, we have prepared a brochure, which I am sure most of you have read. If you haven't, I suggest you do." He glanced at Judy, taken with her good looks, but quickly focused on the others and moved closer to Beau. "You wouldn't be here if you didn't want to experience the unexpected thrills that the river has to offer. But, always keep in mind the old motto, 'don't fool with mother nature.' As far as the seating arrangements in the pontoon go, contrary to what most of you may feel, it isn't always in your best interest to sit next to your friends or spouses. You need to know how to work with strangers. Not only will we develop camaraderie by learning to work as a team, it will also ensure your safety."

Pamela put her arm through her husband's and squeezed it. "Well, kids, I think this is going to be a real gas," she said, directing her gaze at the guide.

Picking up his clipboard that held the roster of names listed, he said, "We are now a family, and as a family, we have to watch out for one another. I already know that you are well acquainted, so I'm sure there is no reason to say anything more. But first, I would like to open a bottle of... well, it was going to be wine, but Santiago suggested Dom Perignon, with Mr. Carr's compliments, instead of our regular mountain Chablis." He turned to Santiago who popped the cork and poured the champagne. After they toasted to their trip, he checked the clipboard, "It's alphabetical," he joked. "Okay. Kaitlin Bartoni. You are the first to sign the roster." He walked to where she sat and admiringly looked into her eyes. "You are first. Write your name on the first line, please." Stepping toward Lawrence, he handed him the clipboard and said, "And you must be Lawrence Bartoni."

"Guess I'm next," Beau said, taking the clipboard from Lawrence. "And here, darling," he said to Judy, "You're next."

"May I?" Tom intervened. "Just checking to see we're signing on the correct lines, mate," he said. He feigned checking the list and handed it to Judy. "I know I've seen you somewhere, maybe on a magazine cover? Or on television?" he asked.

"Commercials. I do commercials," she said, handing him the clipboard.

"That's it, I never forget a pretty face," he declared, handing the board to Trevor, who chuckled at Judy's remark.

"You're out of order," Beau said accusingly. "I am a Blessing too, and Blessing is before Carr."

Trevor gave Beau the finger. "Too late, Beau. Want to go a few rounds to settle it?"

Pamela walked to the rattan bar and poured another glass of champagne. Tom sidled up to her and handed her the clipboard, all the while eyeing her cleavage. "You have a preference concerning the pontoon seating?" he asked.

Staring down at his crotch, she said softly. "You've got to be kidding. I'm with my husband and these other nerds. That's enough family for one trip." She ran her tongue over her lips. "I need a stranger's warmth and friendship like you were just touting, Tommy."

He smiled, knowing he was going to score. "I'm sure I can fill your needs," he whispered.

The group chatted amicably, every so often sneaking a glance at Pamela and Tom. Trevor eyed the pair. *Let her have her fun. It's going to be her last.*

CHAPTER 30

After dinner, Lawrence and Tom Floater schmoozed about the trip down the river.

All through the meal Pamela's thoughts were preoccupied with the virile guide. After making light conversation with the group at the table, she excused herself saying, "Look, there's a jukebox at the far end of the dining room. Does anyone have loose change?" The men dug into their pockets, Beau coming up with the quarters first. All eyes were on her as she sashayed her way to the nickelodeon.

"Oh, I better get over there," Tom said, pushing his chair back. "The damn thing has a lock on it. Some teenagers hold jam sessions after dark, and a few of the older rafters complain. I need to unlock it."

"And I suppose you have the master key to all the locks on the island," Judy said facetiously.

He smiled at her wishing it were she, and not Pamela, who came onto him, but knew better than to push his luck. Pamela was a hot number, and for a one-night stand, she would more than satisfy him.

Pamela didn't turn when she heard Tom's voice. "Have to unlock the box," he said, bending down and inserting the key in the lock.

"Cute butt," she said watching his pants tighten about the cheeks of his rear end.

He smiled knowingly at her as he stood up. Her full breasts brushed against his arm.

She spoke low. "It's my first time, Tommy. I mean going down the rapids, of course."

"Of course," he said, his eyes intense upon hers. "Maybe you need a few lessons, just to make sure you get the hang of it."

"I thought you'd never ask, Tommy."

"You come on pretty strong, don't you?"

"When I see what I want I go for it. Any objections?"

"I'm just a country bumpkin, Ma'am. All I know is what I read in the papers."

She inserted a quarter into the juke box and selected a record, glancing at the others, who pretended to be unaware of them. "Well then, maybe we could teach each other a few things."

He stared down at her breasts, wondering if it was his imagination or if they were rising and falling rapidly. Smirking, he said, "I'm always willing to learn. How about your husband?"

Her head snapped back and she laughed. "Why? You want a threesome?" They both laughed. "Where and when, Tommy?"

"Anytime after ten. Room 7. The door will be unlocked."

"You got it." She turned to the others, winking at him. "Don't start without me, Tommy."

Cautiously lifting the bedcover, Pamela inched her way off the bed and slipped into her negligee. She stood at the foot of the bed listening to Trevor's deep breathing. Satisfied he was sleeping soundly, she silently closed the door and tiptoed down the hall to room number 7.

Trevor, who pretended to be asleep, slipped out of bed, opened the door a crack and watched his wife enter room 7. He knew he should go back to bed and forget about her indiscretions. After all, her screwing every man she could was nothing new. *So why lose your head now he thought, when you're so close to putting an end to it all?* But for some reason he couldn't control, he became incensed at her for having the gall to pull a stunt like this so blatantly.

Pamela closed the door and leaned against it, allowing her negligee to slip from her shoulders onto the floor.

On the other side of the door, Trevor, rested on his knees and peered through the keyhole. He watched as his wife walked to the bed where Tom Floater lay, his arms extended, his penis bulging in his shorts with anticipation, waiting for her. "Turn out the light," he said, grinning from ear to ear.

"No, Tommy baby," she cooed. "I want to see every inch of you." Wasting no time, she climbed on top of him, pinned his hands above his head and rubbed her pelvis up and down the length of his penis, teasing him. "You *did* start without me, didn't you?"

"Take it easy, baby," he said moaning. "I'm too hot. You're going to make me come. Let me cool off. I've been playing around waiting for you and..."   But she kept taunting him and before he could control himself he had an orgasm. "I'm sorry," he said, "but I warned you.

"Oh, I'm sure you can rise to the occasion after you satisfy me, don't you think?"

"All night long, if you're up to it."

"I'm up to it. Now show me how the Aussies go down under."

Trevor, still on his knees, watched as the guide spread his wife's legs and went down on her. *Slut,* he thought, as he stood up and walked back to his room.

Lying in bed, he polished off a half bottle of scotch. He stared up at the ceiling picturing Pamela and Tom, their bodies writhing with passion. His mind switched to Judy and he fantasized about having torrid sex with her. He thought if he could only have her, he'd be one happy guy. His mind flashed back to his wife and Tom. *What's wrong with me? I don't give a shit about her anymore.* Pissed off as he was, he found himself turned on, visibly intrigued by watching them fornicate. He imagined the four of them in a state of heated passion as he fondled himself until he climaxed.

At three o'clock in the morning Pamela crept silently into the room to find Trevor awake. Noticing the half empty bottle of scotch, which she knew was full when she left, and the stale odor of liquor on his breath, she became suspicious. "What's the matter dear? Restless? I went down to the kitchen for some iced tea. I just couldn't shut my eyes. I think the rafting has me a little nervous. Can I get you something?" she asked, wondering how long he was awake, and if he knew how long she was gone. She slipped into bed, her body touching his.

"You're sweating," he said flatly.

"I know. I can't seem to cool off in this heat. And the ceiling fan doesn't do anything but circulate hot air. This isn't exactly the Ritz, is it?"

He tried curbing his anger. "You knew before we came the accommodations would be primitive. Just one more day, and we'll be back on the yacht. You'll have all the conveniences you want," he said, slurring the word *conveniences,* suggesting he meant her screwing whoever was in her reach.

"Does my warm body annoy you?" she asked, not wanting to get into an argument.

"I never complained before, did I?"

She was exhausted from her session with Tom, but she sensed his strange behavior, and it worried her. He turned towards her, his hardness pressing against her. "Now I understand why you waited up for me," she said. "Give me a minute in the bathroom and then I'm all yours. In the bathroom she swallowed a pill and washed it down with bottled water. When she returned she snuggled up to him. "You little stud-muffin," she said, cuddling closer to him.

Trevor rolled her over, spread her legs and plunged inside of her before she realized what was happening. "God, you're so wet," he said. "Like a well-oiled prostitute who's been fucked by the whole damn football team." Perspiration dripped from his forehead as he slammed into her with a vengeance, all the time calling her obscene names.

The drugs she took kicked in. "I love when you talk that way, T.J.," she said. "Don't stop, it makes me hotter. Tell me I'm your fucking whore. Admit it. It turns you on knowing I fuck around. You'd like to watch as they screw me, wouldn't you?"

His anger increased, and so did his memory of all the years he stupidly overlooked and forgave her cheating on him. He visualized all the men she'd had intercourse with. The liquor and the frustration of again realizing what a fool he had been hit him hard. His breathing increased as he pumped into her at a frenzied pace. Panting heavily, he whispered hoarsely. "Do they fuck you as good as I do? Did you take Tom the way you take me? You're not only my whore, you're everyone's whore." He tore into her relentlessly, calling her a pig, and a slut, and anything else that came to his mind, when suddenly he felt an agonizing pain in his groin and rolled off her, onto the floor.

Thinking he was joking around, she spun from the bed and tried to mount him.

"You're unbelievable. Who's been teaching you? I want you more than ever, T.J. Why didn't you make love to me like this before? I never would have wanted anyone else. You're a different man. A real man." Realizing his erection had softened, she rubbed against him trying to arouse him. "It's the booze," she said. "Not to worry. Pamela knows how to get you hard again."

He grabbed her and pulled her down by her hair, then straddled her. "You don't want a man. You want an animal. You're the lowest kind of human being," he said, slapping her hard across the face. "Is this what you want? I can give you that, and more. How about we try some bondage? That's something you must have jotted down in your vast portfolio of sexual experiences. Is it filed under Tom, Dick, or Harry?"

Not sure if he was serious, her half smile ambivalent, she looked up at him, unsure of herself. Barely audible, she said, "I've tried bondage, and it was very exciting. But not many men are into it. I'd love you to try."

"Well, Pammy baby, you just found another candidate," he said, his eyes ablaze with rage, the sweat pouring from him onto her. His fingers applied pressure to her throat. With the pain shooting through his groin, he still managed to have an erection and plunged into her despite the discomfort mingled with pleasure he derived from punishing her. "Am I man enough for you now, bitch?" he cried, his voice gravelly.

"Yes, oh, yes. Harder, squeeze the life out of me."

"Make this orgasm the best you ever had, it's going to be your last." Perspiring profusely, he watched as her eyes widened and her face flushed crimson red.

"Now, now," she mouthed, her breath catching in her throat. "Oh yes my love, now, oh, I'm going to..." Her body shuddered.

He pressed his fingers firmly around her throat, shutting her air duct. Her mouth dropped open, and her eyes rolled back in her head.

CHAPTER 31

As concerned as Ceil and Meyer were about Trevor's arrest, when their private jet touched down at Mariscal Sucre Airport in Quito, they were relieved to be greeted by an old friend, Agent Fernando Hernandez, head of Quito's homicide division, who whisked them through customs and into a chauffeured limousine.

Agent Hernandez pressed a button and the glass separating the passengers from the driver slid into closed, allowing them privacy. Sitting across from them, he leaned forward and shook Meyer's hand and smiled warmly at Ceil, kissing her on both cheeks.

"When Mrs. Blessing told me that she had called and that you were coming down, I couldn't believe my ears. I was very surprised."

Ceil, smiled at the agent. "No more surprised than we were when we spotted you. It was Meyer, who said, 'That man is a dead ringer for Agent Hernandez.' And I said, 'How could it be? He's in Columbia, exterminating the drug lords.'"

"Well, I sought a transfer because Maria was getting very nervous about my safety, and especially for the children. So, I pulled some strings and asked to be transferred." He removed a packet of cigars, but quickly shoved them back in his pocket, remembering Ceil's aversion to smoking. "What is your interest in Trevor Carr? Is he an acquaintance of yours? Couldn't be a relation, could he? I mean, a Spiegel related to someone named Carr?"

Meyer tossed his head at Ceil. "Get him, Ceil. They gave him a promotion and now he thinks he's the League of Nations. Hernandez, old buddy, did you ever think it might have been Carvensky? Most immigrants who passed through Ellis Island had their names shortened, misspelled, or cut in half."

"Oh, I'm sorry. Then he is a relation of yours."

"No, he's not," Meyer said, grinning. "I was just making a point."

Hernandez rolled his eyes towards Ceil. "I forgot about Meyer's unusual sense of humor."

"Unusual? Try strange. It's a long story, Fernando, so I'll cut to the chase. You know the business Meyer was in before we were married – and before I made him a partner in the hotel and casino." Meyer screwed up his face at her, which she ignored. "Meyer made a deal with some unsavory characters in the mob, and the deal went sour." She faced Meyer. "Want to tell the story, or should I finish it?"

"Hey," Meyer said, shrugging. "You want your fifteen minutes of fame, be my guest. You always get the last word anyhow."

"As I was saying," Ceil went on, "Meyer couldn't use his contacts, and Trevor, who had a few of his own, was able to save Meyer's ass. We became good friends. Personally I like Trevor, but his wife, forget it! A tramp, what you call in Spanish, a puta, from trailer town. Knowing him, it's hard to believe he could kill anything. A shark in business, but the sweetest man you could want to know. If he did it, and mind you I'm not saying he did, he must have had a good reason."

Meyer turned to Ceil. "Is it possible someone else could get a word in this one way conversation?"

She winked at Hernandez, but her voice was targeted at Meyer. "So who's stopping you? If you have something to contribute, the floor is all yours."

Hernandez laughed. "I see we are back where we left off. I didn't realize how much I missed you both until now. Getting back to Trevor Carr. I hate to say it, but all the evidence points to his killing his wife. Be it as it may, she very well could have been a bitch, but the man confessed to strangling her. Or as he says, 'tried to strangle her.' And the bruises on her neck."

Ceil spoke up. "You said the key word. *Tried* to kill her. That holds a lot of water."

"So you're here to prove me wrong, eh? You're going to have a tough fight on your hands."

"Have they performed an autopsy yet?"

"It's in the works as we speak, but what good will that do?"

"Nothing is certain until all horses are in the barn," she said with conviction.

"You might not be aware, my dear lady, but in Quito we do not have a jury. The judge makes the final decision after he hears all the evidence."

"Maybe that can work in our favor," Meyer said.

Hernandez shook his head disparagingly. "And if you will pardon my English, the judge that presides," he said lowering his voice, "is a real hard on."

CHAPTER 32

I n the wake of Trevor's incarceration at the local prison in Quito, his friends detained on the chartered yacht had to find a way to cope with the predicament they found themselves in.

Ceil and Meyer held tightly to the ropes on either side of the gangplank as they walked up the ramp of the yacht and were greeted by the captain. "Buenos dias. Co'mo este' usted?" Meyer asked.

The Captain smiled and extended his hand. He replied in perfect English, "It is a pleasure to meet you, Senior Meyer. Very well, thank you. Welcome aboard."

Ceil giggled at Meyer's attempt to speak Spanish, and in an undertone, whispered to him. "You can throw away the Berlitz tapes, Meyer, your Spanish is pure perfection."

"And you talk like Queen Isabella, I suppose," he answered challengingly. "You're cruising for a bruising."

"Where can we find the hostages?" she asked the captain, ignoring Meyer.

Laughing at her use of the word 'hostages,' he pointed to the upper deck where Judy, Beau, Lawrence, and Kaitlin stood leaning on the railing, looking down at them. "Thank you, Captain," Ceil said. "We would like to have a word with you later on. You'll be available," she said, posing it as a statement of fact, not a question. "And all of your crew, as well," she quickly added, awaiting his reply.

"Absolutely," he said. "We are at your disposal. Agent Hernandez has instructed me to remain here until further notice, and to cooperate with you in every way."

Looking up at the group staring at them from above, Ceil and Meyer ascended the steps knowing they had their work cut out for them.

Judy, smiling with relief, approached Ceil and extended her hand. "I'm Judy Blessing, I spoke to you on the phone, and this is my husband, Beau, and Kaitlin and Lawrence Bartoni." Ceil nodded, switching from her Miss Congeniality hat to her sleuthing hat, as Meyer, taken with Judy's good looks, shook hands with the men. "I feel so much better since you came," Judy said. "This vacation has turned into a nightmare. Do you think we'll be detained for very long?"

Taking a seat across from them, she hesitated, taking a moment to size them up, mentally referring to the report filed on the group.

Kaitlin nicknamed Kat: Pretty, waif-like youngster. Shy, guilt-ridden, sweet, amiable. Unfortunately afflicted with a grave illness.

Kaitlin's husband. Lawrence. Known to the group as Lar. Muscular, Attractive. Overly emotional. Means well. Has to mature.

Judy. Extraordinarily beautiful. Insecure, honest, too trusting.

Judy's husband. Beauregard. Beau, to his friends. Elderly, stately suave, handsome gent. Easy-going, promiscuous.

Trevor Jase. Successful tycoon. Handsome. Tough businessman. dedicated husband to Pamela.

Pamela, a very attractive, but depressed, maniacal sex-driven woman.

She focused to the group. "I'll be frank with you," she said. "We've been retained by Mr. Carr and have researched your backgrounds, so if we know more about you than you might like us to, don't be surprised. This information is necessary if we are to prove Trevor Carr's innocence."

"*If* he is innocent?" Beau cut in.

"That goes without saying, Mr. Blessing," Ceil said, continuing as if Beau's comment was of no consequence. "But I can assure you that we are not here to dig up your past or embarrass you. Our job is to see if we can uncover evidence that will prove that Trevor Carr did not murder his wife."

"How long will we be detained?" Lawrence asked. "My wife is not well."

Ceil grimaced. "That is not up to us. It's a decision that only the judge can make. Look, we're here on Mr. Carr's behalf, but since you are all Americans in a foreign country, we will do whatever we can to expedite the progress. Luckily, the government officials in Quito and Agent Hernandez are considerate, fair-minded citizens. And the American Ambassador has volunteered his help. The down side is that the judge who is going to preside over Mr. Carr's hearing is, from what I am told... difficult." She sighed, her eyes settling on Kaitlin's troubled expression and her large saucer shaped eyes. "And Mrs. Bartoni, as far as you are concerned, you will have to be checked into the Hospital Metropolitano, here in Quito."

"I won't permit it," Lawrence said. "I'm not going to allow Kaitlin to be in some rat- infested hospital with doctors who don't know her condition and probably don't have a license to practice."

"Take it easy, son," Ceil said softly, but with authority. "We have already contacted your doctor in New York and he has given his approval, considering the unforeseen circumstances you find yourselves in. And you can call Doctor Ludwig if you don't believe me. You are wrong about the hospital, Mr. Bartoni. It is one of three state-of-the-art institutions in South America and fortunately for you, it happens to be right here. And Dr. Ludwig, if he hasn't already, will be monitoring Mrs. Bartoni's progress with the doctor at the hospital. There's very little you can do about it, since you cannot go back to the states until further notice. The laws of Quito are quite specific on that particular point. Witnesses or suspects must remain until the court is satisfied." Pointing a finger at Kaitlin, she added, "From my conversation with Dr. Ludwig, he was not thrilled about consenting to this trip. You will check in today, my dear," she said, with authority. "Otherwise, you will be escorted there. And that is totally unnecessary, don't you agree?"

"Yes," Kaitlin answered.

"I'll go with you," Judy said. "Mrs. Spiegel is right. And, you have to tell them..."

Ceil cut in. "There can be no secrets between us if we are to work together. It so happens that we are aware of Mrs. Bartoni's pregnancy and so is her doctor who was, to put it mildly, extremely upset when he found out."

"But how could he have known?" Lawrence asked.

Ceil shook her head. "Mr. Carr told us when we met with him and I passed it along to the good doctor. Holding back information about your wife's health when she is diagnosed with Hodgkin's disease, and is pregnant is playing Russian roulette with her life."

"You're right," Judy said. "We were stupid not to realize the danger she could be in."

"Stupid is an understatement," Ceil said, "but let's go forward. Arrangements have been made for all of you at the Swissotel Quito. Mr. Carr insists on footing the bill for whatever expenses you incur while you are here. The sooner you leave the yacht, the better. And if you have to contact anyone at home, I suggest you take care of it now. Remember as far as anyone is concerned, you are extending your stay here, since ten days is not enough time to take in all the beauty of the Galapagos Islands, right?" Her eyes searched their faces. "Good," she said soberly, "as long as we understand each other we'll get along just fine."

The second Meyer closed the door of their room at the Swissotel he turned to Ceil. "How do you suppose those youngsters came up with the money for ten days vacation on a yacht? The kid's a pharmacist. If he clears fifty grand, it's a lot. Yachts like that one go for at least fifty to seventy-five grand per week. Even if they split the costs, where would he come up with a third of that?"

She let his question fall by the wayside. "I'm having a soda. You want something?"

"Yeah, I'd like a cooler room if that's possible. The air conditioner sucks big time."

"You're not in the honeymoon suite in the Shangri-la sweetheart. Take a cold shower, or better still, take a dip in the ocean."

He grimaced. "I'll take a shower, and stop patronizing, me. Why is it whenever we take on a job you become my boss? You know Ceil, sometimes you make me feel like I'm your lackey."

Realizing he was right, that she did become aggressive and domineering, she set the soda on the table and went to him. "I know," she said putting her arms about his neck and pulling him closer. "It's just that I become so wrapped up in a case, I lose myself. Forgive me."

He encircled her with his arms and held her tightly to him. "How about losing yourself in me? I could forgive you a lot easier if you consented to fool around."

"Later," she said, kissing and slipping away from him. "We've got work to do."

"In every movie that 007 makes, he manages to have sex while he's solving a crime? Are we so different?"

"The difference is that he's not married to any of those fillies and he has to make sure he gets it before the movie ends."

"And how come I never win an argument with you?"

"Because you like it that way, only you're too stubborn to admit it. Now my little stud, I have to ask you to forgive me for something else."

"What now?"

"Well, we've been so nuts getting information and the like, that I didn't tell you about the rest of the conversation I had with Trevor, while you were on the phone with the hotel."

"So, tell."

"A minute ago, before you started coming on to me, you wondered how the Bartoni's could afford to vacation on the yacht. Trevor told me that Pamela and Beau, who is married to that pretty lady, Judy, were lovers in New York, before they came here."

"Hold it! Hold it!" Meyer said puzzled. "You mean to tell me that they are swingers and came here to play house as a foursome? So where does the couple from Brooklyn shine in? Sounds like a six-some."

"I did a little research and it seems there's more to the three couples than meets the eye. And the poor kid Kaitlin, had a bad experience."

"How's that?"

"Her mother, a drunk, killed her boyfriend, and Kaitlin witnessed it. She was only four at the time."

"That's heavy. Too bad. What about the others?"

"If you'll give me a chance, I'll tell you what Trevor told me." She sipped her drink.

"So?"

"Mrs. Carr, Pamela, set the whole thing up. She paid the travel agent to book the two couples on the same yacht without them knowing. It was high-season and if they didn't share the yacht they'd be out in the cold, and their vacation would be ruined."

"Back up a minute. So the pretty lady, Judy, didn't have any idea that her husband and Pamela were lovers?"

"You catch on quick," she said in jest, as he squinted at her. "But he told her that he regretted what he had done and begged her forgiveness."

"Sounds as if this Beau was scoring all over the place. Stupid move on his part although he might not have known of Pamela's arrangements."

"Exactly what I was thinking. From what Trevor said, Pamela spiked the drinks with a drug called Ecstasy and everyone let their hair down."

"Let their hair down? You mean they had what we call in the old country an old fashioned gang-bang."

"I like your choice of words, Meyer. So articulate."

"Don't be such a prig. I've heard you say worse. I could have been more descriptive you know."

"I'm sure. Anyhow, Trevor told me they met the Bartonis while they were sightseeing. Kaitlin took ill, and being fellow Americans, they took them under their wing and invited them to stay on the yacht. Of course, the youngsters jumped at the chance and the rest you know. Except that Pamela made it with a couple of the crew, not to mention her old lover, Blessing, and Bartoni."

"Some guys have all the luck. How come I never get women throwing themselves at me?"

Ignoring him, she said, "From the info we have so far, I'm beginning to think that Trevor didn't murder Pamela. She gave everyone on the yacht a reason to want her dead. First, she concocts the Ecstasy cocktail that put everyone into a sexual frenzy. She does this without regard to Kaitlin's shaky health knowing it could possibly kill her, and on top of that, she screws Kaitlin's husband. All that adds up to more than enough motive to put the lady over the edge. And let's not forget, the walls are paper thin."

"I can see where you're coming from. Anyone could have heard the arguing, and after they knew that Trevor left, they snuck into the room and seeing she was still alive, put the finishing touches to her. They would be home free since all the evidence pointed to Trevor."

"Bingo," Ceil said. "But who? It seems to me that they all hated her and had a reason to do away with her. Let's put Kaitlin aside for the moment, although she had a damn good motive. And I think first names would make it easier to relate to the group. Take Lawrence, they call him Lar. He could seek revenge knowing Pamela endangered his wife's life by letting her drink the drug. Or, there may be other underlying logical explanations we have to uncover."

Meyer nodded his head in agreement. "And Beau had more than enough of Pamela, and wanted to be free of her. Maybe she wouldn't let go of him. Now, that's a real putz if I ever saw one." He smiled quizzically at Ceil. "Imagine schtuping Pamela when you have a beauty like Judy."

"Proves what I always said. The male animal thinks with his dick instead of his brain. Present company excluded, of course."

"Of course, of course," he said mimicking, her. "What I don't understand is why they participated in the orgy."

"Did you ever take drugs?"

"What kind of question is that? You know better than that."

"I can't swear for anyone, even you. I knew you from when we first came to the states but afterwards, I had no way of keeping track of you. Maybe you tried a little when you were... connected. Happens. I wasn't around then. People try lots of things, doesn't mean they become junkies."

He flinched, hurt showing on his face. "I can swear for you, how come you can't swear for me?"

"Don't get so touchy. No one's accusing you, which means maybe you're holding out on me?" she said posing it as a question.

"You know what I hate about you Ceil?"

She threw up her hands. "What?"

"That you can see through me. Makes me very uncomfortable."

"Guilty would be a better word. I don't care. I know and love you for the man you are now. No one's perfect."

"You are. I never met anyone like you."

"I wouldn't be too sure about that. So, want to get the heavy load off your chest? I promise I won't report you to the Pot Police."

"You're making a big joke out of it, but it wasn't at the time it happened. I know I can tell you."

"So, tell already, we have a closet full of work to do."

"Well, it wasn't pot. It was cocaine, and it happened when I was with the mob. There was a big drug bust and one of the boys brought a packet of it to one of our dinners on Mulberry Street in New York. I guess they were into it and knowing I wasn't, they kidded me until I snorted a few lines, just to get them off my back."

"Naturally. Just a few lines, right?"

"Stop with the interruptions or I'm not going to finish."

"I'm sorry," she said tying to keep a straight face.

He eyed her skeptically. "Well, I got real high and probably made a fool of myself because they were laughing uproariously. Anyhow, after a while I had this horrible sensation that I had no control over my mind and it scared the shit out of me. And that, Ceil, was my vast experience with drugs."

Kissing him on the cheek, she said, "For coming clean and cleansing your soul as a reward tonight, you're mine. Okay? Now back to reality. Let's see, where were we? Oh yes. You asked why they participated in the orgy after they drank the cocktail Pamela made. And I asked you if you ever did drugs. So, tell me, what is the answer to my question?"

He shrugged knowingly. "That you have no control over your faculties if you indulge."

"Good boy," she said pinching his cheek.

"We have a rough outline on Lar, Kaitlin, and Beau. Now what about Judy?"

"Stop thinking with your you-know-what and stop drooling over her. She had the best reason to kill Pamela. She's a woman scorned. We ladies don't forget too easily when our man has cheated on us. It's hard to forgive, but it's a lot harder to forget. I think we have to have a heart to heart with Judy. That is, if you can concentrate on why we're here and not on la femme."

CHAPTER 33

Beau lay on the bed, his hands behind his head. His eyes followed Judy as she unpacked her clothes, arranging and rearranging them in the closet. He patted the bed motioning for her to come over. "I've been watching you for ten minutes," he said. "You're moving like one of the Stepford wives. What's on your mind? The two private eyes?" When she didn't come to him, he sat up. "You're acting very cool towards me, Jude. Still holding a grudge because of my affair with Pamela? I swore I'd never see her again. Don't you believe me?"

She held his gaze, and blew out a deep breath. "She's dead. How lucky can you get? Now you can actually keep your word."

"I meant before she met with her accident."

"That's one way of putting it," she said. Her heart told her something had gone out of their relationship the moment he confessed he and Pamela had an affair for over a year. How could she have been so blind? She thought she had the perfect marriage.

Walking toward her, he placed his hands on her shoulder with tenderness, but withdrew them when he felt her body stiffen. "You hate me, don't you? I can feel it."

"I don't hate you; I'm just disappointed in you. What do you want me to say?

I forgive you, darling? I could understand if I were someone like your dearly departed oversexed girlfriend, who slept with anything that moved. But I gave myself only to you, and that's what hurts so bad. How do you expect me to feel? If I did it to you, how would you feel?"

"Okay, I admit it. I made a mistake. I fucked up. It's done. You want to leave me? You want a divorce? Tell me what you want me to do and I'll do it."

"I don't know what I want. This vacation has been a disaster. I'm humiliated, embarrassed, and disillusioned. I can't think straight." Tears welled in her eyes. "Actually, what I need is another vacation to get over this one." Her eyes stared through him, but her thoughts were of Trevor and the pain he must be enduring in prison. Shaking her head, she focused on Beau again. She took the clothes she spent ten minutes rearranging and threw them in her suitcase.

"What are you doing?" he asked. "Stop and think for a minute. At least wait until we get back to the states. This hasty decision of yours is only going to cast a shadow over us. Can't you see? If we split up now, they'll think that we conspired to do away with Pamela."

Her eyes fastened on his. "What the hell are you rambling about? That doesn't make sense."

"Listen, Jude, it makes a lot of sense. Don't you think they'll find out about the orgy? Any one of us could have planned to do away with Pamela. We all hated her enough to want her dead, and have said as much."

"Yes, I did say it, and I know you and your cohorts, Trevor and Lar, also planned something. So what? Are you going to run to the authorities and tell them we all wanted Pamela dead?"

"No."

"I didn't think so."

He stood facing her, his hands defiantly on his hips. "I'm not going to say a word, and neither are you or the others, but my sweet, you're forgetting the Captain, the steward, the chef, and the rest of the crew who I'm sure had a hell of a good time making fun of us... they would just love to tell all to the authorities. And last and certainly not least, there is Santiago, who stuck to us like a magnet." He walked up to her, "And, I have my suspicions about him. I think he might have participated in our little soiree," he said, flicking his eyebrows imitating Groucho Marx, "the night we all got stoned. So, my love, you must agree that we should join forces in order to protect ourselves."

She plopped down on the bed. "I suppose you're right. Santiago? Jesus. Are you making this up, or do you have some ulterior motive in that devious head of yours?"

"I remember as much as you do," he said leering at her, leading her to believe she might have had sex with Santiago too.

"I may just throw up," she said. "I have never felt so cheap. I feel like a bargain basement item marked down for the last time and destined for the Salvation Army. But, you're right about not making waves. Okay, let's call a truce for the time being. But get this through your head, Beau; you may be able to put all this behind you when this nightmare is over, but I can't promise you I will be able to just pick up where we were before."

"Fair enough. Shall we shake on it, or is touching verboten?" he asked extending his hand. Cocking his head to one side, he quickly lowered his arm as she backed away from him. "Okay, okay, I can take a hint. I'll keep my distance, although it's not going to be easy," he said, his sigh suggesting that he had really screwed up big time and how stupid he was to have let this beautiful creature slip away from him.

A knock at the door startled them. They looked at each other wondering if the visitor had overheard their conversation. "Are you decent?" Ceil called out.

"Well, I am," Judy answered. Her glance at Beau implied he wasn't. "Move, move," she mouthed, pointing to the bathroom. "Come in, Mrs. Spiegel. The door is open."

The door creaked as Ceil entered. "Not the Ritz, is it," she declared, smiling congenially. "If I were you, I'd have them oil the door. Gives me the chills." She continued before Judy was able to answer, "And I would lock my door. Things are not like they used to be. No place is safe today. I see you're still unpacking." She sighed. "Gorgeous suit. I tried it on at Armani, but it didn't do a thing for me," she said, patting her hips. "Now you, you could wear a paper bag and look stunning." Certain her interruption was inconvenient for Judy, she asked, contritely, "Is this a bad time for you?"

"Not for me, but my husband is in the bathroom. Truthfully, I'm glad you came. I..."

Ceil's hand flew up like a policeman directing traffic. "Enough said. I was wondering if you would like to accompany me on a walk around town for an hour or so. I thought it would be nice for us to get acquainted."

"I'd love to; just let me get my bag and hat. The sun is not one of my best friends. I'll just tell Beau I'm leaving."

The bathroom door opened and Beau, who had been listening, walked out toweling his hair. "Oh Mrs. Spiegel, I didn't know you were here. Excuse my appearance. Are you going out? Give me a minute and I'll escort you ladies."

"Thanks, but no thanks," Ceil said with a hint of sarcasm. "Just girl talk. You would be bored. After you," she said, holding the door open for Judy.

"Oh, by the way," Judy said, half-way out the door, "Have them oil all the hinges and fix the lock on the door, will you, dear?"

Beau pressed his palms against the closed door. "Sure thing darling," he called, thinking this woman was going to get Judy to say things she shouldn't.

Lawrence greeted them at the entrance to the hotel, a puzzled expression on his face at seeing them together. Before he could speak, Ceil said, "How's your wife?"

"Oh, hi," he said, his eyes going from Judy to Ceil. "Well, she was very nervous, you know, not looking forward to telling the doctor she is pregnant. And, of course, concerned about the Hodgkin's disease, and if there was a change in her condition." He frowned. "I feel responsible for letting her talk me into taking this trip."

Judy felt his discomfort. "Did the doctor say anything or didn't he see her yet?" she asked, trying to put him at ease.

"Well, Dr. Ludwig in New York was real upset, but after speaking to the doctor here, they decided there wasn't much they can do. I mean, since she's here, and can't leave the country... I'm so confused. But, after an examination, the doctor assured us that from his conference with Dr. Ludwig that her condition was the same. Except..."

"Except what?" Judy asked, putting her hand on his arm.

"Except that, it was not the best time for her to be pregnant. Something about the baby taking the necessary nutrients from her, which would lower her resistance. It could be dangerous."

"That's too bad," Judy said. "But your first concern is to have Kaitlin recover. You can think about children later on."

"That's just what I said, but Kaitlin went berserk. You wouldn't believe how she carried on. I never saw her so upset. Not even when we were first told that she had the disease."

Ceil broke into the conversation. "What you're saying is she wants to have the baby."

He nodded dejectedly. "Not only is it a risk to her health, but the baby could be, well, not perfect."

Judy winced. "Someone has to talk her out of it."

"But who?" Lawrence said. "My mother is in Brooklyn and her aunt is, from what Kat has told me, not the warmest person. She has no one else."

"Well, she has me," Judy said, "We sort of bonded. Anyhow, I could try." She looked at Ceil. "What do you think?"

Ceil smiled warmly. "Sure. She needs a little T. L. C. and motherly love."

"I feel better already," Lawrence said. "They said they had to run some tests. You should check first, to see if they would let you visit."

"Check? Not to worry. We'll get to see her. Now, why don't you get something to eat, or take a shower, or keep Beau company? Judy and I will see to it that your wife is in good hands."

Relieved, Lawrence smiled, waved and headed into the hotel. "Good idea. I'll see what Beau is up to."

Judy shook her head. "You have a way of taking over."

"Comes from years of bossing people around. In my other business, which is running a hotel, you have to be kind but tough, or the help will be running you. Anyhow, he was glad to get a reprieve for a while. He looks like a grown man, but he's still just a kid."

"You know, Ceil. You come across like a real hard-nosed gal, but I think you're all mushy inside."

"Let's skip the taxi," Ceil said, taking Judy's arm. "I can use the exercise. Keep the mushy stuff to yourself. Okay? I wouldn't want it getting around that a private eye was a softy. Could ruin my reputation."

"So, I was right."

Ceil stared hard at Judy. "Don't let my demeanor fool you. I can be a real bitch when it's necessary. Ask anyone in Atlantic City. I'm lucky. I can pass as the little old lady from Pasadena, only I don't ride a shiny red Super Stock Dodge."

CHAPTER 34

The nurse at the reception desk glared at Ceil and Judy, eyeing them with distrust. Her attitude let them know she was in command, and no one was visiting anybody while she was in charge, especially since visiting hours were over. However, when Ceil mentioned she was working with Agent Hernandez, her disposition changed from the Wicked Witch of the East to Glenda the Good Witch as fast as a magician pulls a rabbit out of a hat. Smiling sweetly, she said, "Have a seat, I'll see what I can do." She pointed to a hand-carved bench that read, in Spanish script, 'Donated by Senor Leonardo Montevecchio,' on the backrest.

"Oh boy," Ceil said sighing. "Not a good sign."

Judy looked at Ceil puzzled. "What's not a good sign, the hard bench? I think it's cute. I love handcrafted work."

"The bench I admire, but the name on it doesn't sit well with me. It's the name of the judge that's going to decide Trevor's fate, and I'm told he is one son of a bitch."

The oncologist, a tall, well-built man with piercing blue eyes, in his mid-forties approached. They started to rise. "Please, remain seated," he said. His face looked drawn and tired. "I am Doctor Estanza. And you must be Mrs.

Spiegel, with whom I have had the pleasure of speaking with on the phone." His face brightened, and the tired drawn appearance he had shown a second ago vanished the moment he observed Judy. "And this young lady?"

"This young lady is Mrs. Judith Blessing," she said, aware of his ogling Judy. She made sure to emphasize "Mrs."

He tore his eyes from Judy and focused on Ceil. "I have good news and bad news. Mrs. Bartoni's Hodgkin's disease is the same, but the patient is, as you know, pregnant. At this particular time, it is not a good thing. As I have explained to Mr. Bartoni, his wife's system is rather delicate, and carrying the baby would only weaken her condition further." He raised his hands in a hopeless gesture. "She refuses to have the baby aborted." He sat down next to Ceil. "I'm afraid she is signing her own death warrant." He pressed down on his thighs with his slender fingers and blunt cut nails, the trademark of a skilled surgeon. Cocking his head to one side, he vented a low sorrowful groan. "If the patient's condition should worsen and she is in need of radiation, we will have to abort the baby – which should have been done before. She told me about her drinking and feeling ill on the yacht."

"We all had a little too much," Judy said.

The doctor faced Judy. "I will keep my doctor's confidentiality oath and not reveal what was in the drink everyone ingested. A half of a glass can be half a glass too much." He eyed Judy. "Don't you agree?"

Judy sulked, knowing Kaitlin told him of the Ecstasy Pamela had mixed into the cocktail. "Yes," she uttered, "I agree," She faced Ceil. "I was going to tell you about the drinking, but the good doctor beat me to it. I felt so guilty knowing her condition. Pamela had revealed to Kat and I of her lacing the drinks with..."

Ceil waved her off. "I know all about it," she said, reasoning that this lady was not only pretty, but cunning as well. Turning to the doctor, Ceil asked, "Can we see Kaitlin now?"

"I'm afraid not. She is undergoing tests. Give us an hour or so, and I'll leave instructions so you can visit her. I have to scrub up for a surgery," he said, glancing at his watch. He smiled graciously at Ceil, but his smile at Judy was more than cordial.

Ceil, intent on pumping Judy for information about Pamela's murder, led her out of the hospital and into the heat of the day. Spotting a small bistro with an outside patio, she suggested they spend the hour under the shade of the umbrella, thinking this was the perfect opportunity to get Judy to open up. "How do you manage to ward off the men?" Ceil asked, studying Judy.

"I could show you pictures of me when I was young and you wouldn't recognize me, but those pictures have been destroyed, along with the negatives. I was always a few pounds overweight and inherited my dad's nose. To make matters worse, my mom constantly came up with, 'you would be so pretty if only you lost a few pounds and had your nose fixed'. After mother had her nose done, and not too well, I might add, I thought long and hard. At sixteen, I did have a nose job. I couldn't believe the difference it made. The weight loss helped also. But I still have a problem."

Ceil smiled knowingly. "Shall I venture to make a guess?" Judy nodded. "You still don't see yourself as you are. You haven't accepted the messages that your brain is sending your subconscious. The mirror tells you you're pretty, but you have trouble believing it." She looked at Judy for confirmation.

"You're *so* right on, it's scary. I would like to see pictures of you when you were younger. I bet you were a knockout. Not that you're not attractive now, but..."

"I'm older now, and one's looks tend to fade as time leaves its imprint on you." A far away look entered Ceil's eyes as she thought back in time. "I suppose I was pretty then. Of course the standard of beauty is much different today. In those days, one did not have to be tall and have thighs that measured the size of your arm. A little meat on a woman was considered sexy. The Latin men have the right idea. They like their women zaftig."

"Well, I think you're a stunning woman by any standard."

"Flattery will get you everywhere. So tell me, what did you do in New York? Model?"

"I did have offers, but I was too insecure. I went to fashion design school. Having a little talent as an artist, I got a job in the garment center. That's how I met Beau. He sold and I bought. I guess you can say I fell for his line." She stopped short, the words, 'fell for his line,' whirled around in her head. "I was surprised when he asked me on a date."

"Why? Because of his age?"

"Actually, I never gave his age a thought. He always spoke about this lady he was seeing and I imagined it was a done deal. My thing was dating older or married men. I know if you're going to tell me I have a father complex you'd be right. I guess I was afraid of making a commitment. For what reason I don't know. We hit it off, and after three months from the time we first dated, we were married. In City Hall, no less."

"I hate to get personal, but knowing myself, I will. Did I detect regret in your voice when you just mentioned, he sold you?"

Judy fanned her face with the handwritten menu that had seen better days, and stared down at the rattan table. "I might as well tell you. You're going to find out sooner or later, that is if you don't already know. The party Kaitlin told the oncologist about – the one on the yacht. As you know, Pamela laced the drinks with drugs and we all became uninhibited – sexually. To tell you the honest to goodness truth, I, and everyone else, remembers only flashes of what went on that night. But what got me was what my husband told me. Pamela had originally arranged for the four of us to share the yacht and..."

"You don't have to go any further," Ceil interrupted. "That he and Pamela were lovers – and he was sorry for what he did – and realized his mistake – and would you forgive him."

Surprise shown on Judy's face. "I guess I shouldn't be shocked. You seem to know a lot more than..."

Ceil cut her off again. "... than you would have liked me to know. Funny thing about lies. They always find a way of boomeranging at the liar. Go on."

"I won't pretend. Yes, I hated Pamela. Hated her enough to want her dead. But I didn't do it. Kaitlin and I planned to punish her because of her affair with Beau, and also for taking advantage of Lar. Practically raped him and every man aboard the yacht."

"You don't have to tell me about Pamela. I knew the Carrs, quite well. As much as I sympathize with you, murder is murder, and no one is beyond suspicion." Her eyes narrowed and she shrugged. "Even you, my dear."

CHAPTER 35

A stale mustiness permeated the air in the dimly lit anteroom of the Quito prison. A small shifty-eyed man, his face partially hidden by a newspaper, pretending to read, sat watching Ceil and Agent Hernandez walk up to the guard, who saluted snappily and unlocked the prison door.

The agent inclined his body toward Ceil and whispered. "Don't look back, but you may have an additional problem to contend with." Once on the other side of the door he led Ceil into a room normally used for interrogating suspects.

"What?" Ceil pondered.

"Did you happen to notice the little man behind the newspaper we passed in the lobby?"

"Yes, so?"

"He's called *Pepe el Narigudo.* Which means Pepe the Nose. He works for the daily newspaper in Quito. He can be very annoying, especially since nothing of any consequence has happened here, until now." Stroking his chin thoughtfully, he added, "I wonder if his nose picked up the scent of a story."

Ceil sighed. "Damn it! Wouldn't you know it? The one thing that we didn't want was publicity. Do you think he might be on to us?"

"I'm not sure. I have instructed the guards and everyone who works for me to keep Mr. Carr's arrest confidential for the moment, but you know as well as I that people, no matter how trustful, will talk. Anyhow, as soon as Mr. Carr is arraigned, the world will know. To have Mr. Carr hidden somewhere is something I cannot do. As much as I would like to help you, I would not break the law."

"And I wouldn't want you to," she said, biting her lip. "I hope we can stall for time until I can get more information to help Trevor."

"I understand your plight, Ceil, but you know this will be public knowledge very shortly, and the evidence against Mr. Carr is overwhelming. Time is short, but we do have one shred of hope."

"Which is?"

"Fortunately, this is the time of year the judge takes his family on holiday for a week. So you may have a week's grace, so to speak. That is, unless he cancels his plans, which I doubt, since he takes his children to visit his wife's parents the same time every year. So fortunately, you could have a week's reprieve."

"That *is* a break, but what about the snoop? If he suspects something, from what you say about this being deadsville, he's sure to jump at a chance to get his fifteen minutes of fame."

"There is a possibility I could convince him otherwise, but it would only be until the judge returns. Perhaps I can hold him off for the week, and promise him an exclusive on the story, with photographs he can sell to the world. He would be a fool to pass up the notoriety and money that will come to him."

"You're a life saver."

"I don't forget what you and Meyer did for me," he said, thinking back to the time when they were consulting on a case and Meyer had taken a bullet meant for him. His eyes shined with gratitude at Ceil. "And now, I will let you confer with Mr. Carr, while I check out what the little man with the nose for news is up to." When Agent Hernandez entered the waiting room it was empty. Pepe el Narigudo was gone.

CHAPTER 36

Ordinarily, the housekeeper at Judge Leonardo Montevecchio's home had a buoyant, effervescent disposition, but today her demeanor was that of a woman trying to fit thirteen eggs into a twelve-digit carton. When the front doorbell chimed she shut her eyes tightly and let out a deep sigh of frustration. Hoping the maid would answer the door she waited a few seconds. Laying the children's clothes she was packing on the bed, she scurried down the stairs, all the while muttering obscenities under her breath. Peeking between the curtains of the alcove window, her face darkened at the sight of Pepe el Narigudo. Her eyes narrowed as she opened the door. "Have you lost your mind? You should know better than to come knocking at the judge's door. He has a secretary who makes all his appointments. We're preparing to go on holiday, so please go away. I'll do you a favor and not mention to the judge that you came here so disrespectfully."

She tried closing the door, but he stuck his foot in. His face took on an icy expression. "Listen, Flora, I knew you when you were cleaning toilets for a living. I have very important news to tell the judge and he will not take it lightly if you turn me away. I must see him before he leaves on holiday."

Her impulse was to slam the door in his face when suddenly an official vehicle suddenly pulled up to the curb. Pepe turned quickly to see who it was.

Agent Hernandez, a menacing look in his black eyes, motioned a 'get over here right now' gesture with his index finger. Pepe walked apprehensively towards the agent and cringed as he heard an avenging giggle from Flora's mouth.

"Get in!" Agent Hernandez said. "You didn't speak to the judge, did you, Pepe?"

"No sir."

"Good. Relax. I'm not going to arrest you for breaking the law, although I do know about the illegal card games you're running in your house."

Pepe blew a breath of relief. "Just friendly games, sir. No money changes hands. Helps to pass the time." Afraid the agent was suspicious as to why he was at the judge's house, he swallowed hard. "I thought it would be nice if I featured an article about the judge taking his family on holiday."

Agent Hernandez laughed mockingly, poking his driver playfully in the ribs. "Did you hear that, Santos? El Narigudo is not only a newspaper reporter and gambling aficionado, but also a comedian." Pepe trembled. Agent Hernandez threw his arm about Pepe and clapped him on the back. "Take it easy, I'm not going to do anything to you. I have a proposition to make that I know you will not refuse."

CHAPTER 37

Trevor fought the urge to vomit as the stench from the prison cell lodged in his nose. *Breathe shallow, he told himself. This fiasco is a dream. No, it's a nightmare. One day you're on top of the world and then kerplunk, the bottom drops out, and you're drowning in shit.* He swallowed hard as the sour bile rose in his throat. The bedsprings pushed their way though the scrawny mattress and into his buttocks. Grimacing, he thought, *beware evildoers, you that find yourselves in a foreign prison.*

His eyes dropped to the dirt floor, spotting a mouse at the foot of his cot. The rodent stared up at him, an expression of sorrowful empathy in his eyes. Trevor wanted to reach down and scoop the mouse up, just to have someone to share his misery with but aware of the viruses that animals carry, he dismissed the thought. The mouse sat up, his eyes searching his newfound friend, a low, pleading squeak emanating from its sad turned down mouth.

Doom enveloped Trevor as his eyes locked with the mouse. It sent a chill throughout his body, causing him to shudder convulsively. A nauseating feeling wracked his system, as he, imagined that he was covered with crawling vermin.

An ear-piercing screech disturbed the stillness of the cell as the iron door opened. Upon seeing Ceil, Trevor's face lit up and he sighed with relief.

The mouse, frightened by the unexpected visitor's bad manners in disrupting the bonding with his friend, scurried into his abode, an opening in a crack in the wall.

Ceil, startled by the mouse's appearance recouped quickly and announced, "If I had known you were entertaining I would have had the caterer prepare a tray of cheese." She held up a paper bag, "I guess we'll have to settle for leftovers." Eying the hostile guard, who stood sneering at them, she dismissed him with a wave of her hand. "I'll call you if I need you," she said. The cell door closed with a distinctive CLANK as the guard, showing disdain, spit on the dirt floor.

"Well, that finishes today's etiquette lesson," she said, stretching her arms out to Trevor, who quickly stood and embraced her.

His voice gruff and cracking, he held tightly to her and uttered, "I can't tell you how good it is to see you. But Ceil, it's hopeless. They're going to crucify me. I don't have a chance. They're uncivilized animals."

Pushing him back, but holding on to his shoulders at arms length, she stared at him with intense determination. "Now you listen to me, T.J.," she said with conviction. "Get hold of yourself. You're not in this alone. This isn't the T.J. I know." She motioned for him to sit, trying not to show her disgust at the filthy cell and frayed mattress. She sat on the cot close to him. Knowing she had to get him out of his depressed state, she held his hand and smiled warmly at him. "I've arranged with Agent Hernandez to have you moved to a cell where the guards live. It's not the Plaza, but it will be better then this vermin-infested cell. At least it will be clean and you will be served decent food. And it will be safer there, too." He cringed.

His silence was loud. Then he said, "So you heard about it?"

"Heard what?"

"About the guards and what they made me do."

Surmising that he might have been raped, she forced herself to suppress her emotions, and waited for him to speak. The fear in her eyes told him what she was thinking. "No, they didn't rape me, but they damn near did. You don't want the down and dirty blow by blow description do you?" She didn't answer. "I thought not." A look of disgust crossed his face. "I will tell you that they tried to make me do things against my will, but they were called off by a guard who told them to lay off me." He half-smiled. "Guess you and your agent friend saved me."

At that moment Agent Hernandez approached the cell holding two guards by the scruff of their necks. "Are these the two that forced themselves on you?" he bellowed.

Trevor turned to Ceil, not knowing if it was in his best interest to finger them. She shrugged. "Let it rest for now," she whispered. "Save it for later."

Trevor's face darkened as his outrage boiled over. Staring at the two terrified guards with intense hatred, he tore his eyes away from them and faced Agent Hernandez. "I'm not sure, it was dark."

Agent Hernandez nodded knowingly, and pushed the two guards against the wall and smacked them hard across their faces. "Take them," he spewed to the guard in charge. "I'll deal with them later." He hesitated, certain Trevor did not want to accuse them for fear of repercussions. "I can't take back what was done, but I *can* apologize for them." He scowled at the guards. "We are trying our best to discourage this type of behavior and create a more civilized environment, but it is not always easy to control the people who work here. And now if you will permit me, I will make arrangements to have you moved to other quarters." He and Ceil waited for Trevor to exit, but Trevor stopped, opened the bag that Ceil brought, and removed a slice of bread. He placed the bread at the opening where the mouse had scurried. Aware Ceil and the agent were watching him, he proceeded to leave, but he heard a squeak and looked back. The mouse stared up to him, pulled the bread into the crevice, peaked out and squeaked again. Trevor imagined it a "Thank you."

CHAPTER 38

Judge Leonardo Montevecchio stared apprehensively out the window of his limousine. He was just beginning to settle down after an irritating visit with his in-laws. By nature, the judge was a dedicated family man who loved his wife and children, but to the prisoners who stood trembling before him, he was known as a merciless tyrant who handed down the harshest of sentences. Problems had occurred at his in-laws home and word of Trevor's incarceration did not help his already disgruntled state of mind.

Foreigners, he thought. Why do they always come to us and make trouble? This Carr character, I'll throw the book at him. Upsetting our tranquil way of life by murdering his wife in my principality. If he had to kill her why did he have to do it here? Why not back in America? Their homicides are catching up with their divorce rates. What a laugh, land of the free. They wouldn't have so many misdeeds if they let the punishment fit the crime. If we managed our country as softly as they do, the criminals would be in charge, and we'd be the prisoners. Just give them time and they will have a civil war on their hands by being so permissive.

His twin boys hassling one another jarred his thoughts. One scornful glance and a raised brow immediately put the fear of God into them. He stretched his long legs and stroked his goatee.

His wife, a dark-haired woman with a plump figure but a pretty face that radiated tolerance and kindness, tugged lightly at his sleeve. Recognizing his annoyance, she asked, "Where are you, Leonardo?"

Silence.

"I was thinking, Leonardo. The twins are growing so fast and they seem bored and restless at my parent's when we visit. I thought, with your permission, that we go elsewhere on our next holiday."

He broke his silence and smiled dubiously at her. "You're being quite tactful Rosetta. Let's face it. Your parents don't like me – never did – and I never cared for them either. It's nothing new. From the first moment I courted you and cow-towed to your arrogant father and socialite mother, they let me know that I was not good enough for their precious daughter. But I fell in love with you, and you didn't give a damn what they said, or how they tried to discourage our relationship. Even now, when I have proven myself to be a highly respected judge, they make me feel like one of the hired help." She started to speak, but he raised his hand. "Pablo," he called to the driver, "Pull over and take the boys up front with you."

As the limousine sped along the countryside, the judge clasped his wife's hands in his and tugged her closer. "It's not only your parents that have me upset. That's nothing new. Let's put that aside for now. I have a case coming up that presents difficulties."

Surprised, she looked at him. "You mean you're actually going to discuss one of your cases with me? Well, that's a first. Not that I'm not flattered but..."

"I know, I know. But I've been thinking. Perhaps it was selfish of me not to have included you before, but whatever the reasons, I admit I was wrong. You are a well-educated, highly intelligent woman. It was wrong of me to shut you out."

Her eyes filled with tears. She held tightly to his hands. "Thank you Leonardo, that's the best compliment you have ever given me. There were times that I would have died just to have you ask my opinion, especially when you seemed so baffled or unsure of a decision you had to make."

"I knew it all along, and you were right," he conceded. "And now I'm going to ask for your help, but I want to make you aware, you may be sorry I brought you into this case. You could feel responsible and guilty, if we should condemn an innocent man to death."

CHAPTER 39

Although Judy and Kaitlin had been strangers, fate somehow predestined their lives to intertwine. Perhaps out of friendship, perhaps because they were in a strange country, but more than likely, they clung together, each suspecting the other of killing Pamela. After all, they had consorted and planned to get rid of Pamela, expressing their hatred for the woman who drugged them and seduced their husbands.

Kaitlin shifted on the hospital bed. Her wide eyes searched Judy's face hoping to find an answer. Judy turned away, avoiding Kaitlin's puzzled expression and rearranged the flowers she had brought. "You look much better today, Kat," she said. "What's the latest word from the doctor?"

"The Hodgkin's is looking better, but there's the problem of my pregnancy. I just can't come to grips with having the baby aborted. It's a life that I'll be ending before it begins." She shuddered.

Judy set the vase of flowers on a nightstand and sat down at the edge of Kaitlin's bed. "I know it's easy for me to give advice, but you'll get through this. You can have children later on. You have to think of Kaitlin first. You can't carry the baby and maybe undergo radiation. To be blunt, Kat, it's suicide. I know how hard it is for you alone, without a mother or father to comfort you. And

Lar. Think of what he's going through."

Kaitlin sighed hopelessly. "Lar is such a baby. He gets so damned emotional." Her sad eyes met Judy's. "I feel so alone, except for you. You're the only one I can confide in."

"Good, then think of me as your surrogate mom and listen to me. We'll do what the doctor thinks is best. That means, saving you and having the abortion." She waited for Kaitlin to answer.

Silence.

"Listen, Kat. You don't have a choice. Stop driving yourself crazy with what is right and what is wrong. There is only one consideration here, and that's your health." From Kaitlin's expression, she doubted Kaitlin would abort the baby. "Look, Kat," she began, but stopped short as Ceil and Meyer entered the room.

"How are you doing, young lady?" Meyer asked of Kaitlin.

"Anxious?" Ceil asked, noticing Kaitlin's forlorn appearance. She continued, not giving Kaitlin a chance to answer. "Don't tell me you're thinking of having the baby."

Meyer cut in. "I hate to sound rude, but we have to talk. Judge Montevecchio is due back tomorrow and we have to be prepared for any questions he or Agent Hernandez may ask of anyone connected with the murder. Don't think because Trevor Carr is being arraigned that you all will not be implicated, perhaps arrested. This is not the States. They don't have a jury that decides the fate of the accused. The judge does the whole kit and caboodle. And if he doesn't like the way you part your hair, or the way you breathe, he can and will throw the book at you. They are not happy about foreigners disrupting their way of life. You have no rights here. And neither does Ceil nor I. Trevor will be assigned a lawyer who will defend him and we will be permitted to enter evidence on his behalf. That is, if the judge is in a good mood and allows it. None of you are home free. Not yet. Inform your husbands that we will all meet at six tonight to have dinner and discuss the aspects of the case. I have conferred with your doctor Kaitlin, and you will be permitted to leave the hospital for the meeting, and will return here afterwards. I have also received permission; with lots of persuasion and expense I might add, to have Trevor there, too.

Judy registered fear. "You mean we could be brought up on charges?"

"I mean we can't take anything for granted. We have to be prepared for the worst."

CHAPTER 40

Caution and precise tact were foremost on Agent Hernandez' mind as he stepped into the foyer and handed his coat to the housekeeper. She smiled politely and curtsied, a glint of admiration showing in her eyes. "Good to see you, Flora," he said, their gaze locking for a moment.

"Judge Montevecchio is expecting you sir," she said coolly, extending her hand toward the sitting room. "Make yourself comfortable, I will tell the judge you are here." As she turned to leave, she felt his eyes burn at the back of her neck causing a sensual tingling sensation that sent shivers down her spine.

At that moment the judge entered the room. He glanced at the housekeeper with concern. "Flora," he said. "Are you ill? Your face, it's so pale."

"It's nothing, sir," she said as she scurried out of the room.

Making sure she was not within hearing distance, he turned to Agent Hernandez and sighed as they shook hands. "You broke her heart, Fernando. She still cares for you."

"Surely you joke, Leonardo. That was many years ago. What makes you say that?"

"We do not treat Flora like a servant, but as one of the family. She and Rosetta talk a great deal as it is with women. Come now. Don't pout. It is one of those unfortunate circumstances that could not be avoided."

"I do think of Flora..."

The judge raised his hand, adding quickly, "No need to explain. It happens." Upon hearing the dishes on the breakfast tray rattling as Flora approached, he immediately changed the subject. "Ah, Flora, just what we needed." He turned to the agent. "You are in for a treat. Flora is the best cook in the whole of Ecuador. Maybe the world."

Flora set the tray on the table and poured the coffee, served the judge, then hesitantly served Agent Hernandez. Avoiding her one-time lover's eyes, her voice flat, quavering slightly, she addressed the judge. "Thank you for the compliment, but Fernando is well aware of my talent as a cook." She left the room, her head held high.

The men sipped their coffee, their eyes focused at the floor. Suddenly the judge patted his mouth with his napkin and snapped to attention. "Back to the business at hand, Fernando. I must tell you, my friend, I'm adamant – no, I'm Goddamn sick and tired of these strangers coming here and adding to our problems by committing heinous crimes. You know as well as I what is going on in our overcrowded prisons. The knifings, the fighting, the gangs opposing each other, the sodomy, and ..." He stopped short knowing that they both understood the trials and tribulations of the penal system and the corruption that existed. Lowering his voice, he said, "How can we upgrade our standards when the outsiders add to the mayhem?"

Agent Hernandez finished chewing. "I agree wholeheartedly with you, Leonardo. Crime is a problem that must be dealt with, and soon. Still, there are circumstances that arise concerning foreigners." He reached for a cookie, and then retracted his hand. "If you will permit me as a friend with no intention of going against your... uh... better judgment, which I have always held in the highest esteem, and your position, which I know you give your heart and soul to. Still..."

"So far, you're sounding like a college professor lecturing his students. What's your point? Ordinarily, I would not have let you get this far, but we have been friends for many years and I trust you. Let me tell you what you are trying to say so tactfully? If I'm wrong I will apologize and let you continue. If I'm right we will still remain close friends since I do respect and value your opinions, and your friendship. After all, we both strive to make our country a better place to live in. That is the reason we have brought you here." He hesitated and looked long and hard at the man he admired. "But, if you're going to ask me to keep an open mind and allow this murderer to enjoy privileges above and beyond what the court allows because you have some attachment to these private investigators ... forget it. I will not let anyone interfere with my court. Not even if they are my blood relatives."

Agent Hernandez half smiled. "I wouldn't do that, and you know it. I want only what is fair."

The judge raised his voice. "And I'm not fair?" Is that what you think?"

"I didn't say that, Leonardo. I ... I thought perhaps that you and I could meet with Mr. and Mrs. Spiegel, off the record, to talk things over before you hear the case. We could ask the prosecuting attorney to join us. Keep it official. Just so you have a better understanding of the situation."

The judge rose and paced the floor. He turned on his heels and walked up to Leonardo, his face just inches away from his friend – so close their noses almost touched. His voice was gentle but his eyes showed anger. Agent Hernandez' face tensed. "Did I hear you correctly?" the judge cried. "A better understanding of the case? Not only are you trying my patience, but also treading on dangerous ground. That is something I will not condone. It is unheard of to have this kind of meeting. It just isn't done. You must be out of your mind. Meeting with a suspected criminal's benefactors is not only against the law, but against all the ethics I swore to uphold." He shook his head, disappointment showing on his face. "How clever of you coming to my home as a friend trying to influence me, suggesting I invite the prosecuting attorney to make it appear legitimate. Why, to ease your conscience?" His agitation rose. "You think I'm a hard-nosed, sadistic, tyrannical bastard who has served too long on the bench and wants to punish each defendant just for the hell of it." Leonardo smelled the coffee on the judge's breath as he inched even closer and raised his voice. "You are right! That is how I get my kicks."

They froze with embarrassment as the judge's wife, Rosetta, stood in the doorway, her hands on her hips, and an expression of bewilderment on her face. Unsure of how to handle the situation she said, "Forgive me for intruding but the conversation is so titillating, I just had to ask if I could join in and perhaps...arbitrate?"

CHAPTER 41

"Please, give me your attention," Meyer said. "This is serious business!"

Beau's facial expression immediately changed from jovial to serious. "I'm sorry. For a moment my thoughts were elsewhere."

Seeing that Meyer was upset at the group's carefree attitude, Ceil stood and gestured to Meyer to sit down. "Keep your thoughts focused. For those who think this is just a game that will be over soon, I suggest you think twice. Better still, take a look at Trevor and what he's going through." She watched as their expressions became somber. "We have gone to the American Council, and the best we can hope for is a fair and just trial for Trevor. It all boils down to one person, Judge Montevecchio. He rules his court with an iron hand. The fact that Trevor is on trial does not excuse any of you from being charged as accomplices to drug trafficking."

"Drug trafficking?" Lawrence asked with alarm, his color draining. Ceil talked over him.

"You're not in the States where you're innocent until proven guilty. They can *and will* accuse you of anything that comes into their heads. You have no rights here. You came here on vacation, and in doing so disturbed their tranquil way of life. This kind of fiasco not only humiliates them, but also turns tourists away, adversely affecting their economy. And that, my friend, is not a good thing. Especially since the biggest source of income is tourism. Our government will not intervene, which puts us at a greater disadvantage. To add to our dilemma, the officials have spent years trying to eliminate the criminal element. They do not take it lightly when anyone, especially foreigners, tear down what they worked so hard to attain." She searched their eyes. "I'm not saying this to put the fear of God into you, but to make you aware that you are all in a very precarious, if not dangerous, situation." The air echoed stillness. "The trial is set for a week from today, and you will be on alert in case you are summoned for interrogation. And that's why we are here. Fortunately, Agent Hernandez, whom Meyer and I worked with before, has arranged for Trevor to join us. He had to skirt around the law, and it took a lot of finagling for him to accomplish it. He could be in big trouble if the authorities find out. This will be short, since we must get Trevor back to his quarters as quickly as possible. I'll say this once and only once. If you conceal any information, or lie, it will be found out eventually. So take heed. If they think you're not sincere, it will not be pleasant for you. Think about what you've read or seen in the movies of how foreign countries torment and torture outsiders."

She sat down beside Meyer. "Okay, Trevor," Meyer said with empathy, "Are you ready?"

"I'm numb, but that's okay," Trevor said, his voice scratchy and hoarse. His bloodshot eyes looked hollow and his expression was that of a helpless man who was to be executed for a crime he didn't commit. Raising his head, he focused on the group and spoke in a hushed tone. His voice dropped to a whisper. He raised his eyes to see tears rolling down Judy's cheeks. "Listen to what Ceil and Meyer are telling you. The realization of living through this hell is unbelievable. Some of these guards are animals. They made me do things that... well... disgusting things, until they got the word to lay off of me from Agent Hernandez, and that was only because of Ceil and Meyer's relationship with him. Personally, I don't think the agent knew what was happening. Or if he did, I doubt whether he could control it." Staring at Judy intently, he continued. "Thanks for telling the authorities we walked on the beach after my scene with Pamela. Trouble is, they'll think you are trying to confirm my alibi. They'll say she could have been dead after I left her and met you."

Ceil said, "Let us worry about the details. You admitted you wanted to strangle Pamela, but you didn't, and she was alive when you took the walk on the beach to cool off. We know you were enraged because you saw her having sex with the tour guide, Tom Floater, and when she came back to your room you were drinking heavily. Take it from there."

"It's ironic that I would get so upset. I knew she was cheating on me. It had been going on for years, and it happened on the yacht with the steward and..."

"Lar, and me too," Beau, broke in.

"Yes, yes," Ceil said impatiently, ignoring Beau's comment. "We are well aware of the Ecstasy cocktail that Pamela cooked up, but explain how you knew she was alive when you left her."

Trevor, visibly shaken, looked from Ceil to Judy. "It was just too much, her fooling around with every man she met. I was ashamed knowing everyone laughed at me behind my back. I had too much to drink, and after I saw her having sex with Floater, I just snapped. Yes, I tried to strangle her, but she was alive when I left." His body shook and he started sobbing. "There's not much more to tell." Holding his tear stained face in his hands he uttered, "I do remember her going to the fridge and nibbling on the food she hadn't eaten at dinner. How could she eat if she was dead?" His head bowed, Trevor started to sob. "Please, no more, I can't talk any more...I just can't."

CHAPTER 42

Rosetta Montevecchio was an eighth of an inch short of five feet, discounting the three inch Manolo Blahnik heels, but her stature was tall, and her composure self-assured. She smiled at the saleslady behind the Hermes counter. Her husband, the lord high executioner as he was known, due to the harsh sentences he handed down from the bench, had taken her into his confidence, giving her a sense of satisfaction she had not felt for years. A Harvard graduate who had dreamed of becoming the first woman lawyer in Quito, after her marriage to the judge found the competition between their related fields too conflicting, and so being a women and second class citizen, she regretfully bowed out to become a dutiful wife and mother. And so she wrapped her dreams in a cloud of hope and stored them in the back of her mind with the rest of her hopeful memories – and marked them, *do not open until...*

Her pretty face beamed as she held two silk scarves up to her cheek and looked into the mirror, trying to decide between the two.

She turned around abruptly upon hearing a woman's voice say, "When I'm confronted with a dilemma such as you seem to find yourself, I just buy both. Saves the frustration of making difficult decisions."

Rosetta sized up the attractive woman, noting the chic Chanel suit and her well-groomed appearance. "Now why didn't I think of that," she said admiringly. Finding herself slightly embarrassed, she added, "On holiday?"

"I wish I were. No, strictly business. I've traveled the world over, but for some reason I never got to the Galapagos Islands. Now that I'm here on... well, as I said, business, I wish I had the time to enjoy it."

Rosetta eyed the stranger suspiciously. "I can't imagine what business a lady like you would have in Quito, unless you are connected with one of the couturier shops. You have a charming accent, and the look of an entrepreneur." She turned to the saleslady, and said, "I'll take both scarves." Turning back to the stranger, she smiled. "Thank you for your help. Was I right? Are you in the fashion business?"

They walked out of the shop like two old friends. "May I introduce myself? I am Ceil Spiegel." She waved her hand at Rosetta. "You don't have to tell me who you are, Mrs. Montevecchio. I already know. Let me be perfectly honest with you. I'm in Quito on Trevor Carr's behalf." Rosetta showed annoyance and her look grew distant. "Please," Ceil continued, "Don't take offence. I took a few minutes to shop and when I saw you I just had to introduce myself. My husband says I'm too pushy, but at this stage of my life it's too late to change my ways."

Rosetta half smiled, "If you are associated with the accused, Mr. Carr. You must know that I'm forbidden to discuss anything that pertains to Mr. Carr's case."

"I'm well aware, Mrs. Montevecchio, but I'm only interested in your friendship and I'm not looking to influence you, or put pressure on your husband for Mr. Carr's sake. I own and operate a hotel and gambling casino back in the states. Mr. Carr happens to be a dear friend who I think is being accused of committing a crime that he... well, I won't go any further. You know, of course, that the court assigned a public defender to represent Mr. Carr, and I wouldn't want you to think that this meeting was planned, or that I'm devious enough to think that I could persuade you to influence your husband in any way."

Rosetta hesitated thoughtfully for a moment, her eyes studying Ceil. "This has become a very litigious society, my dear," she said coolly. "It's getting so that one must be very careful in whom one puts their trust. It's quite sad."

Ceil frowned. "Very sad. You would think that as time passes we would be more understanding and trustful of one another, but from my experience it is getting worse, not better." She waited for Rosetta to speak.

"I have good vibrations about you, Mrs. Spiegel."

"Please, call me Ceil,"

"All right, Ceil, and call me Rosetta. I'll be honest with you. I don't have too many friends. Would you like to stop for a coffee or snack?"

"I'd love it. I really appreciate your honesty and I promise I won't discuss anything pertaining to the case, just girl talk. I'm dying to know about the Galapagos Islands and their inhabitants."

"It's a deal," Rosetta said, extending her hand. "If you promise to tell me about how you run a casino. Sounds fascinating. Oh, and by the way," she advised, "we must use the utmost discretion and not let the judge in on our ... friendship. I wouldn't want to lose a husband in order to gain a friend."

"Stop at the next corner," Rosetta said to the taxi driver. She turned to Ceil. "After the dessert, which you can see I don't need," she said, patting her plump thighs, "it will ease my conscience to walk a few blocks. I can carry my shoes." She searched the street to see if anyone she knew was about, and dug in her purse, but Ceil placed her hand over Rosettas.

"You insisted on paying for the demitasse and lunch. At least, let me take care of the fare." Her look at Rosetta was congenial. "It *was* enjoyable, wasn't it?"

Rosetta returned Ceil's gaze. "Yes, it was. Very much so. Aside from my husband taking me into his confidence, this was the highlight of my day and..." Thinking she was divulging personal information, she stopped short. "Don't think me pushy, but I'd like to visit with you again if it's agreeable with you." She nervously searched the street again. Feeling safe, she extended her hand to Ceil and alighted the taxi. Holding on to the open door, she said tentatively, "It would be better if I got in touch with you, don't you think?"

"I understand," Ceil said. "Just leave word that *Tatiana,* from the garden committee called, and where and when you would like to meet to discus the floral arrangements." Rosetta, fascinated by the deception of having an alias, an interesting friend, plus the newly acquired confidence of her husband all in one week, hastened up the street feeling more fulfilled than she had in years.

Ceil wondered if she had gone a little too far this time by making friends with the judge's wife. "The Swissotel, driver," she said, a chill running though her as she pictured Meyer, waving a threatening finger at her, saying, "So, you did it again, Ceil. When are you going to learn to stop being so pushy?"

CHAPTER 43

Under normal circumstances Judge Montevecchio would have had his précis finished, neatly clasped with a binder clip, waiting in his briefcase ready for Monday morning's nine a.m. pre-examination of Mr. Trevor Jase Carr, of the United States, who was being held for the murder of his wife. He stood staring down at the gardens from the open window of his home office. It was an austere, dimly lit room, which he shared with no one until recently, when in a moment of weakness he decided to include his wife into his work.

He knew these were not normal circumstances and he admonished himself for thinking he had made a mistake by taking Rosetta into his confidence. *Was Agent Hernandez sending me a message? Was he becoming a hard-nosed, ruthless judge, who was trying to cleanse the country of these vermin who want to destroy the safe, secure way of living?* The thought kept running through his mind. Should he have invited Rosetta into his sphere of judgment?

His eyes lingered on his twin sons as they threw a baseball back and forth, wondering when the last time had been when he tossed a ball or played a game with them.

A gentle tap at the open door startled him. "Leonardo, I brought you a tray," Rosetta said. "Flora said you haven't lunched and it's past three. Are you feeling ill?"

He did not reply.

She set the tray on his desk and walked to the window. She looked down at the twins and back at him, searching his eyes. Puckering her lips endearingly, she blew a kiss at him. "I'm in too happy a mood, Leonardo. You don't want to spoil it for me, do you? Is the case weighing heavily on your mind? Want to talk about it? You did say you were going to include me in your work." She looked at him questioningly. "Having second thoughts?"

He looked at the woman who had given up a career, raised his children, and selflessly took care of his every need. Surrounding her with his arms he held her close and said softly, "I have had second thoughts and third thoughts and have come to the conclusion that I was a fool for not having the right first thoughts. I have never lied to you, my dear. I need you now more than ever. Yes, the Carr case is disrupting my usual inerrable sense of judgment. As of late, I find myself unsure and hesitant. That is something that has never happened before."

"Is that the reason you want my ear?"

"Yes and no. Talking things over with you is something I should have done long ago. It wasn't fair of me to shut you out." Turning from the window, he motioned for her to sit. "I've been giving it a great deal of thought and have come to the conclusion the reason I did not include you in the court hearings is... well..."

"If you're thinking discussing the cases with me was unethical, I understand."

"That is not what bothers me. When was the last time I played with the boys or took them to a soccer game... or took you out to dinner or dancing? Besides that, I have pangs of guilt. I have sent men to prison even when I was not sure they committed a crime. The chaos was getting out of hand, and I wanted to punish anyone that came before me." She started to speak, but he waved her off. "Hear me. The honest to goodness truth is that... I knew you were more tolerant and intelligent than I... and I was afraid to let you voice your opinion. Now, what do you think of the most upstanding, respected judge in all of Ecuador?"

"Your trouble is that you are a perfectionist, and that can be a hardship. Nothing you do is good enough. You have to learn to, as the Americans say, 'chill out.' Look where you came from, and what you have accomplished. What brought all this on? Was it your disagreement with Fernando? He has been our good friend for... well, it seems forever. I'm sure you'll do the right thing when you hear the Carr case." She took his hand and squeezed it. "I know you will. I can see it in your face. You got it out of your system, and now you're going to be able to think clearly."

"You've always been there for me, haven't you? Tell me the truth. Have you regretted not continuing your law studies?"

"Yes, but if it was a choice between you and the twins or the law, I'd do it all over again, hands down. Let's do something different tonight or do you have to prepare for the hearing?"

"Whatever you say. And by the way, why are you in such a good mood? The moment you walked in, you seemed so cheerful, so exuberant... until I burst your balloon."

She felt trapped. "Nothing of the sort, silly. I ran into Tatiana at the Hermes counter, and we had lunch... and talked... well what ladies who lunch talk about."

"Tatiana? I don't remember you mentioning her before. Is she connected with the bridge club or the church?"

"Uh...neither. Just an old friend I went to school with many years ago," she said matter-of-fact, feeling guilty for lying.

"If you had such a good time with her, perhaps we could invite her and her husband to dinner, or to a restaurant. This could be a good beginning to enhance our social life. We haven't entertained in quite a while. Is she married? What does her husband do?"

Caught in a lie, she quickly changed the subject. "Enough about me. I have a better idea. It's Friday. Why don't we let Flora take the boys to her daughter's house? They love to play with her daughter's sons. And we could be alone." She raised her brows suggestively. "We could light the candles and have a picnic in the den. Flora could fix us a cold supper with a bottle of your favorite wine, and we could go swimming... remember how we used to?"

"How did I get so lucky to have you for my wife?"

"You always say that, but I'm the lucky one," she answered, but her thoughts were about phoning Ceil and leaving a message that Tatiana called, and would like to meet with her.

CHAPTER 44

A cool gentle breeze blew in from the terrace. The judge shivered and exhaled a low moan of satisfaction as he caressed his wife's long, jet-black hair. He snuggled closer, and breathed in her ear. "Rosetta, that was wonderful." She turned her head away, blushing. "I allowed the years to go by, not realizing what I was missing. How could I be so blind?" His voice was filled with regret.

Turning on her stomach, she playfully made circular ringlets with the hair on his chest and pressed close to him savoring the warmth of his body, thinking that if he pulled away he might fall back to the stern, cold judge he was a few hours ago. She said, "You are a very caring man, Leonardo. Your position as a judge and what you have to contend with is not an easy task. You did what you thought was best – more than most men who claim to be humanitarians in Quito. "And," she added, "with Fernando's aid, the two of you can be proud of your accomplishments. People can walk the streets without fear... in most neighborhoods." She propped up on her elbow and stared, her eyes dark on his, the guilt of her disloyalty nibbling little bites at her conscience. "And, what is done is done and what has passed... let it stay where it belongs... in the past." She searched his eyes for confirmation. "Let's not dwell on it, Leonardo," she said, wondering if his sudden change of heart was sincere, or simply temporary. "I'm going to take advantage of your prowess. God knows, once we start on the case there won't be time."

He sat up. "Did you have to mention the damn case? We were on cloud nine and you have to go and spoil it by talking business. Why couldn't you leave things as they were?"

She positioned herself at his side resting her head on his chest, aware that she had brought him face to face with reality at a time he wanted to forget what lay ahead. "How about a fire?" she suggested, although the temperature was at least seventy-five degrees. She knew the flames and shadowy characters that danced around the hearth somehow mesmerized him into a state of tranquility and he had suggested lighting one or two in the past when he felt upset.

"If you want," he said, his eyes showing regret. Rosetta draped a serape around her, walked to the fireplace, and struck a match, igniting the kindling wood. She refilled the wine glasses and handed him one. Looking deeply into her eyes he said, "You know just how to push my buttons, don't you?"

"Your buttons are easy to push, my dear. They are made out of hard candy. Hard on the outside but soft and sweet when you get to the center."

The phone rang and she hesitated answering. "It's all right it might be important," he said. "Could be the boys or perhaps Fernando. He asked if we could meet with the Spiegels before Monday just to get acquainted. I resent his intervening, but he is a good man and a true friend, and he's never asked a favor before. I wanted to discuss the matter with you first." Seeing her reluctance, he added, "I'm mellowing out. I can discuss the case now. I've gotten over my tantrum."

"Oh yes," she said, hugging him. "It could be entertaining, and we wouldn't have to discuss the hearing. We haven't had company over in a long while. Please?"

He conceded. "Keep pushing the right buttons, Rosetta. Now answer the phone."

"Hello," she said. "And a good evening to you, Fernando. No, you didn't interrupt us. No, no, it's not a bad time. Leonardo was expecting your call. Send your wife my regards. Hold on, here's Leonardo."

"Good evening Fernando. Stop standing on ceremony. Yes, I have thought it over. Hold on a second." He covered the mouthpiece with his hand and looked questioningly at his wife. He spoke in a low tone. "Are you sure we should do this? You do understand they will try to persuade us to go easy on their friend. Ordinarily, I wouldn't tolerate such tactics, but Fernando did ask and..."

The thought of meeting Ceil again, excited her, but hiding the fact from her husband, troubled her. "Ask him to invite them to lunch with us, tomorrow at two. And ask him to get in touch with the prosecutor. Legally, he should be there too. Don't give me that look, Leonardo."

He winked at her, showing his approval, certain he made the right decision by making her his confidant. He spoke into the phone. "After much consideration Fernando, I have agreed to honor your request to meet with the Spiegel's. Shall we say tomorrow afternoon at two, for lunch? Here, at my home. And, ask the prosecuting attorney to join us. Thanks are not necessary. I look forward to seeing you too, Fernando. Goodbye."

He walked up to Rosetta, and watched as she stoked the fire. He took the andiron from her hand, and bent to kiss the nape of her neck. Pulling the serape from her, he lifted her gently and placed her on the sofa. Running his fingers lightly around her breasts, he drew her closer and said, "Now where were we?"

"Where we should be," she answered.

He called out her name as they made love, telling her how much he loved and needed her. She responded to his every touch, but her mind whirled with fear, her heart warning her she was going down a strange precarious road.

CHAPTER 45

Dr. Evan Levy hesitated to pick up the phone. The call waiting button flashed, 'Ceil Spiegel.'

The trans-continental phone call meant one of two things. Either his grandmother needed medical advice, or she called to wish him a happy birthday, and he was sure it wasn't happy birthday. He swiveled his desk chair and looked at the expansive view of New York City's skyline. She was his idol, his special confidant – and visa versa.

"Grandma, is something wrong? Mom told me about your trip to Quito. When are you and Meyer going to settle down? You're always saying that running the casino and hotel is a full time job. So how come you two are pursuing another adventure? Sounds to me like you overruled Meyer, once again."

"Listen, you little pisher, big time toxicologist, you forgot who changed your diapers and taught you to bluff your way with a poker hand full of nothing, so don't give me a hard time. Are you trying to tell me I'm getting too old, and should retire to a nursing home?"

"Don't snow me, granny. I'm onto you. If I learned anything about b-s-ing, it came from you. And it's not my birthday, so what's on that devious mind of yours?"

"If there's one thing I hate, it's someone who can see through me. Seriously, Evan, I need your help. I suppose from my last call you're aware of Trevor Carr, the man who's accused of strangling his wife. Well, it's not the open and shut case everyone seems to think it is. I know Trevor, and although I won't rule out that in a fit of desperation a man could be driven to kill, I feel in my bones that he didn't do it."

"Uh oh. Here we go again with what you're bones are telling you, and your woman's intuition. No, I take that back. You have been right nine out of ten times."

"Thanks for the left-handed compliment. When was the tenth time I was wrong? If this old woman's grey matter hasn't turned to dust, I seem to remember it was you who had psychic inclinations."

"That was a long time ago, granny, and they have never returned. So, what's on your mind? If you're thinking of asking me to come down there and do an autopsy, the answer is no in fifteen languages. I have three lectures, a seminar, and the book I'm almost finished writing."

"You're turning into a super nerd, Evan. What happened to the handsome sexy guy who had to fight off the girls?"

"He left when Elvis overdosed, granny. What's wrong with the coroners in Quito? They're not good enough for you? You do have a history of probing into situations farther than necessary, you know."

"Evan, darling, sweetheart. Do I ever ask you for anything? Can't you have it in your heart to do granny a little favor? Just this one time. You are my favorite grandson, you know. I promise I'll leave you the hotel and casino and all my possessions. I'll even throw in the cabin in the Poconos."

"I hate to be disrespectful, granny. But you're so full of shit. What a pitch. The last time this only grandson was promised your worldly possessions I ended up in the swamps of Florida with alligators nipping at my ass."

"Don't be so sensitive. You helped solve the case and you're putting it in your book, aren't you? How can you say I did nothing for you? You ungrateful, brat."

"I give up. Trying to win an argument with you is like – I can't even begin to describe it. Okay, what's the deal?"

"You're the best, Evan."

"I didn't commit to anything, granny."

"Of course not, sweetheart. I've been checking up on the coroner who did the autopsy on the victim, and there's something not kosher about him. Listen, I can't talk over the phone. I'll explain everything when you get here. You can pick up the tickets at the airport. First class, of course. The plane leaves at eight a. m. tomorrow morning."

"You're one shrewd, pushy broad, Grandma. You knew you'd talk me into coming, didn't you? Don't bother to answer. Just have a signed affidavit stating that I'm entitled to all the hundred dollar chips I require for the rest of my life at your casino."

"I'll go one better. You'll inherit the hotel and casino when I'm gone. For now you can have the condo in Boca after you help us close this case."

"Pass on the hotel and casino. You'll outlive all of us, and did you forget you signed the condo over to me last year."

"Oh, so I did. Well, whatever."

"Give me a break granny. You pulled that one on me two years ago."

"Listen, you promised to find a lady and settle down. I'm not going to the other side without at least seeing one great-grandchild."

"Can we cut the cord now? There's a room full of toxicologists waiting for me. See you tomorrow. Love you, you finagler."

"I love you bigger," she countered.

Pleased with herself, she clicked the phone and dialed Agent Hernandez. "Fernando," she said. "I hate to bother you, but how do I get permission to bring in my own toxicologist? And one more thing; can we get the autopsy records on Mrs. Carr?"

"You will have to go before the judge for permission to bring in a toxicologist. I don't think that is a problem. By law, the prosecuting attorney, Mr. Penya, must give you copies of any and all pertinent evidence he has in his possession, which he intends to present as evidence at the hearing, or trial, if it should go that far. The D. A.'s office most likely has it prepared for you. Incidentally, I've seen the coroner's report, and it states the deceased died of strangulation. Nothing unusual, as far as I can see. There are rumors about the toxicologist though."

"I think there's more to him than meets the eye. By the way, I can't believe how much I forgot about the law and its procedures. I thought of taking a refresher course before I came but there wasn't time. I'm going to ask the judge's permission to bring my grandson over. He's a noted toxicologist in the states.

"Ceil, can I ask you something?"

"You know better than that."

"I know your capabilities, but perhaps you undertook a bit more than you bargained for, this time. I mean, going up against a sharp, seasoned, formidable D.A. such as Mr. Penya, and with..."

She finished his sentence for him. "...So little evidence and even less experience? Yes, I have thought about it more and more each day. Meyer would agree with you. I've gone this far, and I can't just give up and leave Trevor in this mess. Not when there is one shred of hope that he is innocent."

"I'll help in any way I can, you know that. Your problem may be that the judge will say you're pushing too much. I mean, Mr. Carr will be appointed a lawyer from the principality, and you're acting like you're the attorney."

"I know. But we're in a strange country, and Trevor is going to need all the help he can get. In the States we are innocent until proven guilty, but here, who knows? I wonder if I'll be able to confer with the appointed attorney? Well, I'll do the best I can. I'll get through this. I've gone through much worse. Piece of cake, right?"

CHAPTER 46

He was not the gracious host who only two nights ago entertained the Spiegels, Agent Hernandez, and the prosecuting attorney at his home, but a judge whose demeanor suggested to those at the hearing that the condemned had very little chance of being acquitted. He nodded to the bailiff, who signaled to the attendees in the courtroom to be seated. His starched black robe crackled emulating his acrid mood.

He thought the meeting with the Spiegels went quite well – still he felt trapped, manipulated. He should have never conceded to the meeting. It was Rosetta who forced his hand, playing up to them, even suggesting they get together again at a later date. Raising his head, he listened intently to the media who gathered noisily outside the courtroom. The press had gotten wind of the American, Trevor Jase Carr, C.E.O. of one of America's most prestigious technical companies. Was Rosetta right? Was he looking for recognition? The trial of the year, perhaps of the decade, he mused. His eyes flicked from Ceil to Meyer to Judy to Lawrence and rested on Rosetta for an instant. She quickly broke eye contact with him. Still, how could he blame her? It was he who brought her into this case, and rightly so. He knew she wondered why he seemed disturbed. She glanced down at her lap, avoiding his eyes. She was too brilliant a woman to just fill her days with garden clubs and charities. He did the right thing, however it was not only wrong, but also unethical to have gotten involved with the Spiegels.

Straightening his shoulders, he struck his gavel, narrowing his eyes at the spectators. He nodded at the bailiff, who signaled the guard to bring in the accused.

Head bowed, his face pale and drawn, with hands cuffed and feet chained, Trevor shuffled into the courtroom. The guard motioned for him to take a seat adjacent to the assigned attorney.

"Leonardo Montevecchio, presiding primary judge of the principality of Ecuador, in the township of Quito this twenty fifth day of May, docket number 1265. The accused known as Trevor Jase Carr of the United States of America, herewith, charged with the murder of his wife, Pamela Ann Carr." The bailiff looked to the judge for approval of his rehearsed English dissertation, and then faced the spectators. "The prisoner will rise and face his honor," he announced.

"Remove the manacles," Judge Montevecchio ordered, his tone quiet, but firm. "Although the trial will be held in English, I have assigned an interpreter in case difficulties should arise. I will now hear the opening statement from Mr. Penya, the prosecuting attorney. I suggest you make your discourses short and to the point." Concerned by the attorney appointed to defend Trevor, he stood, his face showing annoyance. Para motivo del dios," he grumbled in Spanish. "Senior Pravda, como usted consiguio ser lawyer de Sr. Carr? Usted no habla una palabra del ingles? The lawyer started to rise, but the judge motioned for him to remain seated. The lawyer smiled, and shrugged indecisively. The judge sighed. "This will not do. I'm not about to have a translator going back and forth deciphering from one language to another all day long."

This is starting off badly, he thought, as he caught his wife's eye. He turned to the bailiff. "Who else is available to act as the prisoner's counsel? Approach the bench please." They huddled as the spectators whispered amongst themselves. "I know that Guido," the judge droned. "He is on an extended holiday? What exactly does that mean? Leaving? Without giving us notice? Well I'll attend to him later. For the present, we need a counselor who speaks English." He glanced at his wife, acknowledging a self-assured, smug look on her face. He shook a -no – with his head at her. She returned a, *'you have no choice gaze,'* back at him. He conceded, and motioned for her to approach the bench. "I'm in a bind, Rosetta. I don't want to prolong this damn trial longer than I have to. Do you think it's wise for you to take the position of Mr. Carr's counsel? By this afternoon the world press will be all over us. They will make mincemeat out of me – castrate me for letting my wife defend the accused. They will say we planned it to get publicity."

"You should have thought this out beforehand, Leonardo. I have an idea."

"What is going on in that devious head, Rosetta?" He frowned.

"How about the Spiegels? I understand she is a lawyer."

"Are you out of your mind?"

"Why not? She's smart, and it would move the case along. Isn't that what you want, to get this case over with as quickly as possible?"

He grumbled. "She has to have the proper qualifications as an attorney to defend the accused, and has to be granted a pro hac vice admission. A motion to accept her has to be made by a local member of the bar."

"Listen, Leonardo, she mentioned she had taken the bar exam years ago, and surely the other details can be dealt with."

"Previous conversation? You two aren't becoming fast friends, are you? Unbelievable. She runs a notable hotel and casino, was a spy for Interpol and is an attorney also? My God what other tricks has this woman up her sleeve? It wouldn't surprise me if she were a magician also. Very well. I'll call a fifteen-minute recess. There are legal procedures that I must look into before I make any decisions. Have Pepe take pictures before we adjourn – for the court's gallery. We might as well give our town an exclusive before the rest of the media are permitted into the court. And have your new friend and her husband in my office during the recess." He eyed her suspiciously. "I'm not so certain I like the idea of her representing Mr. Carr. And take that smug expression off your face."

"Like you, I only want justice upheld. Leonardo, I'm proud of you for having an open mind."

He ran his hands over his face, and covering his mouth, said mockingly. "Watch your mouth woman, or I'll bar you from the courtroom and put you back in the kitchen."

"It's too late, Leonardo. You have given me the chance to work alongside of you, and you are a man of his word…"

Speaking through clenched teeth he declared, "It's only a trial run for you, my dear. I will not tolerate any disturbances. I want this hearing to run like clockwork. Tomorrow I must make a decision about allowing the media into the courtroom. I don't want my constituents to think I've suddenly gone soft. One more thing. Just remember, I'm running this show, not you. I'm still in charge."

Her nose crinkled up, and a tolerant expression crossed her face as she smiled at him. "Of course, your honor," she said wondering if he would keep an open mind, or if he would revert back to the judge who severely punished ninety nine percent of the accused who stood before him.

The judge motioned to the three cane-back chairs opposite his desk. "Please, take a seat," he said, to Ceil, Meyer, and Mr. Penya, the prosecuting attorney. His wife stood to his left. He addressed Ceil and Meyer, seriously. "The court finds itself in an awkward position. The attorney assigned to Mr. Carr does not speak a word of English, and it would be frustrating to have a translator going back and forth repeating every sentence. And sadly, the other attorney who speaks English is out of the country on holiday. The attention this case has generated raises an issue. How to move the hearing along expeditiously and legally. I will not postpone the hearing." He glanced at his wife. "So in all honesty, and against my better judgment, I have asked you here to consider standing up for Mr. Carr. That is, to represent him." His wife smiled, and he immediately admonished her. "Rosetta," he said. "Stop standing over me and find a chair."

Releasing a long frustrated sigh, he focused on the Spiegels. "Before you accept or refuse my proposal, there are legalities with which we must deal. Aside from the diverse interests, business and social entities that you entertain, are you practicing attorneys?"

"I'm not an attorney in any shape or form," Meyer said. "But my wife is."

"Then let's not consider you," the judge said, waving a hand of dismissal at Meyer. Meyer started to rise, but the judge waved him down. "This is informal Mr. Spiegel, you may stay."

"Mr. Penya. Have you any objections?"

The D.A. grinned, pleased to find the opposition inexperienced. "None, whatsoever, your honor."

Tilting his face toward Ceil, the judge asked, "Is this true? You have tried cases in court?"

Ceil fidgeted in her chair. "I've never tried a case, but I did pass the bar exam. In fact, the first time I took it."

The judge thought of his wife, and her years of studying, and then finally getting her license to practice and she, like Ceil, for whatever reasons, did nothing with it. He stroked his chin thoughtfully. "Still if all you say is true, and I don't doubt you, you can't practice here in Quito. That is unless we get an attorney to sponsor you."

"Well that's not a problem, your honor," Mr. Penya advised. "Senor Pravda can easily do that. Of course, with your permission," he immediately added.

The judge regarded Mr. Penya, knowing the D.A. hoped Ceil would accept the judge's offer. "Yes, it would simplify things. Thank you for suggesting it."

Taking advantage of his generosity, Mr. Penya asserted, "It's called pro hac vice. It is spelled v-i-c-e, but pronounced, veechee."

"Of course, of course," he said, humoring him. "Well, now that we have settled our problem, I will postpone the hearing until tomorrow so that I can get everything in order. Can you have the proper papers on my desk by tomorrow morning, Mrs. Spiegel, so we can get on with the trial?"

"As long as the telephones are working, and the fax machines are running, I don't see why not."

Ceil and Meyer walked hand and hand, out of the courthouse. "So how does it feel to be a big shot shyster, Ceil?" Meyer joked. "You realize this is going to get back to the States. You'll be famous. You'd better not fuck up."

"Shyster? Meyer, you're as crude as ever. You know, I never thought I'd actually try a case, much less in a foreign country, but if it gets T.J. out of this mess it will be worth it. God, I'm nervous as hell."

"Don't be nervous – remember that movie, *My Cousin Vinny*? He never tried a case and he won. You can pull the same shtick he did."

CHAPTER 47

On Monday morning, sheets of rain beat menacingly against the stained glass windows of the courtroom. The ambience in the room might have seemed austere until Judge Montevecchio briskly exited his chambers and was met with a loud sneeze from one of the spectators.

"All rise," the court attendant roared. Muffled giggles were heard from the onlookers. A cold stare from the judge quickly put an end to their merriment.

The judge had a sleepless night, and during breakfast he toyed with his food, wrestling with his conscience while discussing pertinent facts with his wife about the trial. Now viewing the courtroom, filled with worldwide media, a wave of euphoria swept over him.

Only the pounding of the rain was heard in the quiet room as the spectators awaited the judge's opening words.

Stone-faced, he nodded to the court stenographer and growled, "Be seated." He scanned the room, eyeing the accused, and flicked his gaze from Lawrence to Beau to Judy, and lingered for a brief moment on Ceil, who now represented Trevor. *If she thinks she is going to con me into a fast dismissal with her glib American jargon,* he thought, *she'd better think again.*

A photographer's flash went off, and the judge rapped his gavel. "Picture taking is forbidden, and be so kind as to turn off all cellular phones. This is a courtroom, not a circus. Be forewarned if my rules are not followed, I will not hesitate to clear the room of all media." He called to a uniformed guard. Pointing to the photographer, he said, "I want the film from that camera."

Ceil swallowed hard. His demeanor struck her as somewhat different from the man who had entertained them so graciously only a few days ago. She turned, and glanced at Meyer, who shrugged, and to Rosetta, who avoided her eyes. Meyer, who sat behind her in the first row, nudged her, whispering. "What's with him? Something's not kosher. Yesterday he was all sugar and honey, and today..."

"Shush. He's running the show."

"Was Evan able to get into the morgue without any trouble?"

"Thank God, the judge didn't veto it."

"I'm sure he's not pleased to have an outsider taking the place of the appointed coroner."

"From what Fernando told me a minute before we came here, the judge did object, but quickly decided if he stopped Evan's examination of the body, people would think the court was covering up something."

The judge glared at Ceil and Meyer as he watched them chitchatting. "If the defense is quite finished, the prosecuting attorney may present his opening argument," he said tersely.

Meyer mumbled as he leaned back in his seat.

"Bring the prisoner in," the judge ordered.

Head bowed low, hands cuffed, feet shackled, Trevor, led by two guards, shuffled wearily into the room and sat next to Ceil.

Ceil's heart sank as she looked at him. Touching him affectionately on his shoulder she whispered, "It's going to be okay, T.J. Looking desolate is a good thing. Just keep a poker face, and don't smile. We want sympathy from the judge."

The judge observed Mr. Penya, wondering which of his many faces he would wear. "Mr. Penya, your opening statement."

The D. A., a tall, emaciated man with narrow eyes resembling two slits etched into his long skeletal face, and a jaw that jutted to a V, rose aloofly from his chair. "Your honor, the state will prove that the accused, Trevor Jase Carr, with willful intent and beyond a reasonable doubt, did murder his wife,

Pamela Ann Carr, on the night of May 25, in the year of two thousand and eight. The defense will try to convince you the accused is an honorable upstanding pillar of his community. Donates millions to charities and assorted philanthropic organizations, and, is of course, an innocent man. The state has no qualms with this line of commendation, or praise if you will. But the honest to goodness cold fact is that he strangled his wife. The defense will spin a tale, degrading the deceased – painting her as a deceitful, mendacious, loose woman who took too many drugs, and slept with too many men. Why would they use those tactics? It's simple. There is just too much evidence against Mr. Carr. Their case is weak. So, they must rely on the murderer's spotless reputation to exonerate him of the heinous crime he committed. Now, what will they attempt to do? Just this. Defame her. That is their only hope – to scandalize the strangled woman's character so the court will have pity on him because he had to endure a wife who had problems. The state will prove that Mr. Carr, by his own admission, did indeed strangle his wife. The evidence is clear, as is proven by the black and blue impressions on the victim's throat." Mr. Penya scowled at Trevor, and turned towards the judge. "We will prove that Mr. Carr drank himself into a stupor, and in a fit of rage choked the life out of his wife. Your honor, this is an open and shut case." He strolled to his table, rested his palms on its surface, and said, "Thank you, your honor."

Judge Montevecchio sat back in his chair. "Mrs. Spiegel, you may deliver your opening statement."

In sharp contrast to Mr. Penya, Ceil was a combination of grandmother and Joan of Arc. Shoulders back, head held erect, her stature appearing taller than the five feet she measured, she rose from behind the defense table, smiled at Trevor, and addressed the judge. "Your honor, the prosecuting attorney has painted a picture of the accused, and the deceased, that truly touched me. That is of course, if one believes what he so eloquently tried to portray. I don't, and I'll tell you why. To begin, he wants you to think of Mr. Carr as a wealthy tycoon. A man who is beyond reproach. A man who can, because he is wealthy, get away with just about anything he chooses – in short, painting a negative picture in order to make you dislike him before you've had a chance to hear all the evidence. It's what we call mind-altering persuasion. Yes, Mr. Carr is the head of a large computer firm. Yes, Mr. Carr lives lavishly. Yes, Mr. Carr controls the lives of thousands of employees. And yes, Mr. Carr gives to charities. He can afford to. But what Mr. Penya failed to tell you, is that Mr. Carr was not always wealthy. In fact, he was born in the slums of Washington, D.C. He had to leave school to support his mother and sisters. As a youngster he delivered papers, among other menial jobs. He obtained a job with a computer corporation as janitor. And your honor, the man who sits here before you is now the C.E.O. of that very corporation. As far as the victim is concerned, we will not try to defame her. She did that herself. Mr. Penya says we have a weak case." Walking alongside the prosecutor's table, she stared at Mr. Penya squarely in his eyes. "I beg to differ. The prosecutor must present evidence, which proves beyond a reasonable doubt that Mr. Carr is guilty of the crime of which he is charged. And according to the laws of Ecuador, if there is any reasonable doubt about Mr. Carr's guilt, he must be found innocent. Mr. Penya states that this is an open and shut case. I challenge him to prove it." She turned back to the judge. "Your honor, I have finished."

Judge Montevecchio felt the perspiration drip from his armpits onto his undershirt. "The court will take a fifteen minute... no, a half hour recess, after which time the prosecuting attorney will call his first witness.

CHAPTER 48

Mr. Penya arrogantly eyed Ceil, announcing, "The state calls Captain Alberto Rodriguez."

The captain rose slowly, glanced at the press, adjusted his jacket, and smiled sadly at Trevor as he passed him on the way to the witness stand. After the Captain took the oath, Mr. Penya wasted little time in getting to the text of his questioning. "You are the captain of the yacht, Isabella, which was chartered by Mr. and Mrs. Carr, and Mr. and Mrs. Blessing?"

"I am."

"As Captain, one would ascertain that aside from commandeering the yacht, you make sure that the guests are properly attended to?"

"Oh yes, indeed. More than just properly attended to. The company that employs me has a five star rating, and we cater to our guests' every wish. With the exorbitant amount of money they are charged, one would hardly expect anything less than perfection."

"And expecting anything less than perfection, would your position include becoming intimate with them?"

Ceil rose. "Objection. Mr. Penya is making assumptions about the witness's character."

"Your Honor," Mr. Penya countered. "My intention is to show that the accused had a motive to do away with his wife."

"I'll allow it."

"Captain Rodriguez, were there instances when your duties or responsibilities dictated that you become intimate with the guests... of course, in order to serve them properly?"

"I don't know what you mean."

"Then, let me phrase it so you can understand the question, and remember Captain, you are still under oath. Withholding evidence would put you in jeopardy. Were you privy to any conversations among the guests about harming the deceased?"

"I minded my business. How the guests conducted themselves was strictly their affair. They were on holiday. My job was to make sure the yacht was properly maintained, the chef and stewards were attentive to the guests, and that the crew was up to snuff."

"Captain Rodriguez, I did not ask you for a résumé of your position as captain, only if you overheard, or had conversations with the guests which pertained to the death of the deceased."

"I pride myself on my discretion. Like a doctor with a patient/guest confidentiality."

Mr. Penya threw his hand into the air showing frustration. "Your honor, really! Please, instruct the witness to answer the question directly, and not skirt around the issue."

The judge viewed the Captain. "Captain Rodriguez, your integrity is not being questioned. We are aware of your excellent reputation and appreciate the confidentiality you share with your guests, but you are not a psychiatrist, lawyer or doctor or priest. If there is information, however private, apropos to the trial, you must divulge it to the court."

Captain Rodriguez' eyebrows formed a question as he looked at Trevor, and then cast his eyes downward toward his lap.

"We are waiting, Captain. Should we take the Captain's hesitancy as a sign that his memory has miraculously returned?"

Ceil raised her hand. "Your Honor, is it necessary for Mr. Penya to insult the witness? I find this line of questioning inappropriate."

"Mr. Penya. We have hardly begun. Save the eloquent orations for your closing argument. Rephrase, please."

Mr. Penya nodded at the judge. "Of course, your honor. Thank you, your honor." He walked away from the witness box, turned, and confronted the Captain in a loud voice. "Captain Rodriguez, wasn't there a time when you became involved, or overstepped your duties with a guest while you commandeered the yacht?" Before the witness could answer the district attorney snapped, "Do you deny having had sex with the deceased?"

The captain stuttered. "I...I... It was not of my choosing."

"In other words, this woman, who weighed an alarming 110 pounds, overwhelmed you, and forced you against your will to copulate with her. Really? Do you expect us to believe that?"

"I was stupid. She told me she would pay me handsomely. I had heavy debts – gambling debts, and my wife was going to leave me. I didn't harm anyone. The money would solve my problems." His eyes drifted toward Trevor, who smiled wryly back at him.

"Wasn't she concerned her husband would find out?"

"No. To my knowledge, she was a nymphomaniac. In fact when I left her cabin after we... well... I bumped into Mr. Blessing, who was on his way to see her."

"I object, your honor," Ceil said. "I don't see where this is going. In fact, Mr. Penya is painting a picture for the defense, not the state, and -"

Mr. Penya cut her off. "If my learned colleague will permit me to continue, I will endeavor to show her where this is going."

"You may continue, Mr. Penya, after I overrule. Do you understand?"

"Sorry, your honor."

"Overruled. Continue."

"Now, Captain Rodriguez. Did Mrs. Carr pay you handsomely for your... uh...services?"

"Yes...uh... no. I mean..."

"Come now, Captain. It's not a difficult question. Did she, or did she not, pay you as she promised?"

"She did not."

"So, she stiffed you, so to speak?"

"No."

"Captain Rodriguez. A moment ago, you said she did pay you. Well, anyhow, you hedged, leading us to believe that you did receive money. Please, help us unravel this tangled web you have spun."

The Captain squirmed in his seat, his face reddened, and his eyes watered. He agonized, "She didn't pay me. Mr. Carr did...but..."

"Ah-ha," Mr. Penya said, empathically. "The spider has finished spinning his web. Your honor, I have no further use of this witness."

Captain Rodriguez' mouth remained open as the judge asked, "Mrs. Spiegel, you may cross examine."

Ceil's voice was gentle and reassuring as she smiled pleasantly at the Captain. "No one is faulting you for trying to keep your family situation from deteriorating. I'm sure even Mr. Penya will agree we've all made mistakes, and that for a family to prosper and survive, there must be understanding, overlooking, and forgiving. None of us is perfect. Tell us. Why did Mr. Carr pay you for his wife's indiscretion with you?"

"She asked him to."

"How strange. Are you suggesting he knew of your tryst with his wife and condoned it, by paying you for servicing her needs?"

"Oh no. He might have been aware of her cohabiting with the crew and the steward, and probably suspected me too, but he made no mention of it at the time he paid me. He said she asked him to give me the money. In fact, he even thanked me."

"Didn't it strike you as odd?"

"Odd? I don't know what you mean."

"Odd that Mr. Carr would pay you for sleeping with his wife. What was the sum?"

"I didn't question what she might have told him. To me, she was always sort of... flighty...more than likely... high."

"Objection!"

"Noted. Mrs. Spiegel, get to the point."

Ceil grinned. "Captain Rodriguez, please continue."

"All I thought about was paying the two thousand dollars to my creditors, and making peace with my wife. I do remember thinking they were so wealthy, two thousand dollars to them probably equated or seemed like no more than twenty dollars to me."

The judge tapped impatiently on his desk.

"One last question, Captain," Ceil said. "Did Mr. Carr make any arrangements with you by offering you money or other gratuities, so you would spread the word that he was an aggrieved husband and she a nymphomaniac?"

"No. As I said before, it was common knowledge that Mrs. Carr was promiscuous. The crew chaffed about it all the time." He glanced at Trevor adding, "Mr. Carr didn't seem able to control her. Mr. Carr did not make any arrangements with me. If the trip had continued, I would have followed the customary procedure, which is for the guests to tip the Captain, the guide and the chef, and the stewards, if they care to, at the conclusion of the holiday. I only accepted the monies I had been promised."

"Thank you Captain Rodriguez. No further questions, your honor."

"Mr. Penya," the judge said. "Do you wish to question the witness further?"

"No questions, your honor."

"Then the court will recess for lunch and convene at two o'clock."

Meyer squirmed in his seat. "These courtroom seats are hard on my ass, Ceil. You would think they would pad the courtroom benches. Make it more comfortable for the spectators."

She didn't reply.

He leaned closer to her. "I could turn up the volume on your hearing aid."

Still, no reply.

He took her hand in his. "What's wrong, baby? You didn't eat a thing for lunch."

"I'm okay. Just worried. Eating is not one of my priorities at the moment."

"I think the trial has gone to Scrooge's head. He's playing to the press."

"I know," she countered. "But it could work in our favor."

"Don't trust him for a second, sweetheart. He's going to nail T.J. to the cross."

His voice pleasant, the judge said, "Mr. Penya, if you would be so kind, we would like to begin."

Mr. Penya stood and faced the row of spectators as the court artists sat sketching. "Will Mrs. Judy Blessing take the witness stand," he announced.

After being sworn in, Judy, dressed in a subdued white linen suit with matching shoes and wide brimmed-straw hat, her flawless complexion complimenting her beautiful face, looked at Trevor, then lowered her eyes. She fought to hold back tears viewing the expression of hopelessness that shadowed his face. As she passed him, he slowly raised his head and locked eyes with her, an inaudible gasp of silent pain catching in his throat.

Like a bolt of lightening, the events that led up to this day flashed through her mind – the walk on the beach when she found herself drawn to him like a magnet. She remembered how he begged for her understanding because he had no one, and how she was there for him when he needed someone so desperately. How she gave in to him with tenderness and let him take her, as the gentle breeze tried in vain to cool the heat of their passion, and the gigantic Ecuadorian moon warned of savoring forbidden fruit. Having sex on the beach had never entered her mind – *it was meant to be – why fight it?* It was then she decided her marriage to Beau was over. Perhaps Trevor clouded her mind – *but so what, how could something that feels so good be bad?*

The rustling of the artist's sketchpads broke the stillness as they turned the pages, switching from Trevor to this beautiful woman. Their heads buzzed with the thought that this was going to be more than an ordinary murder case – a murder involving three couples that played a game of more than just intrigue.

She looked up quickly upon hearing Mr. Penya's sharp voice. "Mrs. Blessing, were you with Mr. Carr on the night he was accused of strangling his wife?

"Yes."

"I suppose you're going to tell us it wasn't prearranged – that you met by chance, even though the two of you are married to other people."

Ceil raised her hand. "Objection, the counsel is not asking a question. He is suggesting one."

"Mrs. Spiegel," the judge said flatly. "I realize this is your first court appearance, but try to state your objections in a more professional manner." He smiled solicitously. "Mr. Penya, rephrase the question."

Ceil swallowed hard. She ignored the prosecuting attorney's snicker, and the judge's reprimand. "I'm sorry, your honor."

Mr. Penya gloated. "Mrs. Blessing. Can you tell the court how you happened to meet Mr. Carr on the night Mrs. Carr was found strangled in her room?"

"I couldn't sleep, so I decided to take a walk on the beach. At the water's edge, I spotted T.J., uh, I mean, Mr. Carr, sitting on the sand. He seemed distraught – he was whimpering and I became concerned. When I approached, I heard him crying."

"Did you ask him why he was upset?"

"Yes. He told me he had a fierce fight with his wife and that ... he became so enraged when he found her having sex with the rafting guide, Mr. Floater, that he lost control and almost strangled her."

"Did you say, *almost* strangled her?"

"Yes."

"How do you know he didn't strangle his wife?"

"He told me before he left her, she was hungry and wanted him to come back soon because ... she wanted to have sex again ... with him."

"Didn't it seem odd that he had consensual sex with his wife, and tried to kill her afterwards?"

"Objection, your honor. The witness's opinion is not relevant. Can we deal in facts and not the opinions of the witness?"

The judge grumbled. "Mr. Penya, can we avoid the melodrama and confine our questioning to reality? Mrs. Blessing's thoughts about Mr. Carr's personal life are not relevant to this case. Get to the point of your interrogation. I don't intend to have these proceedings go on forever." A chuckle was heard from the spectators, but quickly ceased as the judge narrowed his eyes at them.

Judy faltered. "Just what I said before. I can tell you from my personal experience with Mrs. Carr, she was a manipulative, selfish, self-centered woman who took drugs constantly and..."

The prosecutor cut her off. "Objection. The answer is not responsive to my question. I move to strike. The statement is an opinion of a lay witness, which is not relevant to this case. The witness should only testify as to the facts of the case."

"Overruled, Mr. Penya. You opened the door to this line of questioning. I'll permit it."

The prosecutor's voice was shrill and tenuous. "Mrs. Blessing, wasn't your meeting with Mr. Carr planned, and not by chance, as you previously stated?"

Ceil rose. "Objection. The District Attorney has not laid a foundation for this statement."

The judge screwed his mouth thoughtfully to one side. "I'll allow it. Let's see where this is going."

Mr. Penya gave Judy a long serious look. "Perhaps the witness has good reason for not telling the truth. Perhaps there was more than just a walk on the beach, or just a chance meeting. Perhaps it was planned."

Ceil spoke up. "Objection, your honor. The D.A. is speculating as to what might have happened, not what actually happened. It's only fair the witness be permitted to speak for herself."

"I'll allow it." the judge said, aware the D.A. was playing to the press. He pointed a warning finger at Mr. Penya. "This court will not be subjected to these flowery speeches. Kindly conduct your questioning in a more professional manner."

"I beg the court's pardon. Mrs. Blessing, is it not true that you and Mr. Carr had a previous affair aboard the yacht?"

Judy's face flushed and she hesitated, looking at Ceil for direction. Ceil shrugged, knowing the D.A. had interrogated the captain and crew, and lying would only make things worse. She nodded a yes to Judy, as she heard Meyer mutter, "Fuck."

"We are waiting, Mrs. Blessing," the D.A. said. "Shall I rephrase the question?"

Her voice quavered. "No," she stuttered. "We did engage in sex on the yacht, but it just happened accidentally and -"

He cut her off. "Did I hear you correctly? It just happened by accident? Really. Isn't it more logical to say that you and the accused were lovers, and that you conspired to do away with the victim in a very carefully thought-out scheme, so you could be free to carry on your love affair?"

Judy whispered. "No."

The silence in the courtroom was deathly still as the spectators leaned forward in their seats. Tears welled in Judy's eyes. Ceil, knowing she had to do something, spoke up. "The D.A. is badgering the witness," she complained.

The judge motioned for Ceil to sit, and directed his attention to the D.A. "Mr. Penya, you are making serious accusations at the witness. If you persist along these lines, you better have proof to back up your allegations."

The D.A. addressed the judge. "Your honor, what appears as a simple matter of a man strangling his wife is more complex then meets the eye. I have witnesses who will attest to sordid sexual encounters on the yacht that led up to, and possibly culminated, in the murder of Mrs. Carr."

Ceil's heart sank. She put her hand on Trevor's shoulder as he expelled a long painful sigh. "He's digging up all the dirt he can," she said sympathetically. "Don't worry T.J. Having sex and being promiscuous doesn't prove you did it. It only proves that you misbehaved."

"They're going to find me guilty no matter what you say, Ceil. The deck is stacked against me."

The judge rapped his gavel. "Mrs. Blessing, you may step down. Mr. Penya and Mrs. Spiegel, I will see you in my chambers, now."

Ceil started for the judge's chamber, but Meyer stopped her short. "It's only the beginning. Don't lose your cool. You'll make it up." He squeezed her hand as Mr. Penya approached them.

Bowing his head, Mr. Penya said, "After you, my dear."

Smiling cordially, she said, "Quite the gentleman, aren't you?"

He held the door open. "It is a rarity to come up against such an attractive and astute adversary. I'm honored."

"Thank you for the compliment," she answered, thinking it wouldn't hurt to humor him a bit, aware from his manner that he was flirting with her.

The judge motioned for them to be seated. He glanced at his wife who stood at his side. "Look," he said with frustration, addressing Ceil. "I understand this is not easy for you – this being your first case – and in a foreign country, defending a man who happens to be a friend, and the evidence so clearly not in your favor. But please, as frustrating as it may be for you, try to keep to court procedure and avoid the theatrics you displayed." He glanced fleetingly at his wife who smiled tentatively.

Turning sharply to the D. A., and scowling, he spoke in a soft, but angry tone. "Mr. Penya, you are carrying on like a pompous actor performing for an audience, which at the moment happens to be the media. I notice you have gone to the trouble of having your hair restyled, and are wearing a designer suit, tie, and shoes – a far cry from the soiled shirt, faded tie, and same wrinkled suit you have worn for years in court. This leads me to believe you are trying to achieve star status from this trial." The D.A. opened his mouth to speak. The judge waved him off. "No, you don't have to go home and change to your usual clothes, but I'm putting you on warning. You are not prosecuting O. J. Simpson, only an American citizen who is accused of murder. Although this may prove to be a boost to your career, I advise you not to keep up this charade. Just go about proving your case without all the theatrics. Do we understand each other?"

"Yes, your honor."

"Good. Mrs. Spiegel, are you prepared for the unsavory allegations that may arise?"

"Such as?"

"Please, don't play that game with me. What went on aboard the yacht is common knowledge."

"Yes, I know the crew told stories, and even if there was sexual promiscuity, it does not mean that my client is guilty of murder."

"Well said. But, it is yet to be determined. You'll have to convince me, won't you?"

"I intend to."

Rosetta moved toward her husband, an indication of 'that's enough for now' crossing her face. "There's a horde of media and curious bystanders converging about the courthouse," she said. "I think the courthouse and the immediate area should be roped off to avoid media frenzy, and also for the protection of the witnesses."

"Please see to it, Rosetta, and have the court official extend the lunch hour to two p.m." He rose to look out the window at the paparazzi setting up the TV cameras on the courthouse grounds. "You are right," he said. His eyes went from Ceil to the prosecuting attorney. "Let us try to be professional. This case is starting to take on an air of sensationalism, and I'm not certain I approve."

CHAPTER 49

eil, Meyer, Beau, Lawrence, and Judy sat in a remote corner of the bistro. "Ceil," Meyer said, concerned. "Stop playing with the food and swallow some of it. You need all your strength."

"I don't need strength, I need a miracle. That Penya is some painya in the ass. He's using this case to make a name for himself and at Trevor's expense." She forced a fork full of mashed potatoes into her mouth. "And the strange thing is, I can't blame him. It's a once in a lifetime chance for him to get into the big city."

"Well, I for one can blame him," Judy said acidly. "I was so flustered and embarrassed on the stand. He made me feel so cheap. I thought I would die. I wanted to help Trevor, and I fell apart."

"Well," Meyer intervened, "we can expect a lot more. This is only the beginning. If they proceed with the same line of questioning and bring up the sexual aspects of what went on at the yacht, all of you are going to be labeled promiscuous. If the judge allows Penya to continue with his insidious line of questioning it will certainly hang Trevor. The crew must have given them an earful."

"But," Beau said. "We were not to blame. Pamela is to blame. She laced the drinks that made us... lose control."

"We were all to blame," Lawrence said. "I for one, now that I think back, could have put a stop to my behavior, but I wanted to... have sex with her. The drug only gave me the courage to carry it out. But I can only speak for myself."

Ceil pushed her plate away. "Let's not get into what turned you on, or if you could have prevented your behavior from getting out of hand – it happened and it's over. We have to deal with the present. And what is important is to prove that Trevor is not guilty, beyond a reasonable doubt."

"Boy, oh boy," Judy said. "I have never felt so helpless."

Ceil rose, straightened her skirt, and rested her hands on the table. "Look, feeling sorry for ourselves is not the answer. Let me ask you something. I want you to be honest with me even if it kills you." Everyone leaned forward. "I'm going to give each of you a slip of paper and on it will be one question. The question will be a 'yes' or a 'no' as to whether you believe Trevor strangled Pamela. No one will be the wiser. Just put a check next to the yes or the no."

"What will that prove?" Beau interjected.

"Maybe T.J. didn't murder Pamela. Maybe one of you did. Anyhow, yours is not to question why," Meyer said. "You are in no position to question Ceil's motives. Just do as you are told. She has her reasons."

A messenger approached the table and handed Ceil a sealed envelope. "I was instructed to wait for an answer," he said.

Ceil opened the envelope and read:

"Ceil, something unpleasant has come up. Can you meet me behind the Topanga Bistro immediately before court convenes? I will be in the rear gardens under a blue parasol. We must talk!"

Tatiana.

CHAPTER 50

T he tiny flake of soft snow gathered momentum, and then sped faster and faster, picking up more flakes that adhered to its growing bulk. Recklessly plunging down the icy slope as a huge mass, it stopped at Rosetta's feet just in time.

Shaken by the illusory mental image, she looked up, startled to see Ceil standing by her side. "You were in another world, Rosetta," Ceil said. "What's the problem?"

"Sit down. I've taken the liberty of ordering ice tea – it's so hot today. I was careful to select this out of the way bistro for our... uh... rendezvous. I don't know quite where to begin. There isn't much time, and frankly, I'm feeling at a loss."

Looking around, Ceil sat down and spoke remorsefully, "I know. You opened up a whole can of worms, and you can't get them back in the can, right? The guilt of befriending me and going against your husband is weighing heavily on your conscience. I have to take some of the blame. It was wrong of me to encourage our friendship, but when I spotted you in the department store, I didn't think of the consequences. To be honest, Rosetta, maybe I didn't think. I'm known to be aggressive, and a little too pushy at times."

"We can share the blame. To tell you the truth, I've been living in a shell so to speak. After I graduated law school, I thought I had everything a woman could want. Like the independence to be able to break the old traditions we have in this country, by starting my own law practice. But then I met Leonardo and fell in love. And with his macho insistence, I gave up all my dreams, and decided to raise a family, and be the dutiful wife this society calls for. It is only of late that my husband has taken me into his confidence, and probably because he was overburdened by problems and judicial decisions he had to make. So I jumped at the chance. It gave me a reason to live again – to come out of my shell. When we met and talked, my dream was completed. Everything fell into place. I told myself, 'here is a woman with great success – a woman who is respected, and has proven that she is as good as any man.' It awakened the spark I thought was gone forever." She took Ceil's hand in hers. "Be the aggressive, pushy person you are, Ceil. Don't blame yourself. I'm glad it happened. You made me come alive again." She withdrew her hand from Ceil's and glanced around the garden. "But that's not why I asked you to meet me. I'm sure the guilt I feel by consorting with you will dissipate in time."

She felt Ceil's anxiety level rising. "It's about your grandson. They have put a halt to his examination of the victim's body."

Ceil was taken aback. "How is that possible? He had the judge's permission to do the autopsy."

"I know. But I have yet to find out the reason he was barred from the mortuary."

"They're hiding something. Otherwise, why would they take this action? This worries me. Are you sure your husband is aware of this? I'd hate to think your husband..."

"...Is involved in this? It isn't like Leonardo to do anything unethical. He's committed to the law. Still, he has been under a great deal of pressure. I used to be able to know what he is thinking, but now..."

"There has to be some logical explanation, Rosetta. Think. Is there some reason they would stop Evan from redoing the autopsy? Perhaps the medical examiner complained about someone else, especially a foreigner making him appear to be adequate at his job."

"You may be on to something. I remember Leonardo telling me that he wanted to replace him with a new medical examiner because there was talk about him being an alcoholic, and relatives complained about him being abusive to his wife. What I can't understand is my husband's involvement in this. I know him. His heart and soul are woven into the fabric of the law."

"Did you ever think that he might not be aware of my grandson being barred from the mortuary?"

Rosetta glanced at her watch. "My God, court convenes in fifteen minutes. We better fly."

Ceil's cell phone buzzed. "Yes, Meyer, I heard about Evan. Never mind where I am. Yes, I realize I have to be in court. Yes, I ate. Let me go, I'll explain when I see you. Yes, I'm fine. Lighten up, will you? Now say goodbye."

CHAPTER 51

"*This can't be happening*," Ceil told herself. She brushed past the annoying media, who crowded her and took her picture, and hurried up the courthouse steps. Meyer stood shaking his finger warily at her. "Where have you been? I've been going out of my head worrying about you."

"Later," she snapped. "Let's get inside."

He took her arm and led her into a secluded corner of the hallway. "What the hell is going on, Ceil? I just got word. They closed the door on Pamela's autopsy."

"Who told you?"

"Evan, of course. Who else?"

"Where is he?"

"In the courtroom. We better get a move on. They're just about to start."

"Damn! I wanted to talk to Evan before court convened."

"Too late now. Here comes the judge."

"Your sense of humor is not appreciated, Meyer. I have enough to deal with."

"You better get to your seat. Don't give the bastard any more reasons to degrade you. Who do you think Penya will call?"

"At this point it doesn't much matter. They're going to tear apart any one of the witnesses. I wish I could talk to Evan before we start. I could ask for a recess."

"Ask for a recess? Don't do it. The judge will castrate you. He's had it in for you from the moment you opened your mouth."

"Screw him. There's something going on. I feel it."

The judge entered from his chambers and smiled slyly upon seeing Ceil and Meyer scurry to their table. The bailiff announced, "All rise, the court is now in session." The judge took his seat and the bailiff said, "Be seated."

"Bring in the prisoner," the judge said as Trevor, showing no emotion, shuffled in. His handcuffs were removed, and he turned to Ceil, a hopeless expression crossing his face.

She squeezed his arm. "We believe in you, T.J.," Ceil whispered. "Have faith. Expect a few setbacks – it can't be helped. They're going to try to portray you as Jack the Ripper. If you are called, be strong. No matter how they try to degrade or put you down, don't let them get to you. You can take it. I know you can."

He bit his lip. "I'll try."

"Is the prosecution ready to continue?" the judge asked.

Mr. Penya rose slowly, his shoulders back, his head erect, ready to charge like a bull.

"Will Beauregard Blessing take the stand?"

D.A. Penya decided to play up to the press, though warned the judge would take action against him, should he try theatrics. He decided to take the chance. *He can't take me off the case now. He wouldn't dare. It would give the press reason to doubt the judge's clout. That's the last thing old sourpuss wants. This is my chance to get out of this rattrap of a town and into the spotlight. And if he does take me off the case, by then I'll be in every newspaper around the world.* He watched as Beau took the oath. Mr. Penya proceeded to glare at Beau. "Tell us Mr. Blessing, how did you and your wife come to be on the same yacht as the Carrs? I understood that it was originally chartered for ten days to only one couple, but somehow ended up with three couples."

"Mrs. Carr arranged the bookings for her and her husband. My wife coincidently made the same reservations at the same travel agency."

"In all of New York, the biggest city in the world, the deceased made bookings at the same travel agency that your wife did. And you all ended up on the same yacht at the same time? Mmm, how convenient. And how was it that it became a threesome? I mean, of course, three couples." He walked toward Ceil, smiled arrogantly at her, quickly turned on his heels and barked at Beau. "It was my understanding that you all met after you arrived at the Galapagos Islands. Do you want us to believe this was not prearranged so that you all could participate in one big festive sex orgy? Mr. Blessing?"

The air in the room hung heavily, the silence was loud. Beau's clenched knuckles turned white but he held his ground looking to Ceil for support. Her slight nod told him the opposition had done their homework, and he might as well come clean.

Trying to make Beau uncomfortable, Mr. Penya shifted his weight impatiently from one foot to the other. "Well, Mr. Blessing, we're waiting."

From the many books he had read, and the grueling hours of research and writing, Beau, unnerved by his wife's humiliating testimony on the stand, decided this was the opportune time to spin his saga for the defense of what took place aboard the yacht. In a remote corner of his subconscious an idea formed of what a spectacular novel this vacation would make. Encouraged by this new notion, he sat back in his seat and addressed the judge. "If your honor permits, I would like to make a statement on behalf of the accused."

Mr. Penya jumped to his feet. "This is utter nonsense, your honor. The witness is out of order."

Ceil countered with conviction. "Your honor, the prosecuting attorney is suppressing the witness's right to speak. Is he afraid of what the witness may say?"

Judge Montevecchio pondered for a few seconds thinking that instead of the string of the witnesses that Mr. Penya intended to call, Beau could speak for them all. *Might move the hearing along and at the same time watch him dig a hole too deep to climb out of.* "I'll allow it," he said. "Please, Mr. Blessing, make it short. You understand that you are under oath?"

Beau looked at Judy, at Ceil, and sighed as his eyes rested on Trevor. Facing the judge, he spoke softly and calmly. "Yes, I foolishly did have an affair with the deceased in New York, but I had no idea she bribed the travel agent to book both of us on the same yacht. We met Lawrence and Kaitlin Bartoni when we toured one of the islands. When Kaitlin took ill, being fellow Americans and feeling sorry for the youngsters, we invited them to join us on the yacht. There was plenty of room. Mrs. Bartoni has Hodgkin's disease and is pregnant. They had third class accommodations. All went quite well until – until Pamela, Mrs. Carr, concocted a cocktail from a drug called Ecstasy. Not aware of what we were drinking, we lost control, and like idiots, participated in a night of uncontrolled, blind, sexual promiscuity. The next morning, everyone, too embarrassed to talk about the goings on of the previous night, pretended like nothing had happened."

Mr. Penya rose. "Really your honor. Must we sit here and listen to the saga of three couples having a sex orgy?"

Ceil stood to respond. "Perhaps Mr. Penya has led a sheltered life. Will your honor permit the witness to continue? He is trying to give us a synopsis of what led up to the death of the deceased."

A ripple of chuckling echoed through the courtroom. Judge Montevecchio knew Mr. Penya was playing to the press but he felt he could keep him under control. "Mr. Penya," he said, "collect yourself. You don't want to run out of steam so early in the trial."

"But, your honor..." Mr. Penya insisted.

The judge roared. "But what?"

"I..."

The judge's face contorted with anger. He glared, red faced, as Mr. Penya swallowed his words.

Mr. Penya spoke sarcastically. "Mr. Blessing, is there much more, or are we going to run into the dinner hour?" He enjoyed the banter, knowing it was a good thing for the press to think him impartial, yet righteous.

"Not too much, your honor," Beau said. "The next day we left for a ride down the Rio Toache River. That's when Mrs. Carr made a play for the river guide, Tom Floater. And that night, Mr. Carr peeked through Mr. Floater's keyhole, and saw the guide and Mrs. Carr having sex... well... he saw red... and as he said, drank too much, and almost strangled his wife when she returned to their room."

"I object," the D.A. shouted. "Pure conjecture on the witness's part. The witness did not see the couple having sex, and was not in the room when the accused strangled his wife. And..."

"And neither were you," Ceil spouted.

The judge announced. "Mrs. Spiegel – Mr. Penya – please. Let's not make this a contest. Turning to Beau, he asked. "Have you anything more to add?" Beau nodded. "The court stenographer cannot enter body language. I'm sure she would be most appreciative of a simple yes or no."

"Yes, your honor." Beau hesitated. "Well, Mrs. Carr appeared unstable. I suppose from all the drugs she'd inhaled. But her husband was a gentleman at all times."

Mr. Penya's hand froze in mid-air. "But not unstable enough for you to stop carrying on the affair with her before and during your holiday, was she?"

"Objection," Ceil said coolly.

"I think we have had enough for one day," the judge said. "Unless the attorneys think there is some dire question that has been overlooked. I thought not." He raised his hand to rap his gavel as Ceil spoke up.

"I would like a brief conference with the prosecuting attorney and his honor in chambers at the close of this session, for a moment."

Judge Montevecchio's shoulders dropped with frustration. "I think we've had more than enough for one day, Mrs. Spiegel." But he caught his wife glaring at him and quickly added, "Ten minutes, and not a second more."

CHAPTER 52

eil was weighted with uncertainty as she entered the courtroom. Last night, sleep never came – it was out of the question. She had tossed and turned relentlessly using every ounce of her mental power thinking of a thousand ways to convince the judge of Trevor's innocence, but in her heart she knew there was too much evidence against him. Her last minute plea with Judge Montevecchio for a temporary adjournment so she could get information from Evan in order to strengthen her case had been refused.

This morning, in the courtroom Ceil was still morose. "Stop taking it to heart, Ceil," Meyer said. "You're doing the best you can with what you have to work with. Stop frowning; they're bringing T.J. in. No sense letting him see how depressed you are."

"He seems almost cheerful. As if he has nothing to worry about."

"He's putting on an act."

The judge entered, and the courtroom became silent. "Good morning," he murmured. "Let's begin where we left off. Mr. Penya, your next witness."

Mr. Penya stood. "Your honor, it has just come to my attention a witness who is critical to this case has been located. I realize this comes as a surprise since routinely I would have conferred with his honor, and the defense, but the witness has not made himself available until now.

"Approach, please. Where the hell has the medical examiner been all this time? Didn't he know he would be called to testify? Is this another one of your unethical stunts?"

"I'm sorry, your honor. He said there was a sudden illness in his family, and he was so distraught, he didn't think. He just left to see them."

"Did his family go with him?"

"I didn't have time to question him."

The judge eyed Mr. Penya with reservation. "And you discovered all this just before court convened and you are now telling me you haven't interrogated him? Did you advise Mrs. Spiegel of this?"

"I didn't have a chance. It happened only a moment before the court convened."

"Mr. Penya, you have crossed over the line of legality. The least you could have done was to ask for a conference so Mr. Spiegel could be aware of what was going on. You should have known better than to pull this kind of maneuver. Really, Mr. Penya. Bring in the witness."

"The state calls Dr. Pablo Rodriguez, medical examiner for the principality of Quito."

Ceil quickly sized up the coroner thinking, from his neat appearance, a recently purchased suit and highly polished shoes, no doubt sponsored by the devious Mr. Penya, that the District Attorney knowingly contrived to spring the witness on her at the last moment.

Dr. Rodriguez kept a cool demeanor, his eyes focusing solely on Mr. Penya from the time he was sworn in, to the first question he was asked by the district attorney.

"You are and have been the coroner for this city for the last three years, have you not, Dr. Rodriguez?"

"Si, tenyo."

Ceil's hand shot up. "Excuse me your honor. Does the witness speak English?"

Dr. Rodriguez kept his eyes on Mr. Penya and said, "I do."

Mr. Penya continued. "And did you perform an autopsy on Mrs. Pamela Carr?"

"I did."

"And as a result of the autopsy performed, were you able to come to a conclusion within a reasonable degree of medical probability as to the cause of death?"

"I did."

"And would you be so kind and tell the court what those findings were?"

"The victim died of strangulation." His look grew distant, but upon catching Mr. Penya's intense stare, he quickly regrouped. "Yes, there were definite signs that she died of asphyxiation."

"We are not as versed as you are concerning the elements of asphyxiation. Can you clarify your last statement?"

Dr. Rodriguez sat up proudly, his eyes still glued on Mr. Penya. "There were characteristic ruptured blood vessels in the whites of her eyes, which have been documented in many cases of this type, and can be attested to in the medical journals."

"Then, Dr. Rodriguez, are you testifying that in your opinion the deceased died of strangulation?"

"I am."

"Is there anything else you can add to prove that the deceased was strangled?"

"One has only to view the imprints and bruises on the victim's throat to conclude the obvious."

Mr. Penya, his characteristic magnanimity on display, gestured with his hands. "Your honor, the witness has been with the city for over three years. I'm sure the court will agree we have established that the deceased was indeed strangled, and will find the accused guilty of the murder of Mrs. Pamela Carr. I have no further questions for the witness."

"Mrs. Spiegel?"

"Dr. Rodriguez. I understand that you were not available to testify at the beginning of the hearing. Can you explain?"

The coroner, his eyes still fastened on Mr. Penya, squirmed in his seat. "I...uh...I received a letter from my uncle, advising me of my aunt's illness."

"So you went there to pay your respects?"

"Yes."

"Did you drive your car, or take a bus?"

"Objection. I fail to see what means of transportation has to do with anything."

"I'll allow it. But not for long."

"I drove."

"Did you take your wife with you?"

"No."

"Is this aunt from your side of the family?"

"Uh... no. She's my wife's sister."

"You went alone. If the lady is your wife's sister, why didn't your wife go?"

"Uh... she gets car sick."

Ceil positioned herself between the doctor and Mr. Penya, as the coroner swayed in his seat trying to view Mr. Penya. "Doctor, do you have a problem with your vision?"

"No, I see twenty-twenty with my glasses."

"Really. Then I would appreciate you focusing on me and not follow Mr. Penya's every move."

"Objection. Mrs. Spiegel is trying to unnerve the witness."

Ceil fired back. "Your honor, the witness has not taken his eyes from the District Attorney from the moment he took the witness stand. I find it odd that he looks to Mr. Penya constantly. Is he taking guidance from our esteemed colleague?"

"Objection. I take offense to Mrs. Spiegel's insinuation. If Mrs. Spiegel is proposing something devious might be transpiring between the witness and me, she'd better have proof to back up her insinuations. I take offense at the innuendo she is putting in front of the court."

"You do realize that you are treading on dangerous waters, Mrs. Spiegel."

She thought, *"Open your eyes, judge. The man is a liar and a pervert. You know of his shady reputation, better than I. Weren't you looking to replace him for that very reason?"* But to the judge, she smiled sweetly and spoke demurely. "I'm sorry, your honor. Forgive me. I found it disconcerting to have the witness avoid my eyes." She quickly turned to the coroner. "You don't by any chance have the letter your uncle sent you, do you?"

"No."

"I thought not. Dr. Rodriguez, did your autopsy show proof that the deceased might have been poisoned?"

Beads of perspiration appeared on his forehead. "None, whatsoever."

"Or, perhaps an overdose, the deceased could have consumed?'

He wiped his brow with his handkerchief. Weakly, he said. "No."

"I'm sorry, Doctor. Did I hear you correctly? Was that a 'no'?"

"Yes. That was a 'no.'"

Aware of the judge's displeased body language and knowing she couldn't prove the coroner's dishonesty, she decided to quit before she got into more trouble. "No further questions, your honor."

The judge looked at Ceil, then the D.A. "Are there witnesses yet to be heard, or can we bring this session to a close?"

"I'm finished," Mr. Penya said. Ceil, likewise agreed.

"In that case, we will break for lunch. Will the attorneys approach the bench?"

Looking from one to the other, he said, "I would like to move this trial along. Could we have your summations perhaps after lunch?" His eyes searched theirs. "Or possibly by tomorrow morning? Mr. Penya?" `

"More than ready, your honor."

"Mrs. Spiegel?"

"Forgive me your honor, but I've changed my mind. I have a witness to call."

The judge protested politely. "Very well." he said.

Mr. Penya faced Ceil. "May I be informed as to whom you intend to call or are we to hold our breath with anticipation?"

The judge growled at the district attorney. "Mr. Penya, watch your step!" Turning to Ceil, he asked, "Mrs. Spiegel, the court will hear the witnesses' name."

Ceil faced Trevor. "The accused, your Honor. The defense calls Trevor Jase Carr."

CHAPTER 53

A s pleasant and hopeful as yesterday had been, the grey clouds and heavy rain that battered against Kaitlin's window seemed to be an omen of tragedy, confirmed by the concerned expression on the doctor's face.

Kaitlin smiled broadly. "Lose a patient, doctor? Or are you working a twenty-four- hour shift again?"

He pulled a chair close to the bed and took her hand in his. Her eyes disclosed a change from cheerful to frightened. "Something's wrong with my pregnancy, isn't it? Is it the pains in my stomach? Don't tell me you want me to abort the baby. I know I can get through it. Please not the baby."

"I wish it were as simple as that, Kaitlin. I shouldn't have let you talk me into trying to save the baby – not with the Hodgkin's, and the possibility of chemotherapy you may be facing, but only you can make that decision. And, another thing, young lady; I'm very upset with you. You have seriously compromised your condition by not being honest with me. You've been hiding your stomach pains. Your blood is too weak. Taking the baby is the least of our problems."

"What are you trying to say, doctor?"

"We have no choice but to abort the baby immediately. You're becoming toxemic."

He looked around as the nurses entered. "You're a brave lady, Kaitlin, but as much as you resist, I think your husband should be notified. You can't do this alone, and it's unfair of you to hide this from him. It is, to be blunt, selfish."

"You don't understand, doctor. Lar's squeamish when it comes to sickness. Especially when it comes to me. He'll fall apart. He cries at the drop of a hat. He's that sensitive. I don't want him to know. Not now. He's got his hands full with Trevor's hearing. They might even call him to testify. No. Definitely, no!"

"Okay, okay. Calm yourself. We're going to prepare you for surgery. The nurse is going to give you a shot to help you relax. You won't feel a thing, and when you awaken you'll be sedated."

The injection took hold, and Kaitlin began to drift off. "Remember, you promised not to tell him. You promised... promised... prom..."

He turned to the head nurse. "What did the latest white blood cell count reveal?"

"I'm sorry, doctor... the peritonitis is progressing rapidly."

"Get in touch with her husband immediately! Too damn bad about his sensitivity. It's time for him to grow up." She turned to leave. "And nurse," he called after her, "see if you can arrange for a few of their friends to accompany him... just to be on the safe side."

"Take this, Mr. Bartoni," the doctor urged. "It will calm you."

Judy, Beau, and Ceil stood anxiously by.

"It's not going to calm me," Lawrence said, attempting to look undaunted. "I'm okay. Why did you summon us here so suddenly? Has Kaitlin taken a turn for the worse?" He plopped into a chair, running his hands over his face, wiping the tears from his cheeks.

"Take the pill," Judy insisted, her arms on his shoulders.

He held out his hand, swallowed the sedative, and washed it down with water. "The bed is empty," Lawrence said, alarmed. His voice cracked, his eyes searched the doctors. "She's not..."

"No, she's in I. C. U. We had to abort the baby."

"She's okay, isn't she?"

The doctor winced. "It's not as simple as that. She has complications."

Lawrence turned ghostly white. "Is it the Hodgkin's we should be concerned with? Is it getting worse?"

"Please, will everyone take a seat?" The doctor called on his many years of experience of telling concerned relatives that the patient had less than a seventy-five percent chance of surviving.

The doctor eyed Lawrence, aware of his sensitivity. "It's a complex situation." Lawrence opened his mouth to speak, but the doctor waved him off. "Hear me out. There will be time for questions when I'm finished. The Hodgkin's has been arrested, for now at least." The group sighed with relief. "But, because Kaitlin insisted on holding onto her pregnancy, complications have set in. I'll try to simplify it for you by avoiding the technical terminology. The Hodgkin's lymphoma involved the bowel wall. She has developed a perforation of the bowel leading to peritonitis. We had to take her for emergency surgery to remove the involved segment of the bowel and reconnect it. Naturally, the pregnancy had to be terminated because of the intricate operation. Pregnancy causes some suppression of the immune system, so there are fewer problems with the immune systems of the baby and the mother interacting. If the mother has cancer, and is pregnant, the cancer often grows faster because of the diminished effectiveness of the immune system."

'But," Ceil interrupted, "she must have shown characteristic signs of peritonitis before this."

"The symptoms of peritonitis depend on the virulence, or the relative ability of microorganisms to cause disease, and the extent of the infection. It was only this morning we discovered Kaitlin has had severe stomach pain, and headaches, and bouts of vomiting that she somehow concealed, all of which have been going on for a while. How she endured such pain and how she hid it from us, is beyond us. She was obsessed with carrying the baby for the full nine months, even if it cost her life. I had to make an immediate decision. Every minute counted. Ordinarily I would have had you sign the proper papers, but... I'm sorry."

"You did the right thing, doctor," Lawrence said. "How critical is she? Can I see her?"

"I won't lie, Lawrence. It's very serious. At this time, I would not suggest visitors. As to her condition, we will have to wait and see. Rest assured we are doing everything we can possibly do for her." He rose. "I'll be watching her constantly." He clapped Lawrence on his back. "You may call as often as you like."

"I want to stay."

"If you insist, but I wouldn't advise it. You won't be able to see Kaitlin for at least twelve hours. There's much to be done."

"If I may ask," Ceil said, "now that the baby is aborted, how do you deal with peritonitis?"

"We inject antibiotics into the vein, or the peritoneum, the serous membrane that lines the abdominal cavity. The antibiotic chosen is one specific to the organism recovered in cultures of her blood. People, I suggest you take Lawrence back with you," his voice urged.

"I'm staying," Lawrence protested.

"I need a cup of coffee," Judy said. "Let's go to that little bistro down the street. We can regroup there."

"I'm with you," Ceil agreed. Beau took hold of Lawrence's arm, and firmly raised him from the bench.

"You're coming too, Lar," Beau insisted. You're too upset to stay here alone. Don't give me a hard time, buddy." Lawrence, still in a daze, let himself be led.

In the hallway, the doctor called after them. "By the way, how is the hearing going?"

"Don't ask," Ceil moaned back. "Couldn't be worse. Between the hearing and Kaitlin, if the earth swallowed us up, it would be a plus."

Shadows from the passers-by crept eerily across the faded stucco walls. Judy and Ceil sat at one table, Beau and Lawrence at another.

"Ceil," Judy, asked. "How in the world did the events of this vacation turn into a tragedy? I was so blind, or rather naive, not to suspect Beau's indiscretions? Now that I think back, there were times I wondered about his staying out late under the guise of going to authors meetings and the like. In the instances when I questioned him, he seemed so vague, so elusive. Being the trusting idiot I am, I believed him. Now it all comes together. Too little too late? Now there's T.J., who I think I'm in love with. One thing I did achieve. Pamela is out of his life, and I know T.J. needs me.

"Listen, Judy. No one can predict what the future will bring. Today you're floating on a big white cloud. Then, tomorrow the cloud suddenly bursts, and with every drop of rain, your hopes and dreams get flushed away."

Judy turned toward Beau, watching his furrowed brows leave deep creases in his forehead. Turning back to Ceil, she said. "How could he have been so foolish, so deluded, by taking on someone like Pamela, when he had me? And look at what it did to our relationship. I don't think I can respect him, or take him back. Not the way it was before. I hate for T.J. to be blamed for her death."

His eyes closed, Lawrence exuded a low painful groan, and realizing the others heard, silently looked from one to the other, too out of it to feel embarrassed. Tears streamed down his cheeks. He held his hands to his face, and wondered why he had not been strong enough to insist on putting his foot down when Kaitlin pushed him into going to the Islands. He remembered her words: *"We didn't have a honeymoon, Lar. Now with the Hodgkin's thing who knows when we will be able to. Don't fight me, Lar. Do this one thing for me."* He couldn't refuse her. Not when he looked into those eyes. Her words echoed repeatedly in his mind, bringing back her words – *don't fight me, Lar – don't fight me, Lar.* The guilt consumed him, his head spun. He felt a burning, gnawing sensation in the pit of his stomach. Then he collapsed.

CHAPTER 54

Meyer's fist slammed down hard. The table wobbled precariously. The bottle of Vodka teetered, and the glasses fell to the floor. He raised his voice at Evan. "What do you mean they threw you out of the room? Who did this?"

Agent Hernandez intervened. "It's not his fault, Meyer. The coroner who originally performed the autopsy on Mrs. Carr, in all probability, took it upon himself to order the guards to remove Evan."

"But we had written permission from the judge," Ceil said. "Can he do that – override the judge's consent?"

"I should think not. I've been trying to get hold of the judge. For some reason, which I don't understand, he's not accepting calls or visitors."

"But you're close to him," Meyer said to Hernandez. "You've been friends many years. You talked him into letting Evan do an autopsy after the county coroner did one. Why would he give Evan permission to work on the body, and suddenly change his mind?"

Agent Hernandez shrugged. "I can't get to the judge to find out. I intend to do a bit of investigating on my own. Maybe I made a mistake."

"How is that?" Ceil asked.

"Maybe, just maybe, the judge knows nothing about this. I do know that the present medical examiner is on his way out. It is common knowledge that he is an alcoholic and abuses his wife and children. Give me a little time to get to the bottom of this."

"Evan," Ceil asked. "How far did you get on the autopsy before they stopped you?"

"You know, Grandma. It was like in a movie. I had my scalpel set to make an incision and suddenly the door opened and in they came, shouting in Spanish. Words like, – *license* – *imediatamente.* I had the scariest feeling they were going to handcuff me and throw me in some rat infested cell, to torture me."

The agent smiled. "What the guards said was *get out, leave immediately."* He faced Ceil and Meyer. Stroking his chin, he said, "The more I think about it, the more I'm convinced this did not come from Judge Montevecchio. He can be stern, and perhaps severe at times, but he is an honest man, and upholds the law to the letter."

Ceil chimed in. "Could've fooled me. The way he's been treating me, you'd think I was public enemy number one."

"Let me go now," the agent said. "I want to get to the bottom of this."

"Thanks, Fernando," Ceil said. "There's something fishy going on. There has to be a reason Evan was tossed out. They're either afraid he will discover something, or the medical examiner has screwed up. From his history, I think it might be the latter."

The telephone rang. "Hello," Ceil said. "Oh, Judy. What? Are you serious? When did it happen? Does Lar know? I'm on my way."

CHAPTER 55

A delightful cool breeze, hinting of fragrant cacti and rampira palm trees, swept across the ocean from the Galapagos Islands, and lifted Ceil's skirt above her knees as she climbed the steps to the Quito hospital. The second she entered the hospital, the medicinal odor filled her nostrils, causing her to shudder.

In the visitor's waiting room, she met with a mournful Judy. Lawrence sat crouched in a chair, his chalk-white face buried in his hands. "How's Kaitlin doing?" she quietly asked Judy.

Judy took Ceil's arm, and led her to the far end of the room. "She's taken a turn for the worse. I just spoke to the doctor." She wiped a tear from her cheek. "It looks bad. Real bad. The peritonitis has spread through her system." She glanced at Lawrence, and back at Ceil. "He's a basket case. I hope you don't mind. I had to call you. I didn't know who else to turn to. Beau is no help when it comes to illness, and I feel so alone."

"You did the right thing. After all, you are in a strange country, and although you care about Kaitlin – worrying about her, and," she motioned towards Lawrence, "coping with him, is a bit much. Besides, I'm an expert when it comes to tragedy. What exactly did the doctor tell you? Is it hopeless? – A matter of days or hours?"

"He wouldn't commit to an exact time. He did say to be prepared for the worst. Lar just about passed out. Then, he plopped into the chair and hasn't said a word. I tried talking to him, but I can't reach him. The doctor says he's in shock. I'm sure he blames himself for her condition. Kaitlin always worried about his stability… I mean his being so emotional."

"Let me try. Do you know what the doctor gave him?"

"He said it was a mild sedative, and he would be back in a few minutes to check on him. It's been about fifteen minutes."

Ceil went over to Lawrence. "Lar," she said softly.

He didn't respond.

"Lar," she said again, her tone sharp and louder.

Still, no response.

Lifting his chin with her finger, she focused on his eyes, forcing him to look at her. His stare was blank, his eyes glazed. He looked through her. She sighed heavily, gritted her teeth, and raised her hand. A loud distinct CRACK! erupted as her hand came down hard across his cheek.

An expression of bewilderment sprung from his eyes. "What was that?" he exclaimed.

"Welcome to the world," Ceil said. "I'm sorry, but you weren't with us. How are you doing?"

"I can't believe she's going to die. It's a nightmare. She was supposed to get better. They said if they took the baby, she'd be okay. They lied to me. Why is all this happening? We only wanted to have a honeymoon. It isn't fair. It isn't fair. It's my fault. I let her get pregnant. She wasn't supposed to. I hate myself. I hate myself."

"Listen, Lar," Judy said. "It happens."

"You don't understand. You don't know. I didn't use the proper contraceptives. It was my fault. My fault."

Ceil pulled a chair adjacent to his. Gripping his shoulders she said, "Now listen to me, Lar. Face up to it. It's done. Stop thinking of yourself and what was. Start thinking about making Kaitlin happy. Falling apart isn't going to accomplish a thing. It isn't going to make Kaitlin better, only more concerned about your welfare after she's gone. But you can show her in her hour of need that you are man enough to stand by her, and give her the love and security she now needs. This is the one time, maybe the only time you'll be able to prove to her you're not the emotional cripple she worries about – but a strong man. You're going to have to be strong for her. If you have to let her go – wouldn't it be better if she left with the peace of mind that you were okay? It won't be easy for you, but she'll go without having to worry about you, and you'll feel a lot better. Well, not right away, but in time."

Lawrence stood and raised Ceil to her feet, embracing her as a child with his mother. Pulling back, he locked eyes with her. "Thank you. I'll try. I'll really try."

The doctor entered the waiting room. His face was gray with the news he was about to tell them. He took a chair and motioned for them to sit. Eyeing Lawrence warily, he frowned and said, "We are trying our best, but only time will tell. She's in the recovery room and you may visit, but I must offer a word of caution. Don't expect too much. She's holding her own, but for how long, we don't know."

Lawrence stood and took Judy's and Ceil's hands. He half-smiled at them. His hoarse voice cracked, but with determination, he said, "I'm going to do it for Kaitlin."

CHAPTER 56

The sunlight streamed through the window of the private room, but failed to brighten Kaitlin's expressionless face. She lay motionless, heavily sedated. Only the beep... beep... beep... of the heart monitor broke the dismal silence.

Judy and Ceil remained silent as Lawrence fought to hold back the tears, determined to show Kaitlin he had the courage to face her illness – to cope with the tragedy that was yet to come. The doctor entered the room, his expression grave.

The threesome stared questioningly at the surgeon, and was answered with a concerned frown, and a negative shake of his head. Ceil turned away, Judy sobbed openly, and Lawrence waited impatiently as they read the doctors expression.

Kaitlin's eyes fluttered open. Lawrence moved close to her, taking her hands in his. The resolve he tried to maintain quickly disintegrated, along with his promise to be strong for her.

Knowingly, Kaitlin weakly raised her hand and brushed away his tears, her fingers lingering on his cheek, letting him know she understood. "It's going to be fine, Lar." Her breath came in labored, short spurts. "Come closer. You don't have to pretend, Lar. I know what you're going through." She held tightly to her teddy bear, Pinky. "Promise me you won't blame yourself. I talked you into the vacation, and in spite of what went on... on the yacht... you still gave me the best honeymoon, and whatever time we had together...before... it's worth the..."

He put his fingers to her lips. "Stop talking like it's the end. The doctor said there's a lot that can be done for you," he lied. "There are new treatments being discovered every day. You'll see. You'll get better."

Kaitlin opened her eyes halfway. "I'm here," she managed to say.

"Save your strength Kat."

Kaitlin attempted a laugh, but only managed to lift the corners of her mouth. "One last thing."

"Anything. Just tell me."

She moaned low. "Make sure my teddy is buried with me. Now, kiss me goodbye, Lar. I feel... my strength... leaving..."

Lawrence kissed and hugged Kaitlin. The nurse edged closer, then scurried out of the room to fetch the doctor.

The doctor rushed into the room. "Lar," Kaitlin breathed. "Hold me."

He sat on the bed and lifted her into his arms, rocking her back and forth. "I'm here darling. I'm here," he sobbed. "I'm here – I'm here – I'm here, my love."

"Don't worry... I'm... not ... afraid. Promise me you'll go on with your life ... try... please... for me."

His heart breaking, his voice hoarse, he said, "I promise... I promise... oh Kat... oh Kat... my love... my love." He held her fast, rocking her back and forth. "I promise... I promise... I..."

Her eyes smiled up at him as she went limp in his arms – and then she was gone.

CHAPTER 57

I lift mine eyes unto the mountains: Whence cometh my help?

My help cometh from the Lord who made heaven and earth.

He will not suffer thy foot to be moved; He that keepeth thee doth not slumber.

Behold He that keepeth Israel doth neither slumber nor sleep.

The Lord is thy keeper; The Lord is thy shade upon thy right hand.

The sun shall not smite thee by day or the moon by night.

The Lord shall keep thee from all evil: He shall keep thy soul.

The Lord shall guard thy going out and thy coming in from this time forth and forever.

The crisp air and sunny morning that had shown promise of clear skies now gave way to a gray overcast sky as the mourners shivered, and the press behind a barricaded area, zoomed their lenses as the priest gave his eulogy.

So typical of funerals, Judy thought looking up at the threatening nimbus clouds. A chill ran through her. She tightened her grip on Lawrence and Beau's arms.

Rain began to fall. Beau let go of her hand to open a tent umbrella. Inclining his head toward Lawrence, he asked, "How are you holding up, buddy?"

"Between the pills I've been downing, and the shock of losing her, I'm numb." His weight shifted unsteadily from one foot to the other.

"Lar, what made you have the burial here?" Judy asked.

"I wanted to have her shipped home, but she insisted on having it here."

"Did she say why?"

"She said she was happiest in the Galapagos Islands."

Beau, aware of Lawrence's wavering, handed the umbrella to Judy. "You don't have to stand, Lar," he advised. "I'll get you a chair. Okay?"

"No. The least I can do for Kaitlin is to show her I'm going to be a man, not a crybaby." Beau gripped Lawrence around his waist to support him.

"Don't be so hard on yourself, Lar" Judy said. "Kaitlin loved you, and loved your sensitivity. You don't have to prove you're a man. She loved that quality about you. Not many men can show their feelings. It's a good thing. She was more concerned about you getting on with your life without her. That's where she wanted you to be strong."

"Sure... yeah...without her. I wish I could wake up from this nightmare and see Kaitlin, just one more time."

Ceil leaned forward from behind them. "Can I be of any help?"

Lawrence tilted his head sideways at her. "Kaitlin liked you," he declared. "She said that you and Judy really cared about her. She didn't have any friends to speak of. And now, when she finally made some... she doesn't have the time to..."

Suddenly, the skies opened up, and sheets of rain drenched the mourners. Most ran for cover but Judy, Beau, Ceil, Meyer, Rosetta, and Santiago remained.

In a secluded setting, Trevor, accompanied by Agent Hernandez, sat in a police wagon, his hands cuffed, face immobile, the tears streaming down his face, wishing it were him in the casket, not Kaitlin.

At the far end of the cemetery, hidden under a camouflaged clump of magnolia trees, Judge Leonardo Montevecchio kept a sharp eye on the proceedings. He tapped at the window separating him from his chauffeur, and signaled him to motor on.

The instant Lawrence laid a rose on Kaitlin's casket, the rain stopped, the sky cleared, and the sun warmed the chilled bones of the mourners. "It's an omen, Lar," Judy said. "I can feel it. She's content."

They stood somberly watching the casket being lowered into the grave. After a few shovels of dirt were thrown, Lawrence turned to Judy. "I want to spend a few minutes alone with her, please." She eyed him suspiciously, but he took her hand to reassure her. "Don't worry, I'm not going to throw myself into the grave. I'll just be a minute."

"Sure," she said, "and if you feel up to it, Lar, I thought it would be nice to have a little get together. You know. Sort of a farewell to Kaitlin."

"Thank you. She'd have liked that."

The group walked to the limousines except for Beau, who hung back. "I'm cool, Beau," Lawrence called out. "Go with the others." Beau looked at Judy, who gestured with a nod, as he reluctantly joined them.

Lawrence stood staring down at the earth, then up at the azure sky and the puffy white clouds that hung low. "Hi, Kat," he said. "I know you can hear me. I love you, and miss you so much. Remember when you told me you thought when someone died you could see them because they turned into clouds? Well, you're the pretty white one, way up over there." He raised his hand and pointed to the cloud. "Yes, the prettiest cloud in the entire sky. You don't have to worry about me, cause I'm going to be all the things you wanted me to be. You'll see. You're going to be real proud of me. You know how I know that? Because you are a part of me. You're inside my heart and wherever I am, or whatever I do, we'll be doing it together. This way I'll never be alone, and neither will you. That's why I'm not going to say goodbye. I'm glad you wanted to rest here in the Galapagos Islands. It's so pure and peaceful, just like you. I better go now." Turning back, he looked at the cloud he called Kaitlin. His heart swelled, envisioning her beautiful brown eyes smiling down at him.

CHAPTER 58

"What's happening?" Meyer asked of Ceil, checking his watch. "The trial was supposed to start a half hour ago, and the judge hasn't shown up yet. That's not like him. Guess Mr. Perfection is not so perfect."

Ceil ignored him. Turning to Trevor, she said, "Your color is coming back. I'm glad, but I was sorry you couldn't be at Kaitlin's funeral. She asked about you before she passed on. She was worried about the trial."

Trevor sighed. "She was a very special lady." He looked around and caught Judy's eyes. "I was at the funeral, but no one saw me."

"No kidding," Meyer offered. "Wasn't it good of Scrooge to let you attend the funeral?"

"It wasn't the judge. It was Agent Hernandez who arranged it. I'm lucky he's a friend of yours. I'm getting decent meals, and no one touches me, thanks to you and your association with him. You wouldn't believe how the prisoners are mistreated. I guess it's who you know around here that counts." Trevor looked over his shoulder at the guard and lowered his voice. "The food they get is disgusting, and if they step out of line they're punished severely."

"How?" Meyer said.

"It depends on their behavior. They hold back their food sometimes for days. But when there's an inspection, usually by Agent Hernandez or one of his deputies, they make sure the cells are cleaned, and the prisoners are warned to keep their mouths shut, or else. I've seen beatings and sexual abuse going on."

"How horrible," Ceil said. "In this day and age."

"You know, Ceil," Meyer said. "You're talking like a child. You forgot what happened to Trevor before we got him new quarters."

Trevor winced. "That still goes on. Most of the inmates are heartless men who think killing is a way of life. Slitting someone's throat, or shooting a person, is an everyday occurrence. They get off on it. They're like animals. No conscience or sense of right or wrong."

Ceil shrugged. "I suppose that's why the judge hands down such stiff sentences."

"That's what I'm afraid of," Trevor said darkly. "He's not going to make an exception of me, either. That's probably the reason he took your grandson off the autopsy inquest. There had to be more to discover about Pamela's death. I didn't kill her. Someone's covering something up, and it's going to be my demise."

"What makes you so sure it was the judge who put a kibosh on Pamela's autopsy?" Meyer questioned.

Trevor hesitated. "I... I think Agent Hernandez mentioned something," he stuttered. "I forget. Anyway, it was real decent of him to let me go to the funeral. Personally, I don't think the judge was aware of my presence. We hid in a station wagon behind a clump of Magnolia trees and left before anyone could recognize us."

Ceil frowned. "If the judge did stop Evan's investigation, I should think he would have told us. It just doesn't fit somehow. He may be ruthless when it comes to doling out punishment, but he's legitimate when it comes to the law."

Meyer rebuffed her. "What are you talking about? He's gone from hot to cold, nice to downright mean, and back to nice, over and over again. I think he's got too much on his mind. And between you and me and the lamppost, my darling wife, I think you and his wife have a lot to do with it."

"All right, all right," Ceil whispered. "I know I made a mistake by getting close to her, but I thought I could get information from her. Although, we did hit it off, and she is a lovely person."

Meyer shook his head with disgust. "Sometimes I think your being too smart gets you into trouble. Your making friends with Rosetta only infuriated the judge. You put him in an awkward position. She shouldn't be giving you information. She's his wife, and he's the judge, remember?"

"Stop carrying on. So I took a chance. We had nothing to go on." She faced Trevor. "Forgive me, Trevor, but you know as well as I, this is going to be an uphill battle. I have to find a way to prove you didn't kill Pamela, and we have so little to go on." She stared at Meyer. "I'd do it all over again if I thought it would help our case."

"Ceil, you can be stubborn as a mule. Okay, okay, let's not get bent out of shape. We all want the same thing."

She smirked. "That's right. For a moment I was afraid you were thinking of defecting."

"Well…" he began, but a messenger interrupted, and handed Ceil an envelope.

"No answer is required," he announced, and left in a hurry.

Ceil looked from Trevor to Meyer. "It can't be bad news. It just can't be."

She opened the letter and read:

Ceil, as you probably have surmised, my husband and I have been at odds. Our friendship – his position with the court – the paparazzi, and the media breathing down his neck has made him quite irritable. It is upsetting him. As of late, he has asked for my help, but since you and I have become closer, and because you are defending Mr. Carr, he's shut me out. I'm sorry, but I promised him I would end our relationship. More important – I have convinced him to let your grandson continue his investigation into Mrs. Carr's autopsy. I can tell you, it was not easy. I too feel, for reasons I will not go into at this time, the coroner who performed the first autopsy is incompetent. Please, if you are truly my friend, you will destroy this letter. Tatiana

Ceil leaned forward and looked across the aisle at Rosetta. Nodding her head, she tore the letter into small pieces, stuffed them into her mouth, chewed, swallowed, and washed them down with a glass of water. Rosetta stifled a giggle and returned a nod of acknowledgment.

Meyer's jaw dropped. "What the hell was that all about?"

She coughed and said, "I didn't have breakfast. Do you mind?"

"Everyone, rise," was heard loud and clear. The judge entered the courtroom, his eyes focused menacingly at the defense. He directed his voice to Ceil, but his eyes poured over the papers in front of him – shuffling them nervously.

"Mrs. Spiegel, your witness please."

Having second thoughts about calling Trevor to the stand, hoping Evan would come up with evidence to help him, she avoided the judge's eyes, and spoke apprehensively. "Your honor, the defense apologizes, but I have reconsidered calling the witness to testify at this time."

Judge Montevecchio's face flushed the color of a ripe tomato. He glared at Ceil. Using every ounce of his self-control, he labored a false smile at her. *This trial, like everything else in life, will come to an end, and I will conduct court in a normal fashion. I will retain my sanity, and continue to remain calm no matter how the district attorney provokes me, or Mrs. Spiegel, with her unorthodox court procedures, exasperates me.*

"Mr. Penya, you do have a witness?"

"Most assuredly, your honor," he said, glancing arrogantly at Ceil. "The state calls Thomas Floater." After the witness took the oath, he sat fidgeting with his key chain in the shape of a rafting boat. "Would you state your full name and occupation, please?"

"Thomas Edison Floater. I'm employed as a rafting guide by the Ecuadorian Sightseeing Company."

"Were you the guide in charge of the rafting trip Mr. and Mrs. Carr arranged?"

"Yes, sir. But the Carrs did not make the arrangements. Their guide, Santiago, made it and we never made the run down the river."

"And why was that?"

He raised his head, surprised by the question. "Well, because Pam... I mean Mrs. Carr, was uh... not alive the morning the trip was scheduled."

"You mean she couldn't take the run down the rapids because she was killed the night before? And how do you know she was killed the night before?"

"Objection," Ceil called. "It is well documented the deceased was not alive the next morning."

"Sustained. Mr. Penya, keep your questions to the point.

"I'm sorry, your honor. I'll rephrase the question." He edged closer to the witness stand, and dramatically pointed his finger at the witness. "You had sex with the deceased, did you not?

"Yes, we had sex."

"Are you quite sure it was Mrs. Carr who suggested you sleep together?" Mr.

Penya said, his voice soft. Then he approached Tom and shouted, "Or was it Mr. Carr, who put you up to seducing his wife, thereby giving him a credible reason to strangle her in what he called a fit of anger?"

Ceil jumped to her feet. "Objection, your honor, Mr. Penya is badgering the witness, and putting words in his mouth to suggest Mr. Carr purposely and willfully planned to strangle his wife. It's pure conjecture on his part. Furthermore, I propose that Mr. Floater having admitted he had sex with the deceased, now has nothing more to offer, and should be excused from giving further testimony and -"

Mr. Penya broke in. "Your honor, Mrs. Spiegel evidently is lacking the experience one gets from years of trying court cases, as is proven from her last statement. My line of questioning will show the accused hated his wife so much, he worked out a scheme to do away with her, and to play on the sympathy of the court so he would be found not guilty."

"Mr. Penya," the judge responded. "Unless you have proof Mr. Floater and Mr. Carr had conspired to, as you said, do away with the victim, I don't see what you are driving at. Let me cut to the chase and save the court some precious time." Facing Tom, the judge asked, "Mr. Floater. Please remember you are under oath. Was there a conspiracy between you and the accused to harm Mrs. Carr?"

"No, your honor. I never met Mr. Carr until a week ago, when their guide introduced me to him and the others."

"And you thought nothing of having relations with Mrs. Carr knowing her husband was in the room down the hall?"

"I have to admit I was wrong. But she came onto me so intensely, and convinced me he didn't care, and that she wasn't about to tell him. There was something irresistible about her. She just oozed sex. Of course, now I know I used bad judgment." He wrung his hands, focusing on Trevor. "Actually, I thought Mr. Carr was an all right guy."

"Unless Mrs. Spiegel wants to interrogate Mr. Floater, I see no reason to detain him," the judge said, his eyes narrowing at the attorney.

"Mr. Penya, you were finished with your interrogation, I take it?"

"Uh... yes your honor."

"Mrs. Spiegel?"

Ceil folded her arms defiantly while smiling triumphantly at the district attorney, enjoying his embarrassment. "I have no questions for the witness, your honor."

"Mr. Floater, you are excused."

From the street, shouting and merriment interrupted the courtroom procedure. "I see the festivities for tonight's holiday festival have started, and since it will be difficult to continue with any sense of decorum, the court is convened until nine o'clock tomorrow morning." Then he brought the gavel down.

The guard stepped up to Trevor, who extended his wrists to be handcuffed. "Who are you going to call tomorrow Ceil?" he asked.

She gathered her papers, folded them neatly, and placed them in her briefcase. "The one person who can save you."

"Who's that?"

"You, Trevor. I'm going to call you."

CHAPTER 59

Early that evening after the exchange between the judge, Ceil sat at the local bistro with Beau, Judy, Meyer and Lawrence. Each was unusually quiet, lost in his or her own thoughts.

All eyes focused on Beau as he broke the silence. "I want to be fair, and I would love to give T.J. the benefit of the doubt, but the more I think about it, it just doesn't add up."

"We're listening," Ceil said.

Beau leaned closer to the group. "Let's bring it out into the open. We're all thinking the same thing. Did he, or didn't he? We all had a motive to do away with Pamela. She drugged us, and lied to us."

"That's right," Lawrence cut in, "and she knew of Kaitlin's fragile condition. I could have killed her myself for being so insensitive."

Beau reclaimed the conversation. "In fact, we talked about it openly. The woman was a horror. Still, the fact remains that T.J. admits trying to strangle her, and that seemed to me to be a point Mr. Penya scored on when he said T.J. might have planned all this, and thought he would get away with it by invoking the sympathy of the judge."

Judy disagreed. "You can't honestly say that you think T.J. purposely killed

Pamela, can you? He's the most gentle, kind..." she said, stopping short, realizing that by defending him, she was exposing her true feelings.

"Well," Beau snapped. "Aren't we protesting a bit too much? He's not your husband, you know. Why are you defending him so adamantly?"

Her face flushed. "I'm not defending him; I'm just trying to see things through his eyes, which is more than you care to do. From your attitude, you seem to want him condemned."

She rose. "If you'll excuse me," she said to the group, her eyes casting daggers at Beau, "I've suddenly developed a throbbing headache."

"Just as well," Meyer commented, as Beau ran after her.

"Right on," Ceil said. "Family squabbles are best done in private. How about another round? Meyer? Lar? Good. Now, let's think about putting Trevor on the stand."

Beau caught up with Judy. Taking hold of her elbow he swung her around. "Come on, Jude. I thought we promised to call a truce until this was over. I apologize if I spoke out of turn back there, but it just got to me when you started slobbering over T.J. You as much as told everyone that you care for him, and I lost it." She tried to pull away, but he held tightly to her. "Listen, I know my affair with Pamela came as a shock to you, and I made a humongous mistake – I know you'll never forgive me, but I do love you. I always have, and always will. We did have some great times, didn't we? Don't they count for anything? Maybe what you feel for T.J. is pity, not love. I'm not asking you to forgive me... not now. Maybe in time you'll understand how much I regret what I did and how much I love you. I know there's no excuse." Tears filled his eyes, and hers too.

"Yes, we did have a wonderful relationship, Beau. But I trusted you. It hit me so hard. I'll be honest. Right now, I'm confused. The trial, plus our lives being so disrupted... so unsettled... and Kaitlin's death. You not only disappointed me, you hurt me deeply. As far as T.J.'s concerned, I don't know how or why – it just happened. I fell for him. Okay, I'll go along with our little charade of pretending we're a happy couple, but the minute this is over, I'm going to leave you."

"What if he's convicted, and spends time in jail, or you change your mind in the future?"

"I can hardly cope with today, much less tomorrow," she said, suddenly remembering her promise to Kaitlin to watch over Lawrence. "I'm going back to the bistro to make sure Lar is okay."

"Do you mind if I go with you? I promise to behave. Please."

"Sure. We may as well go on with the pretense."

"Would you permit me to take your arm?"

She nodded, her eyes locking with his. She still loved him, and wondered if, when the time came, she would be able to leave him.

CHAPTER 60

The prosecuting attorney chuckled to himself as he scrutinized the paparazzi that sneaked pictures of the courtroom scene. The guards stationed in the courtroom moved towards them, but the judge entered, and they quickly positioned themselves at their posts. The usual protocol of rising and being seated took precedence and the judge called the trial to order. Glaring at the photographers, Judge Montevecchio leaned forward, nostrils flaring, and said, "This is a court of law gentlemen and it will be treated with respect. Evidently there are those in the media who choose to disrespect it." Growling at them, he added, "If one more picture is taken I will remove the entire gallery for the rest of this trial."

As if I didn't have enough to contend with – now these foreigners, and the damn publicity – my face plastered on all the tabloids like a court jester, he thought.

The stillness of the courtroom brought him back to reality. He pointed his gavel at Ceil. "Although it is not usual procedure, the prosecuting attorney has relinquished his questioning of the accused, to you." He threw a suspicious eye at Mr. Penya, but directed his voice to Ceil. "Mrs. Spiegel, you may proceed."

"Your honor," Ceil said. "I need one moment to sort out my notes. Please, just a few seconds." The judge nodded with impatience.

Trevor and Meyer exchanged glances. Ceil shuffled a few papers on the table. Meyer looking perplexed, asked, "What's going on? You have that funny expression on your face, Ceil. Aren't you going to call T.J. to testify?"

"No. I think Mr. Penya, the pain in the ass, is trying to pull a fast one. He's up to something, letting me question T.J. first. I need to stall for time. I'm hoping Evan will find something to help us. The judge is either bored or fed up with the trial and is pushing for a quick end. I can taste it."

"What could Evan possibly come up with?"

"I don't know, but I'm going to delay putting T.J. on the stand. We're finding out very unsavory information about the previous coroner."

Trevor added, "Your instincts are right, Ceil. I feel it, too. I hope Evan's going to come up with something."

"What are you, psychics? So how come I'm not feeling what you two are?" Meyer asked.

"Later Meyer," Ceil responded. "The judge is looking quite agitated."

"Frothing at the mouth would be a better way to describe him," Meyer quipped.

Twitching his nose, Judge Montevecchio lowered his head, narrowing his eyes at Ceil. "Are we quite finished sorting out our notes, Mrs. Spiegel?"

"Yes, thank you, your honor. The defense first calls Mr. Santiago."

After Santiago was sworn in the bailiff asked him to state his name. "Alvarez Roberto Santiago."

"Be seated."

Ceil smiled warmly at the witness. "Good morning, Mr. Santiago." He returned the greeting. "What is your occupation sir?"

"I am a guide for the Ecuadorian Tourist Bureau. I take tourists to different islands of the Galapagos and point out the animals, birds, and natural beauty the surroundings have to offer the visitors."

"Were you hired as a guide by Mr. and Mrs. Carr?"

"Oh, no, ma'am."

"No? I don't understand. Didn't you escort the three couples, and stay with them on the yacht?"

"Yes, but I was not hired by Mr. and Mrs. Carr. I was assigned to Mr. and

Mrs. Blessing. But there was confusion as to who should stay on the yacht, because it was supposed to have only one couple. There was a mix-up. Both couples were booked on the same yacht."

"How was this resolved?"

"The captain was very disturbed. He was not sure how to handle the situation. He asked them on board and served them hors d'oeuvres and champagne. They talked about how to work the situation out, and agreed to share the yacht. It had eight cabins and six would be empty. Besides, it is high season, and finding such exclusive accommodations again would be impossible. All the yachts were engaged months in advance."

"And they agreed to share the yacht. Did anyone say how the mix-up occurred?"

"No. I guess it was blamed on the travel agency."

"Are you sure it was blamed on the travel agency?"

"Objection. The witness has no way of knowing the actual workings of the travel agency."

"Rephrase, Mrs. Spiegel."

"Mr. Santiago. Do you have any proof that the agency mishandled the bookings?"

"Only, what I overheard."

"Objection, your honor."

"I'll allow it. Mrs. Spiegel, let's not drag this out."

"What did you overhear, Mr. Santiago?"

"I overheard Mr. Blessing and Mrs. Carr quarreling loudly."

"Don't you mean Mr. and Mrs. Carr?"

"No. It was Mrs. Carr and Mr. Blessing having an argument in an unoccupied cabin."

"Why in an unoccupied cabin?"

"They met there secretly many times."

"And why do you think that was?"

"Objection."

"Overruled. I'm interested to know just where the defense is going with this line of questioning." He stared down at Ceil. "I hope we are not casting a net to find there are no fish to snare," he said flatly.

"What did you overhear that makes you so sure the bookings were...

uh... fixed?"

Santiago looked at Beau, who sat shrinking in his seat, his face pale. "Mr. Blessing told Mrs. Carr he was sorry he got mixed up with her, and that she was not acting rationally, and doing too many drugs. And that if she ever told his wife about their affair, he would kill her with his bare hands. She yelled back at him that she would never let go of him and he could go and... I can't say the word. Then he said, 'you paid the travel agency to double book this vacation,' and she said, 'so what? I thought you would be glad to have me and your precious Judy. I was even thinking of a threesome, or maybe a foursome.' He raised his voice again, and I'm not sure, but he might have slapped her. Then he said, "It's over between us. You can't hold a candle to Judy. You're nothing but a slut. You've screwed the captain, the steward, and half the crew. You're really a sick f...'"

Mr. Penya sprang to his feet. "Objection, your honor. This man is either an aspiring actor, or has been prompted to make up this senseless, absurd story."

Santiago flushed. "I am not a liar. I was not brought up to lie. I am a God fearing man. I am telling the truth. Ask anyone on the islands about me."

The judge raised his hands, waving Mr. Penya to sit. He observed Santiago. "I'm sure you are a God fearing man, Mr. Santiago, but you seem to know intimate details about the passengers... how can you explain it?"

Ceil sighed with relief, hoping things were going to shift in her favor. Santiago eyed the prosecutor with contempt and held his head erect. "I can't remember everything I heard word for word. I can only tell you the way I remember it best. Living on a yacht is like living in the same room. The walls are not thick. When the water is calm, and the yacht is anchored, you can hear a whisper from stem to stern. I was with the group night and day, practically. The three couples were fun loving people, and I was included in most of their activities."

"Mr. Santiago," the judge asked, "when did it become three couples?"

Mr. Penya rose, then stopped in mid air, and quickly fell into his chair, deciding not to risk another reprimand from the judge.

"Let me think. It was the day we had seen the boobies, and giant sea turtles. Mrs. Bartoni suddenly fainted and Mr. Carr caught her. It was very hot." He hesitated, crossed himself and sighed painfully. "May she rest in peace. She was an angel. Mr. and Mrs. Bartoni were on a commercial boat, and the others, upon hearing that she was pregnant and sick with Hodgkin's disease, agreed to invite them to stay on the yacht. Mr. Carr arranged to have their belongings moved to the yacht. He took care of all the bills and financial expenses the group incurred. He even paid off the other guide. He was very generous."

Mr. Penya insisted. "Your honor, Mr. Santiago has painted a wonderful canvas of Mr. Carr and his philanthropic nature, but I fail to see the connection. Even the most exemplary men have been known to do misdeeds."

The judge shrugged. "I agree. Mr. Santiago has given the court an admirable account of Mr. Carr's character, but I fail to see the relevance to this case. Mrs. Spiegel?"

"I'm finished with the witness, your honor."

Mr. Penya smiled smugly at Ceil.

"Do you wish to cross examine the witness, Mr. Penya?"

Mr. Penya was not going to be upstaged. He was a graduate of Harvard law school and was not going to be intimidated by this common armchair lawyer. "No. I do not wish to cross-examine the witness. Your honor has spoken for me. We are aware of the deceased's loose morals, but, I must repeat, it does not justify an act of strangulation. It is a waste of the court's time to prolong the discussion of Mr. Carr's contributions to society." He smiled glibly at Ceil, "Unless the defense intends to bring forth another witness who can attest to Mr. Carr's upstanding, charitable, and benevolent character." He turned and held a pose for a moment, making sure the artists captured his profile.

"Mrs. Spiegel," the judge said, "we are going in circles. If you have a witness who can bring to light some shred of evidence to show Mr. Carr did not commit this crime, the court will allow it. Otherwise, I see no reason for this trial to continue, except for the summation by the prosecutor and the defense."

In a last ditch effort, knowing she was grasping at straws, Ceil, said, "Yes, your honor. I do have one last witness. I call Trevor Jase Carr to the stand." The courtroom buzzed with excitement.

Mr. Penya raised his hands in frustration. "Really, your honor, are we to go through another tireless accounting of Mr. Carr's self imposed image?"

Ceil hit back. "It would be unfair of the court not to let the condemned man testify on his own behalf."

The thought of another long drawn out argument between the lawyers did not sit well with the judge. *What was Mrs. Spiegel trying to accomplish by putting her client on the stand? She is too smart to have him repeat what had been alleged – unless she is playing for time. But why? It's time to put an end to this trial. As he started to speak, he felt his wife staring at him. Their eyes held* for a moment as he read her mind.

"Very well, Mrs. Spiegel, the court will grant your request, but I must warn you, if it is going to be a repeat performance of previous testimony, I will suspend the trial, and set a time and date for a final summation.

"He's right, Ceil," Meyer whispered. "What can T.J. tell the court that hasn't already been said? You're going to look like an ass. All you're going to do is antagonize the judge."

"I know, I know, but I can't think of anything else to do. We need time."

Suddenly, a cough and a loud gasp for breath was heard. One of the spectators fell to the floor. "Oh my God," someone yelled, "he's having a heart attack."

The judge banged his gavel and announced, "Court is adjourned until ten o'clock tomorrow morning. Bailiff, call an ambulance."

Ceil, Meyer, and Trevor looked over each other as a spectator – a doctor, ran to the stricken man.

"Saved by the bell," Meyer said remorsefully.

CHAPTER 61

As she sat in the courtroom waiting for the judge to enter, Ceil thought of the previous night – a night imbued with distress and anguish. Prolonging the trial was foremost in her mind. She prayed Evan would come up with something – anything – to help Trevor's deteriorating defense, but he only put her off with, "Stall them, Grandma. I'm onto something, but it will take time." Prolonging the trial was foremost on her mind. She tossed and turned, thinking of a hundred ways to convince the judge of Trevor's innocence – at least to establish a reasonable doubt in the judge's mind. Meyer had shaken her. "It's three a.m. We might as well wait for the sun to rise. Let's get out of bed. We're not going to sleep tonight, anyhow. You're so wired."

The bailiff called the court to order, and she snapped back to the present.

Judge Montevecchio surveyed the room, taking in the attentive spectators and the eager press. He too, had not slept well, and after a tug of war with his anxious mind, and with the urging of his wife, he took sleeping tablets and closed his eyes – but his mind would still not shut down.

His tone was gentle, but firm. "Good morning." He motioned to a guard who tapped on a door where Trevor, accompanied by another guard, stood waiting to enter the courtroom.

Trevor, the epitome of a broken man, face waxen and expressionless, hair in disarray, hands cuffed behind his back, feet shackled in chains, shuffled toward the defense's table.

"Remove the gear."

Easing his body, as if in pain, he sat beside Ceil and placed his hand over hers. His eyes swollen, he smiled weakly at her, observing her shocked expression at his chaotic appearance. "Are you up to this, Trevor?" she said in a sympathetic tone.

"I'm numb, but I'm okay." His voice sounded scratchy and hoarse, his bloodshot eyes looked hollow, his presence that of a helpless man who was to be sentenced to death for a crime he didn't commit.

"Mrs. Spiegel, call your witness, please."

"Will Trevor Jase Carr take the stand?" she said. After he was sworn in, Trevor sank heavily into the witness chair, his head bowed.

Her palms resting on the defense table, Ceil posed her first question. "Mr. Carr will you please state your occupation and position with the corporation where you are employed?"

Mr. Penya spread his arms, his face expressing annoyance. "Objection. Must the court go through another rumination of Mr. Carr's virtues? We have already established that Mr. Carr is an outstanding pillar of the community. Are we to be subjected to more of this self serving testimony?"

The judge agreed. "Mrs. Spiegel, move things along. Mr. Carr's reputation has already been established."

"Very well then," she said. "If the court permits, I will ask Mr. Carr to tell us what actually happened leading up to, and concluding, with the death of his wife."

Mr. Penya raised his hand to protest, but the judge waved him off. "Mr. Penya, you will have ample opportunity to object and cross-examine. At this rate we will be here forever."

Ceil threw the district attorney a false smile. Turning her attention to Trevor, she said, "Mr. Carr, please begin."

Lowering his head sorrowfully, he focused on his hands, which were folded in his lap. "I don't know where to begin," he said inaudibly.

The judge faced Trevor. "Mr. Carr, please speak up."

"Tell us about your relationship with your wife," Ceil prompted.

Suddenly, his mind cleared and he spoke coherently. "It's so ironic, I mean that I would get so upset. After all, I knew she had been cheating on me for years. This was nothing new. We took this vacation to patch things up. We hadn't been getting along. She was on all kinds of medication and it was no secret she had fits of depression. Her behavior could be...well...erratic at times. Even her mother admonished her for... but that's another story." He looked from Ceil, to Judy, to the judge, and back to his hands, which were now tightly clenched in his lap. Speaking as though he was reliving the scene, he continued. "Yes, I wanted her dead. I was at my wit's end. I felt ashamed...degraded... with her cheating so blatantly. I knew she was playing up to this stud, Tom, and I knew she was going to get him into bed. I don't blame him. She had these pheromones she exuded that drew men to her like a fly to flypaper. He was only one more conquest to fill a void that couldn't be filled. And for me, it was just one more time. But when I followed her and peeked through the keyhole, and saw them having sex, I became enraged. It was then that I broke down. I went back to my room and started drinking. The more I drank the more infuriated I became. When she finally came back and slipped quietly into bed I just couldn't contain myself, and I confronted her. By then I had finished off a half bottle of Scotch. I was so incensed at her having sex with Tom that I forced myself on her." Trevor's voice was harsh, and he stopped to drink a glass of water. "The funny thing is, she enjoyed my aggressiveness." Trevor hesitated as he eyed the judge. "Can I be frank when I repeat her conversation, your honor?"

The judge shrugged. "Nothing would surprise me. But I think it would be better if you used the first letter of the obscenities when necessary."

"She said, 'Who's been teaching you, T.J.? You want to know a secret? If I knew you were so animalistic, I never would have screwed another man.'

"For the life of me, I'm not sure. Maybe it was the booze, or the times she cheated on me, or her egging me on. I'm not sure, but I wanted her badly. It was then that we got into a frenzied sexual encounter." Trevor's eyes widened as he relived the scene. "The rougher I became, the more she enjoyed it. She screamed, 'Harder, harder! Make me know it, you brute!'"

He looked from Judy, to the judge. "I'm omitting the obscenities, your honor. I thought my heart would burst. She panted as her excitement rose and she said, 'Show me how much of a man you are. Put your hands around my throat. Choke the life out of me.' I became crazed. All the hatred I felt for her welled up in me, and it sent me over the edge. I remember yelling, as I tightened my hands around her neck. 'Is this what you want? Is this the way they do it to you?'

"'Yes,' she moaned, my fingers gripping tighter – Suddenly, she gasped for breath."

Trevor looked down at his colorless knuckles as he clenched his fists. "I panicked when I saw her face turn chalk-white and her breathing stopped. I was overcome with fear. I gave her mouth-to-mouth resuscitation, but she didn't respond. As a last resort, I slapped her hard four or five times, and she started to breathe. We had ended up on the floor, so I lifted her, and carried her to the bed. I held her in my arms, when suddenly, her eyes fluttered open, and she smiled at me. I couldn't believe it, and to say I was relieved is an understatement. She startled me even more, when out of the blue, she said, 'T.J., you were incredible.'

"I sat dumbfounded . . . stunned . . . in a daze . . . not believing what I was hearing. It was like she had never passed out . . . like . . . nothing had happened. It sobered me up real fast. Confused and disoriented, I asked if she was all right, and if I could get her water, or anything.

"She said, 'I'm fine. Stop carrying on. I only was out for a few seconds. I'm hungry. I didn't eat dinner, remember?' She sat up. 'I'm famished and I have that delicious fish we doggie bagged in the fridge. Want to join me, you stud-muffin?'

"I was overwhelmed by her quick recovery. I wanted to get out of there in the worst way, embarrassed if others had heard us. I told her I was going to the beach to clear my head and walk off the booze. I was almost out the door when I turned back, and asked if she was sure she was okay, and how was she going to explain the marks on her neck. By then she had the fish out, and was munching on it.'

"'Stop worrying,' she said. 'I can cover it with makeup or wear a scarf. I've had hickeys before, silly.'

"'Those marks are more than just hickeys,' I called back through the closed door. Then I heard her voice trailing. 'Don't be too long. I may want some more of the new you.'"

Trevor's voice softened, and he released a deep breath. "I remember how relieved I felt, knowing she was alive. On the beach, I happened to meet Judy. That's the truth, your honor. I swear it is."

Silence pervaded the courtroom, as everyone waited – no, hoped, Trevor would continue. The sordid details of his sexual encounter titillated them, and as he uttered, "I swear it is," he viewed the judge with wounded eyes, his voice faltered.

The judge turned to Ceil. "Mrs. Spiegel?"

Ceil blinked back tears. "No questions, Your Honor."

The judge called. "Mr. Penya, I'm sure you want to cross-examine."

The district attorney rose, his manner showing exaggerated self-assurance. He sauntered toward Trevor. "Mr. Carr, you have painted an admirable portrait of a man wronged. You've described your wife as a sick, psychopathic, sex-driven woman, and quite cleverly tossed in a few touches of compassion, leading us to believe you stood by her, as a dutiful husband should. Did anyone witness you on your knees as you spied through a keyhole while you watched Mr. Floater and your wife embracing?"

"It was three o'clock in the morning. Everyone was asleep."

"Mr. Carr, please listen to the question. I did not ask what time it was or if people were sleeping. A simple yes or no will suffice. Let me repeat the question so it will be clear in your mind. Did anyone witness you peeking through a keyhole while your wife and Mr. Floater, as you claim, embraced?"

"First of all I was not spying. Not in the sense of the word, spying, and secondly, they were doing more than just embracing."

Mr. Penya spread his arms in frustration. "Your honor, can we direct the witness to answer a simple yes or no, to the question?"

"Mr. Carr," the judge said. "Don't avoid the question with an explanation. Your counsel, I'm sure, will rectify any and all dialogue the district attorney has queried. Now answer the question."

"No."

Mr. Penya's eyes widened. "No, you didn't see anyone to witness your actions, or no, you won't answer the question?"

"Yes, to the last part of your question, and no, to the first." Giggles were heard throughout the room.

Mr. Penya tapped his foot impatiently. "Really, Your Honor. I think the witness is being hostile."

"Mr. Carr, please," he said, dryly. He nodded to Mr. Penya to continue.

"Very well, Mr. Carr. Two can play this game. Did you put your hands on your wife's throat and leave black and blue imprints of your fingers on her?" He quickly added. "A yes, or no, will suffice."

"Yes."

"Good, we're catching on."

Ceil rose. "Objection, your honor. Is it necessary to insult the witness?"

"Counselors approach," the judge whined.

Judge Montevecchio tapped his fingers anxiously on his blotter. "My patience is at an end," he said, through clenched teeth. "Mrs. Spiegel – Mr. Penya – In my chambers, now! Mr. Carr, you may step down. Guards, take the prisoner out." Noticing the wall clock nearing the lunch hour, he said, "The court will recess early, and reconvene at one o'clock." He gently brought the gavel down gently on the pad, remembering how it had splintered when he had previously lost his temper. *Enough is enough. I'm going to put an end to this free-for-all mockery of the law.*

Mr. Penya and Ceil sat pensively, uncomfortable under the judge's glare. His body language revealed they were going to be chastised. He glanced at his wife, who stood at the far end of the room, fearful of what he might say.

"I'm trying hard, very hard, to contain myself," he began. "In all the years I have been on the bench I have never witnessed such outrageous behavior from counsel. I know this is your first case, Mrs. Spiegel. But your objections and manner of questioning do not live up to the professional standards of courtroom procedure. I'll be lenient with you, because I know you hadn't expected to try this case when you arrived. Your job is to help the accused, but keep in mind, this is a court of law, and I will not excuse incompetence." She opened her mouth to speak but he shook a 'no,' at her. He scowled at his wife for convincing him to let Ceil defend Trevor. She turned away and looked out the window.

Gritting his teeth, he faced Mr. Penya. "You, Mr. Penya, have stepped over the line of ethics. You've let yourself get carried away by delusions of grandeur. You, no doubt, see yourself as the greatest lawyer to come upon the scene this century. You think this case is going to skyrocket you into the hall of fame and fortune – that because of the notoriety the trial has stirred up, the demand for your services will escalate. Well that may be true – if I allow you to continue as the prosecuting attorney. You have shown yourself as a pompous, arrogant, and unprincipled member of the bar. You know I can remove you, declare a mistrial, or bring you up on charges for unethical practices to the tribunal's Ethics Court. You know what that means. But you're in luck, for the moment, anyway. I want this trial to be finished and done with. The municipality has suffered financially from loss of the tourist trade, and the media has made a spectacle of this trial. I'm not singly blaming you, Mr. Penya, or you, Mrs. Spiegel – I too have contributed to this fiasco. But, I intend to make it right, and I expect the same from both of you."

"I understand, and will cooperate in every way," Ceil responded.

"And you, Mr. Penya. Will you conduct yourself in a lawyerly manner? If you don't, I'll take you off the case, and have you disbarred. You can go back to chasing ambulances for a living."

Mr. Penya's face drained of all color. "May I speak?" he asked, timidly. The judge nodded.

"Perhaps this comes after the fact, but your honor has struck a chord in me. I see things more clearly now. I ask the judge's forgiveness and apologize for being such an overbearing obnoxious ass. If I strayed from the oath I swore to uphold, I sincerely apologize to the court and want to thank your honor for making me see the error of my ways."

"All said, I think we understand one another," the judge declared. "After lunch, we will go into the courtroom and conduct ourselves in a manner that is befitting of our profession and bring this damn trial to an end. Mr. Penya, will you want to continue cross-examining, Mr. Carr?"

"No, sir. I feel there is sufficient evidence to convince your honor of Mr. Carr's guilt."

"No witnesses to call?"

"No, your honor."

"Am I to understand that you are ready to present your summation?"

"Tomorrow morning would be time enough to prepare, unless Mrs. Spiegel has witnesses she would like to call."

"Mrs. Spiegel, are you in agreement?"

She would have liked to stall for time, but Mr. Penya had forced her hand

and she knew unless Evan came up with new evidence, which now seemed unlikely, she had to agree. "Tomorrow morning is fine with me," she said confidently.

The judge stood to indicate their dismissal. As the door closed, he faced his wife. "Rosetta, was it difficult for you to stand by and not say a word?"

She walked up to him, stood on her toes and reached for his face so she could kiss him. "I'm so proud of you, Leonardo. You were masterful and considerate at the same time. Like the old Leonardo I know." She hugged him.

"Stop," he said. "I haven't changed. It's you who has changed." He looked at her seriously. "Tell me, Rosetta. What is your take on Trevor Carr? Do you think he meant to strangle her?"

"I've been wondering about that, and to tell you the truth, I don't know. If he didn't, who did? Stop scowling. I know you want this over with. You're right. You have to put an end to this trial, and get the principality and our lives back to normal again."

"You're being evasive."

"Yes. But I have faith in you. I know you'll make the right decision."

He frowned. "I hope so, Rosetta. I sincerely do."

CHAPTER 62

Mr. Penya, beaming a smile of triumph, rose, walked toward the first row of engrossed spectators, stopped short, and turning on his heels, confronted Trevor. Looking directly at Judge Montevecchio, but pointing his finger menacingly at Trevor, he voiced, "Your honor, the evidence against Trevor Jase Carr is so overwhelming, I'm baffled as to how to commence my summation."

"Force yourself, Mr. Penya," the judge said, glibly. A trickle of laughter crept through the room, but ceased like a shot as he eyed the courtroom.

The judge's remark agitated the D.A., but no one, not even the lord high executioner was going to spoil this, his moment of triumph. He would have liked to address the spectators, and more so, the media – show them his genius as a lawyer, and bypass the judge, but it was the judge he had to win over, not the public. The judge was furious with him, but he also knew he would not stop the case at this point. Mustering all his nerve, he smiled respectfully at Judge Montevecchio, and began his closing argument.

"Your honor, this is not a complex case. All the evidence points to just one fact – that Mr. Carr did strangle his wife. True, the deceased's reputation and credibility were not ... savory, but that is hardly an excuse for murder. Aside from that, all the events leading up to the death of Pamela Carr, point to one, and only one, person." He walked to Trevor, leaned over him, their noses almost touching, and eyeballed him. Then, he raised his voice and said, "And that person is Trevor Jase Carr."

Ceil jumped to her feet. "I'm sorry, your honor, I know objections during a closing argument are improper, but I must protest to the District Attorney's close contact with Mr. Carr."

"Noted," the judge said. "Mr. Penya, it is not necessary to approach the accused at such close proximity, as you well know. This is not a cross-examination. It is a summation." He wished he could leave the bench, take Mr. Penya by the scruff of his collar and throttle him for displaying such theatrical antics after his previous warnings, but completing the trial was his foremost priority, so he gritted his teeth and swallowed hard.

"Sorry, your honor. I was caught up in the moment. Nevertheless, the facts are the facts. Mr. Carr has admitted becoming enraged at seeing his wife and the tour guide engaged in each other's arms."

Trevor turned to Ceil. "Engaged in each other's arms, that's a laugh. They were fucking."

She nudged him. "Shush. We'll have our turn."

Mr. Penya continued, "He went back to his room, where he admits drinking half a bottle of Scotch. It doesn't take a rocket scientist to conclude that half a bottle of Scotch will surely cloud a person's judgment." Mr. Penya paced back and forth, still playing to the media. Running his eyes from Trevor to Ceil, he paused momentarily to make eye contact with the press, and shifted his attention back to the judge. "Mr. Carr admits, and I quote his very words, 'Yes, I wanted her dead.' He uses the excuse that his wife slept with every man she could get her hands on. And why? Because he hasn't a credible excuse. He does this to justify his actions, hoping this tactic will play on the court's sympathy, and therefore vindicate him. If Mr. Carr was the loving devoted husband he claims to be, would he sit back and watch while Mr. Floater flirted with her so brazenly for everyone to witness? Would he sit back and allow his wife to entice men to have sex with her?" Mr. Penya's eyes held tightly to the judge's. "Would you? I think not." He turned and concentrated on Trevor. "This man, your honor, had a cleverly thought out plan, or scheme if you will, to do away with his wife. It might not have started before the holiday. After all, they were there to work on their relationship. But it took shape as the trip unfolded, which fell in flawlessly with his strategy. Oh, make no mistake. This handsome, cultured gentleman, who sits before you so rational, so humble one moment, and in the next displays his other side – that of a beaten, wronged man who has lived through hell because of a wife with a personality disorder. This man is not the person you think he is." Mr. Penya paused, making sure he had everyone's attention. When he felt enough time had elapsed, he locked eyes with the judge, then swung around and pointed at T.J. "In a fit of rage he strangled his wife. Why? Not because of her infidelities – not because she drank too much – and not because she took drugs – and not because he was sick and tired of her ways. He, himself, admitted he endured her problems for years."

Mr. Penya turned and stared at Judy. "Because he found new fresh, exciting, passion enter his life. What was this bliss? Love in the form of an enchantingly beautiful woman. A woman who captivated, bewitched, and mesmerized him so intensely he could think of nothing, or no one else, but her. That is what motivated him to carry out his scheme. This man thought of a plan, carefully devised it, and executed it."

He stopped and poured a glass of water, slowly lifted it to his mouth, and drank, holding the attention of his audience with every swallow. He placed the glass down gently and turned toward the judge. "Your honor, even if you disregard every word I have spoken, we cannot erase this one glaring fact. He, the accused, signed his own death certificate when he said, 'Yes, I did strangle my wife.' What better evidence is there than the bruised impressions of Mr. Carr's own hands imprinted on the throat of the slain woman, as was testified to by the medical examiner?" Mr. Penya shrugged and gestured with his hands towards the sky. "Your honor, I rest my case."

Impressed with the district attorney's summation, but still annoyed by his theatrical display, the judge glanced at his watch hoping the defense would respond with a short summation in order for him to hand down a verdict and bring the trial to an end. "Mrs. Spiegel?" he inquired.

"Your honor, I will continue where Mr. Penya left off. His strongest point being that Mr. Carr admitted strangling his wife. Let me repeat the district attorney's words verbatim. Quote, 'Mr. Carr said. 'I drank too much, became enraged, and when I caught her having sex with Tom Floater, I strangled her.' That is misquoted. It is not what Mr. Carr said. What he did say was, 'I drank too much, became enraged, and when I caught her having sex with Tom Floater, I lost control. Afterwards we had sex, and I tried to strangle her.' This was given as testimony by Mr. Carr, and is documented by statements taken by Agent Hernandez at Mr. Carr's inquest, which can be obtained if the court deems it necessary. The act of having sex is hardly, and I quote again from Mr. Penya's silver-tongued verbalization 'Mrs. Carr and Mr. Floater were engaged in each other's arms.' I find it hard to believe they were playing a game of hide and seek."

Ceil resumed. "Let's review the facts. First, we have shown that Mr. Carr did not admit strangling his wife, but admitted trying to. There's a world of difference." She viewed the court, and turned back to the judge. "Keep in mind, the word, *strangle*, to which I will return shortly. Secondly, finding your wife having intimate relations with another man is not an everyday occurrence, as Mr. Penya would have you believe. Yes, he did go back to his room and did drink a half bottle of Scotch. He was distraught. Wouldn't you be under the same circumstances?

'Thirdly, the fact that Mr. Carr may have been attracted to Mrs. Blessing should come as no surprise to any normal red-blooded man." Facing Judy, Ceil pointed to her. "Mr. Penya was correct when he said she is an enchantingly beautiful woman. One has only to look at her to come to that conclusion." Judy shrank in her seat. Turning back to the judge, Ceil paused as the artists quickly sketched Judy.

"Granted, Mrs. Carr was a promiscuous woman. Why did he stay married to her for fifteen years? He is wealthy, handsome and successful. He could have easily divorced her and had the pick of any woman he desired – yet, he stayed with her. The reason is simple. He loved her. Time and time again he tried to understand her problems, overlook her infidelities, her indiscretions, and her drug abuse, and with all that, he still forgave her. That doesn't sound like a man who would intentionally strangle his wife. It's more like a man hoping the woman he loved would eventually come to her senses, or get some help, and until she did, he'd stand by her, no matter what. Isn't that what we say when we take the marriage vow? There are other issues to be considered. Before judgment is passed on Mr. Carr, may I point out there could have been others who had motive to want the deceased out of the picture. She had many enemies, as you have heard from previous witnesses. This was a self-centered, callous woman who thought nothing of endangering the lives of her friends by giving them dangerous drugs in order to seduce their husbands. I know what you're thinking. *That is no reason to kill her.* No, it isn't. But how can we be certain Mr. Carr did? There isn't a single person who can testify that he, or she, witnessed the crime. Why? Because he did not commit the crime. The only thing Mr. Carr can be accused of is losing his temper and trying to strangle his wife. There's more to the story than meets the eye.

"A moment ago, I asked you to remember the word strangle." The spectators leaned forward eagerly awaiting Ceil's next words. "The truth is, as Mr. Carr has testified, Mrs. Carr was into what is called near death sex, or in technical terms, autoerotic asphyxiation. Also called 'scarfing.'" A low murmur resounded throughout the room. "I understand that those of us who were brought up with decent morals may not be aware of the more exotic sexual practices, but, they do exist." She looked at the judge for his affirmation. He, in turn, eyed his wife, and nodded approvingly at Ceil.

The spectators sat on the edge of their seats. Ears listened intently to her every word. Even Mr. Penya, taken aback by Ceil's comment, showed interest in what she was about to disclose.

"Although most of us are not aware, there is such a thing as strangulation sex. Mind you, this is not a usual practice, and can be dangerous, in fact, to the point of death, due to the lack of oxygen. Still, there are those individuals who go to these lengths to achieve a heightened orgasm." Except for a few gasps, the courtroom air stood at a standstill.

"Can I be perfectly candid, your honor?" He nodded.

"This is not a subject I would ordinarily choose to discuss, but, it being germane to this case, I have no choice but to explain it to the court." She inhaled a deep breath and let it out slowly. "Mrs. Carr was one of those individuals who enjoyed this kind of sex. To her, having a normal orgasm was not fulfilling. Somewhere in her sexual encounters, she learned of a method whereby one intensifies the thrill of the climax by having their partner clasp them tightly around the neck until they either pass out, or nearly pass out."

The judge's eyes widened with amazement. "Mrs. Spiegel, I take it for granted that you have researched this, uh, technique?" Before Ceil could answer, he quickly added, "Of course, you must have. You wouldn't have the nerve to make up anything so outrageous." He scratched his head wondering if, being the cunning woman she was, she just might have.

"Thank you for those kind words, your honor. Rest assured I have researched the subject and can, if necessary, present the text."

"Go on."

"Mr. Penya had all the right moves, but not all the right facts. Number one. Mrs. Carr, thinking her husband is asleep, sneaks out of their bed and steals her way silently down the hall, where she enters the unlocked door of Mr. Floater's room. We have testimony of this from Mr. Floater. Number two. Mr. Carr, who feigned sleep follows her, and peeps through the keyhole to see the aforementioned couple having intercourse. Infuriated, he goes back to his room and consumes half a bottle of Scotch. Mrs. Carr, after two hours of, uh, frolicking with Mr. Floater, returns and slips quietly into bed. When her husband asks her where she was, she laughs playfully and says she was unable to sleep and went to the kitchen for a glass of iced tea. She asks if she can get him something cool. He's sweating and reeks from liquor. Infuriated by her taking the matter so lightly, and his feeling aroused for some unknown reason, he pounces on her, trying to prove that he can satisfy her just as much as Mr. Floater did. She, being the passionate nymphomaniacal lady she was, encourages him, saying, 'if I knew you could...' Ceil hesitated... 'screw me so well, I'd have never gone with any of those other men.' The angrier he became, the more forcefully he made love to her, and the more turned on she became. In fact she begged him. 'Do it like the others do, and I'll never cheat on you again. Don't be a pussy. Come on, put your hands around my throat. Squeeze the life out of me. Prove you're a man.'

"Her constant challenge to his masculinity, compounded by the liquor he consumed, incensed him to the point of no return, and he gave in to the unnatural sex she craved."

Trevor turned to Meyer. "Your wife's unbelievable."

Meyer responded. "That she is, that she is."

Ceil walked two steps closer to the judge. Speaking softly so that everyone strained to hear her, and said, "All the years of putting up with her and her endless problems came to a head in that moment, and he pressed harder and harder until she lay lifeless in front of him. But the shock of seeing his wife in a state of death sobered him quickly. Artificial respiration did not work. Slapping her did not work. He held her in his arms sobbing, when suddenly she opened her eyes and smiled up at him. And do you know what she said?"

Everyone, including the judge pressed forward.

"She said, 'T.J., that was the best – I'm starving.'

"Relieved but confused, Mr. Carr turned to take a walk on the beach, and figure out if all that had happened was real, or a bad dream. She was at the refrigerator picking at the fish, which she couldn't eat for dinner since she had been too worked up, thinking about her date later that night with Mr. Floater, when she called out to him, 'Hurry back, I may want some more of the new you.'"

Ceil fell silent for a moment. "Those were the last words he heard her say. 'Hurry back, I may want some more of the new you.'" Ceil placed her hands on the table. "She was alive when he left, and that, your honor, is God's honest truth. I fail to see where the district attorney has proven there is sufficient evidence to convict the accused. Clearly, there is reasonable doubt."

CHAPTER 63

She was halfway up the courthouse steps when a voice called to her. "Ceil, over here."

"See you inside, Meyer. I'll see what she wants," Ceil said. She turned and walked toward a side entrance adjacent to the steps.

Rosetta tugged at Ceil's arm, drawing her into the shadows, out of anyone's sight. "I just had to see you," Rosetta said, her voice hoarse. "You don't think the media saw you come here, do you?"

"No, I'm sure it's okay."

Rosetta shivered. "Things have not been going well for me. The tension of the trial, the untried cases that are piling up, the negative publicity, and the pressure from the Ecuadorian counsel to end the trial because it is killing the tourist trade... I don't know what else – he's like a Jekyll and Hyde. A stranger. He's shut me out. Hasn't asked for my opinion, or discussed the case with me, as he promised. He eats very little, hardly sleeps, and keeps to himself. I used to be able to read his thoughts, but now – I don't know what he's thinking. There are times when I catch his eye, and know he's befuddled, like he has come to a fork in the road and doesn't know which road to take. He knows what I'm thinking, and at times does listen to my opinions, but I dread to think of the decision he will pronounce on Mr. Carr." Ceil's heart skipped a beat. "I'm sorry to burden you, but I feel that you are a friend and I just had to talk to someone. I can't talk to my so-called friends. I can't talk to my parents. They never liked Leonardo from the time they met him. I have no one."

With those words she threw herself into Ceil's arms and wept. "I didn't mean to burden you, especially now, when you have so much on your mind. But, I feel so alone."

"You have me," Ceil said, trying to comfort Rosetta. "You have me. Go ahead and cry. After the hearing, we'll get together and work everything out. At the moment, he's confused. It's understandable. He's a dedicated man sworn to uphold the law, and the pressure has gotten to him. He'll snap back. Have faith." Patting Rosetta on the back, Ceil held her friend at arms length, and dabbed at her tears with a tissue. "Meanwhile, stand by him, and give him your support."

"Thank you. I feel better already."

"Listen, Rosetta. I better get into the courthouse immediately or the judge will have another one of his tirades. Just keep calm, and remember, your husband needs you now more than ever."

"I won't forget your kindness."

"We'll talk later, when all this is behind us. Right now I have to face the music, and I don't think the judge is going to be playing my song."

CHAPTER 64

The air hung heavily over the spectators in the courtroom. Ceil sat nervously tapping a pencil on the desk while Meyer tried to console her. "Stop making yourself crazy. You're carrying on like you lost the case. I've never seen you like this. It was Rosetta, wasn't it? She told you something that unnerved you. What was it?"

"Rosetta has problems, but it's not that. She told me the judge's state of mind is not good and to add to that, I haven't heard from Evan."

"Jesus, when it rains it pours. That's bad news, Ceil. And what about the judge?"

"He's not himself. He's confused."

"Give me a break. The judge, confused? I don't believe it. All of a sudden he's confused. What is he having, a mental breakdown? He seems perfectly normal to me, except for his resentment toward foreigners. To tell you the truth, I don't hold that against him. Want me to tell you what's eating him?"

"That would be nice," she said.

"Go ahead. Roll your eyes. I'll tell you anyhow. The truth is, he's not sure if Trevor did strangle his wife. He's indecisive. That's why he's acting strangely. He hates the hoopla and wants to get this headache over with. Look at it this way, Ceil. The judge is a big shot. He's looked up to. He's used to getting up every morning, having his breakfast served to him, having the valet lay out his clothes, enjoying his family, being chauffeured to court, and locking up every criminal he can. Trevor disturbed his comfy nest. But his problem is that he's an honest man, and he's having one hell of a struggle with his conscience."

"Maybe you should be defending Trevor. I understand what you're saying, Meyer, but his struggle, as you said, is not going to help us. His posture is going to be negative. Whether he lets Trevor go free or convicts him, either way he's caught between . . . "

"A rock and a whatever place," he finished for her.

"Another thing. Why haven't we heard from Evan?"

"Stop with the worrying, will you? Evan's brilliant. He'll come through. Compose yourself. The judge is coming out of his chambers."

Judy, Beau, and Lawrence sat anxiously watching the judge enter, trying to read his facial expression. "That's a real sour puss," Lawrence said, and turned to watch Trevor being led into the courtroom, his hands cuffed behind his back, a guard holding his arm. "Well, T.J. seems to be holding up. Is that a smile or a grimace he's sporting?"

Judy studied Trevor. He searched the room until he spotted her and his smile broadened when he caught her eye. Her returning smile held more than an acknowledgment. It spoke of deep affection.

Watching them exchange glances, Beau said, "What the hell has he got to smile about?"

"What do you expect him to do?" she snapped. "You're being bitter, and we both know why."

Lawrence spoke up. "*I* don't know why. What's going on?"

Beau spoke across Judy. "Don't pretend, Lar. Everyone knows that Judy has the hots for T.J. You've been with us long enough. You know what's been going on." He faced her, but spoke to Lawrence. "She's leaving me as soon as the trial is over. Judy is going for the big bucks. This has-been husband is stepping aside so she can sit outside T.J.'s cell, even if it takes forever. If he gets off, she'll be dining on caviar, instead of pretzels and beer, and chauffeured around in a Ferrari, not the old jalopy I gave her. I'm too poor, and too old for her to waste her time with me. Right, Judy? Why don't you admit it? The secret's out and the trial's almost over. Isn't this what you've been waiting for?" She started to rise but Beau pulled her down. "It's too late to leave, the judge just came in, and the verdict is about to be handed down."

Her eyes filled with tears, Judy's stare at Beau held anguish and abhorrence. "Lar," she asked, "Please change places with me."

Judge Montevecchio leaned forward, the worn-out leather chair groaned from too many years of service. In a flat, raspy voice, he said, "Good morning." His face was pale and drawn, his eyes appeared to be sunk deeply in their sockets, emphasizing the dark circles under them, and giving him a haunted appearance.

The spectators, taking notice of the drastic change, whispered to one another. The artists, quick to seize the opportunity to capture this sudden transformation, sketched frantically.

Annoyed by the buzz in the courtroom, he slammed his gavel down and spewed at the onlookers. "One more outburst, and the courtroom will be cleared," he growled. "This is a court of law, and will be respected and treated as such."

Except for a light cough or clearing of one's throat, the room was silent. "This case has brought the principality of Quito and the Galapagos Islands into the limelight, but not for the right reasons. It has cast a dark shadow upon us. The peace and tranquility of the islands that bring thousands of tourists who enjoy the untold treasures found only on our shores, has been disturbed by thrill seekers and the media who encourage this hysteria in order to sell their scandalous publications." He cleared his throat. "As this hearing comes to a close today, all will return to normal." He drank water from a glass and continued.

"The defendant will stand to hear his judgment. Trevor Jase Carr, you are accused of strangling your wife. The court has heard from the council for your defense, and from the district attorney representing the principality of Quito. They both have eloquently presented their cases." His eyes flicked from Trevor, to Ceil, then to his wife, and back to Trevor. "Mr. Carr, we do not employ a jury like you do in your country. The laws of Ecuador give the judge the authority to make the determination and arbitrate the case at hand without prejudice or malice, leaving it to his discretion. Therefore, Mr. Carr the court finds you guilty of murder and..."

After reading a note a messenger handed her, Ceil, leapt to her feet. "Your honor," she broke in, "I beg your indulgence, but I have just received information that is crucial to this case."

His eyes narrowed with irritation. That she should have the gall to interrupt him at the moment he was disclosing his verdict threw him into a rage. Bristling with annoyance, he slammed his gavel so hard, the wooden holder the gavel rested on splintered, sending the fragments flying in every direction. He jumped out of his chair and shouted. "Mrs. Spiegel, we are well aware of your lack of procedural expertise, but to interrupt the court so rudely at this time is inexcusable. Please sit down."

Ceil stood her ground. Challenging him, she said, "I will not sit down, your honor. I have just been handed information that will find Mr. Carr innocent of the charges against him."

The judge's face colored beet red. He again slammed the gavel but this time on the bare desk, shouting at the top of his lungs, he repeated, "I SAID SIT DOWN, MRS. SPIEGEL!"

Not backing down, she lowered her voice to a whisper and said, "If your honor does not permit me to enter this evidence, he will have to live with the pain of having unjustly sentenced an innocent man."

The silence in the room was loud.

She held his gaze, bravely defying him. Their eyes locked as she waited, watching his expression gradually alter from contempt to resignation. Almost in slow motion he positioned himself back into his seat. "Mrs. Spiegel," he said with great control, "it is highly irregular to present new evidence or call more witnesses to the stand at the closing of a trial, but in this instance I will reluctantly give in and hear the prodigious new evidence you have to offer the court."

The district attorney stood with outstretched arms. "Your honor I ob..." he started to say, but the judge stared mercilessly at him. He plopped into his seat in frustration.

Ceil smiled and turned to the gallery. "His honor has shown that he is an unbiased, fair-minded, unprejudiced member of the judicial system by allowing new evidence to be presented to the hearing. With his honor's permission, I would like to call Dr. Evan Levy."

The judge rolled his eyes. "Approach counselors."

"What the hell is going on? Are you two taking turns by trying to put me in an early grave? First, Mr. Penya, out of the blue, locates the medical examiner, and now you disrupt the court by asking to put a new witness on the stand when I'm ready to hand down a verdict? Both of you claim the same excuse – the witnesses who just happen to be of the same profession have materialized as if by magic, unexpectedly. In all my years on the bench I have never witnessed such unprofessional behavior."

Mr. Penya interrupted. "Your honor, I object to this new witness, who was barred from performing a new autopsy on the deceased."

Ceil opened her mouth, but the judge waved her off. "Now listen to me, you pompous ass," the judge barked at Mr. Penya. "I let you get away with putting Dr. Rodriguez, that perverted, maniacal idiot, on the stand only because there is no evidence to prove he is incompetent. I have stood by watching you perform for the media. I have serious thoughts about reporting your outrageous behavior to the bar. As far as you are concerned Mrs. Spiegel, may I inquire as to why Dr. Levy has not come up with his findings before this, and then quite suddenly, he was barred from the mortuary. Who did that?" Mr. Penya's face reddened.

"I have no idea," Ceil said. "He finally managed to gain access to the mortuary, and has come up with some astonishing evidence. If I may offer my opinion?" The judge nodded. "I would venture to say that Agent Hernandez had something to do with it."

"Figures," the judge mouthed. "Very well, let's continue."

The judge announced, "The witness will be sworn in, give his full name, occupation, and take the stand."

Ceil wanted to run up to her grandson and smother him with kisses, but knowing it to be an impossible dream, she only enjoyed the thought of doing it. "Doctor Levy," she inquired, "what is your profession?"

"I am a medical doctor, specifically in the fields of pathology and toxicology. At present I am the executive director of the toxicology department of Georgetown University, Washington, D. C., the United States of America."

"Can you tell us briefly about your background?"

"I graduated from Harvard College with a Bachelor of Science Degree. I have a masters and a doctorate in toxicology from the University of Pennsylvania. I spent one year in general residency at John Hopkins, and a five-year residency at the New York Presbyterian Hospital."

Ceil's heart swelled with pride. "Your honor, I offer this witness as an expert in pathology and toxicology, with information pertaining to the cause of Mrs. Carr's death." She glanced at Mr. Penya knowing he wouldn't object.

"Is there an objection to this witness, Mr. Penya?"

"No," the district attorney said reluctantly.

"Then the court deems Dr. Levy qualified and he may testify. Mrs. Spiegel, please continue."

"Dr. Levy, did you examine the body?"

"Yes."

"What did your examination reveal?"

"The bruises around her neck were not intense enough to do permanent damage, only temporary asphyxiation. It can be compared to blacking out, or fainting, but recovering after a brief period."

"Objection, your honor," Mr. Penya said. "Is the witness alleging there wasn't the most remote possibility that the deceased died from strangulation? I find this very hard to believe."

The judge sat back, thoughtfully stroked his chin, and with raised brows, addressed Evan. "Dr. Levy?"

"My opinion is based on what is reasonably probable, and not on remote speculation unsupported by facts. I did not, from my autopsy, feel the deceased died from strangulation. After a more extensive search of the body, I found new evidence that made me suspicious of the previous coroner's report."

"Objection. Does the witness have proof of his assertions?"

"Indeed I do," Evan said. "And they are not merely assertions."

"And they are?" Ceil asked.

"The coroner abused the corpse."

The judge leaned forward, surprised at what he heard. "Dr. Levy, are you serious? Did you say the county coroner abused the dead woman?"

"Yes, your honor."

"How?"

"May I be candid, your honor?"

"At this point, one more revelation will be welcomed."

"The coroner had sex with the cadaver. Well, actually, he tried having sex, but the cadaver was too rigid and he couldn't enter her... so he ejaculated on her. Then, he tried to hide any evidence that might incriminate him. He wiped the semen from her with a towel, but without success. I found the towel, which he carelessly left in the trashcan. With the help of your law enforcement agent, I acquired pubic hairs from the towel, and the corpse. D.N.A. tests were run from blood samples of the coroner previously on file."

The judge thought of calling a recess to digest the information, but he knew the medical examiner's background of wife abuse and his history of alcoholism. "The Prefect of Police, Agent Hernandez will apprehend Dr. Rodriguez," he ordered. "I will issue a bench warrant for his arrest."

The courtroom buzzed with whispers. Mr. Penya stood. "Your honor, I'm not questioning what Dr. Levy has just conveyed to us regarding the coroner's appalling behavior. Doctor Levy no doubt, is correct, but I fail to see what the sexual misconduct of Dr. Rodriguez has to do with Mrs. Carr being strangled."

"A point well taken," the judge said. "Mrs. Spiegel?"

"Dr. Levy, did your examination of the deceased prove anything more than what you have told us?"

"As I said before, I didn't believe from my examination that Mrs. Carr was strangled, because upon further examination of her stomach and intestines, I discovered the true cause of her death." Evan hesitated.

The air stirred in the courtroom, and the eager audience waited for the professor to continue. The judge broke the silence. "Doctor Levy, is there a reason for your hesitation? Now that you have piqued our interest, please don't keep us in suspense."

"She was poisoned."

"That's not enough information," Ceil advised. "Please explain."

"The medical examiner's autopsy was less than thorough," Evan said. "He signed the usual death certificates proclaiming that the deceased died of strangulation, and at some point, he must have realized the extent of his mistake, which is why he was not available to testify earlier."

"Does that mean someone poisoned her?" Ceil asked.

Mr. Penya rose. "Objection, your honor. The doctor may have an arms length of degrees in his profession, but he is not qualified to speculate as to who poisoned the victim. Or is he moonlighting as a detective also?"

"Noted, Mr. Penya. But let's see where Mrs. Spiegel is going." The judge half-smiled at Ceil. "Rephrase the question please."

Trevor smiled broadly. "Go, Evan," he said smugly. "This is what I've been waiting for."

Ceil looked at the judge meaningfully, thinking it was the first time he showed her respect.

She continued. "Dr. Levy, you said the victim was poisoned. Was it perhaps a chemical like cyanide or another toxin?"

"Toxin? Yes. But not the kind of chemical customarily associated with most poisons. Mrs. Carr ingested what is commonly known as puffer fish. I took the liberty of speaking with a few members of the group who were at the same dinner. It was served at dinner on the night of her demise, but Mrs. Carr did not eat the fish until some time later that evening."

"You mean to tell us that by eating this puffer fish you can die?"

"Yes."

"Doctor Levy," said Ceil, "I for one have never heard of puffer fish, and I'm sure many of the people in the courtroom are as ignorant as I with regard to this subject. Enlighten us. If it is so toxic, why for heaven's sakes, would anyone sell it, and serve it, much less eat it?"

"That is a perfectly sensible question, and one asked for many years. Puffer fish, also known as fugu, blowfish or globefish, have long been a gastronomic prize in many countries. Japan, Singapore, Hong Kong, and Hawaii among others. Puffer fish have long been recognized as a dangerous delicacy, albeit sometimes a deadly one. In Japan, eating the honorable fugu is epitome of gourmet dining, and the cooking version of Russian roulette. It is one of the most expensive foods in Japan. A single fish can bring 50 to 140 dollars. Cut up and served in a restaurant, a serving can cost 200 dollars. At a certain restaurant in the Tokyo Ginza District, a complete meal made up of blowfish hor d'oeuvres, blowfish sashimi, blowfish stew, blowfish and rice soup, and fruit, easily costs 230 dollars a head. And, it goes way back in time. Artifacts recovered from an Egyptian tomb indicate puffer fish poisoning has been known since approximately 2400 to 2700 B. C. The puffer fish and related species may contain a tetrodotoxin, an extremely potent neurotoxin, and one of the most toxic substances known, which produces illness, and often death. In Japan, specially trained and regulated chefs choose and prepare the fish correctly, thereby avoiding loss of customers who skirt the edges of toxic reactions to enjoy the tingling oral sensation of the tetrodotoxin. The Japanese harvest the fugu for consumption and export. There are over 200 fugu restaurants in Tokyo, where an average of 100-200 people a year show signs of poisoning. Most deaths result from fish prepared at home. Unfortunately, many deaths go unreported. It is also used to commit suicide. The concern of many countries is that puffer fish might be mistaken and sold for another species of fish. Tetrodotoxin, one of the most toxic substances known, is approximately 275 times deadlier than cyanide and 50 times more potent than strychnine. Because the toxin is heat-stable, the freezing or cooking of affected fish does not inactivate it. And sadly, toxic fish cannot be identified reliably, even by experienced chefs who have been trained to fillet fugu in such a manner that the flesh for consumption is not contaminated with tissue from organs known to contain the high levels of tetrodotoxin, notably the liver and skin."

"It boggles my mind," Ceil declared. "Why anyone would eat something poisonous is more than I can comprehend, but evidently they do. But if they did, and became ill, is there an antidote to counteract the illness?"

"Unfortunately, no."

"It's hard to believe that in this day and age a serum has not been found. Are you saying that anyone eating the fish can die?"

"No. There are gourmet chefs who are schooled in preparing the fish. What I am saying is that symptoms depend on the quantity of the tetrodotoxin consumed. They usually begin within 30 minutes of being eaten, though deaths have been reported in as few as 17 minutes."

"Surely there must be some precautions to save a person from dying."

"I'm sorry to say there are no antidotes, therefore treatment is limited to supportive measures, and the removal of the unabsorbed toxin."

"Supportive measure? How is that done?"

"If spontaneous vomiting doesn't occur, it should be induced. Washing the stomach with an alkaline solution, as well as an endoscopy to remove the poison from the proximal small bowel is helpful. There are other methods, but I feel it unnecessary to go into them at this time."

"Let's get to the heart of your opinion. Dr. Levy, are you testifying that Mrs. Carr did not succumb to strangulation, but from ingesting the puffer fish?"

"I'd stake my reputation on it. All the proof is in Agent Hernandez' possession."

"Thank you. Your testimony was invaluable." She smiled at Trevor, and then turned to the judge. "Your honor, the defense rests."

The judge glanced at the district attorney who sat grimly.

"Mr. Carr, please stand. Under the present testimony presented by Professor Levy, the court reverses its original decision and finds the accused, Trevor Jase Carr, innocent of the charges of murder. Mr. Carr, you are free to leave."

CHAPTER 65

As tense and difficult as the courtroom scene had been on Monday morning, Wednesday morning brought the promise of a new beginning for the group. Meyer's jet lifted off the runway, and soared into the bright blue sky, leaving the shores of the Galapagos Islands to fade into flecks surrounded by the foamy ocean.

Silence prevailed as each of the travelers on board thought of the strange happenings of the past weeks, which had started as a vacation, and had ended in tragedy.

The only movement was the steward walking up and down the aisle catering to the passengers. "Mmm, maybe I will," Meyer said, staring down at the tray of hors d' oeuvres. He poked Ceil lightly. "How about a little finger food. You hardly touched your breakfast."

"Later, but I could go for a glass of grapefruit juice." She smiled warmly at the steward. "You're new, aren't you?"

"Yes, Ma'am."

"I don't take ice in anything I drink. What's your name young man?"

"Lance, Ma'am."

"You don't have to call me Ma'am, Lance."

Meyer smirked. "So what should he call you, hey you?"

She waived a gesture of dismissal at Meyer and spoke to the steward. "Call me Ceil. I hate formality."

"Uh, yes, uh, Ceil."

"I'll take a few of those," Meyer said, pointing to the hors d'oeuvres, "And call me Mr. Spiegel. I like formality."

The steward placed a napkin on Meyer's lap and pulled down the tray table. "I'll be right back with the grapefruit juice. Would you like something to drink, Mr. Spiegel?"

"Why not? Bring me a double vodka with a splash of cranberry juice." He eyed Ceil. "And I like ice in all my drinks."

"I think you're losing it, Meyer." She checked her watch. "Its only eleven o'clock, and you're drinking?"

He slipped his arm through hers. "You think it was easy watching you get your ass kicked by the D.A. and the judge? I need something to get me back to normal."

She teased as she squeezed his hand. "Normal, you'll never be, but I love you just the same. And who kicked who? I won, didn't I?"

He leaned over and kissed her cheek. "I'm very proud of you, baby. You did a masterful job."

"I did the best I could, but if it weren't for Evan, Trevor would be sitting in jail, or shot by a firing squad by now." She turned to wave at her grandson, her heart bursting with pride.

"What are you thinking about, Lar?" Beau asked. Answering before Lawrence, could reply, he said, "Kaitlin, huh?"

"It's the weirdest sensation, going home without her. Like a part of me is missing. I can't believe she's gone." His eyes brimmed with tears. "I try to make sense out of it, but... God just plucked her out of my life, just like you'd pick a flower. She never hurt anyone. She was a very special person."

Beau put a comforting hand on Lar's shoulder. "Yes, she was, Lar. Very special. It's strange, but the longer I live, the less I understand. I guess the saying, 'life isn't fair,' is true."

"I don't think I'll ever get over the loss. I know the right thing is for me to get on with my life. She wanted that. Even with her last breath, she said, 'Lar I won't rest in peace if I know you're going to fall apart.' I want to do it, if it's only so that she'll rest easy, but it's so damn hard."

"Give yourself time. You have the new position as director of the fitness center with Trevor's corporation. That's quite an undertaking. It should keep you busy and out of trouble. I want you to promise me you'll keep in touch with me. Don't make me bug you. If I have to fly down to D. C. and beat the shit out of you, I will. Maybe you'll give me a couple of guest passes to work out in the gym."

"You got it, Beau, and a personal trainer, and anything else you want. You're a good friend. I appreciate the sincere concern you've extended me, not only now but also throughout our trip. You watched over me like my father would." He noticed Beau watching Trevor and Judy, two rows in front of them. "You're hurting too, aren't you?"

"Like a dagger stuck in my fucking heart. I know I was a jerk to cheat on her with Pamela, and there's no excuse for what I did. Honestly, I just can't help feeling she's making a mistake. No sour grapes, but if I wasn't involved, I still wouldn't match them up."

"Just between us, Beau, I agree with you about them not being compatible. He has an extremely strong, almost ruthless personality. And although to look at Judy – I mean, it's no secret she's a knockout – but she's sweet, and even shy. And you know something, Beau?"

"What?"

"I saw you two before all the trouble started. You both looked so right together. I don't see the same chemistry between T.J. and Judy."

"What's the difference? She's going to be his now. I'm history."

"Funny, but when you think about it, most of the successful entrepreneurs are ruthless and aggressive. Seems that's the only way to achieve your goal."

"Don't you believe it for one minute, Lar. For God's sake, don't follow in T.J.'s footsteps, or I'll personally put a hit out on you. Use your head. Would your father agree with that kind of talk?"

Lawrence paused for a moment. "No, he wouldn't."

"So don't fuck up your life with that kind of bullshit thinking. You had a good upbringing. Keep to those values."

"Can I ask you a personal question, Beau?"

"A personal question? You mean screwing each other's wives when we were all stoned on Ecstasy isn't personal?"

Lawrence chuckled. "Gee, that's the first time since Kat's passing that I laughed."

"What's the life threatening question? I can't wait."

"Do you think Judy is in love with T.J.? I mean, really in love."

Beau, looked at Trevor and Judy, then up at the plane's ceiling. "I don't know. She could be. And then, she might be using him temporarily, as an escape from her problems... and me."

"You mean like someone to take care of her until she gets over you?"

"It looks like she's already done that. Yeah, I guess. I really hurt her, so it's possible she's using him as a buffer. That's what I'm counting on – that she'll see him for the... well, what he is, and come to her senses. If I'm lucky, I might get a second chance. What I wouldn't give to have her back."

"Well," Lar declared, "you never know what tomorrow will bring. He's sure drinking up a storm. The champagne hasn't stopped flowing. But that's nothing new, he's one of those guys who can drink all night, and carry on as if it was his first."

"What more could a man ask for?" Trevor said. "I'm free, we're on our way back to D. C., and wait until Washington society gets a look at the gorgeous creature I've snared. They'll burn with envy."

Judy flinched. "Snare? You make it sound like you captured a wild animal."

"You are a wild animal – my wild animal – the most beautiful, sensual, feline in the world."

"T.J.," Judy agonized, "that's your second bottle. Should you be drinking so much while in the air?"

"Come on, Judy, I've just been vindicated. I want to let the whole world know I'm a free man."

"I'm sure they already do."

"That was quite an experience – being locked up in that hole they call a jail – and the shit they call food. The sons of bitches should rot in hell." He knocked the champagne glass off the tray. "Don't be mad at me, baby. Give a guy a break. It's *my* time to celebrate."

She cringed when he called her baby. Somehow, when Beau called her baby, she wasn't offended. In fact, she had liked it. I'm being silly, she thought. *T.J.'s not himself. It's the champagne talking.* When the steward bent to pick up the glass, she recoiled as Trevor grabbed his arm, and slurred, "bring another one, and forget about the glass, it tastes better from the bottle." Judy recoiled.

"Hey, don't pull away from me Judy , I promise to behave." He stared at her. "God you're beautiful. Do you have any idea how beautiful you are? Want to know the first time I fell in love with you?"

"When, silly?"

He snuggled closer to her. "Remember when you and Beau were sitting across from Pamela and me, waiting to board the yacht and we each thought the yacht was ours. I caught your eye. I know you caught mine. That's when I decided you were going to be mine. Little did I know that the bitch had doubled booked the yacht, and that she and Beau were lovers in New York. What a break for me. When she drugged us, and we had sex, I thought I had died and gone to heaven." He kissed her cheek. "Judy , I'm going to give you the world. You just say it and it's yours." He shook his head. "To think you belong to me!"

"Belong to you? You make it sound like you're closing a business deal. And, T.J., I'd like to forget the orgy scene if you don't mind. It makes me feel cheap."

The steward set a bottle of Dom Perignon on Trevor's tray. "Your champagne sir," he said. "And would you care for anything, Ma'am? We have a full kitchen at your disposal."

T.J. answered for her. "Yeah, I could go for a steak, medium rare, and any veggies that are hanging around. Come on, Judy, join the party." To the steward, he said, "Bring this gorgeous creature the same."

Embarrassed by his actions, knowing that he had had too much to drink, she conceded. "Sure, whatever you say, T.J." Looking over her shoulder she caught Beau's eyes fixed on her, and a feeling of remorse ran through her.

"That's my girl," Trevor cooed, "You're just what the doctor ordered. How about toasting to my freedom?" He stood and waved the bottle of champagne, shouting, "Everybody, a toast to freedom. And to Ceil, who fought for me, and her grandson Evan, who proved me innocent, and to my bride to be, Judy." He took a long pull on the champagne and plunked heavily into his seat. "What a day, what a day," he repeated.

Judy placed a pillow behind his head. "Why don't you sleep it off T.J.? You'll feel better, afterwards."

"We haven't had our steaks yet, baby," he garbled. Giggling, his eyes half opened, he inclined his head toward her. "Only you and I know the truth, baby. Only you and I."

She humored him. "The truth? The truth about what?"

"You know. I told you, didn't I? Anyhow, it doesn't make any difference, now."

The champagne's gotten to him, she thought. He's babbling nonsense. "Close your eyes, T.J. We'll talk after you've rested."

His eyes snapped open. "Don't patronize me. I may be drunk, but I'm still conscious." He took her hand in his. "Maybe I didn't tell you. I am a little fuzzy. But since we're going to be one – I mean, married – after you lose Beau, and we share everything – no hiding secrets like Pamela did." Tightening his grip on her hand, he said, "I have to release it. I can't hold it inside any longer, or I'll explode."

"Explode?"

He cackled. "Heh, heh, heh. The trial – the trial – I'm talking about the trial. You know – when I swore I didn't kill Pamela... well..." He poked at her ribs playfully. "I did."

"That's not funny, T.J."

He lifted the bottle to his mouth, but found it empty. "It's funny, very funny." Running his finger along her cheek, he whispered, "Listen to this, Judy. It's going to blow your mind."

"Come on, T.J., I'd rather you got some shut eye."

His eyes narrowed at her. "I promise I will, but first, you have to hear what I have to say. Okay?"

"Okay. Okay."

"Pay attention, sweetheart. This is one for the books. Are you listening?"

"Yes, I'm listening," she said half-heartedly.

"I paid the chef a million bucks to fix the puffer fish so it was toxic. Got rid of the bitch. Oh yeah. Gone forever."

"What in the world are you saying?"

"Remember, at dinner, when Pamela, I mean, Pammy baby, said she wasn't hungry because she was wiped out from the pills she'd inhaled, and she refused to eat? Jesus, I almost died. It wasn't the way I planned it."

"Planned? What are you talking about?"

"Can't you hear?" he said raising his voice loudly. "Don't interrupt, baby. You're spoiling my train of thought. Pammy baby was supposed to succumb at the table, so everyone could see her leave this world. But, I used the old noodle. My daddy didn't raise dumb kids, ya know. The chef made sure the waiter packed a doggie bag, which I took to the room. I couldn't wait. It was driving me nuts. I knew she always snacked at night, and the bitch played right into my hands when she got the munchies after I tried strangling her. What a break. I waited until she stuffed the fish into her mouth and hung around awhile. When I was sure most of it was partially digested, I left her convulsing on the floor, and went for a walk on the beach. That's when I met you."

Judy's mouth dropped and her face paled as she slunk back in her seat, shocked at what he had said. He tilted her chin toward him. "You didn't know you fell for a genius did you?" Seeing her startled expression, he patted her hand reassuringly. "Hey, don't fret, baby, we're in the clear. I've been acquitted. They won't find out, and if they do, so what. They can't try me for the same crime twice."

Upon hearing Trevor's confession everyone exchanged stunned momentary glances.

A smug expression of satisfaction crossed Trevor's face as he closed his eyes and fell into a deep, relaxed, peaceful sleep.

www.ingramcontent.com/pod-product-compliance
Lightning Source LLC
Chambersburg PA
CBHW021335250626
47155CB00002B/712